Praise for *The Gemini Experiment:*

'A dizzying compilation of action scenes and moral quandaries...Pinkerton wields fast pacing and an entertaining, electrifying plot.' *Publishers Weekly*

'Part spy thriller, part SF adventure, Pinkerton's latest is a fast-paced and action packed novel with well-developed characters that will have strong YA and adult appeal.' *Library Journal*

'*The Gemini Experiment* is a thrill ride filled with twists and turns that keep the reader guessing and entertained all the way to the stunning conclusion. Brian Pinkerton has created a wonderfully constructed story, frightening in its believability.... an exceptional read.' *Cemetery Dance*

BRIAN PINKERTON

THE NIRVANA EFFECT

This is a **FLAME TREE PRESS** book

FLAME TREE PRESS
6 Melbray Mews, London, SW6 3NS, UK
flametreepress.com

US sales, distribution and warehouse:
Simon & Schuster
simonandschuster.biz

UK distribution and warehouse:
Marston Book Services Ltd
marston.co.uk

Publisher's Note: This is a work of fiction. Names, characters, places, and incidents are a product of the author's imagination. Locales and public names are sometimes used for atmospheric purposes. Any resemblance to actual people, living or dead, or to businesses, companies, events, institutions, or locales is completely coincidental.

Thanks to the Flame Tree Press team, including:
Taylor Bentley, Frances Bodiam, Federica Ciaravella, Don D'Auria,
Chris Herbert, Josie Karani, Molly Rosevear, Mike Spender,
Cat Taylor, Maria Tissot, Nick Wells, Gillian Whitaker.

The cover is created by Flame Tree Studio with
thanks to Nik Keevil and Shutterstock.com.
The font families used are Avenir and Bembo.

Flame Tree Press is an imprint of Flame Tree Publishing Ltd
flametreepublishing.com

A copy of the CIP data for this book is available from the British Library and the Library of Congress.

HB ISBN: 978-1-78758-487-7
US PB ISBN: 978-1-78758-485-3
UK PB ISBN: 978-1-78758-486-0
ebook ISBN: 978-1-78758-489-1

Printed and bound in Great Britain by Clays Ltd, Elcograf S.p.A.

BRIAN PINKERTON

THE NIRVANA EFFECT

FLAME TREE PRESS
London & New York

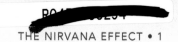

PART ONE
A FEW YEARS IN THE FUTURE

CHAPTER ONE

Aaron Holt didn't believe in alarm clocks. He woke up naturally with the sunrise. He kept his bedroom curtains open so light could spill across the room and declare a new day. He didn't require electronic devices to jolt him with beeps or poke him with music. His body was synchronized with the rotation of the earth. The dawn refreshed him.

Aaron's room was clean and orderly, a foundation of comfort before he confronted the usual spread of mess across the rest of the house. In the past twelve months, his roommates had reversed their priorities and embraced artificial reality over their true living conditions. They had mentally moved out of Los Angeles without physically relocating, reduced to grotesque, vacant shells anchored around the house, indifferent to their bodily needs and deteriorated appearances.

Aaron stripped and covered himself in a robe, an old habit that was probably no longer necessary given his privacy was almost certainly guaranteed. He stepped into the hall and walked past Scotty's room on the way to the shower.

Scotty's door was open, and he was sitting shirtless on his bed, fat hairy belly exposed, wearing a Dynamica eye cover illustrated with goofy, cartoony eyeballs. Creative eye cover designs had become a hot seller in recent months, one of the few physical items to see a rise in popularity as people spent more time with their 'head in the cloud', fulfilling Dynamica Incorporated's marketing tagline.

The odor coming from Scotty's room was inescapably sweat and urine. To extend consumer 'chip time', an enterprising company had come up with an apparatus that attached around the waist and over the groin to collect streams of piss and eliminate pesky bathroom breaks. Prior to retiring to bed, Aaron had witnessed Scotty deep into a chip adventure in essentially the same spot. It was apparent he had been on another all-night chip bender.

"Hell *yeah!*" shouted Scotty abruptly, as speckles of saliva flew from his lips. He was unaware of Aaron's presence or anything else outside of his manipulated brainwave activity. His hands gripped an imaginary steering wheel, knuckles white, and Aaron concluded he was engaged in his favorite adrenaline rush: driving a supercharged race car through a twisty maze of outlandish landscapes painted in his mind.

Aaron was particularly annoyed with Scotty because Scotty wasn't supposed to be a long-term housemate. The modest L.A. rental home initially belonged to just two tenants: Aaron and his longtime friend Desmond. When income streams decreased for both of them for different reasons (Aaron's shrinking client list and Desmond's deteriorating work ethic), they brought in a third roommate and mutual acquaintance, Larry, a struggling restaurant chef coming to terms with fewer people dining out. Larry then talked the others into letting his unemployed brother Scotty stay for a few weeks until he found new work, and 'a few weeks' became a permanent residency.

Upon securing a roof over his head, Scotty stopped looking for employment. He had twice seen his occupation replaced by automation – first as a worker at a manufacturing plant overtaken by robotics and then as a truck driver made obsolete by driverless highway transportation. Once he got hooked on the chip's intoxicating escapism and found a way to sustain basic survival through government subsidies, Scotty placed his job-hunting efforts on an indefinite hiatus. His mental state slipped into a predominately passive mode, and his physical condition underwent a dramatic transformation; formerly physically fit and lean, his big frame now carried the droop of a soft, heavy paunch.

Aaron reached over and closed the door to Scotty's room, gagging for a moment as he stepped too close to the authentic stink produced by artificial pleasures, a sour stimulation for those remaining in the real world.

The sloppy, messy condition of the bathroom increased Aaron's ire. It was lazy and disrespectful, and Aaron knew that while his complaints would initially be met with a sympathetic response, no real action would ever be taken.

Aaron showered, suspecting he was also the last person to set foot in the shower. He brushed his teeth and shaved in the dirty sink. He returned to his room to slip into his gray gardener's uniform and give a quick study to the day's schedule of appointments.

Thankfully, he still had a decent number of wealthy clients with elaborate estates, people who remained committed to maintaining attractive properties. These people were willing to pay top dollar for the A-list treatment. They included celebrities and entrepreneurs, old money and new money. They put Aaron's horticulture degree and landscaping artistry to good use.

While his original client base had dwindled, Aaron picked up new customers as larger competitors folded, unable to sustain themselves when interest in beautifying the physical world diminished. This allowed for an independent, sole proprietor like Aaron to survive as a niche business.

His income was crucial to the others in the house. At this time, he was the only person with a regular job, resulting in a lopsided contribution to the rent. During rare moments of real-world coherence, the other three vowed to find work and help cover costs, but these promises were left behind once they journeyed back into fantasyland.

As Aaron descended from the second floor, he encountered Larry sprawled on the steps, an obstacle to be stepped over. Scrawny with long limbs, Larry appeared to be unconscious, still wearing his designer eye cover (illustrated with a colorful fruit cornucopia). He gripped a mobile device that routed signals to the chip implanted at the base of his brain. This was typically how Aaron discovered his roommates in the morning – dropped in random places around the house, exhausted from lengthy, immersive sessions in their imagination that all but erased their awareness of their real surroundings. Sometimes they passed out while the chip was still receiving an onslaught of data, unable to turn off the feed, resulting in health risks. Heart attacks and shock-like trauma had been linked to overdoses, although the lawyers at Dynamica had skillfully avoided any direct correlation or liability. It was hard to sort out how much of the health risk was ancillary: the result of a population taking less care of its physical well-being through proper sleep, diet and exercise.

Aaron reached down to extract the thin, rectangular remote from Larry's hand. As he did, he glimpsed the screen to see the sensation Larry had ordered up: Flavors. Chef Larry no longer indulged in the taste and aroma of real food preparation; he now fed off the simulation of these things as delivered via satellite and transmission towers to his sensory system. He had sworn to anyone who would listen that the chip experience was stronger and more pleasurable than the real thing. He could blend flavors, meticulously dial them up and down, and choose from a menu of monstrous proportions and variety.

Actual eating for sustenance had become dominated by Body Fuel bars and a selection of pills, bland intakes that were quickly and efficiently absorbed to keep the body operational, like filling a car with gas, while extravagant meal experiences primarily existed as a virtual treat.

Standing over Larry on the steps, Aaron turned off the feed to Flavors. Some of Dynamica's feeds charged by the minute and Aaron doubted Larry had an unlimited plan – or could afford to run up his bill. He placed the remote back down near Larry's hand. At that moment, Larry grabbed Aaron by the sleeve and shouted out loud, startling him.

"*Don't!*"

Aaron pulled his arm away, irritated. "Give it a rest, Larry."

Larry blindly scrambled to regain the remote. Aaron yanked the eye cover from his roommate's face. Larry froze for a moment, staring at Aaron through thin, pained eyes unaccustomed to light.

"I said *give it a rest*," said Aaron, tossing the eye mask down the stairs. "Get up. Go find some work. If you don't start pulling your weight around here, I will have you evicted. Got that?"

Larry's eyelids flickered in a mad twitch of blinking. He was still coming down from hours of stimulation high. "Banana.... Strawberries..." he said, nonsensically, still mentally consumed somewhere else.

Aaron descended the rest of the steps. Two roommates accounted for, one more to go.

Desmond was laid out on the living room couch with his pants down around his ankles. Aaron didn't have to guess very hard at his chipfeed choice. He appeared to be sleeping, chest rising and falling gently under a wrinkled T-shirt. His hair was pulled into a man-bun. He was pale and shriveled, but not dead. Like the others in the house, he was in his late twenties, but looked older.

Desmond worked sporadically as an information technology specialist. As such, he had connections to a lot of gray market hardware and software that mimicked Dynamica's chip sensations without requiring Dynamica's pricey products and services. Desmond currently wore his sensory collar – a black, softshell device that circled his neck and communicated with the chip in his spine through an alternative delivery method. Desmond claimed the collar provided a boosted signal that the satellite couldn't replicate and created superior sensations at an unrivaled strength. The collar had a small slit that accepted thin square 'memory cards' of stored experiences that could be purchased on the black market. While the public had been warned about 'bootleg' feeds, they became popular nevertheless as a lower-cost alternative that offered unregulated experiences that sometimes strayed into sick and twisted fantasies. While it was illegal to buy and sell brain feeds that simulated the act of rape or murder, these cards became widely available and difficult to intercept.

Aaron looked at the scattering of small black squares on the floor next to the couch. He worried about the questionable sensations they offered and the potential for underground products to have bugs and viruses that could damage the brain and nervous system. Earlier in the month, the local news had warned about black-market sensory cards that had been suspected of triggering aneurysms and strokes.

"That's a load of crap," Desmond had responded to the controversy. "Dynamica is a monopoly. They want to give everything else bad publicity. There's nothing wrong with these knockoffs. They're just cheaper, with some different offerings. If you've got a fetish, why not? It's not hurting anybody."

Aaron had long ago learned not to argue with chip users. Their numbers had grown to the majority of the U.S. population in less than eighteen months after the technology's introduction into the marketplace.

"Unleash your imagination," promised Dynamica. "Live your fantasies. Expand your senses."

Aaron's response was a firm 'no thanks'. When everyone else was jumping on the bandwagon and having the chip installed in simple two-hour surgeries, Aaron flat out refused. Some people laughed at him and called him old-fashioned. They considered him a stubborn traditionalist, ridiculing him as they would somebody who still used a typewriter, made phone calls on a landline, or listened to compact discs.

"Get with the times," they told him.

"It's not how I want to live my life," he responded.

Aaron entered the kitchen and made himself a real breakfast of pancakes with syrup, scrambled eggs and melon slices. He drank a tall, chilled glass of orange juice. He did not touch any of the smooth, tasteless Body Fuel bars or Instant Edibles nourishment pills that his three roommates gobbled for convenience. Aaron's food, kept on designated shelves in a cabinet and in the refrigerator, was typically untouched by the others, even the former chef. They didn't have the patience to cook, to clean dishes, to shop for groceries. They claimed flavors and tastes were far superior when experienced through the chip and that it made eating real food a stale and tedious exercise.

Sadly, as the roommates neglected to feed themselves real food, they also neglected to feed the house cat, Paddy. Aaron filled Paddy's bowl with a generous heaping of cat food, and Paddy hungrily wolfed it down.

Aaron reached down to stroke the back of the cat's neck, a smooth sweep of fur undisturbed by the awkward bump added to so many human necks. Paddy purred with appreciation.

★ ★ ★

Aaron and his roommates lived in a rundown twenties-era Spanish colonial-style home in Elysian Valley, a neighborhood in East Los Angeles nicknamed Frogtown after a legendary incident in the thirties where thousands of toads invaded the community following a hard rain.

While swarms of toads no longer posed a threat, slippery humans were commonplace, stealing from ignorant homeowners. Aaron kept his Ford F350 landscape truck and gardening equipment securely locked up in a detached garage on the property. Residential burglaries, often conducted brazenly in open daylight, had become an epidemic as the number of 'zoneouts' – people consumed in lengthy chip fantasies – skyrocketed. In some cases, items were stolen out of rooms while zoneouts lay sprawled in chairs or sofas a few feet away, unaware of anything happening in the real world.

Aaron kept his own lawn watered and neatly manicured – a compulsive routine – and it caused the house to stand out on a block of ugly, indifferent residences surrounded by dead foliage, sparse grass, uncollected litter and bald patches of dirt. Unfortunately, Aaron's cleanliness sent the wrong signal to would-be thieves who deduced this well-maintained home must have some valuables inside. More than one burglar left the house disappointed and empty-handed. While the yard was attractive, the house's interior remained a dump.

Aaron started up his truck. He headed to his first client of the day, a multimillionaire in Beverly Hills who still believed in preserving the beauty of the physical world. The eerily quiet Los Angeles streets continued to amaze Aaron, because he remembered a different L.A. from not that long ago, when traffic was constantly congested and everyone seemed to be on the move from one location to another. Now most work and pleasure took place inside the home, thanks to advances in technology that Aaron was convinced represented a regression in society. *Everyone back to your caves!*

He remembered the heavy traffic on game nights to nearby Dodger Stadium, before baseball went bankrupt from the loss of a new generation of fans. The relaxed pace of the game was intolerable for users of chip technology, accustomed to an accelerated rush of rapid-fire thrills.

Today, most of the other vehicles on the roadways belonged to transportation companies that had perfected driverless technology for home deliveries. The majority of bricks and mortar retail stores had become obsolete as most anything could be ordered online and arrive the same day. Residents only needed to step outdoors to report to a driverless truck stopped in front of their homes, punch in a code supplied during the transaction and accept packaged goods through a service window, much like an ATM withdrawal.

The autonomous vehicles were very good about not striking other vehicles, and when Aaron was younger and more mischievous, he would deliberately swerve his car in their direction to send them off the road and into palm trees.

Driving through the residential streets of Frogtown, Aaron couldn't help reflecting on what could have been. The community had just started riding a development boom that replaced old bungalows and vacant lots with new housing and hipster restaurants, drawing a younger crowd and fresh energy. But when the chip technology took off, shifting allegiance from the physical world to a state of mind, the gentrification movement stalled, then died.

As Aaron drove by the L.A. River bike trail, which ran along the eastern edge of the neighborhood, he could remember a time when cyclists populated the community and groups of children played in the parks. These days, such sightings were rare. You were more apt to see packs of lost, wandering dogs and cats neglected by chip-addicted pet owners who no longer required a furry companion. The tactile experience of pet ownership had been efficiently recreated as a brain stimulation, without the nuisance of buying pet food and cleaning up poop.

Just before he reached Highway 101, Aaron caught a glimpse of something that caused him to do a double take. It was a common sight in his younger days but an unusual spotting in today's Los Angeles: a jogger.

In simple shorts, T-shirt and running shoes, a cute young woman kept a steady stride on the sidewalk, arms locked in forty-five-degree angles, ponytail bouncing, cheeks red, eyes determined and focused. Aaron smiled. Here, in the flesh, was someone who still believed in the outdoors and exercise.

Dynamica offered a chipfeed that replicated the adrenaline rush of a good run, releasing many of the same endorphins, without subjecting the user to physical exertion and the side effects of blisters, shin splints, burning lungs and tired legs.

As he drove past, Aaron waved at her.

She glanced at him for a quick moment and did not wave back, facial expression unchanged.

"God bless you," said Aaron softly, and he headed for the ramp that would take him to the highway.

Highway 101 was a breeze: open and uncluttered. Years ago, this stretch of concrete would have promised bumper-to-bumper traffic inching forward at an agonizing pace. This was one of the upsides of the chip phenomenon: fewer cars on the road, faster travel and a noticeable decline in smog and pollution. Deteriorating and faded billboards, long past their expiration date, still decorated the route, promoting forgotten movies and canceled television shows. The newest billboards mostly advertised Dynamica and the 'mind-expanding' selection of more than one hundred thousand experiences 'just a finger poke away in the comfort of your own home'. With lightning speed, Dynamica had become the number one company in the world, surpassing its beginnings as 'alternative recreation' to become a way of life. On days when he was feeling angry and extra defiant, Aaron would flip his middle finger at the billboards, an old-fashioned physical gesture.

More recently, however, his ire had turned to a resigned sadness.

People were free to live their lives however they chose, and if someone's quality of life was improved by the chip, then he would accept that. But there was no way in hell he would ever get a chip sewn into his own flesh and blood at the delicate spot where the spine met the skull.

Aaron reached his exit quickly and then took Santa Monica Boulevard into Beverly Hills. Every week, he witnessed more businesses shuttered on the long, commercial strip that once drew big crowds to shopping plazas, popular restaurants, trendy nightclubs, fitness facilities and car dealerships. Today, he noticed a newly closed clothing boutique. (Who needs to worry about fashion when the physical world barely matters?) Some of the old storefronts were taken over by groups of homeless people, while others hosted shady, pop-up enterprises selling black-market chip technology that stole or mimicked Dynamica's signal feeds.

Male and female beggars created obstacles in the street, stepping in front of the sparse traffic, holding up cardboard signs pleading for money to maintain their chip subscriptions and shouting offers to do *anything* for renewal funds. Aaron moved around them without slowing down. When stopped at red lights, Aaron had to keep an eye out for ambushes from quick-moving criminals – sometimes gangs of teenagers – who would try to break into the back of his truck and steal his equipment. The cargo area had a thick padlock, but that didn't stop attempts to break inside. The police, hopelessly outnumbered by the rise in petty crooks, could not be counted on to show up and save the day. The ranks of law enforcement diminished as the chip's popularity grew, and Aaron couldn't help but wonder if more of L.A.'s finest were staying home to play cops and robbers in their head rather than place themselves at risk on the city streets.

Construction crews, too, had been abandoning their posts, resulting in stretches of roadway in a permanent state of partial shutdown. Trash pickup was equally unreliable. Aaron regularly swerved to avoid garbage and potholes, as if maneuvering through a minefield.

The most popular addresses on Santa Monica Boulevard belonged to Dynamica. The company's nationwide network of chip installation clinics drew long lines of ticketholders on their big day, assigned to receive what the company's marketing professionals touted as 'The Nirvana Effect'. In less than two hours, a chip could be installed and linked to the satellite feed. Chip types came in a variety of offerings – from standard to premium to 'gold' – with an array of subscription packages to choose from. The first three months of service, known as 'the starter kit', came reasonably priced, and then subscription costs soared soon after to coincide with the inevitable consumer addiction.

Stopped at an intersection in front of a Dynamica clinic, caught in a rare moment of cross traffic, Aaron studied the happy, excited faces of customers lined up at the entrance, awaiting a life-altering change. This particular Dynamica clinic had taken over a large space that previously belonged to a Cineplex movie theater. You no longer had to go to the movies to see Spider-Man when it was much more exciting for Spider-Man to come into your head and take you on an adventure of your choosing.

Unlike the rest of Santa Monica Boulevard, this stretch of block boasted fresh paint, vibrant colors and a clean sidewalk. For a split moment, Aaron observed a cheerful, chatty woman in a long skirt who resembled his wife, Wendy. Her long brown hair and lively eyes reminded him of the way Wendy once looked, years ago, when she had the spark. It filled him with a profound sadness.

Aaron looked away and kept his eyes on the road for the rest of the drive to Beverly Hills.

Beverly Hills remained in better shape than its surrounding neighborhoods, but not anywhere near as lush and picture-perfect as in its recent past. The crumbling of Los Angeles was extending into the upscale areas. It started slow and gradual, then turned swift and deadly, like the spread of cancer. Environmental indifference had reached the wealthy, who retreated into custom designer pods in their homes, paying top dollar for the gold chip and unlimited signal access. For many Beverly Hills residents, showing off an extravagant façade to their neighbors no longer mattered.

Thankfully, a few people still cared about appearances, and some of them remained Aaron's clients.

The saddest sight for Aaron, just before he reached Madison Reddick's mansion, was the local high school. The once handsome campus with its surrounding sports fields had become a shuttered, abandoned building surrounded by stray trash, dead grass and silence. Once Dynamica introduced stay-at-home chip schooling – a huge cost saving for the state of California – physical schools began shutting down. The arguments in favor of the transition pointed to the fairness of every student receiving an identical education, from the same curriculum feed, regardless of neighborhood, family income or other differentiating factors. While it sounded promising in theory, a singular experience eliminated a diversity of instructors and teaching methods, while reducing the creativity and interaction enabled by a classroom setting. Experiential courses like art, music and theater that did not effectively translate into one-way chip downloads were dropped from standard education and halfheartedly made available as a smattering of 'extracurricular' activities.

Aaron drove past the homes of two former clients – residents who previously cared about their lawns, gardens and plant life and now no longer gave a shit – sighing at the ugly sights they had become. He finally reached the stubbornly beautiful and majestic estate of Madison Reddick. He pulled up to the front gate and entered the code that Madison had trusted him with, enabling Aaron to conduct his weekly maintenance even if the eighty-one-year-old entertainment industry mogul was not at home.

The entire trip, door-to-door, had only taken fifteen minutes. When Aaron first started serving Madison as a client, the drive took about forty-five minutes on a good day, and sometimes up to an hour if traffic was backed up.

Yet somehow, someway, this shorter commute felt longer to Aaron. He was too aware of his surroundings.

Aaron parked, opened up the back of his truck and got to work. Vibrant plant life decorated every side of Madison's mansion, a leafy pleasure to the senses. Aaron trimmed and pruned, treated the soil, spread compost, cleaned up the flower beds, checked the sprinklers and irrigation control, applied protection from insects and disease, controlled the weeds and arranged some new life and color to brighten several areas that were beginning to bald.

After a solid three hours of work, as Aaron was packing his truck, Madison called to him from a tall, open window with billowing curtains and invited him inside for a glass of tea.

This had become a tradition.

Aaron understood it. Madison was lonely. Unlike most of the others on his block, he still craved human interaction.

Aaron smiled and waved his acceptance. He was tired and dirty, but you don't say no to a man who provides a considerable portion of your income. And Aaron liked Madison – they were on the same wavelength, literally. They did not surrender their brainwaves to a chip.

"What flavor would you like today?" Madison asked Aaron as he entered through the oversized front door. Madison rattled off a selection of exotic teas, leading Aaron into a grandiose den surrounded with plant life, framed art and stuffed shelves of books, compact discs, vinyl, DVDs and Blu-rays. It was an unusual sight – no one collected physical media anymore.

Aaron made his choice – 'white mango' – and sat in a large, soft chair that immediately felt good against his aching back. He apologized for his sweaty smell, and Madison laughed. "If I wanted a pretty scent, I would chipfeed it to my neurons," he said sarcastically. He was breezily indifferent to Aaron tracking dirt into his house. He didn't care about their difference in class status or age. Madison, at least fifty years older than Aaron, was a retired entertainment executive who had done it all – produced hit movies, managed pop music superstars, created long-running television series and even dabbled with stage musicals.

Famous decades ago, Madison was now irrelevant in the modern era. The entertainment industry had essentially shriveled up since the introduction of the chip. People could experience the euphoria of an exciting feature film or music composition without enduring the actual art. Now it was as easy as the touch of a button on a mobile device.

Madison delivered a tall glass of cold tea to Aaron, who gratefully accepted it and took a healthy gulp. It hit the spot.

"Real human labor and work ethic," said Madison, admiring his visitor. "I deeply appreciate it. I do. Everything is so automated these days. But you bring a personality, a passion, a creativity that a cluster of technology could never achieve. You've continued to stay off the chip?"

As Madison asked the question, he lowered himself into a nearby chair, which signaled this would not be a short conversation. He had trapped a real live human and would make the most of an opportunity for authentic dialogue.

"I will never put that thing in my body," Aaron said. "It's not how I want to experience the world."

Madison sighed. "And I thought it was bad when everyone had their nose buried in an iPhone. We should have known it would get worse – far worse. But maybe I'm just a relic of the past, an old geezer clinging to physical things." He gestured to his walls. "My art collection, my antiques, my Persian rugs and elegant furnishings. I spent so much money on tangible items that I can touch and feel, and now it's all worthless."

A sad smile crossed his face. He was still a handsome man. His clean-cut appearance was at odds with social norms. He was dressed in a maroon polo shirt, neatly pressed slacks and new loafers. He was freshly shaven with short, wavy gray hair carefully styled with gel. He wore round designer glasses with thin metal rims.

"I get it," he said. "I understand what happened – to people, in general. Real life is shit. Who wants to face it? The crime and disorder, the sad state of politics, a spiraling economy, the lack of ethics and moral fiber. We're all just wanderers. There's no longer a sense of community, of personal values. No individual expression. Everything is a one-sided download. Nobody wants real feelings anymore. Our real feelings are bad. So we feed off fake feelings from Dynamica Incorporated. Order me up some exuberance!"

He stared into the ice in his drink and added, "We've lost the art of being human. We no longer communicate in any meaningful way. The young people, they don't even know human interaction, they can barely speak in complete sentences. It's like they still haven't found their voice. This new generation – everyone is growing up fat and lazy. Do you know that for the first time, life expectancy in this country is declining? It's a statistically significant amount. We're living shorter lives. Of course proponents of the chip say, 'Yes, it's a shorter life, but higher quality because of the pleasures of the chipfeed.' What total nonsense. We *are* our bodies, we must take care of our physical health."

"I need to do more to stay in shape," said Aaron. He was a former high school and college athlete, distanced from his peak condition.

"Your work keeps you fit, it keeps you active. You're in good shape. I work out every day in my gym. I go on long walks. I do laps in the pool. That reminds me, anytime you want, you are welcome to use my pool. I mean it. I promise it's more refreshing than the swimming options in the chipfeed. You know they have one for the backstroke? Such nonsense! You can do your own backstroke for real at my house."

"Thank you," Aaron said. He was indeed tempted to bring his swimming trunks next time. All of the public pools around L.A. had closed, and the public beaches were in poor shape.

"Despite all of this," said Madison, "I do have hope. Sometimes things have to get really bad for the pendulum to swing the other way. I have my sources – and they say the government is in serious talks with Dynamica. We should see some intervention soon. I don't know the nature of the conversations, but one possibility is more regulation, more oversight of this nationwide addiction and its health effects. Or maybe they'll load it up with taxes. Make it less affordable. It's too easy to be a do-nothing these days. You have people who are playing the system. They live on the government's Survival Subsidy because it gets them a minimal lifestyle in the physical world: basic housing, food and health care, and everything else goes toward their Dynamica subscription."

Aaron nodded, thinking of his roommates. He had witnessed their slow slide into a minimal, lethargic presence hooked on chipfeeds.

Madison stood up. He walked over to a large picture window with a scenic hilltop view of his Beverly Hills neighborhood. "Look at this. No people, no cars. Looks like a goddamned still-life painting. I think I'll go stir things up. I'm going on a motorcycle ride. I'm going into the mountains and make some noise."

"I should be heading out," said Aaron, putting aside his empty glass. "Thank you for the tea."

"Any time," Madison said. "You'll be back next Tuesday?"

"Of course."

"Good."

At the front door, Madison handed Aaron a black and white booklet. "Here. Take it. You should read this."

Aaron accepted it and looked at the cover, which said *Real Earth Movement* in big letters with a simple graphic of a globe. The tagline underneath said *Chip sense is nonsense.*

"Yes, a paper product," Madison said. "We operate off the grid. Do you think there's any privacy online? Of course not. This is information about a group – a movement – of citizens resisting the chip technology. We're advocating for a deeper appreciation of real-world experiences. People need to return to the purity of a natural life. We need to cut the connections with Dynamica and hit them with stronger controls. We can't afford to accept this new norm. I hope you will join our movement. There's information inside on where to find us, who we are. I'm one of the biggest sponsors."

Aaron nodded. "I'll look at it. I'm not one for organized groups...but I am sympathetic to the cause."

Before Aaron departed, Madison gave him an abrupt, tight hug. "Thank you for being real, my friend," he said.

"I like being real."

"Perhaps we're the last of a dying breed," said Madison. "What happens when virtual reality becomes the new norm? And you and I become the alternate reality?"

Aaron had to shut his eyes for a moment. Madison's innocent musing stung. It hit closer to home than the old man could realize.

★ ★ ★

On his way home, Aaron made his weekly visit to his wife, Wendy. He brought fresh flowers – red and pink roses. She could not see, feel or smell them, but he hoped that somehow she would sense their presence.

He signed in through the front entrance of Tranquility Stay, validating his identity with a thumbprint and face scan. He took the elevator to the seventh floor, walked a long corridor and reached her resting place. He punched in the code for patient #25176.

The room was small and narrow. It was just big enough for her see-through Living Casket, a tangle of tubes and wires connected to her vital organs, and a space for one to three guests to visit with her, observing her unchanging presence in suspended animation.

She looked peaceful.

Aaron set the roses on the clear casket, above her chest, where her arms remained folded.

Her condition made him feel sick inside all over again. She was dead and alive, stuck in a self-imposed eternal bliss or perpetual damnation, depending on whom you asked.

Once, many years ago, she had been full of life and energy. When Dynamica introduced the chip technology, she welcomed the opportunity to experience artificial sensations and emotions as an occasional recreation, despite her husband's misgivings.

She got hooked and her personality changed. She was never the same again. She tried to go cold turkey but swung hard the other way. She abandoned her job, her friends and her family. Their marriage collapsed. She craved the chip's effects above all else.

When she was off the chipfeeds, she was depressed. The declining state of the real world didn't help.

She got hooked on the stronger, riskier, black-market chipfeeds. During one of their arguments, in a fit of rage, she told Aaron she wanted to escape into a chip high and never return. He yelled at her to go ahead, she was already halfway there.

She disappeared soon after. He went crazy trying to find her, fearing that she had gone on a binge and become unaware of her natural surroundings and possibly gotten hurt.

When she returned, she locked herself in the bathroom to avoid him.

Then she did the unthinkable. She downloaded an irreversible chipfeed, sold illegally, that sent her brain into a nonstop loop of ecstasy without ever waking up. This new 'suicide drug' dominated the headlines as authorities tried – unsuccessfully – to remove it from circulation. Thousands bought it.

Wendy entered her stimulated imagination and never came out.

As the number of victims of the 'suicide' feed piled up, enterprising new companies offered mausoleum-like storage spaces to keep these 'patients' on life support until a cure could be found.

Aaron looked down at his wife and wept. He felt the weight of being surrounded by hundreds of lifeless individuals in self-induced comas made possible by the 'exciting advancements in technology' brought to the population by Dynamica Incorporated. When his wife first underwent the chip installation process, he had been both upset and mildly intrigued. But after seeing the effects on her and others, he swore to never allow the evil, coin-sized demon into his body.

He hated it, even as it produced a thin smile across his wife's lips.

"Cure? There's no cure," said a leading medical expert interviewed recently on the news. "You have two choices. You can pull the plug and bury them or allow them to live in a state of never-ending stimulation that, ultimately, is meaningless."

Aaron couldn't bring himself to pull the plug on Wendy. But he did vow to pull the plug on whoever sold her this poison. He would put them in a state of anything but bliss before turning out their lights completely.

CHAPTER TWO

"Please sign this."

Betty Anne, the tall, stringy administrative assistant for Dynamica CEO Jeff Reese, dropped a red folder on Marc Tefteller's desk. Marc, entering his sixth week as Dynamica's Chief Marketing Officer, stared at the folder for a moment, swiveling in his chair. Hand-delivered documents from the CEO came in a variety of color-coded folders, representing topics and levels of urgency.

This was his first red. He knew that red meant 'right now'.

"It's a nondisclosure agreement," said Betty Anne, a woman of minimal words. Her mind always seemed elsewhere. She was relentlessly serious for a thirty-year-old. She dressed in monochromatic pantsuits and always kept her hair up in a tight, controlled bun.

This typically provoked Marc to crack jokes, tease her or otherwise try to break the stoic façade. They were the same age, and he was a pretty boy, currently between girlfriends, and prone to flirting. But for the moment he was caught up in curiosity over the request before him. He opened the folder and skimmed several pages of a legal document containing the traditional boilerplate agreement over material information: do not discuss with unauthorized parties, do not trade company stock, do not redistribute confidential documents.

The topic for all this secrecy was referenced in a simple code name: Project Sky.

"What's it about?" Marc asked.

"You know I can't say."

"How about if I bribe you with chocolate?"

"I subscribe to a chocolate chipfeed."

"Let me guess. Are we expanding into Europe?"

She simply stared at him, so he kept going. "We're introducing a new chipless technology? No more implants, we can send signals directly to the brain. No? We're being sued by Disney for the alienation of their customers' affections? Or the National Restaurant Association? The tourism industry? Or is it a change in leadership? Jeff is buying Hawaii and building a retirement castle? Or maybe – I know – I'm getting fired."

Betty Anne still didn't crack a smile. "Just sign it," she said, impatient and expressionless.

He nodded, signed it with a big, fat signature, closed the folder, and shoved it across the desk at her.

She took it and said, "Thank you" with her back already turned, retreating to the CEO's luxury suite on the top floor of one of Manhattan's most prominent high-rises.

Marc felt excitement – his first red folder. His rise to CMO had happened quickly through a mix of luck, good fortune and circumstance. Nine years ago, fresh out of Yale University, he had rolled the dice and joined a young startup company with big dreams but no track record of success. Jeff Reese had assembled a group of technology innovators, neuroscience experts and creative thinkers to bring the human experience to a brand-new level. Using mathematic modeling, they sought to recreate the full range of human emotions and sensations by manipulating the nervous system and brainwaves through electronic pulses that prompted physiological responses, such as the release of adrenaline, synchronized with a vivid capture of the imagination. The earliest experiences were similar to virtual-reality goggles with important exceptions: the sensations were recognized in the user's consciousness without external equipment and, once connected, there was no underlying awareness that the experience was false.

The magic took place through a small chip installed at the base of the brain. The chip accepted the user's selection of encrypted signals streamed through the airwaves via satellite and transmission towers. Sensations were ordered by individuals through mobile controllers, with a private passcode for each offering.

The first artificial thrill to be tested was a roller-coaster ride. Once a user got comfortable, covered their eyes and triggered the chipfeed, they could not distinguish between an actual experience and a fabricated adventure delivered to their mind.

The simulated roller-coaster trip lasted four minutes and then reality returned in a gentle transition. A team of scientists worked tirelessly to ensure the experience created no damaging physiological effects to the brain or nervous system. Testing and research continued for two years to validate proof of concept.

After safely and successfully crafting a dozen experiential 'highs' – from hang gliding to eating pizza to making love – the floodgates opened and anything was possible.

Reese had the best intentions in the world: providing warm sensations of acceptance for lonely hearts; satisfying hunger for dieters; offering intoxication without hangovers and liver damage for drinkers; and providing a safe outlet for people to engage in activities deemed unacceptable in real-life social settings.

After achieving all the final regulatory approvals, the chip was introduced to the consumer marketplace. Reese and his team expected the product to be greeted with some trepidation and skepticism, followed by a slow acceptance. After all, surgery was required to install the chip and the entire concept was unlike anything ever offered before.

But as soon as Dynamica unveiled its groundbreaking technology, demand exploded. User testimonials were ecstatic. The general population, angry and frustrated with the state of events in the real world, embraced the escapism.

The company shot to the top of the Fortune 100 list of publicly held corporations. It moved into a big home office headquarters in Midtown, New York City. Dynamica's distribution network canvassed the country.

Not everything went as planned. Instead of helping citizens lose weight through virtual feasts, the chip experience added pounds through a dramatic decrease in physical activity. Actual food was still required for general sustenance, so fast and convenient junk food became the norm to cheaply 'fill up the tank' between simulated gourmet meals. The average weight of Americans climbed.

But no one seemed to care.

As a junior marketing representative, Marc experienced the company's rapid growth firsthand. As the company quickly expanded its operations and employee count to keep up with demand, Marc saw his own status rise in the company. All Dynamica employees were required to receive the chip to represent the company, so Marc signed up and received the installation without question.

He liked it.

He sampled a variety of popular chipfeeds and enjoyed them all. At the same time, he wanted to maintain a good balance with the genuine side of life. He continued to explore the sights and sounds of New York City while others mostly stayed in their apartments.

Marc crafted numerous marketing slogans and taglines; all of them were successful because the product practically sold itself. Dynamica became whatever consumers wanted it to be, fulfilling their individual desires and fantasies.

He regularly saw his catchphrases on billboards, integrated into social media streams and dominating television advertising.

Reality got you down? Pick a dream and lift off. Dynamica.

Love. Laugh. LIVE. The Dynamica Experience.

Taste your favorite flavors of life. Get Chipped! Dynamica.

Let us capture your imagination. Dynamica.

Marc grew overwhelmed with his company's ubiquitous presence – it not only consumed his work life, it surrounded him everywhere he went. It thrilled him at first, to be part of such a significant movement, and then he became tired of it. The chip obsession was relentless. It was all his friends and family would talk about. There was no escape.

But the money was really, really, *really* good. And it kept getting better.

Marc did his job well, it was noticed, and Jeff Reese, the CEO, liked him. Reese had a special appreciation for employees who joined the company in its early, uncertain years, stayed loyal and contributed to its current success. Marc's promotion to the C suite took place following the abrupt, unexpected death of the previous Chief Marketing Officer, a robust and jovial man named Steve Bowers. Bowers bragged he had sampled more than one thousand Dynamica feeds and while this was true, it also contributed to his enormous weight gain. He reached three hundred and fifty pounds before succumbing to a heart attack while exerting himself to tie his shoe. He was known to practically live in his office, filling his stomach with ice cream and cheese sticks from a mini fridge when he wasn't binging on chip fantasies to experience his company's products firsthand. Marc was a young choice to succeed Bowers as CMO but the other leading candidate was on an HR watch list for impregnating an intern, a regrettable lapse in blurring his fantasies with reality.

Marc enjoyed his new role, his spacious office and the increased interaction with the executive leadership team. Most of them already knew and liked him. He was particularly close with Brandyn Handley, the head of Distribution Operations. Brandyn oversaw the network of transmission towers, satellite stations and chip implant facilities that continued to spread like wildfire.

A few minutes after Betty Anne had left Marc's office, Brandyn appeared in the doorway with a big grin, knocking on the frame. He wore chunky, rectangular glasses and a full beard, eyes lit up with excitement.

"You sign it?" he said.

"The agreement? Just did."

"This is going to be big."

"So what is Project Sky?"

"You'll find out. Soon. But let me drop a hint. Imagine the biggest thing that could happen to this company. Because it's even *bigger.*"

"Now I'm even more intrigued. And you're not going to tell me?"

"Hey, I signed the papers too."

"Fair enough."

"There's a big meeting notice coming. Clear your Thursday. That's all I'm going to say. See you, man."

Brandyn rapped again on the doorframe and was gone.

Marc shook his head. He looked around at his ridiculously large office. He still had empty shelves to fill, blank walls to hang paintings on. He turned his chair to face the scene outside his window – a sprawling, godlike view of Manhattan culminating in the lush green treetops of Central Park. The people below were represented by tiny dots of life, hundreds in every direction, each representing a customer or potential customer for the 'Nirvana Effect', a tagline he had developed in his first year at the company.

Marc thought, *How much bigger can we possibly get?*

★ ★ ★

Marc arrived early to the top-floor conference room as security personnel concluded a sweep for bugs. They inspected under the large mahogany veneer table, around the high-back leather chairs and behind two widescreen LCD monitors.

Marc stood off to the side, waiting for them to complete their duties before sitting down.

This was only his second meeting in Jeff Reese's executive conference room as a member of the senior leadership team; the first had been a conversation about acquiring a company that had successfully launched a 'pod room' concept to consumers – small enclosed spaces you could build in your home for zoning out and experiencing chipfeed signals in the ultimate comfort. The pod rooms were cushy, soundproof and private with built-in control panels for selecting and streaming feeds.

"We could create our own subsidiary that does the same thing," said CEO Reese, "much like we did to dominate the designer eye mask business. Or we could just buy them."

Since Dynamica's balance sheet was stuffed with outrageous profits, the decision was quickly made to buy the business outright. It was another offering for the new Chief Marketing Officer to pitch to the public alongside the wildly popular chipfeed subscriptions.

This meeting felt different, more intense than the acquisition deal. Reese, via Betty Anne, had stressed that it was in-person only ("whatever you're doing, wherever you are, be here") and required formal business attire ("suit and tie mandatory, we will have an important guest").

Marc sat in a tall chair with his back to the wall. He faced the sky and clouds. The meeting room's floor-to-ceiling windows towered above Midtown. Few buildings were taller.

Gradually the room filled with Dynamica's executive team as they dropped into seats around the table. Eight men and four women. Brandyn Handley sat next to Marc, smiled and said nothing.

There was minimal chatter and full attendance. The room went completely silent when Reese arrived and stood by his chair at the head of the table. A big bronze Dynamica logo dominated the wall behind him.

"Good," he said. His eyes searched the room. "You're all here. Phones put away. Laptops closed. Pens down. This is big news, and we cannot allow it to leak before we are ready to go public. Thank you for signing your nondisclosure papers. You're already under a broad NDA as members of the senior leadership team, but this information is highly material and requires extra stringent precautions. You're officially on the blackout list, prohibited from trading company securities. I know you know the drill, but it's worth repeating. This is very sensitive, and we must control the timing and the messaging. Are we in agreement?"

Heads nodded around the table.

"I am incredibly proud of what we – what *you* – have achieved in the past few years. No one could have predicted this kind of success. We took risks. We broke new ground. We mastered the integration of cutting-edge technology with the human brain. We delivered exactly what the consumer wanted – escapism in a troubled world – and we were rewarded handsomely. Today, our customer base represents a very large portion of the public. We have become a vital part of everyday life. And we are about to get even bigger. How is that possible, you ask? Through total saturation. We are going to serve one hundred percent of the American public. That's right, I said one hundred percent. Getting there requires a special partner. Someone who recognizes and appreciates the value of what we do – and possesses the power to take it to the next level. Someone who can produce a mandate so that no one is left behind when it comes to the miracle of chip technology. This time next year, every man, woman and child across America will be chipped. That's because it is becoming law. In two weeks, we are announcing a partnership with the United States government."

He paused for a moment to let this sink in, enjoying the surprised reactions around the table. "Everyone, I would like to introduce you to Wilbur Kepling. Mr. Kepling heads up the U.S. Department of Citizen Affairs, a federal agency dedicated to the welfare of the people. Mr. Kepling, please come in and meet the Dynamica leadership team."

A tall, gaunt man with white hair and pale blue eyes stepped into the conference room from where he had been waiting just outside the door. He smiled, looked at the faces around the table and stood alongside Jeff Reese.

"Mr. Kepling will now describe this new partnership and the benefits it will bring to society. This is truly a revolutionary moment we can all be proud of. Mr. Kepling, the floor is yours."

Reese sat down in his chair as Kepling began a slow stroll around the room, delivering a short speech in a slight southern accent. Heads turned to look at him as he passed by each corporate leader in the room.

"You may have wondered about our project's code name, which was referenced in the papers you all signed. Project Sky. What does it mean? Well, the sky encompasses all, does it not? It is there above us, around us, wherever we go. It is a constant that unites us. If we took on the perspective of the sky, we would see all and know all, would we not?"

He chuckled. "We've been monitoring your products and services very closely. At first perhaps, admittedly, with alarm. But you can't change the tide of consumer demand – they want what they want. If you deny the people, they'll find another way. If we shut down Dynamica, a thousand imitators would take its place, what we call 'fast followers', who steal your patents and technology breakthroughs and bring them to the market in legal or illegal ways, cheaper, less safe, less controlled. It's like handing over drugs to the drug dealers. Or moonshine to the bootleggers. It's much more powerful if you find a way to work with – not against – the desires of the people. So we looked at your chip technology not as a threat, but as an opportunity."

Kepling stopped for a moment behind Marc's chair. Marc started to crane his neck to look at him, and then simply looked down at the table's shiny wood surface. He kept his reaction neutral. He didn't know yet how he felt about this arrangement. While others already wore smiles, Marc felt a sinking feeling in his gut.

"As Jeff said, we are entering into a partnership that will require all citizens to be chipped. The government is going to leverage your technology for the benefit of the American people. We do not have a clear, accurate account of the population. The Census Bureau is perennially outdated and unreliable. We have a hodgepodge of systems. Social Security numbers. Tax IDs. Voter registration. Driver's licenses. Imperfect at best. For the first time, we will have a uniform tracking system that provides an accurate representation of the people. Everyone is accounted for. Everyone is logged into a master database where we can ensure they are receiving the appropriate allocation of social services and government benefits. Everyone can be treated equally, truly for the first time. We will restore some social order. That includes citizenship rights for lawful immigrants. Equal education credits. Consistent taxation. Balanced allocation of property and other common assets."

Some of the smiles around the room turned into uncertain glances. Kepling began pacing again. "Now, of course, there will be exceptions for exceptional people. Please don't consider this as some kind of socialist programming. That's where the consolidated oversight comes in, a discipline that frankly, has not existed in a proper form under traditional methods. For instance, let's discuss criminal activity. By placing everyone on a common grid, we can maximize the support we give to law officials. We can color-code citizens as to their risk level, meaning the danger they may present to society. We will have a faster, more effective means of stopping and preventing crime. Let me share some scenarios."

Kepling stood at one of the tall windows. He faced a pale blue sky. "A child is abducted. Immediately we can track and recover that child – and apprehend the kidnapper. For criminals, there is no such thing as a hiding place. The chip tells us their location in real time. We will use the chip to find fugitives, to stop those who do harm to others. Another scenario: an active shooter erupts somewhere, spraying bullets at innocent bystanders. Within seconds of being notified of this behavior, we can send a signal to the chip that stops the attacker immediately – paralyzes him – bringing him down before the body count goes up. It's as simple as the press of a button from a government agency receiving countrywide alerts. Another example? The suicidal and mentally ill. We will be able to substitute the toxic torment of a sick mind with happy thoughts and feelings. Again, a press of a button. Think of the wellness clinics we could create. We will have direct access to address disorders of the mind: violence, anxiety, sadness. No one needs to be unhappy. We can be the happiest country on earth."

Kepling left the window to continue circling the room. "Jeff referred to this as a revolution, and while I appreciate this description, it is really more of an evolution. We are already deep into the era of data and analytics. We have smart technology in our phones, our cars, our homes. Now we have it in our heads. It's a natural progression. There should be nothing shocking about it, but we know there will be some resistance when the mandate is introduced. Every citizen of the United States will require the chip. Every child that is born in this country will receive the chip. And, we will enforce it with every means at our disposal. It's only fair – as Americans, we are all in this together. Fortunately, a huge proportion of the population already has the chip. And, as your company has carefully communicated, removal of the chip is extremely dangerous and could result in death, paralysis and all the other footnotes in your television ads. Once it's in, it's in. You don't attach something so intricate to your brain and spine, and then just rip it out. I've heard the stories of those who have tried, and your legal team has addressed the lawsuits with great vigor and success."

Marc winced; he knew the PR team that had worked closely on the reputational issues related to the deaths. It had been very difficult and led to even stronger disclaimers in all marketing materials.

"Dynamica has a very strong team," said Kepling, circling past Jeff Reese and patting his shoulder. "That is why we are so excited to partner with you. You are a number-one company that attracts top talent. You have an extremely powerful brand. At the beginning, I know, there will be some public outcry. The usual noise about freedoms and privacy – too much government, too much information sharing. But it is for the greater good of the people. Let us get one thing clear from the start: this will not be optional. It will be enforced. With that enforcement comes a responsibility that we will take very seriously, to deal with any ancillary health implications. We will establish medical clinics to address chip malfunctions, chip addictions, and anything else that takes away from the full potential of the chip technology. We, as you, are vested in a one hundred percent success rate."

Kepling now stood with the large Dynamica logo behind him. "This will be a true partnership where both sides win," he said. "Washington will not interfere with your entertainment division or influence what you sell to thrill seekers to fulfill their fantasies. Our interests are in tracking and logging citizens, helping them in a more balanced manner and controlling crime. We govern the people. This is a tool to support that. It's obvious, right?"

Kepling clasped his hands together with a big sigh. "That's it, really. We're going to be working very hard in the coming days on all the logistics, a communication timeline, an integration plan, and once this goes public, we'll bring a lot more folks to the table. Talented people with big ideas. The excitement level will be extraordinary. You are the most successful company on the planet. We are the strongest government in the world. Together we are creating something that will change the fabric of society. We will reach out across the United States, from coast to coast, to unite the people under our broad canvas of hope and protection. Yes, we *are* the sky. Every one of us. Thank you."

★ ★ ★

After the meeting, Brandyn followed Marc into his office. He shut the door and gave Marc a stinging high-five. "This is *awesome.*"

"My head is swimming," said Marc.

"We're going to make millions when this goes public. You do know that?"

"I mean, I expect…."

"All that company stock stuffed in our bonus plan is going to explode. We're going to have one hundred percent market penetration."

Marc was already wealthier than he ever dreamt he would be at thirty years old. Most of his friends made far less, even the Ivy League grads. Some struggled to find work as artificial intelligence overtook large numbers of jobs – and many industries took a nosedive as more people chose to stay home and indulge in the pleasures of the chip.

"It's crazy," Marc said. "It's…embarrassing."

In the office next door, which belonged to the Chief Data Officer, Marc heard a wild shout of "Yes! Yes!" Another Dynamica leader expressing post-meeting exuberance in his office.

Marc noticed a folder had been placed on his desk. The cover had an official emblem featuring an eagle, with the words 'United States Department of Citizen Affairs'. He looked down at the folder, almost afraid to open it. He was still absorbing the news.

Brandyn saw it and said, "We all got one. I helped coordinate some of it. It's the game plan. Key messages. Roles and responsibilities. Dates for the rollout. This is going to move very fast."

"Are we staffed for this?"

"No," said Brandyn. "But we have the green light to hire, hire, hire. My team is going to double, easy." Then he let out a laugh. "You're going to have the easiest job on the planet – marketing a mandatory product! Your job will probably change from sales to real PR, you know, reputation management. We're going to be a monopoly. No one else has our expertise and scale, and now we'll have a big, fat government contract. We're kings of the world, buddy!"

Marc thought about the pockets of public resistance to Dynamica – not everyone was enamored with the company. Some people considered it a threat to society – another example of technology ruining the relationship between the human race and the natural world.

"I can't stand still," Brandyn said, moving in small circles in front of Marc's desk. "Let's go celebrate. We'll get out and have some fun, before we get totally consumed by this. It's going to get crazy busy. What do you say?"

"Sure," Marc said. He still felt shaken, and welcomed the opportunity to step out of company headquarters to let it all sink in for a while before digging into the execution phase. "I don't think I can concentrate right now anyway."

"We'll go to CAPE. My treat. It's a few blocks away, just off Seventh Avenue. You been there?"

"Never heard of it."

"Great! You'll love it. Let's go." Then he said, "You're lucky you're not married. Do you know how hard it's gonna be to keep this from my wife? We'll be able to afford the biggest penthouse suite on the East Side, the best of the best. We'll have vacation homes, plural. She's gonna go bonkers."

★ ★ ★

Marc and Brandyn entered CAPE, where a sign in the front window promised 'Come in and Soar' with an intentionally kitschy illustration of a superhero. Once Marc stepped inside, he inwardly groaned. This was not a traditional bar, in the historic sense. It was a Chip Bar.

"Check out the menu," Brandyn said, directing Marc's attention to it.

A list of offerings filled the length of an entire wall behind a 'bartender' who assisted in programming the desired experiences for customers equipped with the chip. The offerings included every possible alcoholic drink, from expensive wines to domestic beer.

"These aren't real drinks," Marc said. He looked around the room, where customers sat in colored beanbag chairs, wearing eye masks, lost in the sensations they had purchased. He saw a young couple sharing an oversized red beanbag, holding hands, united by their chip selection.

"We gotta work tomorrow," said Brandyn. "So we'll get drunk without the side effects. No hangover. No dry mouth. We won't even have to pee."

Marc had experienced alcohol by chip before and felt let down. He missed holding a chilled glass with melting ice, taking measured sips at his own pace, engaging with his environment and companions. This new form of consumption, while safer, was a mostly solitary affair. In addition to the drink selections, users could pick the music genre of their choice to pipe into their heads while they enjoyed their beverage.

Brandyn studied the jukebox options alongside the drink listing. He stroked his beard. "I'm going to have a Black Russian and listen to some hip-hop. Wait, no – electronica. What'll you have, buddy?"

Marc continued to scan the wall at the seemingly endless options. Then he saw one that caused him to do a double take.

"Cocaine?"

Brandyn laughed. "Yeah, they have that, too. Coke. Heroin. You get the kick without the health risks. It's FDA approved. Supposedly it cuts down on real drug addiction."

"Except now they're addicted to the chip."

Brandyn gave his colleague a funny look. "What, now you're on the side of the naysayers? You can't get physically addicted to the chip."

"Physically, psychologically, what's the difference?"

"Hey, this kind of attitude isn't going to help us when the new law goes into effect. Come on, you'll feel better after a drink. There's gotta be something here you like."

"I think I'm going home," Marc said.

"What about our celebration?"

"I'll celebrate at home."

"Yeah, okay," Brandyn said. "I guess it is sort of pointless to pay a premium here for what you can get at home, but this is more social, you know?"

"Is it?" said Marc, looking around the room at the zoneouts who no longer had any awareness of their surroundings – until the chipfeeds expired, like a parking meter. Security personnel were stationed around the room, arms folded and eyes roaming, to ensure that pickpockets didn't take advantage of customers who were lost inside their imagination.

"It's about having a shared experience," said Brandyn. "That still counts for something, doesn't it?"

"I suppose," Marc said. "See you at the office tomorrow."

"Godspeed, brother." Brandyn flashed a peace sign, then he and Marc knuckle-bumped a farewell.

Marc returned outside to the dirty, smelly New York City sidewalk, and it gave him a strange feeling of comfort – or was it nostalgia? Maybe the setting was ugly, but it was real. He walked a couple of blocks, remembering when the streets were more crowded, and found an outside food vendor. While their numbers had dwindled, they still existed for people who wanted an alternative option to bland Body Fuel bars.

Marc bought a slice of greasy pizza and ate it, enjoying every bite: the gooey cheese, the rubbery mushrooms, the chewy pepperoni, the stale crust. He gave the gruff, stocky vendor a big tip and encouraged him to hang in there.

Marc wiped his hands with a paper napkin and walked another two blocks. He passed a shuttered Broadway theater, once a major attraction, now just another empty building. Out front, a short man with scabs on his face had set up a small table filled with crude mobile devices. Marc recognized the gizmos right away – cheap knockoff technology that streamed unregulated, black-market chipfeeds. Essentially, these devices delivered illegal bootleg experiences of dubious quality. Sometimes they carried viruses, such as persistent 'pop-up' advertisements that nagged inside the user's head for days after the initial download.

Marc stopped to look at the cheap devices. A handwritten sheet of paper taped to the table listed chipfeed choices.

"Not everything's on the list," said the scabby man. "I can get you underage girls. You into that? I got underage boys, too. Live the experience. Got a great deal for you."

"No thanks," Marc said. He continued walking. When he got to the corner, he pulled out his phone and reported the vendor to Dynamica's Watchdog Hotline. Within fifteen minutes, the man's operation would be shut down, and he would be jailed.

Marc advanced another block, a dark street with fewer pedestrians, advancing in the shadows until he reached his destination: The Big Be Bop.

Manhattan's last remaining jazz club.

Inside, it was sweaty, and that was okay. It was damp and musty, and that was just fine. The music was performed by real people, from the heart, not computers programmed with common formulas to mimic popular genres, favoring familiarity over originality. On the cramped stage, the Bobby Jimminy Band created a fabulous blend of sounds with joyful improvisations and energetic spontaneity.

Marc ordered a real drink – a martini – and enjoyed the elderly musicians giving their all on the trumpet, drums, bass, saxophone and piano. The audience was small but appreciative. Not every form of stimulation had to be chip based.

Marc reflected on the day's announcement. It had taken some time to settle on a feeling, but now he realized that deep down, he was distressed about the government partnership.

Dynamica's success had thrilled him up to a point. He believed in his product's benefits, but also feared its increasingly dominant presence in society. Making the chip mandatory didn't sit well with him, no matter how much money he stood to make.

Marc sat on a hard wooden chair, enjoyed his spiky drink and soaked in the soulful sounds of live jazz. Halfway through the set, he reached back and touched the small lump on the back of his neck. He felt the company chip he had agreed to insert into his body. He received it free of cost, a lifetime subscription. An employee perk.

He wanted to rip it out.

CHAPTER THREE

Aaron returned home in a foul mood. He had just lost another client to aesthetic indifference and spent much of the day distributing flyers to promote his business, sticking them in mailboxes where properties appeared to still strive for a respectable presentation.

Los Angeles' high temperatures and frequent dry periods already created a challenge for green lawns. Some homeowners installed artificial grass while others turned to moss beds, mulch and gravel.

But too many residents – a growing number – simply let their lawns go to hell. People no longer worried about how their yards looked in comparison to their neighbors', because the odds were the grass *wasn't* greener on the other side.

Aaron secured his truck in the garage. He walked across his cushy lawn, a rare parcel of colorful elegance on a block of ugly neglect. He unlocked the front door and stepped inside, expecting to find his roommates in the exact same spots he had last seen them.

Sure enough, the first sight to offend his eyes was Desmond on the couch, wearing his eye mask and neck collar, perfectly still except for the movement of his mouth, which twitched between a grimace and a smile.

Then Aaron spotted something new and troubling – broken glass on the floor. He walked over to the living room window and saw that it had been shattered, unlatched and shoved open, bringing in a slight breeze.

Aaron heard frenetic movement upstairs: the rapid sound of banging cabinet doors and sliding drawers. It was an unusual level of activity for a typically lethargic house.

We're being robbed!

Aaron raced up the stairs and, in his bedroom, found a strange, wide-eyed man with a wild red beard digging through his things, holding a pillowcase weighed down with bulges. Aaron tore the pillowcase out of his grasp and immediately shoved the man hard into the wall.

Shocked and frightened, the man threw up his hands to protect himself.

Aaron was prepared to land a punch to his face but froze when there was no resistance. The surrender came instantly.

"I'm sorry I'm sorry I'm sorry!" sputtered the intruder.

"What the hell are you doing?"

"I didn't know anybody was, you know, on watch. I wasn't, I'm not bothering anyone, just—"

"People live here!"

"I don't know, you're right, I'm confused." The man was obviously a mess. He smelled like he hadn't showered in weeks. He could barely string together a coherent sentence.

"You're trying to rob us!"

"Just a few things, you wouldn't notice—"

"I *would* notice."

"Just enough, you know, my subscription ran out, I can't, I can't, look at me, I'm not good at explaining this. I need to go back, go back—"

Aaron's voice lowered from an angry shout to simple disgust. "Get the hell out of here. If you come back, I *will* hurt you."

"Please don't." The red-bearded man shuffled out of the room in small steps like a tiny child, hands still raised halfway in a defensive pose.

Aaron followed him downstairs. The man started to return to the window.

"No," Aaron said. "Use the door, God damn it."

The man nodded vigorously and walked past Desmond, who remained on the couch, oblivious, lost in a fantasy.

"Sorry…" muttered the man. "Very sorry."

After the would-be burglar left, Aaron shut the door and locked it. Then he walked over to Desmond and tore the eye mask from his face.

Desmond let out a big scream, followed by, "What the hell, man! She was going down on me."

Aaron grabbed him by the shoulders and roughly sat him up on the couch. "Look at me!"

Desmond winced, as if experiencing daylight for the first time in ages. "Damn."

"Somebody just broke in here. Again! While you were zoned out. They were in my room, taking my things. Right under your God damned nose!"

Desmond's face twisted into confusion. "What do we have to steal?"

"*Plenty!*" Aaron shouted at him. "I'm sick of this – all of you!"

He stomped up the stairs. He slammed through a bedroom door and confronted Larry and Scotty. One was on the bed, the other on the floor, both wearing eye masks, consumed in imaginary experiences and sensations.

He tore off their eye masks. He took away their handheld remotes for activating the chipfeed.

Both of them transitioned slowly to the scene in front of them, as if being shaken out of a daze.

"You asshole," said Scotty, the bigger of the two men.

"Give it back!" Larry said. "It's not yours."

"We're having a house meeting," Aaron said. "Downstairs. Now!"

"Can it wait?" Larry said, in a thin voice, like a child's whine.

"No." Aaron left the bedroom, holding their remotes. "*Now.*" He returned downstairs and knew they would follow, given that he had cut them off from mental escape.

Desmond had retrieved his eye mask; the strap was broken, and he was trying to fix it. "You owe me a new—"

"Shut up, I owe you nothing," Aaron said. "I've been subsidizing you clowns, and it's going to stop."

Larry and Scotty moved down the stairs on shaky legs, holding the banister for support.

"Give it back!" Larry said.

"You're going to listen to me," Aaron said. Now he had the undivided attention of all three of them at the same time, a rare occurrence.

"So speak," said Scotty, "so we can get back to—"

Aaron cut him off. "You idiots, a man just broke into this house. It's not the first time this has happened. He smashed that window. I caught him digging through our stuff with no worries about getting caught because all of you are too busy playing in your heads. You have no perception of what's happening two feet away from you."

"All right," Desmond said from the couch. "We'll get an alarm. One of those new ones that send an alert through the chip. I know a guy—"

"And who pays for it?" Aaron said. "This arrangement started as roommates with equal expenses, equal responsibilities...."

"Sorry I got fired," said Scotty, scowling.

"Are you out looking for work?" asked Aaron. "Any of you?"

"I get my royalty checks," Desmond said, referencing tiny sums related to an old software product he co-created.

"It's not enough."

"We live cheaply," Larry said. "That's the whole point of this. We don't need—"

"Maybe *you* don't need," Aaron said. "But I do. I want more than this…this mess. I still eat real food. And I think someone…one of you…has been getting into my food supplies."

"Why would we do that? We eat fuel bars," Desmond said in a plain, isn't-it-obvious tone.

"Somebody's getting into my stuff," Aaron said. "I don't care, I'll lock it up with a goddamn padlock. But the point is – you need your own food. Real food. Larry, what the hell, you're a chef. Cook yourself dinner once in a while."

Larry gave him a quizzical look. "Man, you are living in the past."

"Because I don't pee in a jar while I'm high as a kite in some kind of land of make-believe?"

Scotty chuckled. This only made Aaron angrier.

"Yeah, funny because you don't help clean up. And you don't even belong here! We let you stay as a favor, because you're Larry's brother, but I'm done. You have one month to get a job, start contributing to this house, or you're out."

"Fuck you," Scotty said.

"Yeah," chimed in Larry. "Fuck you. You don't run the place. You just have one vote, same as the rest of us."

"That's bullshit," Aaron said. "There's nothing equal about this."

"It's a democracy," Larry said.

"I pay most of the bills," Aaron said. "The utilities, the rent, the upkeep that you don't care about. I patched the roof. I'm out there working, getting paid."

"We get our government checks," said Scotty.

"What happens when they keep reducing those checks? When too many people depend on them because they're all like you, hiding out in virtual reality?"

"We can minimize our expenses some more," Larry said. "Be frugal."

"You people are *barely living*," Aaron said, looking around the room at each of them, staring into vacant expressions. "This place is disgusting. Even the cat ran away for a better life. Don't you want to get out of this house, ever? Experience life? Travel, see the world?"

"I travel all the time," said Larry. "I go to Spain, Brazil, Paris...."

"You punch in a code!" Aaron said.

"Right, no sitting around in airports, jacked-up hotel costs, crappy weather, jet lag, stupid foreign languages...."

"That's just crazy," Aaron said.

"To you, maybe," Larry responded. "So go live life the way you want, and I'll live my life the way I want. Deal?"

"Not when it's affecting my quality of life," Aaron said.

"Then lower your standards a little," Desmond spoke up. "Maybe if you got the chip, you would understand. You can't criticize what you don't know. Consider all of this." He gestured around the room. "Consider all of this, right now, as the dream state. Technology has turned it around, brother. The chip state is our primary existence now. Sometimes we step out of the chip state to deal with real-world bullshit, but if you think of this environment – this conversation, the arguing, the house, the neighborhood – as a dream state, maybe more like a nightmare to be honest, then you can improve the quality of life. You can just flip a switch and make your inner consciousness your true self. You can create the ideal environment instead of taking what's given to you. You can choose how you experience life. Do you really want *this*?" He again gestured around the room.

"Yes," Aaron said. "Yes, I do."

"Great," Scotty said. "So be it. Go mow some lawns, if that's what turns you on. And leave the rest of us alone."

"Give back the controllers," Larry said.

"Yes, give them back." Scotty stepped toward Aaron, and Aaron tightened his grip on the devices he had taken from Scotty and Larry.

"You're all negative vibes, man," said Desmond. He leaned forward from the couch to pick up a small, square sensation card from the floor. "I'm leaving this buzz kill."

Aaron stepped on Desmond's hand before he could lift the sensation card. He yelped. Within seconds, Scotty slammed into Aaron, wrestling him to repossess his controller. Larry joined in, punching Aaron in the back. Desmond stood up off the couch and staggered forward.

Aaron fought all three of them simultaneously. His roommates' coordination was awkward from their diminished mobility in the physical world. Desmond could barely throw a punch. Scotty's deteriorated muscles, now mostly fat, weighed him down as he tried to tackle Aaron and wound up entangled with Larry.

This is the most pathetic fight ever, thought Aaron. Within a minute, two of them had fallen down and did not have fast enough reflexes for getting back up.

"To hell with this," Aaron said. He tossed the controller devices to the floor, and their owners scrambled to retrieve them. "You're right, this is all a bad dream."

He watched the three of them scurry back into their fantasies, butts on the floor, anxiously connecting signals to their brainwaves.

"Go play in your head," Aaron said, but they probably no longer heard him.

Aaron left the room. He gathered a few things. Then he left the house.

* * *

Aaron parked his Ford F350 truck by the river bike path on the eastern end of his neighborhood. He took a blanket and lunch into the forest. Egrets and blue herons skipped across the trees. Here he had privacy and a natural setting – well, mostly natural, if he didn't think about the river's concrete flood channels. The surroundings were calm, quiet and people free. Most people preferred experiencing the 'Walk in the Woods' chipfeed in the convenience of their homes, without the hassle of insects and dirt.

Aaron spread out his blanket on the grassy riverbank, sat down and enjoyed a simple meal. He drank lemonade tea from a thermos. He ate a ham and cheese sandwich with a dash of mustard. He peeled an orange and consumed sweet, sticky slices.

He soaked in the surroundings. He took in the earthy fragrances, the spare and delicate sounds, the crisp and gentle breeze. During his last visit here, he saw a raccoon family.

He remembered a few years ago going on bike rides with Wendy. They followed the twists and turns of the river, shouting conversation back and forth, laughing, exploring.

Those first few years of marriage were bliss. And he could trace the decline in their relationship precisely to the introduction of the chip. Dynamica – or 'Damnica' as it was called by virtual reality opponents – changed everything.

Aaron lay back on the blanket, face turned up at the treetops, and once again wished he had prevented Wendy from ever receiving the chip implant.

"It's safe, it's fun," she had told him. "Everybody has the chip. Come on, don't be such an old man."

"No way," he had responded. He didn't like the idea of foreign objects sewn into his body. He didn't even like the concept of tattoos. His body was off-limits to alteration. The whole thing creeped him out, even as his friends and family took the plunge – and came out singing the chip's praises.

He had everything he wanted in the real world. He was a well-paid landscape architect and 'gardener to the stars' with a solid client list and busy days dedicated to his passion, horticulture. He was young, healthy and excited to explore the mountains, valleys and beaches of California, the Golden State and its eternal good weather. And above all, he had a fabulous, beautiful wife who taught second grade in the L.A. County public school system.

She had long brown hair, large brown eyes and a round face with a natural smile. She was five-foot-five of energy and optimism. She read books, she liked plays, and she was great with children, easily connecting with them with her soft voice and quick engagement. She was magnetic.

And then.

The chip craze unfolded fast. The initial customers delivered unanimous rave reviews. Skeptics soon changed their tune. The technology delivered something for everyone. The first wave of users came away hooked, and there appeared to be no negative aftereffects.

It was a minor miracle. The mind could experience *anything*, flooding with realistic sensations, without putting the body at risk.

Wendy's closest friends spent all their time sampling and discussing chipfeed experiences. Book Clubs became Chip Clubs. It became a national obsession.

Wendy tried to convince Aaron that they should get chipped together – a shared experience – and he refused.

They argued about it for weeks. And then one day, she went and got chipped on her own.

He was furious when he found out. She was angry at his ire – "It's my body. I can do what I want. You don't own my body, whether it's the chip or having my ears pierced or anything else."

He hovered over her the first time she scrolled through the ever-expanding selection of sensations. They were divided into categories and lists: Top Sellers, Sports, Adventure, Travel, Aromas, Moods, Entertainment, Intimacy.

She sat in her favorite chair, poked in the code for waterskiing and covered her eyes with a soft mask.

He sat and watched her.

She smiled, she gasped, she laughed, she squirmed, she oohed and aahed, she erupted into shouts of excitement.

When it was over, she pulled off the mask and said, "You have *got* to try this."

"No thanks," he said.

She frowned at him. "You're no fun," she said. She returned to scrolling through the listings, finding dozens of other offerings that grabbed her interest, vowing to sign into more virtual experiences in the days ahead.

Aaron and Wendy soon spent less time together, even though they lived in the same apartment. Mentally, she left him to pursue artificial thrills, while he often sat in the same room, looking at a book or simply staring at her weird facial expressions and tiny jolts of movement.

"You look stupid when you're doing those feeds," he told her.

She swore at him – and she rarely swore.

She lost interest in other forms of recreation. She neglected her appearance. She became less engaged in her job and the students. She stopped having sex with Aaron.

She seemed to fill every spare minute with the chipfeeds.

"I've got ten minutes before I have to leave for school," she said one morning. "Time for a quickie."

"How about an old-fashioned quickie with your husband?" Aaron said.

"Sure, later," she said, already poking through the handheld controller that activated signals to her chip. "But there's a new one on here that I really want to try."

In the months that followed, Dynamica's sales and selections exploded. Beginners received discounts, making the offering affordable to most citizens. The cost of installing the chip was an inexpensive surgery, and then Dynamica made most of their profits off the subscription fees. Renewal rates hovered near one hundred percent. Subsequent rate increases did not hurt retention.

Wendy no longer wanted to leave the house, except as obligated by her job. She slept less to give herself more time to thrill to chipfeeds. Around Aaron, she became irritable and distracted. When she wasn't on the chip, she muddled through emotional hangovers, falling into depressions from reentering the real world.

Then she got fired. She was caught 'chipping' at the school, neglecting the children. A little boy under her care nearly choked to death on a piece of carrot. Fortunately, another teacher entered the room and gave the boy the Heimlich maneuver in the nick of time.

Aaron screamed at her: "You're addicted to this thing!"

She denied it with every ounce of energy in her – because, Aaron knew, she didn't want to get cut off.

He confronted her about a specific virtual experience he discovered in her billing history: sex with 'Mr. Dreamboat', an imaginary, muscle-bound man with a long mane of thick hair. He looked like a cliché from the cover of a lurid romance novel.

"So what?" she said. "Men jerk off."

"You had an affair. This is like having an affair."

"No it's not – it's fantasy. All of it, it's just fantasy. You're going to get jealous of some made-up character?"

"When you were experiencing it, you didn't know it was made up. That's how this thing works. The experience feels real. In your head, in the moment, it was the real thing."

"So what?" she repeated. "If you would get chipped, we could sign up for couple experiences. They have a whole list of things you can share with your partner, they're synced up to happen simultaneously. That guy I had sex with – it could be you."

"You want to have sex with me in your head?"

"Sure. I mean, you're threatened by me having sex with someone else in my head. We'll fix that."

Aaron sputtered for a moment, trying to find the right words. Finally, he exclaimed helplessly, "Listen to yourself! This doesn't even make sense. You're crazy!"

"You cannot call me crazy," she shot back. "You know nothing about this technology, except those op-eds you read from backward thinkers like yourself who can't accept that the world is changing. Do not criticize me or this chip until you have tried it because, guess what, you would probably love it."

"No," said Aaron. "I don't love some chunk of computer technology. I love what's on this earth. The sky, the stars, the mountains, the rivers, the oceans, the flowers. I love real people who really exist. I love *you*."

When this final statement failed to move her, he knew he had lost her.

He had married one person and now she was someone else. The transformation was grotesque. He knew the original Wendy still lived inside her, buried under a lot of crap, her blood poisoned by the mega-corporation Dynamica.

Like any other addict, she needed to go cold turkey. She needed to go into rehab. She needed to clean out her head and beg for her job back.

Late one night, while she slept, limp and drained from another phony stimulation, he took drastic action. He entered her Dynamica account and canceled her subscription.

The next morning, barely awake and already itching for a chipfeed, she quickly discovered his action.

She went ballistic. She attacked him and clawed at his face like a wild animal. He pushed her down to the floor and felt terrible about it. He started crying.

Then she started crying. But not about the pathetic state of their relationship, which caused his tears. She cried because she needed to feel the comfort of artificial good feelings delivered to the base of her brain.

"If you renew the subscription," Aaron said, panting with emotion, "I'll put a block on your signal. I've done research. I know how to do it. Every chip has its own passcode, and yours will be locked out."

Furious, she fled the house.

She reappeared two days later, refusing to say where she had been or what she had done. She simply glared at him. She locked herself in the bathroom for hours. She ignored his shouts.

He felt helpless and confused. He considered leaving her. But the girl he married, the real Wendy, still existed, he was certain of it. She could be revived. He needed to be tough and patient. She would one day realize the extent of her addiction, the hollowness of virtual reality, and desire to climb out of this awful hellhole.

He banged repeatedly on the bathroom door. "What are you doing in there?"

Most of the time, she didn't respond. Occasionally she muttered, "Nothing."

"If you renewed the subscription, under another name or whatever, I will block the signal. Is that what you want?"

"Go ahead," she said.

He was confused. And then he grew alarmed.

He had read about the rising number of pirated and bootlegged chip experiences. Cheap knockoffs that took an illegal ride on the Dynamica technology. Dynamica had worked hard to stop these dealers, but they continued to spring up like weeds. Aaron often saw them pitching their wares from street corners in seedy parts of Los Angeles.

"If you went to one of those street hustlers…you're in danger. They aren't regulated. You could infect your brain with a virus. Or some kind of invasion of privacy that takes your personal thoughts and does God knows what with them. They could fill your head with advertisements, subliminal messages. Wendy, please, tell me you didn't."

"Go away," she said behind the door in a weak voice.

"You need to eat real food. You need to get sunshine on your face. You need to…. Oh God." Aaron felt like he had lost the battle yet again.

"Come out," he said to her. "Come out right now, or I'm going to break down this door and drag you to a doctor. I have names of doctors, people who deal with this, and you'll get treatment. I'll do whatever it takes. This nonsense is over. It's going to end. You're not well, and you don't recognize it."

She refused to open the door.

"Then I'm going to bust in there," he said. "I'm sorry, but this, all of this, it ends today."

Aaron began slamming his shoulder into the door. He was a large man, a former athlete who played football in high school and college. It hurt, but he grimaced past the pain. He pounded repeatedly with all his might.

Finally, the door broke open.

Wendy was spread out unconscious in the bathtub, fully clothed, mouth open and eyes shut.

He tried to shake her awake. He screamed her name. He was overcome by anger and then alarm. He sprayed the shower on her, blasting cold water.

He couldn't revive her. He knew this was bad.

He had always been able to shake her out of a chipfeed. It was typically a slow, unhappy awakening but enough persistence would bring a person's mental state back to the real world.

When she refused to budge, he called for an ambulance.

He rode with her in the ambulance, crying, explaining everything he could to the paramedics. They could not get her to regain consciousness either.

"Her vitals are okay, it's like a deep sleep," one of them said.

At the hospital, they examined her and ran a multitude of tests but were unable to bring her out of her unconscious state.

Wendy had lapsed into a coma.

Aaron sat in her hospital room in a hard visitor's chair, waiting for something to happen, hopeful for some sign of life to flicker back: a movement in her fingertips, a blinking of her eyes, anything.

In the bed, under the sheets, she wore a thin, blue hospital gown. The street clothes she had been wearing were tucked in a large plastic bag placed in a small cabinet in the room.

Aaron opened the bag and went through the clothing. He felt in the pockets and found a clue.

Aaron pulled out a crude flyer, produced by one of the bootleg chip experience vendors.

He studied it for several minutes. Then he fell to the floor, sobbing.

A banner on the flyer read: DR. DELIGHT'S ULTIMATE CHIP TRIP. The text below described a signal sent to the brain that created an infinite loop of 'happiness and ecstasy'. It boasted that 'this loop cannot be broken, ensuring you remain in your ultimate state of joy for eternity without rude returns to miserable realities'. It was essentially a suicide signal that placed the recipient in a permanent coma of artificial heaven. The cost: a measly three hundred dollars.

Wendy had implemented this death wish. On the flyer, in her handwriting, she had written: PASSCODE 46XN38P.

She had purchased and activated the signal to the chip with the passcode. She had triggered it while he was yelling at her through the bathroom door.

Aaron felt sick. He felt responsible. He was screaming at her – and threatening her – and this was her escape.

He knew he had to notify the doctors. Then he had to make a decision. Stop her brain or keep her alive in this make-believe afterlife.

He couldn't halt the feed. He couldn't kill her. He just couldn't.

He soon discovered that hundreds of people, later becoming thousands, had sought out this same black-market suicide solution to depart forever from their undesired states of reality. An enterprising company began offering final resting places for these 'heaven seekers', keeping them on minimal life support in coffin-like boxes to provide family members with an alternative to pulling the plug on those who had 'overdosed'.

Wendy was transferred to an eternal resting place for a reasonable monthly rent. Aaron visited every week, delivering fresh roses.

Dynamica slickly sidestepped any liability for the unauthorized businesses that hacked into their technology. The corporation's PR machine issued press releases condemning such activities and promoting the efforts of their investigation unit to crack down on illegal practices related to their proprietary products and services, but in reality it was impossible to control. Websites of illicit activity were routinely busted and then reappeared online days later with a new URL. Some of them were hosted out of the country and it was difficult to track their ownership. Efforts to sue Dynamica were largely unsuccessful, as the company employed the largest legal team in the world.

Aaron sat up on the blanket in the woods, hurting from the memories. He missed Wendy. He wished she was lying next to him. But he was alone with nature. He watched a black-and-orange monarch butterfly move through the air in circles before landing nearby in the tall grass. It made him smile.

He pulled a brochure out of his back pocket, the one given to him by his Beverly Hills client Madison Reddick. It described the Real Earth Movement. Aaron had become determined to seek out the organization, become a member and meet others who felt the way he did about the intrusion of virtual reality into everyday life. He needed to spend less time in the house with his stupid roommates and more time with people who recognized the ugliness of the chip fad. The brochure said, *Fight the war against Sloth Society*. He liked the slogan.

During his drive back to the house, at the break of dusk, Aaron again spotted the female jogger. "You're not a member of the sloth society," he said quietly as he passed her. She looked right at him, like the other time they had exchanged glances and once more, he waved from the truck.

This time, she waved back. A small lift of her hand, but a returned gesture nevertheless.

She was tan, firm and fit in her loose white T-shirt and blue shorts. Her dark hair was tied back in a sleek ponytail that flopped in rhythm with her feet hitting the pavement. She had a wide, open face and dark, serious eyes.

He continued to watch her in his rearview mirror and saw that she had started to slow her pace. He reached a stop sign and dutifully stopped – despite the total lack of traffic – and then lingered for a moment so he could continue to look at her in his mirror.

She was attractive.

She had concluded her run and walked in big steps on the sidewalk, hands on hips, breathing heavily, sucking in air.

She turned toward the front entrance of a four-story apartment building.

So that's where she lives, Aaron thought.

Impulsively, he decided to circle the block to get a closer look. He advanced the truck.

He took a left, then another left, then a third and a fourth. He returned to the street he had just driven on moments ago when passing her.

He got a good look at the low-rise, block-style apartment building. It was in decent shape. Obviously people lived there who cared.

The property had a nicely manicured lawn, nothing fancy: no flowerbeds, a few hedges, definitely on the plain end of the spectrum. But, unlike many of the surrounding properties, it had not been ignored and left for dead.

Aaron saw a light appear in one of the windows on the third floor and guessed it must be the jogger, returning home. She didn't need to see him lurking out front. He quickly drove away.

He wore a smile on his face.

He liked what he had seen. Her apartment had a balcony. There was a sporty red bike parked on the balcony. And hanging off the rail, she had big flower boxes of bright, healthy marigolds, begonias, chrysanthemums, fuchsias and snapdragons.

It was like a splash of color in a black and white movie.

Aaron returned home feeling better, rejuvenated.

CHAPTER FOUR

Marc drove into upstate New York for an appointment with Dr. Rance Higgins at the Dynamica Research Lab, just outside Albany. Even with his clout as the company's Chief Marketing Officer, scheduling time with the 'Father of the Chip' was no easy task. Marc uneasily accepted the soonest available date of August 15 – which happened to be the same day the government partnership would be announced.

Fortunately, it was a late-afternoon announcement. The news release would go live after the stock market closed to minimize chaos during trading hours, given the sizable impact it was expected to have on Dynamica shares and the equities market. Marc's surgery would take place earlier in the day, before knowledge of the government partnership circulated beyond Dynamica's senior leadership team.

Extracting the chip from the human body was a far more complicated procedure than installing it, and most medical professionals would not even attempt it at the risk of blinding, paralyzing or killing the patient. Citizens who wished to disable the chip would simply have to unsubscribe to its services and leave it dormant.

Marc knew this would no longer be an option when the government began using the chip for its own tracking and citizenship oversight. He wanted the chip removed from his brain stem, pronto. There was only one man he trusted with that hyperdelicate surgery – Dr. Higgins.

Dr. Higgins had no clue the chip would soon be mandatory and that any attempts to remove it would go against the law. Marc had just barely enough time to undergo the chip removal and drop out of sight before the news hit.

He was finished with Dynamica. He did not want to be part of the company's future.

"Wouldn't you rather just have the chip wiped clean?" Higgins had asked him when they arranged the procedure. "It's far safer. We can disable it, neutralize it. Then you can reinstall the feed."

"No," Marc said, and he continued with his carefully constructed story. "I need to have it removed. There's a newer model coming, and as the head of marketing, they want me to experience it firsthand."

"I wasn't told anything about a 'newer model'," said Higgins in a huffy voice.

"Not a major difference," Marc said. "Just some minor enhancements."

"The original chip still works perfectly. Nobody's told me otherwise. There's nothing to upgrade. What's wrong with it?"

"Nothing," Marc said. "Please keep this to yourself. It's highly confidential, and I don't want you to put your job at risk. But there's a *slight* difference in the quality of experience. There's nothing wrong with your original chip. No defects. No recall. Nothing like that. We've expanded so much as a company – we're building on your great work – it's part of our mission to never stand still, to continually look at ways to bring new value to the Dynamica experience."

Marc leaned on his marketing skills to pitch Dr. Higgins the benefits of an updated chip.

Higgins remained skeptical. "I'm going to make some calls tomorrow," he said, bitter about being kept out of the loop regarding a new advancement for his discovery.

Tomorrow is fine, Marc thought. He just needed to keep Dr. Higgins in the dark until after the chip had been removed, and he became a free man.

Marc spent two hours unconscious in an operating room filled with the most advanced medical equipment that money could buy. Dr. Higgins led a small team of expert surgeons in conducting the highly precise removal of the chip without endangering Marc's brain, spinal cord or nervous system.

The procedure was a success.

When Marc awoke, he immediately brought his fingers to the back of his neck. He did not feel the small bump that had resided there for years. He only felt stitches and a lingering soreness.

Dr. Higgins waited for Marc to fully come out of his anesthetic stupor. Higgins was a short, wide man with a broad mustache, thin hair and thick glasses. As Marc stared at him, he looked like a cartoon character until his full dimensions settled in and the clouds dissipated from Marc's consciousness.

The rest of the surgery team had departed.

"Thank you," Marc said.

"Even with me, even with the experts here, you took a risk," said Higgins.

Marc nodded, propped up against pillows.

Higgins tested Marc's movements and reflexes to ensure there was no damage to his nervous system. He asked Marc to conduct simple thinking commands, like reciting the alphabet and counting backward from ten. He did so, cleanly and clearly.

"So the removal was a success?" Marc asked.

Dr. Higgins handed him a small plastic bag. The extracted chip was inside – black and round, like an oversized button with a hard texture.

Marc accepted it. "Goodbye, Mr. Chip."

"I would wait a few weeks before having the new one installed," Higgins said. "You're still going to be tender. You need time to recover and stabilize."

"Of course."

"Who's installing the new chip?"

"Oh…" Marc said. "I don't know yet."

"I need to find out more about this. I find this whole procedure unnecessary, to be honest."

"Perhaps," Marc said. Then he looked at his watch.

It was quarter to four.

"I need to go."

"You need to rest," Higgins countered.

"No," said Marc, sitting up on the edge of the mattress in a thin patient's gown. "Where are my clothes?"

"I don't recommend leaving that bed yet. Your coordination might be off. You could fall."

"I feel great. Really. I feel really great."

Despite Dr. Higgins' objections, Marc got dressed. As he was buckling his belt, the cell phone in his pants pocket buzzed. He quickly pulled it out and read the text alert from Dynamica CEO Jeff Reese.

"We are confirmed to launch at four p.m. Eastern Standard Time. Comprehensive timeline and key messages by stakeholder to follow. Please direct any media inquiries to PR team. Thank you again for your leadership and support with this significant milestone for our company and our country."

"So," Dr. Higgins said, startling Marc's attention away from his phone. "A few weeks without the chip. That's a big lifestyle change. What are you going to do with yourself?"

"Oh, I don't know," Marc said with a forced smile. "I'll find something."

Dr. Higgins joined Marc on his walk to the building's exit. "Are you sure you're okay to drive?" he asked.

"Absolutely." Marc was still blinking back some fog. His muscles felt sluggish, but he would manage through it.

"All right then." Dr. Higgins reached out and gave him a hearty handshake. "Good luck."

At that moment, Dr. Higgins' cell phone buzzed inside his breast pocket. He slowly withdrew his hand from Marc to reach for it.

Marc glanced at a clock on the wall.

It was four o'clock.

Marc quickly left the research laboratory as Dr. Higgins read the company announcement.

Marc ran to his car and climbed in, without looking back. He tore out of the parking lot with an abrupt squealing of tires.

* * *

As Marc sped along I-87S, returning home to Manhattan, his phone ignited with callers from his personal and professional life. He ignored them and punched the buttons on his radio, quickly finding a newscast.

The announcement had reached the general public. "The plan is to chip the entire U.S. population within twelve months…."

Marc listened to a reading of the press release and then skipped across the dial. Every radio station was interrupting its programming to cover the breaking news. On New York's most prominent news network, Marc listened to a live briefing from the White House press secretary.

"The president is very excited for the American people," she said, reading from prepared remarks. "This exciting technology enables us to ensure a society of equality and benefits for all. By unifying our country under the chip, we will see that no one is left behind. Your government stands with you. We understand you, we understand your needs, and we will protect you.

"The government will cover all costs of installation for those who do not yet have the chip. This includes newborns, who will be chipped at the time of birth. Immigrants, who enter this country legally, will be chipped as part of their citizenship. There will be a grace period for chip compliance.

After that, there will be an escalation of fines and other consequences for willful negligence."

Marc began to feel nauseous – a mixture of anxiety over the forced tracking and wooziness from leaving the laboratory so soon after surgery.

The press secretary spoke about the chip's ability to reduce crime by precisely locating inappropriate conduct and identifying criminals in real time. She also said it would ease the burden on the court system by reducing the time and expense of trials when evidence could be readily obtained through the chip's tracking mechanisms. Her speech ended with, "Please hold your questions until we have heard from all of our speakers."

Dynamica CEO Jeff Reese took to the podium next. His familiar voice filled Marc's ears. His speech was highly predictable – it aligned with many messages that Marc himself had crafted about the consumer benefits of the company's offering. Only now it wasn't presented as a choice. The pitch had a different tone: legitimizing the forced acceptance of the chip as a requirement of citizenship.

"The world is changing," said Reese. "We are proud to be part of that change. We built the most popular brand in America on innovation and dreams. We listened to what people wanted, and we delivered. While other countries have blocked this technology through government interference, restrictions and heavy regulations, we have worked toward a true partnership, so that all may benefit. As always, the United States is a leader, not a follower. No other country offers this. No other country will prosper like we do. Dynamica isn't just about sending signals through the air to enhance your state of happiness. We care about your safety and protection. We care about job creation. We believe in broadening our distribution reach and eliminating the cost of entry so *everyone* is equally privileged to access this technology. In the coming year, we will expand our offerings. We will increase opportunity for you to customize your experiences. Live the life you desire. And that gets at the heart of Dynamica. It's our mission statement and a promise to you. Dynamica: Making your dreams come true."

Marc turned off the radio. He muted his phone. He opened his car window and listened only to the sound of the rushing wind as he sped home, prepared for the fact that his life would change in a very big way, beginning with his resignation.

* * *

Marc managed to stay off his iPhone and laptop, getting a good night's sleep in his penthouse apartment on the Upper East Side of Manhattan, overlooking Central Park. For breakfast, he made himself a cheese omelet, hash browns, orange juice and coffee. It felt good to move at a leisurely pace. He stayed in his robe and pajamas. He was not going to work today – or ever again.

The New York Stock Exchange opened at nine thirty a.m. Marc settled into his fat, comfy living room chair, propped his laptop in his lap and watched the movement of Dynamica Inc. shares in real time.

As expected, the news about the government partnership sent the stock price skyrocketing. It very quickly realized a gain of eighty percent, nearly doubling in value. The stock had already been on a healthy trajectory for several years, while Marc accumulated more and more shares through his company's incentive program and retirement plan.

With the news public and his ban on trading over, Marc called his broker. He converted all of his Dynamica shares to cash, including stock options that were still years away from expiring. His broker was delighted, collecting a whopping commission.

And Marc's bank account became millions of dollars richer.

It was just the first move in disconnecting from Dynamica. Next, he entered his company email account. He ignored the download of a huge number of new emails, most of them related to the announcement. There were numerous meeting appointments in the mix, urgent requests to begin crafting a new marketing campaign to shift the tone of the company's message as it moved from an optional lifestyle enhancement to a mandatory enrollment.

Marc composed an email to CEO Jeff Reese and Executive Vice President of Human Resources Carol Sibley. He CC'd the rest of the senior leadership team.

He typed up his letter of resignation.

He reread it several times, felt satisfied with its firm but respectful tone, and pressed SEND.

Then he shut down his laptop before the responses began to flow in. He kept his iPhone off. He didn't want someone to try to talk him out of it. He didn't want to reveal that he was no longer chipped. The media would have a field day with that – it wasn't the type of publicity the company or the White House wanted right now. Because, inevitably, the backlash had begun. Not everyone wanted the government sewn into their head, even if it came with the side benefits of selectable moods and artificial stimulation.

Marc felt free.

Freed from the tight leash of corporate devotion, no matter how lucrative. He had been living and breathing Dynamica for ten years, working all hours, weekends included, sacrificing his social life. While he had several girlfriends over the years, none of them developed into a steady relationship. He regretted that now – in the chip era, a growing number of young, single people rejected the emotional, bumpy waters of true romance and opted to fulfill their yearnings through hassle-free simulations of love and intimacy in their heads at times of their choosing. One of Dynamica's biggest sellers was Romantic Hearts. Marc and his team had created the marketing campaign for it. Now Marc was personally feeling the aftereffects of its huge success.

Marc finally turned on the large flat-screen television filling one wall of his living room. He watched the news coverage across several channels. As he expected, there was joy – and fear.

A camera crew was on hand to celebrate the first newborn baby to be chipped. The parents were happy. The father expressed relief that the baby's late-night crying and restlessness would be solved by sending the baby comforting, sleepy feelings via remote control without having to hold and cuddle the child at four a.m.

Elsewhere, TV cameras captured an angry, older woman who declared her townhouse a 'chip-free zone' and insisted she would never allow the government to interfere with her body.

One of the most vocal opponents of the chip, Senator Dale Sheridan from Massachusetts, held a press conference to condemn the actions of the White House and demand an investigation into the ethics of the deal, citing an unlawful invasion of privacy and overreach of 'Big Government' into citizens' lives.

Marc watched his former colleague, company spokesperson Matt Revord, defend criticisms of the chip's tracking mechanisms. "It's no different in concept than the security cameras and online monitoring that already govern our lives. If you're good, you have nothing to worry about. If you're a criminal, yes, the chip will be a threat. We will dramatically increase the ability to identify, locate and prosecute murderers, thieves and rapists – and that's for the betterment of society as a whole."

Finishing off his channel hopping, Marc landed on a morning news program interviewing low-income residents who were elated because the chip installation was now free, subsidized by the government. Those who financially couldn't afford it would now be chipped with a complementary bundle of mood enhancers – Happiness, Love, Satisfaction and Calm.

Marc turned off the television. He got dressed. He decided to go for a walk. He took his extracted chip with him, shaking it out of the small, clear plastic bag and into his palm. He put it in his pocket.

Along the sidewalk on 79th Street, he encountered numerous people following the news closely on their iPhones or through earbuds. Some were engaged in open conversations about it – pro and con. Marc reached the East River Greenway, a walking and cycling path on the east side of Manhattan. In recent years, the number of walkers, joggers and cyclists had decreased considerably, but he still came here for long strolls to clear his head.

Marc stepped over as close as he could get to the flow of the East River. He took the small metal chip out of his pocket. He side-armed it with a hard toss, like skipping a stone. The black object skimmed the water's surface in a series of hops, then sank out of view.

Marc imagined a fish eating it and then Big Brother tracking his movements, baffled by the strange trajectory that placed Marc in the river, darting around like a manic, underwater swimmer.

Marc continued his walk along the river. Occasionally he encountered people. But for the most part, he felt very alone.

CHAPTER FIVE

Aaron attacked his job with extra vigor following the announcement, trying to block out the horrors of a mandatory government chip. He poured his mental and physical energies into making sure his clients maintained lush, colorful lawns and gardens with immaculately shaped hedges, festive plant variety, elegant decks and working fountains. He spent four hours on Madison Reddick's estate, working himself to exhaustion, not really in the mood for the customary cup of tea and whimsical chat with the lonely old man before departing, but curious about the millionaire's reaction to the big news.

As Aaron was packing his truck, Madison stepped out on his large front porch and waved him over. Aaron waved back, dripping with dirty sweat, and reported to the mansion's entrance after locking up his equipment and supplies.

As expected, Madison was shocked and furious. He directed Aaron to the den and then left to get the drinks.

This time, it was not herbal tea. It was red wine.

Aaron suspected, by the slight stagger in Madison's movements, that he had already consumed a few.

Aaron himself didn't drink much, but he was definitely agreeable to a glass of wine to settle his agitated state.

Madison sat across from him in a plush, high-back chair and did most of the talking, as usual.

Aaron was a sympathetic ear.

"I am appalled," Madison said. "This is worse than anything I could have imagined. I want to love this country but our leaders are making decisions affecting all of us that are so very wrong. I expected them to fight Dynamica, not team up with them."

"They're selling it as a benefit," Aaron said. "But it's a benefit I don't want."

"Yes, they claim it will cut down on crime, it will enable the equalization of government subsidies and citizen credits. They can sugarcoat it all they want. This is how 'Big Government' takes over our lives. By promising to take care of us so we don't have to take care of ourselves. Let us send you happy feelings, free of cost! Let us tell you how to feel the next time we're screwing you over. Trust us! No thank you."

"But we can't say 'No thank you.' It's going to be a requirement."

"I've read through all the fine print, believe me," said Madison, taking a hearty sip of wine. "It's 'illegal to interfere with government protocol'. Getting chipped is the law, like paying taxes. So what will they do to people like you and me who say 'No, my body belongs to me, not the government.' Do they throw us in jail? Do they expel us from the country?"

Aaron was at a loss for words. He truly didn't know what his next move would be, aside from burying himself in his work and, when assigned a chip installation date, being a conscientious objector.

"The government's not stupid," Madison said. "When they have a direct feed into our heads, how will that influence future elections? Oh, they say they would never use it for that, but come on. It's diabolical."

"Won't people fight back?" Aaron asked. "It's one thing when it's optional, it's used for entertainment and getting high or whatever, but do people really want to be tracked to this degree?"

"Ten years ago, no," said Madison. "But the world has changed. There's an entire generation that practically expects it. We're already tracked and monitored every day – what we do online, where we go in our cars, how we engage with our phones, and all the data and analytics in the hands of big business to define our preferences and profiles. This is a natural extension of all that. We're a connected society. Why not connect your soul?"

Aaron stared down at the drink in his hands. "I'm twenty-eight years old. I grew up in a connected society, and *I* don't want this."

"You're unique among the people in your generation," Madison said. "The older folks, people like me, we'll voice our protest and then just die off. Most of my closest friends in the entertainment industry have died, or they are too weak and feeble to put up a fight. So many of them rely on the government for their Medicare and Social Security and what have you, they don't want to endanger that relationship. The younger generation, today's owners of the entertainment industry, they've accepted the new technology with open arms. So instead of plays, musicals, books, movies, live music and all of that, they go right to the end result of how arts and entertainment should make you feel, and they manufacture that and sell it without the 'middleware'. As a result, there's no more creative expression. There's just a delivery of emotion and sensation that's not earned."

Then Madison chuckled, a harsh and scornful sound. "I mean, I stand corrected, a semblance of the art form remains, but it is hardly genuine. They sell movies and books and music that are bundled with a synchronized chipfeed to tell you how to feel. One of my old films, a comedy, can be watched in the privacy of your head, along with prompts that make sure you feel the humor so you laugh in all the right places. I'm told it also comes with the aural experience of a crowd laughing with you. Remember the laugh tracks on old television sitcoms? It takes it to a new level."

"So what do we do?" Aaron asked. "Obviously you can't stop technology. But how do you stop it from controlling every aspect of our lives? Go live in a cabin somewhere? Is that even possible anymore?"

"Did you read the booklet I gave you?"

"The Real Earth Movement?" Aaron said. "Yes."

"I've been funding the resistance. I made hundreds of millions of dollars back in the day, before Dynamica, before everyone spent all their money on one company and pretty much bankrupted everybody else. I sponsor lobbying, op-eds, consumer advertising. The problem is, now that Dynamica is teamed up with the White House, I'll wind up on the government's enemy list, if you know what I mean. They'll probably do everything in their power to stop me and silence my network. Fortunately, I have some allies in the political arena. There's a state senator named Dale Sheridan."

"I've seen him in the news," said Aaron, recalling the tough, vocal opponent of the government deal.

"Dale is our biggest hope," Madison said. "If he can get enough supporters, perhaps we can begin to turn the tide. If not, then look out. Dale is fighting the good fight, thank God. And Dynamica is going to use their government allies and huge financial resources to fight back."

"Doesn't sound like a fair fight."

"Not at all," Madison said, and he finished his glass of wine and somberly stared into it. "I guess it becomes fight or flight. I can't flee. It's not in my bones. I can't leave my house, my things, which I worked so hard for over the course of my life. Call me old-fashioned but I'm not leaving the physical comforts I've built around me."

"I don't have that problem," said Aaron.

Madison looked up at him.

"I mean, a physical environment, a home I want to protect," Aaron said. "I live with three slobs, addicts to this new technology. I hate them. I hate the house we live in. I can…I can flee."

Madison nodded. "You're too young to have accumulated a lot of possessions and a lifestyle you need to protect. Yes, you could flee. And I can help with that."

Madison stood up. He left the room. Aaron waited patiently in the extravagant den, listening to the steady tick-tock of a tall, antique grandfather clock.

When Madison returned, he held a refilled glass of red wine and a folded piece of paper.

He handed the paper to Aaron.

"What is this?" asked Aaron, accepting it.

"Some names and an address."

"For what?"

"Sanctuary."

Aaron stared at the folded piece of paper in his hand.

"First of all," Madison said, "you will need to leave L.A. There are too many supporters of the regime in L.A. County. They've been promised all sorts of things to help turn around the city, clean up the homeless problem, restart the economy after the collapse of the entertainment industry. It's a mess here, and they badly need a good working relationship with the feds."

"I can't leave Los Angeles," Aaron said. "My livelihood is here. I don't have much in savings. That's why I'm forced to live with those idiot roommates…."

"Aaron, you know and I know that what you do is a dying profession," said Madison. He returned to his chair and dropped into it. "Sure, you have me, but tell me, over the past six months, is your client list growing or shrinking?"

"Overall? Shrinking," Aaron said quietly.

"And when *more* people are chipped and giving even *less* attention to the physical world, do you think it will get any better?"

Aaron said nothing. It was a painful consideration he had tried, often unsuccessfully, to block from his mind.

"Well, you don't need to say anything," said Madison. "You know the answer. So let me present you with an option. There is a strong, underground pocket of resistance up the coast. I can connect you with them. They will do everything possible to stay off the radar and protect one another."

"You mean, go into hiding?"

"Hiding with other like-minded citizens. Searching for solutions together."

"But why don't you go?"

"I told you, I'm not leaving my home, my things. It's what defines me. I'm old. Let's leave it at that."

"Where is this, this…."

"Sanctuary. It's in Santa Barbara. I know these people. They're good. They have money. They'll keep you safe. And maybe one day, together, you'll discover a cure to this madness…."

"But what about your lawn?"

Madison laughed. "There are still a few people in Los Angeles who do what you do. They're not as good as you, but I pay extremely well. I'll whip them into shape. Don't worry about my grass. You've been outstanding, and I'll be sorry to see you go. But as a final gesture of my appreciation, please allow me to grant you a severance package."

"A severance package? For a landscaper?"

"Absolutely. You'll need money to relocate. Money to live on, when you reach the sanctuary. I'm prepared to sponsor your escape. I only ask this: find the collective energy of the resistance. Retain some dignity for the human spirit. Flee, yes, but when the time comes to fight, I want you to find strength in numbers. Recruit others. Don't give up hope, do you understand?"

Aaron was struck speechless for a moment. Then he responded resolutely with confidence.

"Yes."

* * *

On the way home, Aaron stopped at his neighborhood grocery store to collect some items for a real dinner. Fruit, vegetables and meat were still sold in small quantities to a shrinking niche market, but no longer commanded a dominant presence on the shelves. More than half of the store was now dedicated to fuel bars. To reduce the hassle of cooking and preparing meals, not to mention cleaning up afterward, consumers gobbled chunky bars of alleged protein and vitamins to quickly satisfy their hunger and increase the amount of time available to enjoy chipping. Since they essentially tasted like nothing, many of the fuel bars came with recommended chipfeed signals to sync up the act of eating with simulated flavors.

As he was inspecting the lettuce – not fresh, but decent – a familiar face appeared in the aisle, carrying a small basket of real food.

It was the jogger, the tanned young woman with black hair he had seen sprinting around the neighborhood and traced to an apartment with a bicycle and fresh plants on the balcony.

As she passed by with her eyes on bunches of spoiling bananas, he smiled and said hi.

She nodded politely without slowing her pace. She advanced ahead to a selection of apples.

I bet she doesn't have the chip, Aaron thought.

He wanted to talk to her, but didn't know what to say. She was plain-faced yet attractive, short and sturdy with serious eyes, a square jaw and youthful curves. She wore a loose, sleeveless top, athletic shorts and white running shoes. Her skin held good color, standing apart from the pale appearance of most everybody else.

He caught up with her at the apples and pushed himself to start a conversation.

"Hey," he said. "Sorry – you look familiar. I think I've seen you around my neighborhood."

She held an apple. She turned and looked at him, not smiling or responding, but attentive.

He said, "I'm on Colfax, not too far from the river, from the bike path. I see you running, from time to time. I'm – I'm Aaron."

"Hello, Aaron," she said, eyeing him with mild suspicion. She didn't offer her name.

"I'm sorry for interrupting, it's just…." He gestured to the wide, empty aisle around them. "It's kind of funny – no, sad, really – we're the only people buying real food."

"Those fuel bars are no good," she said. "It's sugar and fat. People like them because they go down quick and easy. But it's not real food."

"Not at all. I guess I'm a traditionalist…. I like real apples, too."

She nodded. She wasn't turning away to end the conversation, but she was sticking him with most of the talking, and he felt awkward.

"Apples, oranges, bananas," he said. "I like melon. Pineapple. Sometimes the watermelon is good. Strawberries have a lot of nutrients."

He could tell from her steadily, disengaged expression that he was babbling and losing her. So he quickly changed gears and said what was really on his mind.

"I – I don't have the chip. Do you have the chip?"

She shook her head. "No. Absolutely not."

"So what are we – what are we going to do?"

"They can't enforce something like that."

"It's Dynamica teaming up with the government. It might not happen overnight, but I'm – I'm pretty freaked out." He cringed slightly at his word selection, but she picked up on it without missing a beat.

"I'm freaked out too."

"Have you heard about the Real Earth Movement?"

"No."

He realized he was jumping ahead of himself. In that moment, he really wanted to get to know her better. He was lonely, and he dreaded going back to the house to confront his deadbeat roommates yet again.

"There's a movement," he said. "A resistance, it's getting organized, to fight the chip."

"I already fight it by keeping my mind and body healthy," she said. "I exercise. I meditate. I don't allow anything to pollute me physically or mentally."

"Me, too," said Aaron. Then he looked into her cart and gestured toward his own. "You know, we're buying some of the same stuff. Do you want to be efficient…and maybe have dinner together?"

She cracked a thin smile. Her eyes continued to study him. She rotated the apple in her hands.

"I mean, we could find a mutual place," he said. "I'm not inviting you over to my place. I – I have three roommates who are deep into chipping. They've made a mess out of the place…."

"Okay," she said. "But we're not having dinner at my place. You might mistake it for a date."

His heart sank a little at the cool tone in her voice. Still, she hadn't rejected his offer outright.

"Sure, a neutral location," he said. "We can do that. I like to go on picnics, by myself. Be one with nature, all that. Would you like to join me? We could be…two with nature."

Her tone remained flat and cynical, but he could see a slight spark in her eyes. "So, you want to take me into the woods? I don't go into the woods with strangers."

"Well, no," he said. "I have different places that I go. We still have a few hours of daylight. Have you ever been to Becks Field?"

"Oh," she said. "So we're going to play catch?"

"Well, not exactly…."

She tossed him the apple. He caught it quickly, startled.

"Sure," she said, and the smile grew. "Let's have a picnic."

"What's your name?" he asked.

She hesitated, looked him over, and then gave it to him. "Clarissa."

★ ★ ★

Aaron spread out his blanket on the outfield grass of an unused Little League baseball diamond in central L.A. While youth baseball had ended due to low enrollment, the grassy field was still sporadically maintained by one of the remaining employees of the Los Angeles Department of Recreation and Parks.

"I used to play here as a kid," he told Clarissa as they set up a meal of fruit, vegetables and cheeses. "I played shortstop."

"How quaint," she said.

"I loved watching the Dodgers play – back when they played." He popped a grape in his mouth. "It's really pathetic. I hear they're going to use the old Dodger Stadium as a dumping ground for abandoned cars."

"That will be a lovely sight."

"So I told you about my landscaping business," he said. "What is it you do?"

"It's equally old-fashioned, I suppose. I work in an actual, bricks-and-mortar retail store."

"They still have those?" he said lightly.

"Well, it's for clothing. People still need to wear clothes and try them on somewhere. Most of our sales are online, but we get just enough people who come into the store. Little old ladies."

"So…do you live alone?" he asked.

She paused for a moment and then gave a small nod. "I guess so. I had a boyfriend – up until, oh, last month. He moved out. He was, let's say, very much into the chip. The whole porn thing. I finally kicked him out. It didn't take much kicking. I couldn't compete with the ideal girlfriend in his head."

"His loss," said Aaron. With the sinking sun behind her, Clarissa had a soft glow as a light breeze teased with her wavy black hair. She didn't smile much, but when she did, it elevated her natural beauty.

Aaron shared the history of his wife, Wendy. While he meant to do it in the same resigned, matter-of-fact tone that Clarissa had used to share her story, he couldn't help feel a rising emotion tighten his words. He described Wendy's suicide from the real world, downloading the eternal loop of heaven into her head, an irreversible act that devastated him.

"The chip addiction is very strong," Clarissa said. "Dynamica pretends it's taking steps to address it, and now the government's involved, but what do they ever make better?"

"There's a whole black market out there," Aaron said. "It's taking a ride on Dynamica's technology but offering all these horrible, unregulated products and services."

"My younger brother goes to those dealers," Clarissa said. "They messed him up big time. He got into some intense stuff where it's much harder to come back down to reality. Now he's high all day on the chip, living in one of those tent communities you see everywhere. They live outdoors yet barely see the sun. His skin…."

She frowned and stopped talking for a moment. She reached for a pear. She studied it. "He eats those fuel bars all day. They hardly cost anything. What a life. He's going to love the new government deal – free chips for everyone, a free basic package of happiness options. Happiness. I might not be totally happy, but God damn it, at least I'm authentic."

Aaron watched as she bit into the pear. He felt an urge to kiss her but was afraid of her response.

Instead, he chose to tell her about the Real Earth Movement and the secret sanctuary in Santa Barbara. He described everything that Madison Reddick had told him.

"Go into hiding?" she said. "What for?"

"What if they want to chip us against our will?"

"If anybody tries to stick that thing in me, I will fucking kill them."

"Yeah, I don't know if that's a realistic option. Then you go to jail *and* get chipped."

"I need my job," Clarissa said. "It's how I pay the rent and buy real food."

"I have some money," Aaron said. He declined to explain that it came from Reddick. He simply stated, "It's more than enough to relocate and live on for a while. It will get us off the grid."

"Is that even possible?"

He looked into her dark, serious eyes. "I know we barely know one another. But I trust you. I – I have a good feeling about you." The comment almost made her smile, and he kept going. "Here's my offer. We get out of here together. Los Angeles is collapsing all around us. Everybody is lost, they just don't know it. We need to leave."

"Could we bring my brother?" she asked, and her face softened.

"Would he come with us?"

"I don't know," she said. "Probably not. But at least – I want to try. Maybe a new environment and the two of us could persuade him. He's got no one else. Our parents are dead. I'm all he's got."

"Where is this tent community?"

"It's by the highway."

"Is it dangerous?"

"I won't lie to you," said Clarissa. "It's dangerous."

Aaron thought about it for a moment. He thought about Wendy and his regrets over not saving her. It had never stopped gnawing at him.

"Let's do it," he said.

CHAPTER SIX

"Excuse me."

A voice cut through the early evening street noise, commanding attention on the Manhattan sidewalk. Marc looked for the source and his eyes landed on a broad-shouldered man in a suit, wearing dark sunglasses and a tidy haircut. He was standing up ahead in front of the awning entrance to Marc's apartment building.

"Mr. Tefteller?" he said.

Marc gripped his bag of carryout Chinese food. He cautiously approached the man. "Yes?"

"My name is Ted. I'm with National Security. I'd like to ask you a few questions."

Marc felt an immediate tightness in his chest. He had ignored phone calls and texts but knew that eventually someone would come looking for him. He had expected it to be somebody from Dynamica, not the federal government.

Marc was not going to invite this man into his apartment. If there was something he wanted to say, it would take place on the open sidewalk with people and vehicle traffic around them.

"Okay. What do you want to know?"

"Can we go somewhere and speak in private?"

"No."

Ted frowned and stepped closer. "I want to talk to you about your sudden departure from Dynamica."

"I resigned."

"It's not that simple. You have ten years of proprietary information. If shared with outside parties, it could jeopardize the welfare of the American public. You could create unnecessary disruption at a time we need full cooperation."

"That's not my intention, I assure you. I just wanted out."

"You know and have worked with a Dr. Rance Higgins."

It was posed as a statement, not a question, but Marc answered anyway. "Yes. That is correct." He immediately knew where this was going.

"You are fully aware that removal of the chip will be a violation of the law."

"Perhaps."

"There's no perhaps, Mr. Tefteller," said Ted in a plain, even voice. "You were in confidential meetings. You knew that the chip would become mandatory to being a U.S. citizen."

"It was a possibility."

"It was more than a possibility. You had insider information and used it for personal gain. You deceived a company scientist."

"I am within my legal rights," Marc said, and his tone turned forceful. "I chose to have the chip technology removed."

"You acted on information that had not yet gone public."

"I didn't touch my company stock until after—"

"I'm talking about the chip," Ted said. "Very soon, the law will require that you have it reinstalled."

"That law isn't on the books. It still needs to get passed. Why are you bothering with me?"

"Are you part of the resistance movement?"

"I don't know what that is."

"Are you familiar with the recent threats to bomb chip clinics?"

"What? No."

"Who is paying you?"

"No one."

"Have you been talking with Senator Sheridan?"

"This is not a political thing. It's personal."

"You worked on the public relations for some unfortunate flaws in early editions of the chip."

"Yes. Not everything went smoothly. There were some problems, some malfunctions and side effects."

"And you kept it out of the news cycle."

"I supported issues management. That was my job."

"You have certain nonpublic information that would be destructive in the wrong hands. You have trade secrets others will want to exploit. You are not authorized to represent this technology outside of the company. Is that understood?"

"I represent me, that's it."

"You cannot disclose anything about the company's methods, its history, its litigation, its future plans or the government partnership. You are not authorized to talk with the media. You cannot write a book."

"Great," Marc said. "Fine. Listen, my dinner's getting cold…."

"Your dinner is the least of your worries."

Marc studied the man and could only see random shapes of reflection in his dark sunglasses. "That sounds like a threat. Listen, what I did was within my legal rights. I chose to resign from my job as an employee and cancel my company's services as a customer."

"Those services are not optional. You will need to renew your participation."

"Yeah, well, I respectfully decline."

"That's not how it works."

Marc's impatience bubbled over. "Are you here to arrest me or something?"

Ted paused to give his response extra weight. "No. Not yet. But I can and will obtain that authorization."

Finished with the conversation, Marc moved past him to enter his building. "Leave me alone."

* * *

Brandyn Handley lifted his head, nervously glanced around the dark, cramped jazz club, then stared down at his drink again.

"I can't believe I'm in this place," he said. "It smells. The drinks have no consistency. And the music…they're making it up as they go along. I can't tap my toe to this."

"It's improvised. It comes from the heart. Every individual expresses themselves differently," Marc said.

"Yeah, well, I was never much into jazz. Give me verse, chorus, verse, chorus any day."

Tucked deep inside The Big Be Bop, the two men sat at a table in a poorly lit corner behind a pillar, barely visible to the rest of the crowd.

"Listen, this is the best place for a private conversation," Marc said. "We go to one of your places, it will be crawling with company people."

"Nobody from Dynamica hangs out here, you can be sure of that."

"I don't want to endanger you."

"I don't want to endanger me, either," responded Brandyn. "You're a big topic of conversation at work."

"So what's with this 'Ted' character? Why does he care about me?"

"Well, first of all, nobody leaves Dynamica. It's pretty much unheard of. The pay, the benefits, the job security.... There's a buzz you've been recruited."

"By who? Into what?"

Brandyn stroked his beard. "I don't know. It's a lot of speculation. They think you're up to something. You gotta admit, what you did, it was very abrupt. Somebody at your level can't just walk, with everything you know."

Marc sighed and took another swallow from his gin and tonic. "It's not fair. I've earned this. I've been a good soldier."

"But now you've gone AWOL."

"I supported that company for years...stuck up for them every time, even when I wasn't comfortable...but this latest news, this is more than I can accept."

"It's the wave of the future," Brandyn said. "You can't get stuck in the past. You're like this old jazz club. The biggest city in the country, and there are maybe eleven people in here."

"So my values are different. And they're going to make that a crime? I was threatened with arrest."

"Yeah, well, they're working very fast on the regulation plan. People without the chip will go on a list...."

"Jesus."

"Dynamica has nothing to do with it. We're just the manufacturer. But the government, they know it has to be a fast rollout to be effective. They'll come see you again. They'll probably assert more pressure."

"Like what?"

"I don't know," Brandyn said. He nervously adjusted his glasses. "I just know it's going to get more serious. Since you worked at Dynamica, you know everything, warts and all. They don't want you running around rogue."

"Rogue? That is such paranoia."

"Maybe, but they're serious. I took a chance meeting with you. If someone saw me with you and reported it back.... I've got a wife and kids. I can't go on some blacklist."

"Listen, I appreciate you meeting with me. You helped give me some background. It's good to know what I'm up against."

"This is probably the last time we can get together," Brandyn said. "At least for a while. I don't know how this is going to play out. But it could get more dangerous. I don't mean to desert you, but…."

Brandyn studied the club once more. On the small stage, a jazz trio prepared for a new set. Most of the room's focus was on them.

Brandyn reached down and retrieved a plain manila envelope he had tucked out of view, next to his chair. He handed it to Marc. There was something small and square-shaped inside, creating a lump.

"What is this?" Marc asked.

"Go ahead, take it out."

Marc reached into the envelope and pulled out a thin, black electronic device with a small screen. It resembled the device owned by chip consumers to select and trigger chipfeeds.

"Why do I need this?" Marc said. "I don't have the chip anymore."

"I know what it looks like, but it's actually a little different. You might need that. It's for your protection."

"Protection?"

"First, we have to have an agreement. If you get caught with it, you can't tell where you got it. They would come after me. They would come after my wife and kids. If they catch you with it, you'll have to tell them you took it from the company when you quit. That's the trade-off. Otherwise we both go down."

"But what is it?"

"It's a jammer."

Marc continued to study it. It looked no different than the common handheld devices that others used to operate their stimulation feeds.

"It can hack into someone else's signal," said Brandyn. He motioned for Marc to lean in. He lowered his voice. "It's a prototype for law officials, but it works, I assure you. There are only eight in existence. As head of operations, I have security clearances. I took one. I changed some paperwork so there are only seven on record and this one doesn't go missing. But you need to treat it with great caution – only if you really, truly need it."

"This type of thing is exactly what I was afraid of. This technology… being used this way."

"Used appropriately, it's a good thing," Brandyn said. "We arm our police with guns today. This will be a lot cleaner. It's for confronting aggressive criminals – you send them a signal to stop them in their tracks. Just don't screw around with it. It's not fully tested. It's for emergency use only."

"Got it." Marc tapped the screen lightly and it came to life, displaying a simple menu.

"Here's how it works," Brandyn said, crowding closer. He poked at the menu as Marc held the device. "You input the chip serial number of the chip you want to engage with. If you don't have the chip number, it calls up here, on the screen, the active chips in closest proximity."

A short list of nine-digit entries appeared with location data for each one.

"So, there, the top one, that's me. The one below it – says the receiver is four feet away, you can call up a profile – it's gotta be that guy."

Brandyn gestured to a large, balding man at a nearby table, cradling a beer and waiting for the jazz trio to start. He had a small bulge in the back of his neck, a telltale sign of a chip consumer.

"If I wanted to, right now, I could send him signals from Dynamica's library. I can go right to the Dynamica listings, search, find what I want and send it to his brainwaves."

"Oh my God," said Marc quietly.

"Right now, it just works with the current offerings, the stimulations that are already digitized for transmission. But we're working with the government on a collection of special triggers, only for licensed users, that would stun, paralyze, shock, neutralize – basically subdue anyone that would require it. So, in the hands of the police, no bullets. No mess."

Marc marveled over the powerful instrument in his hands with a mixture of awe and repugnance. "No mess physically. But they're messing with the brain. That could be a lot worse."

"It's a big breakthrough. You can pacify a killer," Brandyn said.

"Or you can pacify a resistance," said Marc.

★ ★ ★

Marc awoke to a sudden *bang!* coming from the other side of his apartment. Wearing pajama bottoms and no top, he pulled himself out of bed and hurried across the bedroom in his bare feet. He was fully alert in a matter of seconds, heart pounding and sweat rising.

After a short silence, he heard a bigger, louder crash and immediately sourced it.

Someone was breaking into his apartment. Marc stepped into his living room and could see his front door opened an inch, halted by the chain. The wood at the frame was splintered around the lock.

A glistening pair of bolt cutters entered the crack, jaws wide, ready to snap the chain in one big bite.

Marc's mind raced. He knew this had to be connected with 'Ted' from National Security. His first instinct was to call the police, but he doubted they would help him. They wouldn't interfere with a federal arrest.

Then he remembered the jamming device Brandyn had given him. He was going to need it much sooner than expected.

The only problem was that Marc had stuck the device in the top drawer of a small bureau at the front of the room, close to the apartment's entrance. Any hopes to lunge for it were immediately dashed when the razor-sharp bolt cutters sliced through the security chain, and the front door flew open to reveal several hulking strangers, accompanied by Ted.

Marc had no choice but to flee back into his bedroom.

He raced inside, slammed the door and locked it. The lock was simple and weak, and Marc knew they would quickly break past it. He had just one escape route – outside.

One wall of his bedroom had a stretch of curtains covering sliding doors leading to a balcony. He rarely ventured out on the balcony – while the view of Central Park was spectacular, the height made him dizzy.

There was no time to be dizzy now.

Marc reached through a slit in the curtains, unlatched the sliding doors and split them apart. He stepped onto the balcony and closed the doors behind him. A cool breeze struck his face and bare chest. He felt it ripple his pajama bottoms.

He looked over the balcony rail. The street was sixty-seven stories below. The tops of a few cars slid by in either direction, like small, silent toys. He tried not to focus on the distance to the ground. Instead, he focused on the balcony directly below him. That wasn't so far. One story was doable.

The loud thuds against his bedroom door ended Marc's moment of hesitation. He needed to act fast and not allow his brain to process the insanity of what he was about to do.

Marc gripped the top rail tightly and lifted one leg, then the other, over the side. The rest of his body followed. He slotted his bare feet between the iron bars, planting them firmly on the outer edge. He froze in a standing position, hanging on the exterior of the balcony. He was going to have to lower himself, blind to the scene below, while maintaining a vise-like grip on the balcony's bars. Loud voices coming from inside his bedroom prompted him to finish the climb quickly.

Marc lowered himself to a crouch, sliding his hands down closer to his feet. Then he removed his footing from the balcony's edge and let his legs drop for a moment while clutching the bars for dear life. His body experienced gravity's pull and the weight strained his arms. He kicked his legs, feeling only open air beneath his bare feet. He twisted his body back and forth to create a swinging movement.

Marc heard the sliding doors open above him.

His swinging gained momentum. He timed his drop and prayed for accuracy. He freed his hands at the precise moment his legs, swooping like a pendulum, reached inside the balcony below.

Marc hit the floor of the balcony and tumbled into some deck chairs. He jumped up, gasping. He immediately tugged at the sliding doors to pull them apart.

Locked.

Shit!

Marc hammered on the glass. He knew these people, his neighbors below, the Taylors. This was their bedroom, and he desperately needed one of them to wake up.

His banging was successful. Rather quickly, both appeared at the glass, pushing the curtains out of their way. Their faces immediately shifted from confusion to alarm.

"Marc—?" said Lori Taylor in a nightgown.

"What the hell are you doing out there?" asked her husband, Tim, eyes half-open with sleep, voice muffled in the glass.

"My – my apartment's on fire!" Marc exclaimed. It was a stupid lie but the real reason would take about fifteen minutes, and he needed to expedite their active support. "Please, open up!"

"Fire?"

Marc could hear footsteps directly above, scuffling across his balcony. He nodded vigorously at his neighbors.

The Taylors opened their sliding doors. Marc dashed inside their bedroom.

"I don't smell smoke," Lori said. "Wouldn't there be alarms? This building's equipped—"

"Thank you, I have to leave," Marc said. He ran out of the bedroom as they shouted questions at him. He scrambled across their living room and reached the front door.

"Have you called the fire department?" Tim asked, following him.

"Not yet," Marc said as he entered the outer hallway.

"Are you sure you're not dreaming?" Lori called after him.

"Talk later!" Marc said. He broke into a dash to reach the elevators on the far end of the floor.

Marc poked the down button repeatedly. "Come on, come on." He was breathing heavily, dripping with sweat.

Finally, the elevator arrived with a *ding*. Marc let out a sigh of relief.

The doors split open, revealing Ted standing inside.

He pointed a gun at Marc.

"You're under arrest. You're coming back upstairs."

Marc froze, hands raised. "Okay, okay. I got it. What – what's this all about?"

"I think you know."

Marc, still shirtless and in pajama bottoms, returned with Ted to his apartment. Three individuals stood in his living room, waiting for him. Two looked like well-dressed thugs – extra support to ensure compliance. They said nothing, simply stared at him with grim expressions and prominent muscles. The third person had a much softer, rounder appearance and an almost-sympathetic face. Marc recognized him.

"Dr. Higgins," Marc said.

"Hello, Marc."

Ted shut the door behind them. "You should know you cannot run away from this. It's going to happen, and you might as well accept it."

"What's going to happen?" asked Marc.

"You broke your contract agreement," Ted said. "That's very serious."

"What contract agreement?"

"You signed an allegiance to Dynamica Incorporated. You broke the agreement. You disengaged from your technology. You acted on nonpublic information."

"I don't know what you're talking about. Let me see this contract."

"We're beyond that," Ted said. Then he stepped toward Dr. Higgins. He pointed to a small black briefcase placed on Marc's living room table.

"Let's begin the procedure."

Dr. Higgins snapped open the briefcase. He lifted the lid to reveal a variety of neatly arranged medical tools, sharp instruments for very precise surgery. First, he removed a clear plastic sleeve with a dark, oval-shaped object inside, the size of a quarter.

"We have brought you a new chip," said Higgins, extracting it from the sleeve. "Marc, you deceived me. I don't appreciate that. I handled your request in my professional capacity without realizing your true motive. So now we will return things to the way they should be."

The two thug characters took hold of Marc, each grabbing an arm. Marc struggled but could not free himself from their tight grip.

Higgins reached again into the black briefcase. He extracted a syringe.

"We can't have you squirming during the application. This will help you sleep. When you wake up, you will be compliant. And this time, the chip will be placed in such a way that its removal will, I guarantee it, kill you. There's no going back."

Marc swallowed hard. Higgins stepped toward him with the syringe. Ted watched intently from nearby, arms folded.

"Wait," Marc said.

Higgins prepared to make the injection. One of the thugs had forcibly extended Marc's bare arm for the doctor.

"There's no waiting," Ted said. "Get on with it."

"Dr. Higgins, I'm asking you to show some compassion," Marc said. "I know I'll receive the chip. I'm not arguing with that. But the first few hours will be traumatic. Can you – can you tell me my chip's serial number?"

"What for?" said Ted.

"I want to be synced for service. So I can download anti-anxiety feelings to help me recover."

"This is wasting time," Ted said.

"Hear me out. I just want to program the new chip into my controller. I'll need the benefits."

"You can do it later."

"I'll be a total mess. Think of what I'm going through. I want to get it ready now."

Higgins shrugged. He looked over at Ted. "I don't see why we can't allow that."

Ted let out an exhale of exasperation. "All right, where's your handheld?"

"It's in the top drawer of that bureau…right behind you."

Ted turned around. He saw the bureau and pulled open the drawer. He reached inside and took out the chip-controlling device. "This?"

"Yes," Marc said. "Thank you."

Ted walked over to Marc and handed it to him. "Make it quick."

"Yes. Thank you."

The two thugs loosened their grip on Marc. He turned on the device. Ted continued to keep a watch on him, gun held tight.

"Okay," Marc said to Dr. Higgins. "What's my personal code?"

Higgins told him, enunciating each digit clearly.

Marc pretended to input it. In actuality he was calling up a list of active chips in the immediate vicinity. A listing of ten appeared. The first four, he knew, were the people in the room.

"Oops, wait, say that again, I screwed up," Marc said, working the device, buying himself extra seconds. He kept the monitor facing him in a way that the others couldn't see.

Dr. Higgins recited the code a second time.

Marc quickly ordered a Dynamica stimulation signal for the first chip on his list. He ordered Instant Sleep.

"What's taking so long?" Ted said impatiently.

"Sorry, I think I transposed a couple of numbers."

"That's it. You're done," Ted said. "You're delaying this. Stick him with the injection!"

The thug to Marc's right dropped to the floor. He hit the carpet hard, then curled up, eyes closed, in a limp sleeping state.

"What the hell!" Ted exclaimed.

Marc sent the same signal to the second thug, and he dropped like a rock.

"Stick him, now!" Ted shouted, confused, waving toward Marc.

Higgins came at Marc with the syringe. Marc swatted it away, buying himself precious seconds. He quickly poked a signal for Higgins – missing Instant Sleep and sending him another one on the bestseller list – Hearty Laughter.

Higgins giggled. Then he broke into uncontrollable laughter. He could barely stand, doubled over with guffaws.

"What the hell is going on here?" Ted demanded.

This only made Higgins laugh harder.

Ted charged Marc and tackled him before he could send a signal to divert Ted's brain.

Marc tumbled to the carpet, and the handheld device skipped out of his grasp.

Ted punched him hard in the ribs. Marc coughed in pain, scrambling to retrieve the controller.

Higgins howled with laughter as the two men engaged in a violent tangle on the floor.

Marc regained a hold on the controller. Ted threw more punches and tried to take it away. The monitor displayed a list of Dynamica's bestsellers and Marc poked one at random, as fast as possible, to fill Ted's head.

Ted landed a fist to Marc's jaw, and then his movements turned sluggish. His brainwaves were captured by one of Dynamica's 'Hot New Releases': Bird Flight.

Ted staggered to his feet. He rapidly lost awareness of his true surroundings as his imagination took over his consciousness.

He became consumed with the illusion he was a bird, soaring through open skies.

His eyes drooped half shut. His mouth dropped open in astonishment.

"I'm flying," he said.

Higgins roared with laughter, collapsing on the couch. As he fell onto the cushions, he accidentally stabbed himself with the syringe still in his grip. He grimaced from the sudden stab of pain and his laughter stopped. His eyes traced the source of the pain. He saw the syringe sticking out of his thigh. Then he exploded into more uproarious laughter.

Ted began to walk across the room, arms spread, eyes closed. "I'm flying," he said. Marc watched silently, not about to contradict him.

As Higgins's outburst slowed to a few lethargic chuckles and snickers, Ted became a ballet dancer, moving in dramatic circles, lost in a fantasy flight and no longer grounded in any reality.

"I am the sky," Ted said.

Ted circled the living room a few more times. Then he soared into the bedroom.

Marc turned to see Higgins lose consciousness under the strength of the tranquilizer. He muttered one last "heh heh" and went limp. The two thugs remained in a deep sleep on the floor, cuddled with one another.

"I'm a bird!" shouted Ted from the bedroom. Marc heard him crash into something, probably a lamp.

Marc hurried into the bedroom to see what was happening.

The sliding balcony doors remained open, and Ted was drawn to the New York City skyline. Ted moved past the bed and stepped outdoors, arms stretched out.

"Wait!" Marc said. "No!" He immediately feared what would happen next. He worked the handheld device and prepared to shift Ted's signal feed to something else, anything else, but his fingers weren't fast enough.

Ted climbed the balcony railing. He declared he was soaring above the earth. Then he made an awkward leap into the open air.

Ted did not fly. Ted fell fast and hard.

Before Ted had even landed on the pavement below, Marc started grabbing his clothes. He pulled on a shirt, jeans and loafers. Gripping the controller, he ran out of his apartment, leaving the three sleeping occupants behind.

Outside the building's front entrance, a small crowd had gathered. People screamed and gasped at the bloody mess on the curb. It barely looked human. Teeth were scattered like pebbles. Police sirens filled the air.

Marc picked a direction and ran off into the night.

CHAPTER SEVEN

Aaron had expected to see a lot of tents but the sheer number and density took his breath away – hundreds of colored bumps, predominantly blue and green, settled in the rocky dirt beneath the cement ceiling of a rumbling, multilane highway. Lawn chairs, shopping carts and piles of trash filled the gritty spaces between tents, with few sightings of actual people – they were tucked inside their one-person dwellings, lost in the escapism of chipfeed pleasures. The stench of human waste struck Aaron immediately. While a series of portable toilets lined an edge of the makeshift camp, it was obvious not everyone elected to use them.

"Every time I come here, I don't know whether to cry or throw up," Clarissa said with a hard grimace.

"Do you know which one is him?" Aaron asked.

Clarissa nodded. "Come on."

She led Aaron on a zigzag path, finding the thinnest of trails between tents, stepping carefully with her head down to make sure she didn't plant her foot somewhere regrettable. Aaron could hear an assortment of guttural noises coming from residents enjoying their fantasies.

Clarissa finally stopped at a partially collapsed pole tent, gray and soiled. She regarded it with a moment of grim reflection.

"This used to be his Cub Scout tent, when he was little."

Aaron just stared at it, waiting for Clarissa to determine her strategy.

"You stay here," she finally said. "He doesn't know you, this will already be jarring enough. I'm just going to.... I'm going inside."

She bent down and unzipped the entrance with a rough, persistent tug. Then, with a face full of disgust, she got on her hands and knees and climbed inside.

Aaron listened.

He heard the sounds of a young man being stirred to consciousness. The young man was not pleased and his voice grumbled with irritation, not yet finding words.

After about a minute, he exploded into raw expletives, followed by: "Get out of here! *Get out!*"

"We need to talk."

"No we don't."

"Then I'm taking this."

Clarissa quickly moved out of the tent, scrambling in the dirt with something in her hand: a chipfeed controller.

Clarissa's brother followed immediately, frantic. His skinny arm shot out of the tent to grab her ankle and just barely missed. He was forced to exit the tent.

Clarissa stood next to Aaron.

A bony, shaggy young man emerged. His eyes were wild and his face was covered in a patchy, unkempt beard. He wore a stained, sleeveless white T-shirt, filthy jeans and wool socks with holes in them. He looked to be nineteen or twenty years old.

He gripped a short length of rusted pipe.

"Michael, NO!" said Clarissa, with the forceful shout of an older sister taking control of her younger brother.

He stood fully erect now, over six feet tall, eyes wincing in the outdoor light. He was panting even though he had barely exerted himself.

"You are not going to hit me with that," Clarissa said, still holding his thin, silver controller.

"Then gimme it back," he said. His glance darted to Aaron. "Who's that?"

"Nobody. A friend," she said.

Aaron had mixed feelings about being called both a 'friend' and 'nobody'.

"Why did you come here?" Michael said angrily.

"We want to help you get away from all this," said Clarissa in a plain tone, refusing to elevate to his level of hysteria. "Look around you – this isn't how you want to live."

"We're not having this argument again."

"I'm leaving Los Angeles," Clarissa said. "It's become a sewer. It's chaos. We're going up the coast. Come with me."

"Why does it matter where I live?"

"You need a new environment. You need to clear your head. This thing—" She held up the controller. "It's an addiction."

His hand shot out to grab it, and she pulled back. Aaron stepped forward, ready to intervene if Michael got physical.

"That – that legally belongs to me," Michael said. "You can't take it!"

Aaron doubted Michael could even mix it up with them in a fight. He looked undernourished, wobbly on his feet. There were dark circles under his eyes. It would be like fighting a hospital patient.

Michael seemed to recognize this. His eyes studied them for a long moment. Then he said, "This community, we stick up for one another."

"This isn't a community," Clarissa said. "It's a bunch of loners who happen to be on the same plot of land. When's the last time you talked to your 'neighbors'?"

"We stick up for one another," Michael repeated.

"I bet," Clarissa said scornfully.

Michael turned around and lowered himself to the ground. He climbed back inside his tent.

"Now what?" Aaron said softly.

"I still have this," said Clarissa, holding the controller. "He'll be back."

Sure enough, Michael reemerged from the tent. He no longer held the piece of pipe. He held an air horn. He stood up, gripping the white canister and pointing its red plastic trumpet above his head. He pressed the button on top and blasted a shrill, piercing alert that echoed powerfully through the concrete underpass.

Aaron immediately covered his ears and shouted, "What the hell, man!"

Clarissa backed up several feet, stumbling and fighting to keep her balance as her footing slipped in a nest of empty Body Fuel wrappers.

Michael kept blasting the horn and finally Aaron started to reach for it. He was grabbed by the collar from behind. He swung around to confront whoever had put their hands on him.

He faced a sudden wall of grubby, dead-eyed people.

Clarissa turned and saw them, too.

The residents of the tent community had quickly mobilized to protect one of their own. The air horn must have been some agreed-upon signal strong enough to stir them from their tents.

In the distance, more tent dwellers were coming out of their stupors to respond to the alarm. Aaron saw people approaching from every direction, and it didn't take long before he and Clarissa were surrounded.

"A threat to one of us is a threat to all," Michael said. He stared into the eyes of his sister. "These people will tear you apart if you try to separate us from our technology. Do you really want to set off an angry mob? The police can't arrest everybody. They don't want to. There's no room for us anywhere else. Besides, according to the police, anybody walking into this pack of wild animals, they get what they deserve. Two weeks ago, there was a guy who thought he could come in here and tell us how to live our lives. All I'll say is, he's gone."

Aaron faced a wall of stinking flesh in every direction, cold eyes staring at him with a single-minded obsession to protect. Perhaps these people were physically clumsy and unfit, but their sheer numbers offered no easy escape.

"Now," Michael said, "give me back the controller."

Clarissa locked eyes with him, jaw tight, simmering with anger.

"Give it back," said someone in the crowd in a hoarse voice. Others picked up the chant: "Give it back! Give it back!"

"You don't have to live here," Aaron said to Michael.

"And you don't have to be here," Michael said.

"We're going to Santa Barbara…" Aaron said.

"Well, have a nice time." Michael reached out for the handheld device.

Clarissa gave it back to him, eyes still blazing.

"I'm disappointed in you," she said. "You disgust me."

With the chip device returned to its owner, the citizens of the tent community began to disband and wander back to their tents. Some of them muttered to themselves in raspy, barely used voices.

"I don't care what you think," Michael said.

"I really am leaving the city," she said. "This is your big chance to restart your life."

"I've made my choice. I'm old enough to make my own decisions, sis." He said *sis* in a hard, sarcastic tone.

"This is a miserable existence," she said.

"I think you're the one who is miserable," he countered. "Maybe you could use the chip. It would give you some happy feelings, maybe a smile now and then."

"So you're going to climb back into that filthy hole," she said, gesturing to the tent, "and pretend like the rest of this doesn't exist?"

He smiled. He nodded. He shrugged. Then he said, "Think of it this way. Right now, I'm having a nightmare. You're in it. Fortunately it will be short. Because when I go in there and put on the eye cover and pull a chipfeed from the sky, *that's* when I'm awake. That's my chosen reality. Not this. Not you. You're a bad dream."

"Fine," said Clarissa in a snarl of futility. "Go ahead and rot." She turned and faced Aaron. "Let's leave. We tried. Fuck this."

Aaron felt sad for Clarissa. She refused to shed any tears over her brother's predicament. She was simply angry. She began to lead the way back out, beginning the maze of steps through a vast huddle of tents and garbage. Aaron looked down to watch his footing – and he spotted something that grabbed his eye.

A flyer for Doctor Delight.

"Son of a bitch," he said. He stopped to pick it up.

Clarissa turned to look back at him. "Why are you picking up trash? Let's go."

"This – this—"Aaron said, and his heart began pounding in his chest. "This is the guy who killed Wendy."

Clarissa returned to him. "What?"

"This – Doctor Delight – it's where she got the suicide loop. This is the bastard who—"

She studied the flyer with him. It included a playful cartoon illustration of a jovial, wizard-like fat man in a white beard with rainbows and stars shooting out of his hands. It read: 'The best in ultimate fantasies. Not available from Dynamica! People's choice favorites. Dreams you didn't know existed! Only the best. Discreet and private. We protect our customers' identities. There's no shame in fantasies. Live the way *you* want, not the way *they* want. Kinky! Kooky! Krazy!'

The flyer listed a short sampler of offerings. 'Orgy Party. Killing Spree. Jail Bait. Eternal Heaven.'

Aaron felt his emotions spill over with anger once more about the fate of his wife. The flyer with its silly drawing and goofy promotional language seemed to mock his pain.

"It doesn't say where to find him," Clarissa said. "Those places – they're word-of-mouth."

"Exactly," said Aaron. He spun around to return to Michael, who had slipped inside his tent.

Before Michael could finish zipping his tent closed, Aaron had scrambled into the tight, smelly space to join him.

Michael grabbed for the air horn.

"No, wait! I just want to ask a question!"

"I said I'm not going!" Michael said, backing into a pile of dirty clothes and blankets. "Get out of my house!"

"I will, I will." Aaron waved the flyer. "I want to ask you about this."

Michael looked at it for a moment. "Doctor Delight? What about it?"

"Aaron, what are you doing in there?" Clarissa called from outside the tent.

"He's bothering me!" Michael said.

"I said I'll leave in a minute," Aaron said. "I just want to know – where can I find him?"

"Doctor Delight?"

"Yes."

"That's not…. I only went to him one time. It's whacked-out shit. I don't go there anymore, I swear."

"I don't care if you do," Aaron said. "I need to see him about something else – it has nothing to do with you." The smell inside the tent was so bad that Aaron wanted to retch. Michael gripped his chip controller, leery that Aaron might try to take it away.

"You can't stay in here," Michael said. "You're trespassing. Besides – it's a one-man tent, man."

"You know where to find Doctor Delight?"

"I don't want to talk about it."

"I – I'll make it worth your while. You want money? You want…a new tent? A bigger one…with ventilation?"

"No, I don't need any of that stuff. You don't get it. I don't live in this world. I'm just a visitor, sometimes."

"Okay, okay," said Aaron, trying hard not to breathe through his nose. "How about a chipfeed? There are some really fancy, high-end chipfeeds that cost a lot – what do you have, the basic package?"

"I get by on basic."

"Yeah, but is there one thing you really, really want to try? I'll pay for it. Anything off the menu. A super-duper premium chipfeed of your choice."

"Well—"

"In exchange, you just show me where I can find Doctor Delight."

"He moves around. I mean, I know, but I could be wrong."

"I'll take whatever information you got."

"And you'll get me any chipfeed I want?"

"Don't indulge him!" Clarissa shouted.

"Shut up!" Michael and Aaron shouted back in unison.

In the moment of silence that followed, Michael thought hard. He started to chew on a long, dirty fingernail. Then his head bobbed up, alert. "I know – I know – Chocolate Swirl Orgasm."

"Chocolate Swirl…?"

"Orgasm. It's new. They just introduced it. It's expensive, supposed to be really great. It gets great reviews. I know a guy who knows a guy who says it's the most awesome trip ever."

"You got it."

"Wait – what – really?"

"In exchange for telling me where I can find Doctor Delight."

"I want a six-month subscription."

"Fine."

Michael poked at his controller device. "Do it now. You can put it on your credit card." He called up the selection and then handed the controller eagerly to Aaron, quickly forgetting that ten minutes ago, Aaron had been part of an effort to steal it.

Aaron read the chipfeed's description: 'A delicious blend of the ultimate dessert and a powerful ejaculation'.

Sure enough, the reviews were stellar: a four-point-eight average rating out of five possible stars.

Aaron subscribed Michael to the feed, cringing at the cost, but only for a moment, because, really, there was no price too high for settling a score with the man who took away his wife.

* * *

Aaron explained everything to Clarissa as they stepped their way through the tent community, following a partially trodden path that led out.

"But what are you going to do when you find this guy?"

"I don't know exactly," said Aaron, still absorbing the potential to live out a confrontation he had dreamed about for a long time. "I think – I think my first plan of action is to see if there's any antidote. A way to break the loop. The doctors said no, but they didn't design the thing. Maybe this guy has a way to turn it off. Money is no object – I mean, I have my savings." He stopped short of mentioning the money that Madison Reddick had given him to start a new life and join the chip resistance.

"Oh my God!" Clarissa said all of a sudden. She stopped abruptly in her tracks.

Up ahead, there was a half-dressed man spread out in the dirt in front of a flattened tent. The canvas rippled gently in the wind. The man's eyes were open, unblinking, with his mouth frozen in a silent shout and hands stiffened into claw-like positions.

"Is he dead?" Aaron asked, standing alongside her.

"Chip fatality," Clarissa said, clearly trying to push back an emotional reaction. "I'm sure that's part of the stink around here. How many of these tents have dead people in them? Does anybody know or care?"

"Should we call someone?" asked Aaron.

"I think they bury their own here," Clarissa said, and Aaron couldn't tell if she was being serious or sarcastic.

"Who knows how many of these people are taking illegal feeds and having heart attacks," Aaron said.

"For that, you can probably thank your friend Doctor Delight. Really, if there was any truth in advertising, his name would be Doctor Death."

They resumed walking in silence. Aaron couldn't stop thinking about Wendy. For many months now, he had started to mentally move on, leaving her tragedy behind, refusing to let it paralyze him or worse – cause him to find solace in the artificial good feelings of a chipfeed.

Many mourners of the deceased turned to chip signals to ease their pain, and there was even one called Peace Be With You, specifically designed to comfort people over the loss of a loved one.

Many of Aaron's friends had suggested he try it to cope with his grief over Wendy's suicide.

"No," Aaron told them. "I want this to hurt. Because it should."

CHAPTER EIGHT

Michael had earned his Chocolate Swirl Orgasm.

Clarissa pulled up her car across the street from a former insurance agency office with its branding removed, but the ghost-like outline of the company name was still readable where dirt and sun-faded paint had created a stencil effect above the entrance. Some of the decals had been chipped away from the large glass window, hastily and incompletely, with several of the letters remaining from 'Auto. Home. Life'. Most telling was the movement of a few people in and out of the retail space, as if transactions were taking place inside.

Nothing visibly promoted 'Doctor Delight', but the right vibe was present for a discreet, pop-up operation.

"Now what?" Clarissa asked.

"I'm going in," said Aaron.

"I'll go with you."

"You don't have to."

"I want to."

Aaron wasn't going to get into an argument with her. He nodded and reached for the door handle. "Let's go."

Aaron and Clarissa crossed Sepulveda Boulevard.

They entered the storefront. In the back of the room, a fat man with a white beard sat behind a long desk, talking to a Hispanic man – presumably a customer – who stood before him. They spoke in low, private tones. Another man sat in a wooden chair alongside the desk, turned to face both the fat man and his customer. His appearance indicated a security presence – bald, menacing eyes, a short-sleeve black shirt that placed his cannonball biceps on display, and tattoos of dragons and flames erupting across his skin and reaching up into his thick neck.

He immediately locked his eyes on Aaron and Clarissa, holding up his hand. "Wait. Right there."

Aaron and Clarissa stood obediently across the room from the desk, allowing the customer interaction to finish in private.

While waiting, Aaron looked around the office. It still contained framed posters on the wall depicting the activity of an insurance agent: pictures of smiling people shaking hands; smiling people leaning over paperwork in some kind of meaningful conversation; smiling parents with a teenager, a proud young driver, holding up a set of car keys. It was a lot of smiling.

The scenes felt quaint and nostalgic. These days, fewer people owned cars and those who did traveled less. The increased obsession with virtual worlds and placing assets in 'the cloud' had reduced the accumulation of physical possessions to insure. The main thing people cared about in their homes was the comfort of the pod rooms where they could zone out on chipfeeds.

And if people needed insurance for anything, they would just order it up online without the bother of stepping outdoors to see an agent in an office.

Doctor Delight, however, still required a physical location to reprogram Dynamica's handheld devices to connect with his own offerings and subscription services. It didn't take long, but a physical hack was required.

After the Hispanic customer left, the fat man waved Aaron and Clarissa forward. As they approached his desk, he said, "How may I help you?"

"Are you Doctor Delight?"

The fat man exchanged a glance with the muscular presence to his right. Then he told Aaron, "I asked you a question. I guide the conversation here. That's how it works. Let's try this again. How may I help you?"

Aaron felt his mouth going dry as sweat tickled his skin. "I – I'm here because I require an antidote."

"I don't understand the statement."

"The Eternal Heaven Loop."

The fat man's eyes lit up for a brief moment, just enough to confirm to Aaron that this man, indeed, was the fabled Doctor Delight. After a measured silence, he said, "We don't sell antidotes to anything."

Aaron reached into his pocket. He pulled out a small, printed photograph of Wendy. He held it out to show him. "You sold one of your products to this woman."

Doctor Delight shrugged. "Maybe. I really can't remember. We have a lot of clients."

"I know you did. It doesn't matter if you remember."

"Please get to the point. We're very busy here."

Aaron's heart pounded. Real adrenaline pumped through his veins. He let everything spill out.

"You sold my wife, Wendy, the Eternal Heaven Loop, eight months ago. She's in a coma. I can't – nobody can break her out of this coma. I honestly don't think she meant to—"

"Okay," said Doctor Delight. "Let me stop you right there. If a customer made a purchase, and a customer used that purchase, and you are not that customer, I don't understand why we're having this conversation."

"Sell me the antidote. I'll pay anything you want."

"That's not how it works. There is no antidote. That would defeat the purpose. It would take away the pleasures people paid good money for."

"God damn it!" Aaron lost his temper. "You infected my wife. You ended her life for three hundred dollars."

Doctor Delight made a sour face, as if he had just tasted something bitter. "No, no." He shook his head. "She's in a better place of her choosing."

"That's bullshit. You sold her an illegal feed to her chip."

"Nothing here is illegal. We're a small boutique, perhaps unconventional, but we serve a niche market that our customers want and ask for."

"You murdered my wife. I will report you to the authorities."

The tattooed man observing the conversation stood up straight now and stared hard into Aaron's face.

Clarissa, who had been silent, spoke up. "Don't you care about the lives you impact? You're just a disgusting leech profiting off other people's miseries."

"Yes, they often come to me because they are miserable," Doctor Delight said. "They come to me to improve their quality of life." He eyed Aaron. "Obviously your wife was not satisfied. Maybe you're to blame, not me, for the path she chose. She wanted out. I provide people with the tools they ask for. How they use those tools is up to them. What does it matter to you anyway?" He gestured to Clarissa. "It looks like you've found your new fuck buddy."

"A what?" Clarissa said. "I'm not his—"

"You're a fucking murderer!" exploded Aaron. "I will sue you. I will shut you down. I will bring this to an end. I will mess you up."

Doctor Delight nodded in a sarcastic rhythm to Aaron's words. "Yeah. Sure. Fine." Then he leaned forward and said, "Go ahead. I've been there before. I have my team of lawyers. You can't stop me. Technology moves faster than laws and regulation. This is the wild wild West. All they can do is slap my wrist. If they kick me out of here, I'll find another abandoned store. There are plenty of them. Listen, I know you're upset. I get it. Both of you look like you're losing your shit, so let me help. I can offer you a happier lifestyle. I have chipfeeds that can get to the root of your problems. You don't have to live this way. I can sell you a better mood. Are you familiar with our new product, Mellow Sunrise? It's like waking up to a brand-new day."

"I don't believe this," Aaron said. His voice cracked in defeat. He turned to Clarissa. "Let's just go."

"Before you leave," Doctor Delight said, "would you like a free calendar?" He held up a twelve-month picture calendar branded with the name of the insurance company that previously owned the office. The calendar was several years old, obviously something left behind when the insurance agent moved out. It was a final, sarcastic stab at Aaron's trauma.

And he lost it.

Aaron lunged at Doctor Delight. He heard Clarissa scream. And then the lights went out.

Minutes later, Aaron woke up to find himself dazed and bloody on the floor. Clarissa was on the floor beside him with a hand over one eye, muttering, "Motherfucker."

The muscular tattooed man stood over both of them. He had pounded them to the ground in a fast, fierce beating. Aaron felt blood coming out of his nose and a split in his lip. Clarissa had a black eye.

For the first time since they entered the office, the tattooed man spoke. "You have thirty seconds to leave under your own free will. Or I will remove you, and this time I won't be so gentle."

Aaron spit blood on the floor and rose to his feet, still seeing stars.

Clarissa said nothing, touching her face tenderly.

The two of them left the office without a word, as Doctor Delight and his henchman stared after them.

On the sidewalk, back in the daylight, Clarissa shouted, "What the fuck!" She tried to shake away her stinging pain.

"He hit you too?"

"I was trying to push him away from you!"

"Why'd you do that?"

"Oh shut up." She was clearly angry at the entire scenario, including being mad at him for provoking the attack.

"I'm sorry," Aaron said. He started to reach for her face. "Are you okay?"

She swatted his hand away. "Let's just get out of here."

* * *

Aaron could not sleep that night. Alone in his bedroom, with the door shut to avoid his roommates, he stewed in the dark. He revisited every nasty, sarcastic word that Doctor Delight had hit him with, jabs even more painful than the knockout punches thrown by his bodyguard.

The sleazy fat pig had insulted Wendy, humiliated him and made him look weak and foolish in front of Clarissa.

Aaron clenched his fists, gritted his teeth and channeled every ounce of his fury into plotting his revenge.

He didn't own a gun. But he did have resources that could serve as weapons. He mapped out a plan and obsessed over its steps in a nonstop loop. It gave him some comfort, but not enough to sleep. He witnessed the sunrise through the open curtains of his window. A new day with a new beginning awaited. He was ready to create some closure.

Aaron drove his lawn maintenance truck through the silent streets of L.A. as dawn released a golden glow. He returned to the former insurance office and parked across the street. He wore a baseball cap and large dark sunglasses to obscure his identity. He drank coffee and ate from a brown paper bag of fruit.

And he waited.

And waited.

One hour became two became four.

Finally, around eleven a.m., two men approached the storefront and unlocked the door to start a new day of business. It was short, fat, wobbly Doctor Delight and his tall, muscular bodybuilder friend. They were a comedy of contrasts, although Aaron wasn't laughing.

After the duo slipped inside, Aaron knew he had to act fast before the first customers of the day arrived to complicate things.

Aaron jumped out of the driver's seat, circled to the back of his truck and unlocked it. He chose his method of attack.

The next eight minutes were a blur of rage that later stuck with him like a movie scene he had viewed but not actually participated in. Demons took over his brain. He felt raw and physical and justified.

"You again!"

Those were the words to greet him, and then a loud roar drowned out any further dialogue. Aaron launched his most powerful gas hedge trimmer, the one that could sever the thickest of branches. In a lightning-fast lunge, wielding the tool with years of expertise, he disabled the henchman first, applying the blade to his throat before he could get his hands on Aaron. The green dragon tattoo on the henchman's neck started breathing fire – a wet, red spray – and the henchman's hands no longer had time for Aaron because they were required to clutch a gaping wound to stop the rush of bleeding.

Doctor Delight, while slow and obese, was still an immediate threat. He was fishing in a desk drawer for a firearm. Aaron kept his finger on the trigger of the hedge trimmer and stuffed it as hard as he could into the soft belly of the man who ended Wendy's natural life.

Doctor Delight screamed and Aaron had a tough time pulling the blade back out, tugging hard and exposing a twisted mass of intestines to the open air.

The bodybuilder sputtered and gurgled, clutching his neck as blood escaped between his fingers. Even in this sorry state, he continued to stagger toward Aaron in an attempt to fight him. He removed one of his hands from his bloody throat and reached out for Aaron. He only furthered his own problems when Aaron neatly severed four fingers, leaving only a thumb.

The henchman let out a loud, high-pitched squeal that no longer fitted his hulking macho presence. The loss of the majority of one hand did not help his efforts to stop the persistent flow of blood from his neck. Quickly succumbing to dizziness, he fell to the floor with a big crash, knocking over a coat rack.

With both of his enemies dropped to the ground and seriously incapacitated, Aaron turned off the hedge trimmer.

In the abrupt moment of silence, Doctor Delight began to beg.

"Please…."

He was on the floor in a pool of his own blood, desperately reaching for something that was just out of his grasp.

His chip controller.

Aaron stared down at him.

Doctor Delight looked up from the ground. "Please…hand it to me…."

Aaron didn't move.

"Please...I'm dying.... I just want to make my final minutes...less painful. Can you.... Can you set it to Bliss...or...or...the Eternal Heaven Loop?"

Aaron stepped over to the handheld chip controller. Doctor Delight looked hopeful, but only for a moment. Aaron kicked the device away. "You're not getting eternal heaven," he said. "I'm afraid you're going to that other place."

Doctor Delight had barely enough energy to groan out his response. The bodyguard was no longer conscious; without a grip around his wound he was practically floating in his own blood.

Aaron dropped the hedge trimmer to the floor.

He left the office. He quickly went to his truck, got something out and returned to the two men one last time.

Aaron emptied a red gasoline can around their bodies. He generously soaked the walls and the furniture. He wished somebody had done this before him, before his wife made her fatal purchase, before so many others had to suffer. Nothing could be done to erase the past. But at least now, with the toss of a match, he could protect the future.

★ ★ ★

Aaron drove far away from the blaze. He traveled for miles until the tears overwhelmed his eyes and he had to pull over.

He cried for Wendy. He cried over the savage, impulsive violence that had consumed him. He felt ashamed, when he wanted to feel relief.

It took him a long time to notice the horrible irony of a billboard facing him from down the road. It promoted Dynamica with big, happy smiles from a loving young couple, cheek to cheek, with bold words surrounding them:

Stressed Out? Get the Stress Out!

New from Dynamica: STAY CALM.

The ultimate in emotional well-being. Temper control at your fingertips.

Then, at the bottom, a tagline:

Choose Peace.

CHAPTER NINE

Marc hid in Central Park, listening to the assorted late-night sirens of Manhattan and knowing that at least some of them were because of him and the man he inadvertently sent off a sixty-seventh-floor balcony in a hallucinatory state.

Officially, Central Park had a curfew but these days it wasn't heavily enforced, and Marc was able to stick himself in some bushes and stay the night, although he was too wired to sleep. Back when he still had the chip, he would download Peaceful Slumber to combat insomnia, a gentle sleep aid, but without the chip he was stuck with his default body chemistry for better or worse.

He knew he could never return to his apartment. His only belongings now were the clothes on his back, his wallet and smart phone, and the special controller that Brandyn Handley had given him.

When the sun came up, he walked the park for a while and then spilled out into Midtown. He had two immediate objectives. First he bought a small suitcase. Then he boarded the subway to go to the Financial District. He arrived at the largest bank in New York City as they were unlocking the front doors.

Marc stepped inside the grand, opulent interior of the landmark building and flagship location representing one of the few remaining bricks-and-mortar financial institutions in Manhattan. It was beautiful and stubbornly historic, like a step into the past, before almost everyone did all their banking online. Well-dressed staff members stepped into position, their hard shoes clicking on the marble floor in the echoey acoustics. The bank maintained a neoclassical architecture with decorative Corinthian columns, tall mullioned windows and a domed ceiling, forty feet high, which pulled in dramatic beams of sunlight.

Marc walked with a deliberate casualness, noticing the stiff presence of security guards and trying not to glance at them too long. He advanced past an empty sitting area and a series of long tables neatly stocked with forms and pens. He had twelve teller windows to choose from. Three had people in them. He chose one in the middle.

A lanky, balding gentleman in a crisp white shirt and black tie greeted him with a smile and a nod. He had a big forehead barely topped by the dark lining of a severely receding hairline. "How may I help you, sir?"

Marc placed the suitcase on the floor. He felt a rush of anxiety, as if he was about to commit a bank robbery. But far from it – he only wanted to withdraw a significant portion of his own savings.

Marc provided identification and his bank account information. He stated simply, "I wish to liquidate two million dollars into cash."

The teller half-nodded, as if he hadn't heard right.

"Sir – you do know – you said cash."

"Yes, two million."

"Two million dollars. You want that now, in cash?"

"That's right."

"Okay – it's not as easy as just pulling it out, right now, on the spot."

Marc maintained a pleasant tone, but his words held an edge. "First, this bank, this time of the morning, has that much cash on hand, I'm sure of it. Second, you are obligated to give it to me. It's my money. Legally I can take it out whenever I want. You're just storing it and skimming some interest off the top. You can't deny me access to my financial assets. I know the laws."

"Yes," said the teller, keeping his voice measured and civil, but with a hard stare of authority. "And the bank has its rules. For an amount this high, I need to get my manager."

"Great. Get them."

Marc felt a cold sweat spreading over his body. He thought about the security guards on either side of the vast bank lobby. He needed to conduct this activity quickly, before the government seized his account or, worse, seized him, a sitting duck in the open.

A pear-shaped man, also balding and dressed in a white shirt and black tie, took the first man's place at the teller window. He wore wire-rimmed half-glasses and had heavy wisps of curly hair above his ears. He offered a bigger smile than the first greeter, perhaps with the knowledge that he was dealing with a customer with a significant amount in his account.

"Hello, it's a pleasure to serve you, Mr. Tefteller."

Marc repeated his request.

The manager nodded and retained his smile. "Certainly. We will need identification, a driver's license...."

"I have all that."

"May I ask why you are withdrawing your funds in this manner?"

"Excuse me?"

"This is an unusual activity. It triggers obligations on my part. I can give you your money, but I will need to report an amount this large. It's for security purposes. We need to make sure you're not laundering money or funding terrorism, or perhaps being victimized at this very moment. For instance, perhaps you are falling prey to a fraud scheme. We see it happen fairly often. Or maybe, a man of your wealth, you have been coerced into giving your holdings to a third party. If so, we can handle the situation discreetly to keep you safe. I will make it look like I'm giving you a form to fill out, and you would write down the nature of your predicament, and I would quietly alert the police and our security force. We will make sure you are not harmed."

"I'm not being robbed, I'm not a terrorist, I just need my money," said Marc, growing terse with the delay.

"You haven't answered my question. Why are you withdrawing two million dollars? I need to submit this information to the IRS."

"I'm – I'm buying a house," Marc said quickly, silently cursing himself for stammering as he lied. "I'm buying a house and the seller is very eccentric. He insists on cash, he doesn't trust institutions."

"I can give you a cashier's check."

"It has to be cash."

"Perhaps you could bring the seller to the bank. We could have the funds withdrawn and given to him directly. You don't want to walk out of here with that much cash."

"I have a suitcase."

"That's not the point."

"Do it right now. Get my money out of your vault and give it to me. I know my rights."

"Mr. Tefteller, I cannot accommodate you without making some phone calls. I need to contact my boss at headquarters."

"That's bullshit."

"I don't feel comfortable with this situation."

Marc clenched his fists in frustration. "Don't – don't call anyone. I need to – let me think this over."

"Are you feeling well? Honestly, you don't look well. You haven't been drinking, have you?"

"No. I didn't sleep well last night. It's been – oh for God's sake, it's none of your business."

Marc turned away from the teller window. He knew he was within his rights to withdraw his money at any time. The bank was just giving him a hard time. They didn't want to lose such a big amount.

Why couldn't they simply be more accommodating to a customer request?

He walked across the bank lobby with his head in a daze. More customers were arriving, creating a busier atmosphere, and he really needed to reach a quick resolution that didn't drag him through a day of bureaucracy. He was a wanted man. Every minute was precious.

Then Marc realized he had a way to persuade the bank manager to be more agreeable. It was in his pocket.

Marc sat in one of the cushy, orange lobby chairs. He pulled out the controller device that Brandyn Handley had given him to send signals to chips embedded in other people. The bank manager was probably chipped…and there was one way to find out.

From his years of marketing Dynamica's signal feeds, Marc was very familiar with the company's vast catalog of offerings. There was one called Agree to Please.

He ran a quick search and found it in the menu, along with promotional language that his team had crafted:

Build better relationships!

Keep your inner contrarian at bay at times YOU choose. Avoid unwanted conflict with:

Your spouse

Your boss

Authority figures

AGREE TO PLEASE stops unproductive bickering before it starts and promotes positive interactions for happier encounters. Don't get stuck in the argument loop – Agree 2 B Agreeable!

Marc returned to the teller window and motioned to the bank manager, who returned with a less enthusiastic greeting the second time around.

"Yes?"

"I'm – I'm sorry – just fiddling with my thing here for a minute—"

The bank manager looked at him curiously. “Are you okay? I don’t think you’re okay.”

Marc tapped the closest chip code on the list, assuming it to be the bank manager, and sent him a thirty-minute feed of Agree to Please.

The manager blinked a few times but did not seem aware that his brainwaves had been hacked.

“I think New York City is the greatest city in the world, don’t you?” Marc asked.

“Absolutely. You are so right, sir.”

“Jazz is so much better than rock music or classical or, God forbid, country....”

“I agree with you wholeheartedly. Jazz is the best, Mr. Tefteller.”

“You are going to liquidate two million dollars of my savings into cash in one hundred dollar bills, and do it without any unnecessary delays, wouldn’t you agree?”

“Of course, sir. We can do that.”

“It’s a good idea for me to take out my money, since it belongs to me, right?”

“Absolutely.”

“I think faster is better, without a lot of talking and forms. What do you think?”

“Faster is better. Let’s not worry about talking and forms.”

“Good. Then we are in total agreement?”

“I would say we see things in very much the same way.”

“No argument here.”

“Here neither.”

The bank manager enlisted an associate to help him and soon the teller window counter was filling with stacks of cash. Marc quickly moved the money into his suitcase as fast as it arrived.

Each half-inch-thick stack consisted of ten thousand dollars in hundred dollar bills. Marc filled the suitcase with two hundred stacks.

“Such a pleasure doing business with you,” said the bank manager, shaking Marc’s hand as they concluded the withdrawal.

“I’m glad you could be so cooperative,” Marc said.

“Will you be requiring a security escort?”

“No.”

“That will be fine.”

"Yes it will." Marc left the teller window with a tight grip on the suitcase handle. The weight felt good, about thirty-five pounds. He was careful to look straight ahead, not glancing at anyone, especially the security guards.

He made it outside to the curb and immediately waved for a cab. He kept an eye out for anyone who may have followed him out of the bank. In less than a minute, Marc sat in the back seat of a yellow cab with the suitcase at his side.

"Where to?" asked the cabbie.

The question startled Marc. He realized he didn't know where he was headed next.

For his destination, Marc somewhat randomly picked a street corner in Stuyvesant Town, a neighborhood on the east side of Manhattan. He climbed out of the cab with the suitcase and a mission.

He needed a small, simple, out-of-the-way apartment under a false name. After a few blocks of walking, he found a promising site: a grungy one-room unit above a 'going out of business' tourist shop with a landlord who spoke broken English and readily accepted cash in exchange for maximum privacy.

"I stay out of your business," promised the landlord. "You – no parties. No cops. Pay on time, first Tuesday of the month. We be good to each other, eh?"

The apartment was ugly and dirty, but secure. After exploring the square space and its tiny bathroom and closet, Marc identified a spot where he could open up the floor and stash his cash in a discreet hideaway. His bed would rest on top. He just needed tools…and a bed.

The former he obtained from a nearby hardware store, the latter he bought from an online seller located in the neighborhood. It was essentially an overpriced stained mattress and clumsy metal frame, but it came with the services of a muscular, stubble-faced Italian man who helped carry it out of a storage shack and into Marc's new apartment. The man had no idea he was briefly standing on two million dollars in cash.

Marc took a cab to a theater supply shop, also going out of business, and purchased various items to help him with a physical disguise for going out in public. He obtained a realistic wig of long dark hair that would cover the back of his neck to hide the absence of a bump from the chip.

After stocking up on food and new clothes, Marc stayed inside his apartment with his money and his fears.

He was surprised to discover he was going through a chip withdrawal. In times of anxiety, he had relied on it for a surge of satisfaction, simple corrections to soothe his nerves and elevate his feelings with a Happy Lift. He missed being able to adjust his mood with a few quick pokes of his controller.

Now, instead, he had a device to control the brainwaves of others – something far more powerful.

He could easily imagine government agents breaking into his new apartment for a raid, similar to the last time, and he would be ready to stop them with the power of this device. He kept it within arm's reach while he slept.

Sleep did not come easy, especially without the chip, but he accepted that.

CHAPTER TEN

Scotty was building himself the perfect woman. He sat half-naked on his crusty bedsheets, bent forward, obese and wheezing. On his tablet, he chose from a menu of physical features to define everything from hairstyle to leg length to eye color to shape of the ass to preferred curve of the bosom.

To finish off his creation, he ticked boxes in a quick checklist of personality traits. He desired 'submissive', 'cheerful' and 'moderate intelligence'. He gave her a name: 'Tulip'. He felt it was a pretty name.

Once assembled, she looked scrumptious – bright-eyed, eager and fully disrobed. He quickly uploaded her for a Dynamica virtual reality experience.

Sex, to be specific.

It was the cap on another glorious day of chipfeed sensations that began with Lost in a Candy Factory, continued with Mixed Martial Arts Bloodsport and moved on to the Sniper Zone. Over the course of eight hours, he had sampled a dazzling array of delectable sugar treats, beat the shit out of a series of would-be champion fighters, and then shot several hundred rampaging terrorists. It felt good. Banging the hell out of Tulip in the Dynamica Honeymoon Suite would be a rousing climax, and if rated highly, he would bookmark her in his list of Favorites for future encounters.

Poking the handheld controller, he activated Hot Sex Action and selected Tulip from his playlist. Wearing his Dynamica eye cover to shut out natural light, he leaned back against a stack of pillows and awaited the beginning of a tantalizing stimulation that would start in his head and travel down to his groin.

He smiled. A luxurious honeymoon suite filled his senses – sight, sounds, textures, smells. Tulip was presented before him in a big bed, tucked nude between pink silk sheets, waiting for him with a moist and inviting smile.

"Oh yeah," said Scotty. In his imagination, he stood erect at the foot of the bed, equally naked. His bare feet touched shag carpeting. He could feel it between his toes.

As he stepped toward her, a rush of adrenaline raced through his body. He experienced a jumbo-sized erection of superhuman dimensions.

Then he was hit with a rude interruption. His vision filled with big, bold, blinking red letters.

ALERT.

"What the hell?" he shouted out loud.

Then he received the message: 'DOOR BELL'.

Scotty cursed himself for not turning off alerts before initiating chipsex. The text alerts popped up periodically with annoying reminders for him to empty his bladder and bowels or eat real food to sustain his physical existence.

'DOOR BELL' startled him because he had experienced it so rarely – hardly anyone came to the door.

"God damn it," he grumbled. He trusted that one of the other two roommates was also receiving the alert and would handle it. Hell, he was farthest from the front door. *Let Larry or Desmond deal with it!*

But they didn't. Perhaps they had turned off doorbell notifications. Or maybe they refused to interrupt their own chipfeed experiences.

As the 'DOOR BELL' alert continued to flash, Scotty tried to ignore it. But then he became curious....

What if it was a delivery of Body Fuel bars or Hydration Packs? He needed those things to stay physically stable while engaging in lengthy chipfeed marathons. He couldn't remember if his current stock was getting low.

Or— what if the caller was testing to see if anyone was home and planning to rob the place if no one answered? They had experienced trouble with brazen burglars in the past.

The words 'DOOR BELL' continued to flicker in his mind.

Scotty swore again and paused his chipfeed. He could not enjoy ravaging Tulip with this distraction. He ripped the eye cover from his head. He fumbled and stumbled off the bed and into a standing position. He pulled on some pants.

He went downstairs. Desmond remained sprawled in his usual spot, delirious on the couch, lost in a chipfeed, spewing drool. Scotty silently gave him the finger and then opened the front door.

A slight man in a neatly pressed button-down shirt and wool slacks stood before him. He was well groomed with slicked-back hair, smiling and holding an electronic tablet.

"Hello. I'm looking for Aaron Holt."

Just hearing the name out loud fueled Scotty with a fresh rise of agitation.

"Aaron? He's not here."

"Would you happen to—"

"No. I have no idea where he is. He's an asshole. He stays away from us most of the time." Scotty had a difficult time spitting the words out. He hadn't spoken to anyone in days.

"Am I correct in listing the occupants of this residence as Larry Wellington, Desmond Irving, Scott Wellington and Aaron Holt?"

"What the hell is it of your business?"

"I'm with the government agency of citizenship."

Scotty eyed the little man suspiciously. "What do you want with us?"

"It's only Aaron that I wish to speak with. The rest of you are in compliance."

"Compliance?"

"Yes. You see, we're reaching out to individuals who are not yet chipped to sign them up, free of charge, so they can enter our government database for benefits and services."

"He doesn't have the chip."

"Yes, that is what our records indicate."

"Good luck getting him chipped. He won't do it. He hates the chip."

"Perhaps he just doesn't understand it. New technology can be intimidating for some people. We're here to help. The chip will give him access to Social Security, voter registration, citizenship privileges. There's nothing for him to be concerned about. It's quite beneficial. As you, yourself, have experienced."

"I think the chip is totally great."

"Of course it is. It's the way of the future. Why be left behind? You wouldn't want to still be using a typewriter…or rotary phone…or horse and buggy, God forbid."

"So what do you want from me?"

The little man handed Scotty a business card with a name and number. "This is my contact information. If you could, please ask Mr. Holt to follow up in the next couple of days."

Scotty took the card and shrugged at it in bemusement. "He's not going to call you."

"The chip is mandatory." The little man continued smiling. "He'll come around."

"We'll see."

"There's an incentive for effective referrals. You could receive complementary credits toward future chipfeeds. Say, eight months' worth."

Scotty tightened his grip on the business card and gave it another look. "No fooling?"

"I would hate to place Mr. Holt on our resistance list. That would require more drastic measures. If you could convince him to be a willing participant, I'll make it worth your while. I'm compensated for every person I enlist. I'm sure we could work something out."

"I'll bet we could," Scotty said. He liked the idea of forcing the chip on that snooty, condescending asshole Aaron. Even better, he loved the idea of free credits, since his Government Survival Checks barely covered the cost of living and some of the more coveted chipfeeds, like Build A Babe and S&M Dungeon.

"I look forward to partnering with you," said the little man. His eyes barely blinked and the smile did not leave his face. He left to advance to the next house on his list, clutching his tablet.

Scotty shut the front door. Desmond remained on the couch, occasionally twitching with some unknown delight. Scotty looked at the business card one more time and shoved it into his pants pocket. Then he returned upstairs.

In his bedroom, he loosened his belt and retrieved his eye cover and handheld controller, excited to return to the lovely Tulip. She remained paused, frozen in the exact place he had left her. "I'm back, sweetie," he said. He activated his ideal lover and launched into a fresh adventure.

CHAPTER ELEVEN

Naked, Clarissa rolled off Aaron. For a quiet moment, they lay side-by-side on her bed, dressed only in a thin coat of sweat.

Still catching his breath, Aaron had to ask, "Was that better than a chocolate swirl orgasm?"

Not amused, she responded, "The real thing is always better than some bogus brainfart sent through the airwaves." With the impulsive lovemaking done, she kept a space between them on the bed and emphasized it. "No matter what you're thinking, this doesn't mean we're boyfriend-girlfriend or in some kind of romantic relationship. It was a physical interlude."

"Like your daily run?"

"Something like that."

Aaron wasn't sure if his feelings were hurt. It had happened very quickly, and he had welcomed it. They were in her apartment packing her things for the move to Santa Barbara. They got into a playful tussle over her CD collection. She wanted to toss them all out. Her CD player was broken and new ones were no longer being manufactured since everyone mentally streamed music these days. She was throwing away The Beatles and he rescued them from the trash, declaring, "Hey, I like The Beatles." She became physical in her determination to grab the discs back and return them to the garbage. Somehow their tangled bodies joined in a kiss.

He hadn't expected them to hook up like this, so he just felt confused when she immediately made it clear that the burst of intimacy meant nothing.

As he remained on his back, looking around the room, he ended the awkward silence with a random comment.

"Are you taking your posters?"

The walls were covered in travel posters displaying grand settings in cities around the world – Paris, London, Singapore, Barcelona. Previously she had told him about her youthful ambitions to be a travel blogger and see the world. She studied journalism but wound up bartending in L.A. and even doing debt collection on the side.

He had found the latter surprising, and she told him, "I can be very disarming."

"I don't need the posters," she said. "I've looked at them long enough that they're burned into my mind. Even if I never see those places, I have those images committed to memory."

In recent years, traveling abroad had become extremely expensive – a casualty of people preferring to travel in their minds. Fewer flights hurt the economies of scale in the airline industry, and flying became a luxury of the rich. Common folks went on trips in their heads, no passport required.

Aaron turned to look at Clarissa as she remained at his side, looking up at the ceiling. She was beautiful in that moment; long, dark hair tumbling freely, bare, angular shoulders, thin lips, alert eyes. He wanted to reach out and touch her.

But he held back.

Then she slipped away from him and sat up on the bed. She sighed. "Let's finish this packing."

She pulled on gym shorts and a faded pink T-shirt, going braless. She offered a final acknowledgment of their episode of lust. "That's the last fuck for this bed."

Aaron didn't know what to say to that, so he said nothing. He pulled his clothes back on.

"There's really not that much left," said Clarissa. "My idiot brother stole anything of value to pay for his addiction. My idiot boyfriend took everything we jointly owned, basically to be an asshole."

Aaron pointed to her balcony. "Your bike?"

"My car has a bike rack. The bike is coming with."

At that moment, there was a tapping at her apartment door.

Aaron and Clarissa froze.

Aaron whispered, "Are you expecting anyone?"

Clarissa shook her head. She gestured for him to keep quiet.

Aaron watched Clarissa step silently in bare feet toward the door.

She looked through the peephole.

She gave a puzzled frown. She stepped back slowly and rejoined Aaron. "Some little guy with a tablet."

"Don't answer it."

"I'm not."

The man tapped several more times, then left. But not before slipping a piece of paper under the door.

Aaron and Clarissa exchanged glances.

She slowly stepped back to the door and gazed through the peephole.

"He's gone," she said. She bent down and picked up the sheet of paper. She brought it over to Aaron, and they looked at it together. It read:

Be counted!

Be compliant!

Receive your rightful services!

The United States Citizenship Agency is updating its records in partnership with Dynamica Incorporated in our mission to extend the chip technology, FREE OF CHARGE, *as an American Benefit for every man, woman and child.* DON'T BE LEFT OUT. CONTACT US TODAY....

Clarissa abruptly crumpled the flyer into a ball and tossed it across the room.

"Not going to happen," she said.

"They want to make it as common as paying taxes."

"I'll give the government money," Clarissa said, "but I won't give them my soul."

She moved over to her balcony and cautiously looked through the glass doors.

"He's probably going door-to-door to bug all the people who don't have the chip. Let's stay inside until he's on another block. Then we'll pack the car quickly, go to your place, grab your stuff, and get the hell out of L.A. They'll no longer have a record of where to find us."

Aaron joined her at the balcony doors. After a few minutes, they saw the small man on the sidewalk, heading to another residence on the street. He had a short build, slicked-back hair and business-like attire.

"Should we try one more time for your brother?" Aaron asked.

"What do you mean?"

"To bring him with us. Out of L.A."

"No," she said firmly.

"No?"

"Don't question me," she said in an abrupt, tense tone. "You tried once. I've tried for months – I've probably been there fifty times. He's lost. We can't save someone who refuses to be saved. It tears me up inside but forget it, he's done." Then she moved away from the balcony, brushing past him, and said, "Let's finish packing."

* * *

Aaron and Clarissa entered the rental house and quickly packed Aaron's belongings into boxes and bags: his clothes, food, toiletries and books. The three roommates were curled up and zoned out in their favorite nests in separate rooms.

"It smells horrible in here," Clarissa said, wrinkling her nose.

"Welcome to my world," Aaron muttered.

"It's like the tent city with a roof."

Aaron didn't intend to notify his roommates he was leaving. He had no interest in even writing a short note. He figured it would take them days or weeks to realize he was gone.

That was the departure he wanted.

But then Larry unexpectedly showed up in the upstairs hallway, walking upright in staggered, numb steps toward the bathroom, apparently pulled from a chipfeed adventure by a bathroom break alert.

As his eyes adjusted to the real world, he noticed Clarissa coming out of Aaron's bedroom, carrying a cardboard box. "Who are you?" he said. Then he noticed Aaron following behind her, also carrying a box. "Hey, what are you doing?"

"I'm leaving," Aaron said simply. Aaron and Clarissa moved past Larry and continued on their way downstairs.

Larry thought about the statement for a long moment and then said, "Wait, no, you can't do that."

Aaron ignored him. He headed for the front door.

"But you pay for rent and stuff!" Larry called out after him.

Aaron and Clarissa loaded the boxes into Clarissa's car, a Dodge Charger, which was parked at the curb. Then they returned inside the house for another armload. They discovered Larry rousing the other roommates from their mental retreats, exclaiming, "He's leaving! Aaron is moving out!"

Desmond sat up on the couch and pulled off the collar that hacked into Dynamica's chipfeed services. It took him a moment to find words. His mouth was dry and his brain was foggy.

"Moving out what where," he said.

In the kitchen, Aaron and Clarissa stuffed paper sacks with food: canned vegetables and tuna, fruit, peanut butter, cereal, soup and noodle mixes.

When they reentered the living room, they discovered Desmond crying on the floor.

"You can't go!" he shouted like a child.

"What the hell?" said Clarissa.

"I can't survive on my royalty checks. We need a fourth roommate. I don't want to get evicted." He was delirious with desperation. Aaron had never seen him slip into hysteria like this before. He was acting like a cartoon.

"Get a job," Clarissa said in a hard tone.

"I don't know how anymore!" Desmond howled.

Aaron put down his sack of groceries. He dug into his pocket and pulled out the keys to his lawn maintenance truck. He threw them at Desmond. They bounced off his chest and landed on the floor. "Take the truck. Maybe you can sell it. Take all the lawn equipment. I don't know if you'll find a buyer, but if you do, maybe you can pay one more month's rent."

Desmond picked up the keys from the floor, eyes wide. "Really?"

At that moment, Scotty came barreling down the stairs. He moved so quickly he nearly lost his footing and had to grab the banister for balance.

"What the hell, man, you can't leave!" he bellowed.

"You didn't like me when I was here, now you don't want me to leave?" Aaron said. Then he stiffened, realizing Scotty was rushing straight at him.

Scotty grabbed Aaron by the shirt with a fat fist and screamed in his face, "You're not going anywhere!"

Clarissa dropped her sack of food, spilling its contents to the floor. She delivered a punch to Scotty's ribs and a pointy-boot kick to his shin. He yelled, "Ow!" and loosened his grip. She planted her hands into his big, soft belly and shoved him away. He stumbled and then unwisely lurched back toward her. She was ready and socked him with a small but hard fist to the face.

Scotty put a hand to his stinging red cheek, glared at Aaron and exclaimed, "I'm telling on you!"

"Go ahead," Aaron said. "Whatever that means."

Scotty said, "They're looking for you. You're going to get the chip. You're illegal now. They know about it."

"Who's 'they'?" Clarissa asked.

"Doesn't matter," said Scotty. He reached into his pocket and pulled out a business card. "I'm turning you in."

Aaron exchanged a glance with Clarissa. He immediately recalled the little man going door-to-door to sign up unchipped citizens for the government tracker.

Clarissa stared at Aaron. "Do you think this is part of…?"

Scotty dialed a number on his cell phone.

"What are you doing?" Aaron asked.

Scotty held up a hand intended to silence him.

"I said *what are you doing?*"

Scotty began speaking into the phone. "Yes. I would like to report a resister. He's a runner. His name is Aaron Holt—"

Clarissa grabbed a can of peas from the floor. She lunged at Scotty and smashed it against the side of his head, causing him to drop the phone. He spun away and she hit him again with the dented can, striking him in the back. He shouted at the other two roommates, "Don't let him get away. *There's a reward!*"

Larry tackled Clarissa from behind. Aaron immediately grabbed him and pulled him off, delivering a hard punch to his jaw. Desmond half-heartedly entered the brawl, slipped on some grapes and fell down. Scotty came at Clarissa again, letting out a dramatic roar as if he was participating in some bombastic video game. She stopped him cold with an efficiently placed kick and punch, while Aaron delivered additional body blows to Larry to keep him at a distance.

With the three roommates punched, kicked and pushed back, sufficiently cleared as obstacles, Aaron exclaimed, "Let's go!"

Aaron and Clarissa left the food scattered on the floor and hurried from the house. Clarissa slid into the driver's seat of her Dodge Charger and began accelerating before Aaron had finished closing the door on the passenger side.

The three roommates did not chase them out on the lawn, but remained crowded in the open doorway, peering outside with anxious expressions, as if the world beyond their little house was a frightening and unfamiliar alien landscape.

Clarissa sped down the street, engine roaring.

Aaron asked, "Are you okay?"

"Of course I'm okay, that was like beating up sleepwalkers," she said sharply. "You lived with that?"

"Not anymore, I'm done."

"I wish we had that food."

"We'll be okay."

She raced down mostly empty streets. "I guess you're officially a 'resister' now."

"So are you."

"Sounds like fun." Then she smiled. She didn't do that often, which was unfortunate, because she had a beautiful, killer smile.

CHAPTER TWELVE

Marc stayed hidden in his small, box-shaped apartment until the crush of cabin fever made him feel like his head would explode. On a random Wednesday, he applied a disguise, slipped into a comfortable pair of gym shoes and went on a very long walk across Manhattan. The chip-hacking device went into his pocket for protection. He wore a bulky 'I ♥ NY' sweatshirt and New York Yankees cap bought at a significant discount from the ailing tourist shop in his building. Oversized sunglasses concealed his eyes.

He proceeded west on East 23rd Street until he got to Broadway, and then he headed north through the heart of the Big Apple. In the beginning, he watched faces, paranoid about being discovered. He was a wanted man, accused of pushing a government agent off a balcony to his death.

The rollout of mandatory chipping was moving full steam ahead after a rapid approval in the House and Senate. As he walked the city streets, Marc observed several pop-up chip installation clinics with long lines of eager New Yorkers. Many of the anxious customers appeared to be economically challenged – unable to afford the chip when it was a luxury, thrilled to receive it free from the government, indifferent to or ignorant of the implications of allowing Washington access into their heads.

He wanted to warn these people about the irreversible nature of the chip and the inability to 'turn it off' or 'unsubscribe' once the feed was activated. Looking into their simple, hopeful faces, he felt tremendous guilt knowing he had helped create this monster.

Back at the beginning, he was proud. He was on the team that introduced a thrilling technological breakthrough that could help combat pain and depression while offering innocent entertainment pleasures inside the user's imagination. Marc had built an enormously successful marketing campaign.

"I'm sorry," he now wanted to tell the world.

Marc felt consumed with angst and anxiety, feelings that he previously suppressed with his own mood manipulation through the chip. He knew that if he still had the chip, he would inevitably give in to tapping a few commands on a controller and triggering instant relief.

The chip was addictive. It appealed to impulses, not rational thought. It was too easy, too convenient. The government had already promised free health clinics to rehabilitate people who became hooked on unproductive chipfeeds – like the popular Stoned and Chill Out offerings that held steady in the Top Ten.

When Marc was employed at Dynamica, the leadership team held numerous meetings to discuss how they would fight accusations that the chip was addictive in the same destructive manner as alcohol, cocaine, opiates and heroin. A massive public relations effort was activated to overwhelm the members of the medical community who made the case for psychological dependency even if the biological effects were minimal.

Marc's role in protecting Dynamica simply felt like a job back then: now he felt like he had let down the human race.

As he headed toward Midtown, the numbers of homeless grew. One grizzled man in particular, sitting on a soiled blanket on the sidewalk and begging for change, grabbed Marc's attention.

His cardboard sign said: *Can't Afford Painumb.*

Painumb was a subscription-based chipfeed that fed signals to the brain to block sensations of physical pain.

As Marc stopped to stare at him for a moment, an older woman in a long dress strolled past hurriedly, exclaiming, "Don't give him any money. It's not for pain, he'll spend it on Intox."

Marc was taken aback by the unsympathetic tone of her voice.

Intox was a chipfeed selection that imitated the feelings of being drunk – or intoxicated.

The liquor industry hated it.

"No, it's for the pain in my legs!" the homeless man tried to shout after her in a rough, hoarse voice, but she was already far enough away not to hear him.

Marc turned, facing away from the man.

"Hey, buddy…" the man mumbled from his blanket.

Marc pulled out his controller. He selected the nearest person to him and sent signals for Painumb, choosing the maximum time period.

"Ohhh," said the homeless man, experiencing instant relief. "Oh God. How did that—?"

Marc resumed walking.

He reached Times Square, which had slowly slipped back into a seventies-era seediness, no longer a tourist, shopping or entertainment destination. The sidewalks were messy with gritty characters filling his path. They were chipping under coats and blankets; lurking in front of shuttered storefronts, begging for change; or loudly hawking stolen chipfeed codes or – with brazen descriptions – illegal chipfeed experiences in the extreme sex and violence categories.

Marc walked a zigzag around them, trying not to look into their eyes, but unable to escape the pungent smell. Up ahead, he saw another chip installation clinic with people lined up to have Big Brother inserted into their neck. However, an organized opposition had entered the scene – anti-chip protesters with signs, led by an angry young black woman with a bullhorn.

"Don't surrender your soul!" she shouted. "Keep the government out! Say no to the chip!"

One of the signs read: *We demand the right to choose. My body, my choice.*

Another said: *Take your chip and shove it!*

Marc wanted to join them. He was thrilled to see an uprising against the government mandate. His immediate urge was to approach the woman with the megaphone and offer his services – and deep marketing experience – for the good fight.

But he knew he couldn't. He had to stay on the sidelines, anonymous, or risk being discovered and captured and then God knows what.

He was an enemy of the state.

He had to stay away from gatherings such as this one. It was probably being watched at this very moment, and it was only a matter of time before the police arrived to break it up – and maybe break open a few heads in the process.

He could imagine the woman with the megaphone being clobbered unconscious and then waking up in a hospital with the chip installed at the base of her noggin.

After all, it was the law now.

An enormous, animated advertisement for Dynamica played in a loop on the Times Square Jumbotron overhead. Once a source of pride, the oversized promotion now embarrassed him. It was garish, tacky and obnoxiously bright, like a second sun. He averted his eyes from it.

Marc kept walking, a meandering path, going a few blocks in one direction, then a few blocks in another direction, and so on.

Even with people spending more time indoors indulging in chipfeeds, the New York sidewalks remained fairly busy with pedestrians, though perhaps at half the volume of five years ago.

It felt good to be immersed with flesh and blood human beings, but it also made Marc feel profoundly lonely.

He knew he couldn't – shouldn't – engage with anyone. He had cut ties with all of his friends and even his family.

He had texted his parents in Oregon to tell them not to worry about him but he would be 'dropping out of society' for a while. He disconnected his phone service before they had a chance to reply. He shut down all of his social media accounts. He erased his online presence the best he could.

He needed to steer clear of human interaction.

It made him sad, but then a fortuitous opportunity showed up in his path.

The sign read: *VOLUNTEERS NEEDED!* The lettering was big and desperate.

Marc stopped to stare into the doorway of a pet rescue center. He could hear an assortment of dogs barking inside.

"I can do this," he said quietly to himself. "It's just animals."

He felt better almost immediately – and it didn't require streaming Happy from a transmission tower.

* * *

Marc met with Kathryn Sedak, the manager of the pet shelter, and liked her right away. He gave her a fake name and job history, and she was so anxious to enroll his help that she barely paid any attention to his credentials as she filled out a simple paper form.

"We are in crisis mode," she told him in the back office, her voice permanently loud from always yelling above the cacophony of barking dogs. "This chip phenomena has basically been a disaster for pets. People feel they can get the stimulus, the same emotional fulfillment they would get from owning a pet from some signal sent to their brain cells. There are even some feeds out there that are like Dog Play or Dog Walk – how great, you can play with an imaginary dog or cat and not have to feed or clean up after them. This means real pets get screwed. People are so caught up in their own heads these days – they don't want to bother with an actual living pet. There's been a huge surge in abandoned dogs and cats. They abandon them on the streets of the city, for God's sake. I'm sorry. You might love the chip. I don't mean to rant. But it's been horrible for these animals – they're victims of this technology. Hey, I get the attraction. I have the chip. But I use it sparingly, you know? I don't get all consumed in it. Sorry, I'm doing all the talking. Let's just fill out this form so we can get you started. Question one, I'm sorry I gotta ask this, it's the law now – you're chipped, right?"

Marc nodded. "Of course. I mean – I'm like you. I don't use it a lot. Sometimes if I have a headache or trouble sleeping…."

"Good," Kathryn said quickly, and she checked a box on her sheet. "Technically, we can't hire unchipped workers. The government is supposed to be providing a list at some point, I don't know when that's gonna come. Maybe a couple of months. They're developing a database."

"I see," Marc said, rather than the two words in his head: *Oh shit.*

"Bob, we're excited to have you join us," said Kathryn, and it took Marc a moment to respond because he had already forgotten the fake name he had hastily given her at the start of the conversation: Bob Nielsen.

"I'm glad to be here. I'm happy to do whatever I can to help."

Marc looked past Kathryn to the wall behind her, which was covered in photographs of cute, sad-eyed dogs and cats with their names written beneath in marker. His eyes started to tear up because he felt partly responsible for the abandoned pet crisis, yet another tragic outcome of Dynamica's enormous success.

The photographs were assembled under three category headings: ADOPTED, PRESENT, LOST.

"Lost…?" Marc said.

"Euthanized," Kathryn said. "I have to be honest with you. We used to be one hundred percent kill-free. But the numbers are out of control. At a certain point, if we can't place an animal, they're put to sleep."

Marc covered his eyes with his hand. He felt nauseous.

"I know," said Kathryn. "It's horrible. Sometimes I go home and cry. I could turn off the crying and the sadness with the chip, I suppose. But I feel like that wouldn't be fair to the departed. They deserve a good cry."

Marc started working at the pet rescue center the next day.

The strays spent most of their time in numbered cages with water bowls and disintegrating toys. The cats were quiet but the dogs regularly barked, yipped and howled. Every time Marc stepped into their general vicinity, the noise volume elevated. The dogs wagged their tails, eager for short walks or play periods. When he wasn't interacting with the animals, Marc was cleaning the kennels, taking photos and writing bios for the adoption website, and assisting visitors with adoption counseling. Fortunately, big-hearted people came in every day to open up their homes to abandoned pets. Unfortunately, the number of animals coming in overwhelmed the numbers going out. Some of the latest arrivals had been badly neglected, or even abused, requiring extra time to regain their trust in humans.

Marc worked alongside another volunteer, a portly, pouty teenage girl named Regan, who clearly did not want to be there. She wrinkled her nose at the animals, complained about their smell and called them names like 'shithead' and 'spaz'. She made her involuntary volunteering clear: "My parents forced me to be here. They're stodgy old farts who think I spend too much time chipping. This is their way of making me deal with the real world." She bragged about how she had turned her bedroom closet into a pod space. "There's nothing I like better than to go in there, shut the door, shut out the real world and go on a trip. Because *this* planet Earth, maybe it used to be something back in the day, but right now, it ain't worth living."

"If it's such a mess, you could do something about it," Marc told her. "Be an activist. Don't just sit in your closet."

"Like I'm going to be able to fix this screwed-up planet? Yeah, right. The older generations had all the fun and left the rest of us a big mess – a shitty economy, climate change, corruption everywhere…. I'm not dealing with somebody else's shit."

Her efforts to help around the pet shelter were half-hearted, slow and draggy with the disdain of unwanted obligation. She did not cope well with animals that were extra anxious or frisky.

"Too bad we can't just chip 'em, you know?" she told Marc. "They start getting all crazy and noisy, we could send them 'shut the hell up' signals."

Marc often wanted to send Regan shut the hell up signals and he was empowered to do so – but restrained himself from wielding his hacking abilities, until one day he couldn't hold back any further.

During an extra busy day, while Kathryn was out in the van picking up more lost pets, Marc discovered Regan slumped in a corner of the office, eye mask covering the top half of her face. She was gripping her pink, decorated handheld device, zoned out in a chipfeed experience.

She had a relaxed expression and gentle smile.

Meanwhile, the dogs needed socialization and time away from their cages. They were growing noisy as their inner clocks sensed the time for play.

"You lousy bitch," Marc grumbled. He pulled out his hacking device, selected her chip and found something to give her a harsh jolt – a popular chipfeed signal called 'Roller-coaster Thrills'.

Marc jammed her feed with the new signal.

Regan bolted out of her relaxed position, tearing off her eye cover. She stumbled around for a moment, exclaiming, "What the hell!"

"Is something wrong?" Marc asked innocently, pocketing his device.

"Jesus," she said, breathing hard. "I was all chill and then all of a sudden it's like I'm plunging straight down on a roller-coaster – like I got somebody else's feed."

"Yeah, I heard they've been having problems with the transmission tower in this part of town. Signals get crossed."

"What the hell?" said Regan, pacing angrily. "Who can we sue about that? I just about had a heart attack."

"It's time to walk the dogs. They need us."

"Yeah, yeah, all right," Regan grumbled.

Marc soon lost himself in playtime with the dogs, and even Regan appeared to be enjoying herself. In the absence of human companionship – outside of working with Kathryn and Regan – Marc was becoming close with several of the dogs, frequently talking to them and sharing his feelings, as if in therapy. The dogs listened, nonjudgmental.

Marc's close circle of friends included Mack, a black lab; Tessa, a golden retriever; Winnie, a French bulldog; and Carl, a Rottweiler. He didn't need artificial triggers sent to his brain to give him comfort – these dogs were doing just fine.

While Regan joined Marc in playing with the dogs, she couldn't remove herself entirely from outside distractions. She turned on an old flat-screen television monitor installed on the wall.

A news network popped on. Regan declared her intentions to change the channel to something more entertaining, but Marc shouted at her to leave it on.

His tone was a bit more aggressive than necessary, but it did the trick and she put down the remote. "Jesus," she muttered.

Congressman Dale Sheridan was being interviewed. Sheridan was a major opponent of the government's chip initiative. Marc wanted to hear what Sheridan had to say. He stroked the head of Floyd, a springer spaniel, and locked his attention on the broadcast.

"The administration cannot be trusted to do the right thing with this technology," said Sheridan. "It will become a means to spy on the American people. It is an intrusion on our freedoms, an unparalleled invasion of privacy. Big Brother just got a whole lot bigger. Well, we need to keep an eye on Big Brother."

"I hate this guy," Regan said. "It's the same asshole who wanted to make pot illegal again."

Marc shushed her loudly. "I'm listening to this."

"The government lures people in by offering free surgery and a free 'basic pleasures' kit," Sheridan said. "Nothing is free. You will pay for it through higher taxes – and you won't mind paying higher taxes because the government will send signals to your head that paying more taxes is a good thing!"

"What a paranoid," said Regan. "I bet he believes in space aliens too."

"No," Marc said, "he's right. You can't underestimate the power of this chip." Then he had to bite his tongue to stop from continuing with: "I should know, I worked for Dynamica for ten years."

Instead, Marc turned his attention to Floyd, who watched the television with him, pink tongue hanging out, seated on his back legs.

Marc was jealous of Floyd's obliviousness over the chip epidemic. Floyd didn't demand fancy technologies to keep him happy. All he needed was someone to pat his head, toss a rubber ball and give him a space to run around in.

People had lost the art of simple pleasures, thought Marc. It was something animals could still teach to society.

★ ★ ★

Brandyn Handley sat in total darkness on a hard chair, the fog gradually lifting from his head.

He didn't know where he was.

He didn't know how he got here.

He didn't know who he was dealing with.

"Don't stand up," instructed an unseen voice. "Stay seated."

Brandyn stared through his glasses into the pitch black, hoping to see something, anything, that could ground him. He felt like he was floating.

"What's going on?" he asked. The acoustics in the room sounded closed, confined.

"You have been brought here for questioning."

"What is…here?"

The question hung in the air, unanswered.

Brandyn tried to recall his last memory. He had been in his office, simply working, alone, late afternoon….

Then something filled his head, quickly, like a mental drowning. His senses faded and his head dropped onto his desk.

"How long have I been unconscious?" he asked when he came round.

Again, no answer.

So he gave it some thought and offered his own conclusions.

"You did something to me…through the chip. Right? You knocked me out."

"I can assure you, you have not been harmed," came the reply.

Brandyn tried to identify the steady male voice. He couldn't. It was dry, articulate and unemotional.

"Are you going to tell me who you are?"

"Our individual identities? No. Those cannot be disclosed for security reasons. However, you should know our collective cause and who we represent. You are familiar with the U.S. Department of Citizen Affairs?"

"Of course," Brandyn said. "We have a partnership. I'm with Dynamica, I'm part of the partnership."

"We know who you are."

"We're allies."

"That's right," said the voice. "And we are here to protect that alliance. You are speaking with the Office of Conflict Resolution."

"The Office of…?"

"Conflict Resolution. We are a unit of the Department of Citizen Affairs. We make sure everything runs smoothly. We're dedicated to special cases that require elevated attention, where there's a viable threat to national compliance. We investigate anti-government forces that are potentially harmful to America's future. We take it as seriously as terrorism. Mr. Handley, are you familiar with anyone who might play a role in such a rebellion?"

"A rebellion?"

"An organized threat to the implementation of the chip program."

"No. I mean, isn't it obvious…? I'm on your side."

"How well do you know Marc Tefteller?"

Brandyn felt a shudder run up his spine. He had feared the conversation was leading to this. He had already been on the receiving end of numerous questions about his former colleague, who abruptly quit Dynamica following the announcement of the government partnership.

"Marc and I worked together for many years," he said carefully.

"He left the company rather quickly, didn't he? Were you surprised?"

"Yes. Yes, I was."

"Did he discuss his reasons for leaving with you?"

"No. It was quick. It caught all of us off-guard."

"Have you seen him since he left the company?"

Brandyn swallowed and offered up his most casual tone. "No. No, not at all."

"Are you aware that he broke a contract agreement?"

"I heard…something to that effect."

"Are you aware he stole company property?"

At that moment, Brandyn was grateful the chip in his head only accepted signals in and did not send them out to reveal his current mindset: panic.

He confined the panic to his brain and maintained a calm exterior.

"He stole something?"

"A prototype for law enforcement authorities. A device that can transmit signals to a third party. Surely you're familiar…?"

"Yes, of course. I didn't know one was missing. Are you sure it was him?"

"Yes. He has used it as a weapon."

"Really?"

"Mr. Handley, we have placed Marc Tefteller on the Red Alert list. He is wanted for questioning. He is accused of treason."

"Oh my God."

"Anything you could do to support our efforts to find him would be greatly appreciated. On the flip side, if you are protecting him and not divulging information that would be useful to our investigation, your lack of cooperation would result in your arrest and prosecution."

"I understand. I don't know where he is. I don't know what his intentions are."

"Did he ever talk with you about joining a resistance movement?"

"No. Never."

"Where did you last see him?"

"In the office. Just an ordinary day at the office."

"What was the last thing he said to you?"

Brandyn shut his eyes. "I don't know. I don't remember. Nothing that would be useful to you...."

"Mr. Handley, you have a wife and two children, correct?"

Brandyn opened his eyes and stared forward into the pitch black. "Yes. Why?"

"You understand the seriousness of treason?"

"Yes. Of course."

"And you understand the penalty for lying would be quite severe?"

Brandyn stated firmly, "I'm not lying." His heart pounded in his chest.

"Good. I hope not. For your sake and the sake of your family."

CHAPTER THIRTEEN

The orange Dodge Charger pulled up to the gated entrance of Madison Reddick's Beverly Hills mansion. Clarissa opened her window and started to reach for the buzzer. "You don't have to do that," Aaron said. "I have his code."

He recited the code and Clarissa entered it into the keypad. The gates split open with a metallic *chung*.

"How'd you get his code?"

"He gave it to me. I've been taking care of his lawn for eight years. It's a convenience, he doesn't have to be home to let me in."

In reality, Madison was usually home these days and loved having visitors to share a cold drink with from his collection of exotic teas.

"I'm glad you'll have a chance to meet him," Aaron said. "He's going to like you. It's important I tell him goodbye and thank you."

As Aaron and Clarissa walked the winding brick path that led to the front door, Aaron worried about Madison's ability to find someone else to take care of his lawn and gardens – but it was Madison who had urged him to leave the area, paying him an absurdly large 'severance package', encouraging him to join the chip resistance rebels and giving him instructions for finding a secret sanctuary in Santa Barbara.

Reaching the front entrance, Aaron prepared to poke the door buzzer. Before his finger made contact, there was an abrupt BANG from inside the house. Aaron jumped.

"What the hell was that?" asked Clarissa.

"Sounded like…" Aaron couldn't bring himself to say it.

"A gunshot."

"Holy shit." Aaron pressed the buzzer repeatedly. He banged his fists on the door. "*Madison!*"

After several minutes of pounding and buzzing without a response, Aaron stepped back from the door.

"Now what?" Clarissa asked.

"We're going to find a way in." Aaron was very familiar with the mansion's exterior and searched his brain for the easiest entry point. He pictured the east-side rose garden with its bluestone paving, gazebo and delicate side door of paneled glass.

"Come on," he said. As he circled the house, he pulled a red brick out of the dirt from edging work he had done earlier in the year for one of the garden borders.

Aaron arrived at the side door, glanced through the glass and saw a portion of Madison's long, elegant kitchen. He listened for a moment, heard nothing, then broke into the house. He smashed a square pane of glass with one strike, reached in and unlocked the door. An alarm did not sound – that meant Madison was home.

"Are you sure we should be doing this?" Clarissa said.

"He's my friend," said Aaron, and the statement felt awkward to say aloud because Aaron rarely referred to anyone as his friend these days.

Aaron entered the kitchen with Clarissa close behind. He stepped softly, listening carefully. The house was silent, except for a ticking wall clock. He noticed a block of carving knives on the white marble counter. He glanced at Clarissa, then back at the knives. She read his thoughts and nodded. They each took a knife – the two biggest ones in the set.

"Madison?" Aaron said, cautiously creeping forward with the knife in his grasp.

He heard nothing but the wooden floorboards creaking under his feet.

Aaron and Clarissa advanced down a hallway of framed black-and-white photographs of Madison with various Hollywood celebrities from a bygone era.

They entered Madison's favorite room, his massive den, where Aaron had engaged in countless conversations with Madison after a long day of landscaping. Aaron immediately spotted Madison seated in his favorite, throne-like chair, surrounded by his bookshelves, plants and movie posters. He was unnaturally still and hunched forward.

His arms had fallen to his sides and there was a handgun on the carpet.

"Oh my God, no," Aaron said, dropping the knife to the floor. He rushed over to the old man.

Madison Reddick was dead. Blood leaked from a red hole in his temple. His eyes were shut. His mouth drooped open.

Aaron wanted to shout Madison's name and shake him back into consciousness but it was obvious he was gone. There was a small round table next to his chair. Typically it held a glass of tea and perhaps some books.

Now it held just one thing: a short, handwritten note.

Trembling, Aaron picked up the note. With Clarissa standing over his shoulder, he read it out loud.

"I have lived a long and prosperous life. Now is the time for my departure to whatever waits on the other side. Society has changed into something I do not recognize. I no longer belong. I am at peace with my decision. Do not mourn for me, my day has come."

"Wow," said Clarissa quietly.

"I didn't expect this," Aaron said, gently returning the note to the circular table. He had to turn away from Madison. He couldn't bear to look at him any longer. Madison's color was fading. He was no longer a person, just an empty carcass.

Clarissa continued to stand close to Aaron for comfort but did not put her arms around him. Aaron stared down at the ground, feeling sick with despair.

"I thought he was a fighter," he said. "He was funding the resistance. He was helping to set up sanctuaries. He was outspoken, trying to bring others to his side. He didn't sound like a man who was giving up."

"Maybe it finally got to him," Clarissa said. "I mean, look at this place. It's like a monument to the past. It's everything he's outlived."

"We'll carry on with his mission," said Aaron. "That's what he wanted. That's why he set me up to join a sanctuary. He used to say, if there is a true rebellion, it needs to come from the younger generation. It can't be the past facing off against the future. It's people like us who have to reject what society is turning into."

"There's me, there's you," Clarissa said. "And we know there are others. We can either fight this thing or all wind up like my brother."

Aaron took one last look around the den. It was filled with mementos of the arts as a physical medium. He knew this would be his last time in this room. He would remember his long conversations with Madison Reddick. Madison used to call himself irrelevant, but he wasn't. Madison would live on through Aaron's memories and his mission.

"Let's go," he said quietly. He left the mansion with Clarissa at his side.

★ ★ ★

After Aaron and Clarissa left the mansion, two men stepped into the den. They wore dark, loose clothing. One of them was slim with darting eyes; the other had a puffier physique with an encroachment of gray in his black hair. Both had stoic expressions.

The heavier man made a call on his cell phone.

"The visitors have left," he said.

"Did they see you?" asked a steely voice on the other end.

"No."

"What about your car?"

"We parked down the street."

"Who were they?"

"We're not sure. But we got pictures. We'll send them over for face matching. From what we heard, it sounds like they're part of the resistance."

"Upload those pictures to me now."

The heavyset man did as he was told. "They didn't suspect anything. They took it as a suicide."

"You're sure?"

"I'm sure. They read the note."

"Did they contact anybody?"

"No. They just left."

"Hold on. I'm getting a reading. The woman is Clarissa Harper, Elysian Valley. She is not in compliance. The gentleman is Aaron Holt. Elysian Valley. Also not in compliance. We have recent intel that suggests he might be a runner. It says his roommate reported him."

"You want us to go after them?"

"No. Not now. Finish going through the house for information on his network. Collect his computers. We'll take care of the kids. We have their names and addresses. We'll place them on the Red Alert list and send local regulation enforcement after them."

"Got it."

"Anybody attached to this Reddick character should be considered a threat to the administration and isolated before they can spread the cancer of noncompliance."

"Roger that. We've killed the queen bee. Now we'll break up the hive."

* * *

Before Aaron and Clarissa left Los Angeles County to head up the coast, Aaron directed Clarissa on a short tour of some of his former clients in the Beverly Hills area, reminiscing about his reputation as 'gardener to the stars'. Most of the properties had since fallen into neglect and ruin.

"I don't know what I'm going to do with my life now," he said. "But it's going to be better with you."

"If that's an attempt to be romantic, please stop," she said. It was a typical Clarissa comment, although Aaron noticed that lately she was saying such things with less of an edge – and sometimes even the hint of a smile.

"Okay, I'll stop." The Beverly Hills tour was coming to an end. "How about some music? Does that old cassette player really work?" He pointed to the strange, decades-old cassette deck that fit snugly in the dashboard.

"Open the glove compartment."

He popped it open and a pile of audiotapes spilled out into his lap and onto the car floor. He started laughing. He picked one up at random and read the handwritten label out loud.

"Black Flag."

"Eighties punk, baby. Stick it in."

"Analog physical media," Aaron said. "Delivered from speakers to your ears without satellite chip technology. You are a true rebel."

"Nah. I just know what I like."

He stuck the cassette into the player. She reached over and cranked up the volume knob.

Raw hardcore punk rock pounded out of the speakers and covered the interior of the car in a blanket of organic, human-powered noise.

Clarissa launched the Dodge Charger onto Interstate 405, shooting north at ninety miles per hour. Aaron braced himself in his seat, alarmed by her speed, then gave in to the adrenaline rush that tickled his body. Traffic was light. The skies were blue. The music screamed with a cathartic punch.

Aaron began laughing, not exactly sure why, and lost himself in the moment.

PART TWO
ONE YEAR LATER
CHAPTER FOURTEEN

Grandpa Ed performed 'Maple Leaf Rag' from the *Scott Joplin Song Book* on the classic oak console piano. Grandma Louise sat on the sofa four chapters deep into a Harold Robbins novel, taking a break from her kimono knitting project. Eight-year-old Liam sat on the floor, constructing a country cabin from a bucket of Lego.

"We're eating dinner in ten minutes," called out Robert Sullivan, Liam's dad and the son of Ed and Louise. He was setting the table in the dining room, laying out plates, napkins and silverware. In the kitchen, his wife, Tracy, prepared a meal of ham, green beans and scalloped potatoes that filled the small California home with sweet aromas.

As Grandpa Ed played the opening notes of 'The Entertainer', a loud *BANG BANG BANG* erupted at the front door. The interior of the house immediately went silent. Then:

"Shit," Robert said under his breath. He exchanged a worried glance with his wife, who stood frozen in the kitchen. Grandpa Ed backed away from the piano. Grandma Louise put down her book. Liam remained on the floor, clutching a piece of Lego in his fist.

Robert grabbed his electronic tablet from the counter and called up the security camera aimed at his front porch. He saw four men wearing identical dark suits. One of them carried a black medical bag.

Robert rushed into the living room. "Hide," he said. "*Now.*"

Tracy quickly stepped inside the kitchen's food pantry. She moved a large coffee can to reveal a silver latch. She unhooked the latch and pushed a broad wall of shelving inward. It opened like a door, revealing a small interior compartment the size of a walk-in closet.

Without a word, Grandpa Ed, Grandma Louise and Liam entered the hideaway. Tracy closed the shelving unit on them, careful not to spill its contents. She moved a few food items around to conceal the cracks where the secret door didn't cleanly align with the frame. It had to look as natural as possible.

The banging continued, followed by a loud shout: "Robert and Tracy Sullivan, we know you are in there. We have the authority to force entry."

"You gonna be okay?" Robert whispered to Tracy.

She nodded.

"Act natural."

He left her side and stepped into the front entryway, where he disengaged the locks and chains, shouting, "Hold on. Just a minute."

Robert opened the door.

Four men, in two layers of two, faced him. They did not smile.

"What's this all about?" he asked.

"We have reason to believe you are harboring illegals," said the senior-looking man of the foursome. His hair was thin and silver.

Robert's expression turned quizzical. "Here? You must be mistaken."

"Who lives at this residence?"

"My wife and I. We're compliant. Do you need to test our chips?"

"This isn't about the two of you. Our records indicate your parents, Edward and Louise, also occupy this house."

"Goodness, no. They left years ago. They moved to a retirement community in Scottsdale."

"And your son."

"My – my son?"

"You have a son, Mr. Sullivan. Where is he?"

"How – how dare you...." Robert began to stutter. "You know he's deceased. He was killed in a car accident. Check your records. Why are you coming here, making these accusations?"

"May we come in?"

"No. This is my home. My wife and I are about to sit down to dinner. Go back, check your records, I'm sure you'll find—"

"We're coming in."

The four men entered the house, pushing past Robert. They split off into different directions and started investigating each room.

The silver-haired man stepped into the living room and studied the piano. "I haven't seen one of those in ages. We heard music as we came to the door. It was very good."

Robert nodded. "Yes. We enjoy music."

"So you play?"

Robert hesitated slightly, then nodded.

"Play for me now."

Robert felt a sinking feeling inside. They were toying with him.

"We're eating dinner. I'm not playing the piano."

"Was it you that was playing?"

"Yes."

"Then sit down and show us."

"I'm afraid I don't do command performances."

"And..." said the silver-haired man, looking down at the floor, "you also play with Lego?"

"Those are from when my nephew was visiting. He was in the middle of creating something, so we left it. We didn't want to break it up."

"I see." The silver-haired man stepped over to the dining room table. A stack of plates sat at one end. He ran his finger along the side of the stack and counted.

"One, two, three...four...five."

Robert said nothing.

The silver-haired man also looked at the collection of silverware and napkins not yet arranged for place settings.

"All of this..." he said, "...for two people?"

Tracy stood in the doorway that connected the kitchen with the dining room, giving Robert a worried look. He turned away from her.

The other investigators reconvened in the dining room. One of them said, "We've searched the house...."

"Yes, well, not thoroughly enough," the silver-haired man said.

He stepped closer to Robert. As he did, he removed a handheld controller from his pocket.

"Mr. Sullivan, we are with the California Department of Citizenship. We report to the federal bureau. This team here is dedicated to Thousand Oaks and some of the neighboring communities. Our mission is one hundred percent compliance. You and your wife are in compliance. You have the chip. You are legally enrolled in your country. However, our records indicate your son is not compliant. He needs to be chipped.

You have been contacted about this many times. You received your first warning, your yellow warning, and then your red warning, which places you in the category of harboring an outlaw."

"Our son is dead," Robert said firmly. "This is very painful. Why must I keep explaining it?"

"You must keep explaining it until the truth comes out."

"You're a bunch of bastards," Tracy said from the kitchen doorway.

"I see," said the silver-haired man. He looked down at his handheld device. He poked at it a few times, and then Tracy was screaming.

She clutched her head in pain and fell to her knees in agony.

After five seconds, the pain stopped abruptly. She gasped and choked on the hardwood floor.

Robert took exactly one step toward the silver-haired man and got no further, immediately slammed by a powerful wave of nausea. He clutched his stomach, retching. He crashed into the dining room table, upsetting the stack of plates, which fell to the floor and shattered.

The intense nausea evaporated after five seconds.

"We don't have to play this game. We can arrest you on the spot as an agitator and put you in solitary mindset. Do I make myself clear?"

Robert nodded, eyes watering.

"So, are you going to show us where you're hiding the illegals? I'd really rather not go to the trouble of tearing up this house if you could simply point a finger."

"You can melt the inside of my head for all I care. You're not forcing your technology where it isn't wanted."

"Bad answer," the silver-haired man said, and he sent a powerful electric shock across Robert's body. Robert fell to the floor screaming uncontrollably. Tracy rushed to his side, shouting for them to stop.

Then Grandpa Ed stepped into the dining room with Grandma Louise and eight-year-old Liam behind him.

"That's enough," he said.

All eyes shifted to the seventy-five-year-old man. He scowled with anger and fatigue. "Stop hurting them. I won't allow it."

"Well, well. Grandpa has come out of hiding," the silver-haired man said.

"I'm sorry," Grandpa Ed said to his son. "I know how strongly you feel about this, but it just isn't worth it. If they want to put us all on some stupid tracker, then let them do it so we can be left alone."

"But, Dad, that's the thing. Once they do it, they won't leave us alone. Ever again."

"Save your family arguments for later," said the silver-haired man. He motioned to his three team members. "Let's get this taken care of and move on."

The investigator with the medical bag brought it over to the sofa, placed it on a cushion next to the ball of yarn, and unbuckled the metal latches with two hard snaps.

He extracted a black, handgun-like device with a long barrel.

Robert, still on the floor, buried his face in his hands. "Jesus...."

Tracy started to cry.

The man with the shooting device stepped up to Grandpa Ed, who accepted his fate with a hard glare and deep frown. The barrel of the device touched upon the back of Grandpa Ed's head, just below the base of the skull.

A loud *PPHHTTT* sounded, and he staggered from the impact. In a swift and efficient injection, the chip had been planted in its proper location.

"Let's give it a test," the silver-haired man said. He looked down at his handheld device. "Chip number 454C21309X2. Let's send you a giggle."

And, literally, he did just that.

A gentle smile came to life on Grandpa Ed's face and then he chuckled lightly, face relaxed in a soft haze of amusement.

"Not so bad, is it?" The silver-haired man stepped over to Liam and Grandma Louise next. Tracy continued to cry.

"This won't hurt a bit. *Trust us.*"

* * *

Later that evening, the silver-haired man arrived at the regional compliance headquarters in Oxnard. He met with his superior, Grady Bruckner, a ruddy-faced, middle-aged man with a tie. They stood in a room filled with monitors providing a satellite view of portions of Southern California. The electronic images of various neighborhoods sparkled with points of light representing the presence of individuals logged into the government tracker.

"We chipped three more illegals. The Sullivan residence in Thousand Oaks, 165 Woodland Drive. I've uploaded all the details and some notes. There was resistance, but they came around."

"Let's make sure they're fully registered." Bruckner spoke in a steady monotone. He studied one of the monitors and manipulated a pad of controls, drawing a closer look at a single residential block.

Bruckner nodded with satisfaction. "The house at 165 Woodland. One, two, three, four, five." He called up their names and read them aloud. "Robert, Tracy, Edward, Louise, Liam."

"Yes, that's them."

"Good work." Bruckner moved over to one of the other monitors. He stared into it. "We experienced a blink out today."

"Another?"

Bruckner tapped a small keyboard and called up an archived recording of an earlier live stream of the satellite tracking system, focused on a particular residence in Camarillo at exactly 14:10 hours. Two points of light moved slowly on the property and then, abruptly, they both went dark.

"What's that? A chip malfunction?"

"No," Bruckner said. "These two individuals, Greg and Ellen Jensen, simply disappeared from society. They went off the grid."

"But it's fatal to remove the chip."

"Something else is happening. We've had sixteen blink outs in this territory in the past two weeks. People disappear. Their light goes out on the tracker board, and they can't be found."

"It's a federal crime to go off the tracker."

"There's a vulnerability in the system. The number of blink outs are low, but it's creating alarm all the way back to Washington."

"We're assuming these people are becoming fugitives?"

"That's how I read it," Bruckner said. "We've ordered special resources, bounty hunters, to go find these missing persons. As you make your rounds, I want you to be on the lookout for anything suspicious."

"Absolutely."

Bruckner stood back and looked around the room at the large stacks of monitors pulling real-time information on the presence of chipped citizens, identifying their precise whereabouts from satellite views displaying varying degrees of closeness. The tracking boards sparkled with points of light like a galaxy of earthbound stars.

"We want everyone accounted for," said Bruckner. "It's for their own good. We leave no man, woman or child behind."

CHAPTER FIFTEEN

At precisely seven a.m., a plain white van pulled into a winding driveway tucked in the hills of Montecito, California. The vehicle parked and waited at the foot of a stone path leading to a large, ranch-style home.

Within sixty seconds, a long-haired woman in her forties, wearing sandals and a sundress, scurried outdoors with her lanky, equally long-haired son. Both carried a pair of stuffed suitcases. The son also wore a funky backpack with an abstract graffiti art design.

Miles, the driver of the van, hopped out and opened a side door to let them in. Once they were secured in the back of the van, he quickly returned to the driver's seat. Within two minutes of his arrival, he was backing out of the driveway, leaving the house as fast as possible.

"Put on the robes, put on the helmets," instructed Miles. He was a rotund young man with thick, chunky glasses, curly dark hair and a round baby face. He glanced at his passengers in the rearview mirror and saw them quickly complying, per the set of instructions they had received earlier.

The robes, lined in a silvery, aluminum-like material, covered their bodies. The helmets fitted snugly around their heads, resembling the protection worn by football players back in the days of the NFL.

"Make sure you're sitting in the middle," Miles said. "Stay away from the sides of the van. The protection is stronger in the center."

The teenage boy looked upward at the strange metallic insulation covering the roof's interior. He huddled close to his mother in the middle of the backseat. They exchanged glances from inside their helmets. The mother patted her son's knee with reassurance.

"We're going to be okay," she said.

"You are now officially off the grid," Miles said, rushing the van along an empty road as fast as he could without generating suspicion. "The roof of this van, the materials you're wearing, they're blocking the satellite feed with a barrier of conductive materials – a mesh of metals, magnets – to shield you from giving or receiving any signals. It took nearly a year to get it right – the perfect combination to jam the frequency. I can't begin to tell you how illegal all this is. But this way the government won't have you on a leash. You're reclaiming your independence."

The van arrived in tranquil, downtown Santa Barbara. Most of the shops and attractions had closed as mandatory chipping led to a predominantly insular, indoors society where most sensations were realized in a virtual rather than physical space. The government subsidized basic necessities to support the transition and minimize opposition.

As a result, it was easy to move around town without many witnesses. Miles made certain no one was watching before he approached the simple, windowless garage attached to Surf and Sand, a shuttered coastal store that once sold swimwear, beach accessories, surfboards and sunglasses. He clicked a door opener, entered the tight, cluttered space, and parked the van.

"Hold on," he told his passengers. He clicked the door opener again, shutting them inside the garage with only a faint overhead light.

Once they were secured in the garage, Miles let out a huge sigh of relief. He had worked hard not to express how nervous he was, wanting to keep his clients calm. But he knew the stakes were very high.

"The roof and walls of this garage are protected," he said. "We're going to go through a short tunnel. We'll just have my flashlight. I'll need you to stay close."

They climbed out of the van, leaving the robes and helmets behind. The mother and her teenage son collected their luggage. Miles walked over to a large wooden crate marked Breezeway Paddleboards. He removed the cardboard boxes of sunscreen products stacked on top of it. He creaked open the crate. Reaching in, he cleared away some old newspapers and magazines lining the bottom to expose a small, barely noticeable brass ring connected to a false bottom. He opened it, revealing an underground tunnel.

"Is this going to make me claustrophobic?" asked the mother, peering into the dark hole, fidgeting with her beads.

"Maybe," said Miles. "But don't worry. I'll lead the way."

Miles entered, shining his powerful flashlight. They climbed into the crate after him, slipping through the false bottom and stepping on ladder rungs leading into a crude but effective tunnel. It was barely six feet tall and four feet wide.

"You might see mice," Miles said.

From inside the tunnel, he closed and latched the passageway entrance.

Then he turned to the other two and said, "Stay in the center. Follow me."

They walked approximately seventy feet in musty shadows until they reached a black door, identical in color to the rest of the tunnel.

Miles knocked on it with a deliberate rhythm, like Morse code.

Then the door opened, blinding them with sudden light and color, and a welcoming committee cheered and greeted them into the sanctuary.

★ ★ ★

Seated in comfortable chairs in the east wing of the Santa Barbara Public Library, Aaron and Clarissa met with Lorraine Beaman and her fifteen-year-old son Flynn, providing them with an overview as part of their orientation to the Resistance League. Generator-powered lights made up for the lack of sunlight, as every window had been securely shuttered as part of the library's official closing many months before. Physical books had become irrelevant in the new society, where technology reigned. The government was no longer funding public libraries, funneling the money instead to chipping clinics, chip services and sophisticated transmission towers. The building's vast network of bookshelves remained in place, creating easily identifiable living spaces for the sanctuary residents.

Aaron and Clarissa occupied aisle 900-999, Geography and History. This address housed their modest sleeping arrangements – cushions and sleeping bags.

"The library makes for an ideal hideout since no one comes here anymore," Aaron said. "Everything is available online. No one wants to bother with physical books."

"My son and I still read," Lorraine said. "Print books. Of course, we're ridiculed. They use the 'H' word."

"'H' word?" Clarissa asked.

Lorraine cringed and spat it out quickly. "Hippie."

Flynn nodded with a look of embarrassment.

"That's just a label they use to dismiss people who have different values and don't think the way they do," Aaron said. "They wanted to demean us with words, stick us in a category. They want 'hippie' to become negative slang. We consider ourselves *naturalists*. We believe in the natural elements of the world, and with that comes the freedom to choose real life over a fake existence, living in some abstract cloud."

"We're very lucky we heard about you," said Lorraine. "We've been feeling so isolated."

"We're happy to have you with us," Aaron said. "I know it took a while. We had to have you screened and evaluated. All it takes is one person to blow our cover. We're against the law. Any organized effort to resist the tracking initiative is considered treason."

"It's been hard to escape," Lorraine said. "Because we have the chip. Both of us. We bought into it, we were deceived. We thought we would have control, a final say, in how it was used, but once they got in our heads...."

"I understand," Aaron said. He looked to Clarissa, who sat silently at his side. "Clarissa and I, we're fortunate. We never got the chip. We went into hiding when it became mandatory. But the way this sanctuary is set up, we have room for both types: those without the chip and those who have it."

"We call them inners and outers," Clarissa said. "I know that sounds stupid, but it has to do with how much you can move around. Since you're still on the tracking system, you have limited mobility. Most of your time will be spent here, inside. There are big areas of the library with insulation that blocks the chip signal. It's like the van that brought you here. But once you step outside the shield, you show up on the tracking board."

"And believe me, your absence from the tracking board has already been found out," said Aaron. "You're on a watch list now. You can't reappear. You'll be apprehended, taken away for questioning. They'll do whatever it takes to find out how you fell off the grid."

"I understand," Lorraine said.

"Clarissa and I, we're outers. We can travel the entire library. We can go outside, with caution. We're not registered. We don't show up on some government monitor. But if we were ever captured...."

"It won't happen," Clarissa said firmly.

"No, it won't," said Aaron. "Because the government's greatest weapon is to separate us, isolate us, prevent us from organizing as one force to fight back. And that is the most important message we have for you and your son. This isn't simply a place to hide. This is a headquarters for strengthening the resistance and finding ways to turn this thing around. We have people with money, people with political connections, people who are brilliant at organizing and communicating, people who are fantastic scientists...like

Miles, who developed the shield that blocks the satellite signal from getting inside your head."

"I have money," Lorraine said. "In a secret place that only I can access. I have connections. I know people who are working for Senator Sheridan."

"I know," Aaron said. "Thank God for Senator Sheridan. He's probably our biggest hope. He's going up against the administration, and not many politicians are joining him. He's on our side."

The conversation went quiet for a moment. Flynn was looking around at his surroundings with wide eyes. The long-haired teenage boy had been mostly silent during the orientation. Now he spoke up.

"All these books…" he said. "Am I allowed to read them?"

Aaron smiled and exchanged an amused glance with Clarissa. "Why, of course. Absolutely. That's what they're here for…."

"Awesome."

CHAPTER SIXTEEN

Flynn Beaman paced the section of the library deemed safe for 'inners' due to the protective shield that blocked satellite signals from reaching his head. After a week, the claustrophobia was driving him nuts. He was one of the youngest people in the sanctuary and had no one to relate to. He spent a lot of his time poking in the book stacks, sampling pages and collecting a short stack of reading material. He was already halfway through Tolkien's *Lord of the Rings* trilogy and had started Heinlein's *Starship Troopers*.

There were maybe fifty people living in the sanctuary, most of them over the age of fifty, and they enthusiastically set up events and recreation like any other community, ranging from board game nights to old movies on disc. Right now, a group had cleared space in the children's books section and they were practicing yoga and meditation.

Flynn had his own preferred way to relax. He craved a joint.

The day before, he had attempted a quick smoke between the book stacks and been caught and reprimanded. Two old biddies scolded him and said he was 'breaking the rules' of the sanctuary, which was bogus since the whole idea of the sanctuary was to escape the hovering watch of Big Brother into every aspect of daily living.

There was some legitimacy to their beef: he might set off some old smoke alarm or worse, accidentally start a fire in a building packed with dry paper. But he suspected the real reason was that the old ladies – who drank wine liberally – disapproved on moral grounds. This was irritating, because weed had been largely decriminalized across the United States for years.

Flynn had a decent supply of pot in his backpack and the idea of the tasty buds going to waste was just too grim. He concluded that if he ducked outside for maybe just three or four minutes and had a quick smoke, it wouldn't do any harm. If the chip in his upper neck caught a signal, it would be so brief, it would be meaningless. The connection would break again before anyone could react.

Flynn's mom was part of the yoga group, so he was able to dig into his backpack without her disapproving presence and pull out the well-hidden bag of weed and a lighter. He wore an old hoody and added a cap to his head bearing the Grateful Dead logo of a red, white and blue skull with a lightning bolt. He slipped downstairs and silently slid through an exit door used by the outers for accessing the rest of the world.

Flynn stood outside the door and felt the sunshine on his face. He had missed it. He had also missed the earthy, sweet strain of 'silk dream', his favorite cannabis, handrolled into a chubby joint and now being absorbed into his lungs. He inhaled the vapor and it delivered his own form of stress relief. To hell with yoga.

In the past year, most of his peers had turned to a simulated high offered by the chip technology, but Flynn stubbornly stuck with the original recipe. Real pot was way better than brainwave pot. It was organic and natural and he knew what he was getting versus some creepy, invisible ray from the sky.

He allowed himself four minutes of deep inhalation and felt calm and happy. He ditched the stub and quietly reentered the library, without being observed from the outside.

However, he bumped into Aaron on his way inside. Aaron was a serious dude who was one of the sanctuary council members. His reaction was immediate and very angry.

"What the hell, did you just go outside?"

Flynn's mellow vibe was being invaded by an extremely harsh attitude. He tried to remain chill. "Just for a couple minutes. Hardly anything."

Aaron wasn't letting up. "It doesn't matter how brief you were out there, you probably showed up on the government tracker."

"Like maybe a blink."

"That's all it takes! God damn it, are you high?"

Flynn shrugged.

Miles came over, responding to the shouting. "What's going on?"

Aaron told him, and Miles grew panicked. "The regulation patrol is going to show up here! If you showed up on the radar— This is really, really bad!"

"I'm sorry?" offered Flynn.

"What do we do now?" Aaron asked Miles.

"We need to create a decoy. Immediately," Miles said. He jabbed a finger at Flynn. "You are coming with me."

"What?"

"We're getting in the van and going for a ride."

"Where?"

"It doesn't matter. We're going. Now!" Miles turned to Aaron. "Alert the others. Get everyone to lay low. If the patrol enters the library, hide everyone in the tunnel."

Aaron nodded and left to notify the occupants of the sanctuary of a possible raid.

"I was barely out there," Flynn said meekly.

"Shut up and follow me," Miles said.

They hurried through the underground tunnel that led to the garage. Flynn climbed into the back of the van, and Miles scrambled behind the steering wheel. Miles ordered Flynn to put on one of the silvery robes and a helmet to provide maximum protection from satellite exposure. Then he drove out of the garage and onto the Santa Barbara streets.

"Where are we going?" asked Flynn.

"Lots of places," Miles responded.

Miles drove seven blocks, then pulled in front of a shuttered Starbucks. "Here's what we're going to do," he told Flynn. "We're going to drive around Santa Barbara to a bunch of different locations. At each stop, you will get out of the van, *without any protection*. I will pick you up a short distance away. This way, you will appear and disappear all over town, and it will diffuse the focus on the library and create confusion. We just have to be fast, so they don't catch up with us. We have to stay at least one step ahead. Got it?"

Flynn tried to follow, but his head was somewhat muddled from the big intake of marijuana. "I think so."

"Get out," ordered Miles. "I'll meet you one block ahead." He pointed. "Down there. *GO!*"

Flynn started to open the side doors of the van.

"Take off the helmet and the robe!" Miles shouted. "I want you to show up on the tracker!"

Flynn nodded and did as he was told. He put his Grateful Dead cap back on and stumbled onto the sidewalk. There were a few random pedestrians in the distance, but not many. The Starbucks had recently gone out of business with the rest of the chain. A sad, final attempt to retain customers was on display in a big sign in the window: 'Re-engage with REAL caffeine from yesteryear – it's not just a state of mind.'

Flynn walked along the sidewalk for one block, nervously looking around for any bounty hunters. Miles drove past him, parking at the next street corner. When Flynn arrived, he climbed back into the van and sat under the protective layer of insulation in the roof. He threw the silvery robe over his head.

"Good," Miles said, accelerating the van. "If all goes well, they'll ignore the library and go on this new trail."

"I'm feeling really paranoid right now," Flynn said, fully consumed in a bad trip.

"You should."

Miles drove to the Santa Barbara Bowl, a desolate, concrete outdoor music venue. "Get out, walk around without the robe, I'll meet you on the other side of the parking lot. Don't be out for more than a couple of minutes."

"Okay." Flynn was becoming familiar with the drill.

After the Santa Barbara Bowl, they went to the former Santa Barbara Zoo, followed by a high school, a public park, and then a stop on Stearns Wharf, a long, wooden pier that stretched out into the ocean, once a hotspot for restaurants and tourist shops. The view was beautiful and reached down to the beachfront. Flynn took a long moment to soak in the surroundings before Miles called him back into the van.

"Now where?" asked Flynn.

"A few more places in town. Then a few places out of town. You're lucky I'm letting you back in the van. If this happens again, I will take you somewhere and leave you."

When Miles and Flynn returned to the sanctuary later in the day, Aaron provided an update.

"I think we're good," he said. "There was a patrol car out front for maybe a minute, and then it sped away. We've been listening in on their radio frequency, and they're confused – basically bouncing around from place to place. They don't know why his tracker light is popping on and off all over town. We'll stay on alert in case they come back."

Miles let out a big sigh of relief.

Lorraine Beaman stepped forward from a gathering of sanctuary members. She slapped her son. Then she embraced him.

"Don't ever do that again!" she said to him, and she started to cry.

"I won't, I promise," said Flynn, still in a frightened daze. "Never again."

* * *

At six-foot-seven, all of it solid muscle, Nash Wenzel towered over most people. He had stringy, dirty red hair. He rarely cracked a smile. And he usually got what he wanted.

Today, however, the massive bounty hunter had failed to capture his prey – a missing teenage boy who had gone off the tracker with his mom and briefly reappeared at more than a dozen spots in and around Santa Barbara – never for more than a few minutes at a time.

It was puzzling and infuriating.

Nash had arrived at the latest missed opportunity and realized somebody was intentionally messing with him. And it put him in a rage.

Nash stood in the middle of Calvary Cemetery, the latest in a long string of location IDs for Flynn Beaman. A Grateful Dead cap had been slung over the edge of a random tombstone, as if to taunt his pursuers.

Nash did not like to be toyed with.

He returned to the regulation patrol car pulled to the side of a nearby curb. "Somebody's fucking with us," he told the driver.

The driver nodded wearily and reported back to the local headquarters with the news.

On the other end, Bruckner's voice came loud and clear. "As long as we're getting these signals, you will follow," he said angrily. "He can't remain one step ahead of us forever. Somebody has figured out how to interfere with the system. That is a major offense."

"I'm thinking this is bigger than some random teenager," said the driver.

"Yeah," Bruckner said. "I'm thinking the exact same thing."

CHAPTER SEVENTEEN

The Santa Barbara Sanctuary for Freedom hosted daily social events for its members. On Mondays, one of the two college professors in residence offered lectures in the library's small auditorium on a wide range of topics from art to history to philosophy. Tuesday was book club. Wednesday was movie night, dipping into the library's huge selection of DVDs and Blu-ray discs. Thursday was poker night, with an assortment of board game options for those who didn't want to play cards. Friday was a wine tasting, featuring previously expensive California wines. Sunday offered a nondenominational church service to discuss broad religious themes.

Saturday night, everyone's favorite, was the potluck party.

Several 'outers', unchipped sanctuary residents who could blend anonymously into society, went on weekly visits to a distant grocery store. This store still stocked real food for the diminished numbers of people who continued to prefer true flavors over simulations. The outers filled shopping carts based on a list compiled by the sanctuary members and then each member prepared their food choices in the library's small staff kitchen. In the evening, a large meal was laid out on long library tables. Alcohol flowed freely, pop songs played on a portable CD player, and sometimes people danced. On the first Saturday after Flynn's joint-smoking crisis, his mom baked him hash brownies as a safer alternative, and a few others joined him in consuming the treat, bringing a new meaning to the word *pot*-luck.

Aaron loved the potluck parties. There was something about the rich tapestry of aromas and communal eating experience that triggered happy childhood memories of family get-togethers during the holidays. He and Clarissa drank too much, loosened up and fed off the collective energy in the room. Social gatherings had become rare in the Chip Era, but inside the sanctuary, they lived on with vigor and high spirits. As the party continued into the night, Clarissa would take command of the music selection, transitioning the soundtrack from disco to hard rock. Later, she would take command of Aaron, leading him into a dark and isolated corner of the library for lovemaking between the shelves.

It was in the middle of a potluck party, during a raucous game of charades, that the news arrived that Senator Sheridan had been shot.

The joyous mood immediately crashed. The music was shut down and everyone huddled in one of the library staff offices, where a small television streamed a live report.

The details were still being sorted out, but the shooting took place at a large anti-chip rally in Washington D.C. on Capitol Hill. Senator Sheridan was speaking to thousands of demonstrators when a shot rang out, striking him in the side, reaching his spine. An organized turnout by pro-chip advocates had infiltrated the crowd and mass chaos erupted after the gunfire. Riot police broke up the protest and Sheridan was rushed to the hospital, where doctors reported his condition as serious but stable.

No arrests had been made yet in connection with the shooting.

Washington officials believed it was the act of a lone, unhinged individual. Sheridan's supporters jumped on a broader conspiracy theory that linked the assassination attempt to the current administration.

"Lone gunman, that's bullshit!" said Clarissa, facing the TV with anger. "This was a deliberate hit, and it probably goes all the way to the White House."

The mood in the sanctuary turned glum. Sheridan was seen as one of the few sources of hope in government for naturalists. He had bravely fought the chip mandate while most other politicians went silent. He was a unifying force for the realist movement that was otherwise powerless, a suppressed minority scattered across the country. The violent turn of events shook everyone in the library.

The next morning, the Santa Barbara Sanctuary held its council meeting in a small conference room. The council meetings were open to all residents of the sanctuary, and this one received nearly one hundred percent attendance.

The first item on the agenda: guns.

Aaron headed the Laws and Ordinances Committee and sat in one of seven chairs at the ten-foot-long table. He was joined by Sylvester, the head of budget; Annabelle, the director of social events; Miles, the technology guru; Peter, overseer of membership; Colette, manager of sanctuary property and operations; and Jacob, council president.

Aaron, working from prepared notes, made his case that the sanctuary's anti-gun policy needed to be revisited in light of civil unrest and growing violence between chip proponents and opponents.

"I don't think anyone here believes that the person who shot Senator Sheridan was acting on his own," he said. "This entire rollout has been accompanied by threats, intimidation and violence. Look at how aggressively they pursued fifteen-year-old Flynn Beaman for going off the government radar. We can't be naïve. We should be armed. This sanctuary could be raided tomorrow, and we could all be force-chipped, put in jail and placed under mind control."

"You really think they'd do that?" asked Lorraine Beaman, sitting beside her son.

"Yes," Clarissa said firmly, sitting behind her.

"As far as the feds are concerned, we're committing treason," Jacob said. "We're organized, we're defiant, we're breaking the law and recruiting others to do the same. This isn't a slap on the wrist. Do I need to remind everyone of what happened to the sanctuary in Santa Clarita?" When no one spoke up, he answered his own question. "They were raided, and no one has ever heard from them again."

Ken Ashburn, a former UCLA professor, raised his hand from the rows of attendees in folding chairs. "So if we arm ourselves, where do we get these guns?"

Jacob turned to Peter Whitehead, who managed admissions and recruiting. Peter was a middle-aged man with a tired face and premature hair loss. "I have someone," he said, and all eyes were on him. "We keep records of potential members to add to our ranks, and we do a lot of research and due diligence as part of our evaluation process. I've had someone on my list for some time, Max Ketchum, who lives up in the mountains, alone, no chip, and heavily armed. He collects guns. He's an old timer, and the authorities have largely left him alone because he's one person, probably in his seventies or eighties, and they figure he's not worth the trouble and they'll wait him out. I don't know how successful our outreach would be, but if we could get him to join us, we could also inherit a considerable arsenal."

"Instant arsenal," Miles said. "I like the sound of that."

"I do too. Given the events of yesterday in Washington, I think we should put it to a vote," Aaron said.

"I agree with that," said Jacob, and many others around the room nodded in approval.

"We weren't going to have our next membership vote until the 20th, but we could expedite it," Peter said. "I also have two other candidates at the top of the list, a couple here in Santa Barbara. The Worthingtons."

Jacob looked at his fellow council members and then stared out into the rows of gathered attendees. "Unless someone objects, I think we could move to a membership vote today for both the Worthingtons and Max Ketchum. Do we feel the Worthingtons could offer the sanctuary immediate benefits?"

"Yes," Peter said. "The Worthingtons bring a lot of connections. Sam and Beatrice Worthington, young couple, lots of money, inherited, the right political allies, but with a hitch. She doesn't have the chip, and he does. He's a recovering addict. He was hooked on chipfeeds, the hard stuff, Bliss, Dreamweave, 360 Cocktail, Celestial Knockout – she told her friends it was like living with a drug addict. She also alleges that he's clean now, stays off the chip and is a strong anti-chip advocate because he's experienced the dangers firsthand. So there's some risk, but, again, they can bring a lot of money and influence into the organization."

Sylvester, who managed the budget, spoke up from the table. "Our funds are dwindling all the time. We could really use a new influx of cash, to tell the truth."

Jacob said, "Let's move on this. I say we take it to a vote."

The results were nearly unanimous. The Santa Barbara Sanctuary voted in three new members. Then they lifted the gun ban.

* * *

At the New Member Welcome Party, Max Ketchum and Sam and Beatrice Worthington formally joined the ranks of the Santa Barbara Sanctuary, meeting the full membership and mingling over drinks and food as a classical string quartet played on the antique CD player. People dressed up for the occasion, including Aaron and Clarissa. Aaron made a rare appearance in a sports jacket. Clarissa actually wore makeup, a skirt and heels, an unusual turn that made Aaron smirk. Clarissa immediately told him to shut up even though he hadn't said anything.

Clarissa was younger than most of the other sanctuary women, and attractive, which engaged the seventy-eight-year-old Max Ketchum. He talked with the young couple for forty-five minutes, unleashing years of pent-up conversation.

At the start of recruiting Max for the sanctuary, the council members had doubts he would accept. There were concerns he would prefer to remain on his own in the mountains, living a private life. When first approached, Max was suspicious, even a little paranoid, and armed himself with two handguns when he came to see the library facility and visit with sanctuary members. His ornery defensiveness soon melted away and his true personality came to the surface: he was extremely chatty and craved companionship. His wife had died four years ago. His dog was dead. His son had fled to Europe at the beginning of the chip mandate. He was lonely.

At the welcome party, Max loved being the center of attention. He dressed up in an old suit, leaned on his cane and told stories about his life's adventures, many of them improbable. He flirted with a widow in her seventies. He eagerly looked forward to joining the weekly poker nights and boasted about his gambling prowess. He talked excitedly about his massive gun collection, the right to bear arms, and the upcoming weapons training class he would be teaching.

Leaning on his cane, Max expressed to Aaron that he was particularly grateful to join a commune where they could work together to gather real food supplies. As it became more difficult for Max to leave his house, collecting groceries became an ordeal. He hated eating Body Fuel bars, which were cheap and plentiful but essentially tasteless without the accompanying chipfeeds.

Every so often during his lengthy monologues, Max would erupt into brief coughing spasms, followed by wheezing. He ultimately confessed to Aaron and Clarissa: "You want to know the biggest reason I'm moving in with you rather than staying at my house? I know I'm not long for this world. I don't want to die alone and get eaten by coyotes."

Aaron and Clarissa finally broke off their conversation with Max so they could also spend some time getting to know Sam and Beatrice Worthington. Max immediately found another ear to fill and relaunched his life story.

Sam and Beatrice were in their early forties, wealthy but weighed down by difficult years in their marriage that they discussed openly. The culprit was the chip.

"I despise the chip," Sam said. "It nearly ruined my life. It's funny –

before the chip, I drank, I smoked some pot, I dabbled in other drugs. I was able to do it in moderation, so I never came close to being addicted to anything. Then the chip came along – and it made everything too easy, I guess."

"I remember you telling me, 'This is great, there's no hangover'," said Beatrice. "You could turn it on and off, go to work and not wreck your physical health."

"Yeah, I used to play a lot of sports, so I was into staying in shape and all that."

"The addiction comes fast and hard," Clarissa said. "I watched it happen to my brother. We tried everything and we lost him. He lives in one of those tent communities in L.A., high all the time. It's horrible."

"The only way to really go cold turkey is to cut off from the signal," Sam said. "That's why this place is a godsend. You have this whole section under a shield – as long as I stay here, I'm clean."

"That's our brilliant scientist and technician, Miles," said Aaron. "If it wasn't for him, we couldn't bring in anyone with the chip."

"You're not the only former addict staying here," Clarissa said. "There are four others, and they have a support group. They meet three times a week. You should join them. They keep each other strong...and safe."

"I'll do that," said Sam. "And anything you need – Beatrice and I are here to support the sanctuary. We have money – money we can access without a lot of monitoring."

"We appreciate that," Aaron said. "And I want to thank you for the workout room."

The Worthingtons had paid for high-end fitness equipment – a treadmill, weights, exercise cycle – to create a gym in the former periodicals room, laying out rubber flooring and covering the windows with full-length mirrors.

"Hey, it's the least we can do," Sam said. "That's my new high – exercise."

Beatrice said, "Do you know there's actually a chipfeed for exercise adrenaline? You get the rush without having to exert yourself. How crazy is that?"

"It's fucked up," said Clarissa. "I'm looking forward to using the treadmill. I stopped running outside because I was tired of always looking over my shoulder. I expected to see someone chasing me."

★ ★ ★

Later that evening, as the Welcome Party started to wind down, Aaron took Clarissa by the hand and led her deep into the bookshelves.

"Mm, where are you taking me?" she said, tipsy with California wine.

"I need to show you something," Aaron said, and the serious tone in his voice suggested this was not an invitation for impromptu sex. He brought her to section 973.7.

"The Civil War?" Clarissa said, looking at the spines on the books.

"I figured this section was as good as any – makes some sense, really."

"For what?"

Aaron removed an extra-large volume on Gettysburg. "Can you see back there?"

Clarissa peered into the open space and said, "Oh God."

Aaron replaced the book. "This whole row – behind the books – it's where we're keeping the guns. We're going to announce it later this week, and I think we're going to make it mandatory for everyone to attend Max's weapon training."

"You know how I feel about guns," Clarissa said. "My dad had one."

"I hate guns, too. But I also want protection. If somebody comes after us with aggression, we will fight back. There's a lot of chaos out there right now. If they came after you, right now, to stick you with the chip, are you going to let them do it or are you going to fight?"

Clarissa said, without hesitation, "Fight. Fight all the way."

"I've never fired a gun in my life," said Aaron. "But I'm going to learn. You're going to learn."

"Who would have imagined that one day a library would become an armory?"

"Who would have imagined that one day people would be sticking computer chips in their heads for a Big Brother GPS system?"

"Let's go back to the party," Clarissa said, turning away from the guns. "I think I need some more wine."

CHAPTER EIGHTEEN

Sam Worthington craved Cloud 10.

He woke up in a cold sweat in the middle of the night and stirred restlessly in his cot, alongside his wife, Beatrice, who slept soundly in her adjacent cot, facing the other way and snoring loudly. One of the library's private study rooms had been turned into their bedroom with personal belongings piled on a table, a huge step down in comfort from their million-dollar luxury home in the hills. He fully understood the reason for relocating. It was the necessary thing to do on so many levels.

But all rational thought was shoved aside by the craving that itched mercilessly inside his skin.

Of all the powerful opiate-like chipfeeds he had soaked up in his heavy addiction days, Cloud 10 was his cherished favorite by far. The marketing tagline was 'Soar higher than Cloud 9'.

The elation he felt from the virtual drug was the most powerful, pleasing sensation he had ever known – like being filled with cotton and bathed in the constant shudder of a happy, shimmering warm glow.

Sam had worked very hard to resist the urges and stay signal free. He had successfully kicked his subscriptions to other powerful intoxicants like Bliss, Rapture and Rainbow. Beatrice believed he had been clean for four years, but her definition of clean held zero tolerance for any small relapses. The ugly truth was that Sam still secretly indulged in Cloud 10 on occasion, usually in the middle of the night, while Beatrice slept. He would sneak off into his den, set the timer for a two-hour session, collapse in his big reclining chair and call up a brain feed.

After two hours, happy and exhausted, he would crawl back to bed. If she woke up upon his return, he would claim he had been to the bathroom and make jokes about his small bladder. She never knew what was really going on.

As silently as possible, Sam removed himself from the cot. He reached under a table where he kept extra pairs of shoes. He pulled out a hidden controller that had been tucked inside a brown loafer. Beatrice did not know he had brought the device and would have destroyed it if she had found it.

Sam snuck out of the study room. The library was dark, and he proceeded slowly. Residents slept in groups in various sections of the building. He was careful not to wake anyone.

Large portions of the library had been insulated with special magnetic material to block satellite connections that sent signals to and from the chips. The areas of the library without this insulation were off-limits to 'inners' – residents with chips. If he entered these spaces, he would be spotted by someone in the sanctuary. Sam knew he needed to sneak outside, absent of witnesses, to reengage his chip.

Parts of his brain screamed at him that what he was doing was wrong. He was going against everything that the sanctuary represented. He was breaking the oath he took when he was accepted as a member. He was betraying his wife's trust. He was risking his own sanity and well-being by giving in to his urges and getting mentally blitzed yet again.

He knew it was wrong and hated himself for giving in to temptation. But the winning argument in his head was simple: "You'll get away with it. You always do."

That was the beauty of getting wasted via the chip: no telltale evidence afterward.

No bottles to discard. No stash to hide.

No odors to conceal.

No hangover or other visible physical effects. No puking, no lingering head fog.

Just two hours of ecstasy, flipped on and off like a switch.

Of course, he hated the chip and everything it represented on principle. The government mandate, the sketchy plans for using it to track citizens, the replacement of real-life pleasures with head games. He was against all that.

But Cloud 10 was his friend. Maybe his best friend. It was too complicated to explain the hypocrisy – especially in his new environment.

These people simply wouldn't understand; just like Beatrice didn't understand.

Before going outside, Sam armed himself. He selected a snub-nose revolver from the collection of guns stashed behind Civil War books on a long library shelf. Max had taught the sanctuary residents some gun basics and the Sanctuary Council had shared the hiding place for the weapons for use in emergency situations only.

Sam felt justified in borrowing a gun. If he faced an unexpected threat outside the sanctuary, he wanted to be prepared to protect himself.

The library doors were locked and alarms were set, but Sam had already planned his exit route. In the sanctuary gym, he removed one of the long mirrors he had installed over a window and slipped through, a short drop to the ground.

Downtown Santa Barbara was dark and empty. Sam strolled State Street without incident. He moved at a casual pace and soon reached the beach.

Waves crashed along the shore. The moon hung high, beaming light. Bodies and tents populated the wide stretch of sand. Homeless chip addicts had made the beach their home, setting up a community where no one bothered anyone and the impeccable weather left them alone. Sam knew it would be easy to slip among them and disappear for a while – physically and mentally.

He chose a spot near a children's 'Hello Kitty' tent; inside, a male adult was giggling softly, high on something.

The beach smelled strongly of urine and feces, but Sam was going to escape all that. He got comfortable on the sand. He secured the revolver in the waistband of his pants. He began tapping on his chip controller, heart pounding with anticipation.

He activated Cloud 10 for a two-hour session. Then he unwound. He lifted off the ground, erasing all aches and worries to float away in a state of supreme, unadulterated happiness.

"Away we go…" he said softly, his final words before disappearing into his brain.

★ ★ ★

Euphoria came to a hard stop.

Sam jolted out of his head trip to see a very big, broad-shouldered man, with stringy hair that blew to one side in the wind, standing over him.

The face was not friendly.

Sam quickly sat up and reached for his gun.

"I have it," said the man, backlit by the moon, a monstrous shadow.

Then the man said, "I also have this." He held up Sam's controller device – which he had used to shut off Cloud 10.

"I'm just…getting high," Sam said. "Like everybody else here. Why… are you bothering me?"

"My name is Nash," said the man in a deep, coarse voice. "I work for citizen tracking in a special unit that looks for special people."

"Special…?"

"We know who you are, Mr. Worthington. You've been on our watch list for quite some time."

"I'm not harming anyone…."

"You're funding dissidents. You and your wife, Beatrice Worthington. And you have an irregular tracking signal."

"Yeah, about that, my chip's been acting up…."

"Nice try," Nash said. "Stand up. You're coming with us."

"Us?" Then Sam noticed a small group of men standing nearby, dressed in dark colors, facing him with their backs to the crashing waves of the ocean.

★ ★ ★

Sam was handcuffed, placed in the back of a long black car and driven thirty-five miles along the California coastline with a second car following closely. Nash, a hulking presence in the front passenger seat, sat with his head pressed into the ceiling. He exchanged occasional words with the driver in a low volume.

"Where are you taking me?" Sam asked repeatedly, and he was ignored.

When the vehicle arrived at its destination, a heavily guarded complex of small buildings, Sam caught a glimpse of a sign: *California Compliance Agency.* He was taken inside the main building and escorted down a long corridor. They dropped him into a seat in a small, sharply lit room with a barren table, extra chairs and recording equipment.

Sam sat, wide-eyed and trembling, as Nash and several other men faced him from the other side of the table. A ruddy-faced one, carrying a presence of authority, spoke first.

"Hello, Mr. Worthington. My name is Grady Bruckner. I lead the local compliance team and report to the federal office in Washington. We're here to ask you a series of questions, and I would like to preface by saying honesty is rewarded, whereas dishonesty has serious consequences. And we do things in real time here, do I make myself clear?"

To emphasize the point, Nash held up Sam's controller.

"We can give you pleasure or pain – you choose," said Bruckner.

Sam nodded. He was breathing hard. He thought about Beatrice, back at the sanctuary, probably still sleeping, unaware of what was happening to him in the middle of the night. He looked down at the handcuffs on his wrists, felt the presence of a wall of stern faces, and at that moment he wanted to scream, he wanted to cry, he wanted…

…to be high again.

"You've been on our watch list for treason. You play an active role in an organized resistance to our country's laws and protocol. We're going to have a long discussion about where your money is being channeled. You've been clever about it, but we have a good idea of what you and your wife have been up to."

"Okay, yes," Sam said. "I don't believe in the mandate, and I've been helping…within my rights…to communicate an alternative point of view."

"We'll get to what is within or outside your rights, Mr. Worthington. Let me move on to something more specific and far more troubling. It has to do with tampering with government systems."

"Tampering?"

"Your chip signal. It went out for a period of time. We lost track of you. That's not acceptable. You were off the grid for nearly two weeks. Then, tonight, you reappeared."

"Yeah," said Sam, voice wavering uncontrollably. "I've been experiencing problems getting a signal. That's why I went to the beach, for better reception."

"We're seeing a lot more of these irregularities and there's a pattern – they're taking place on the lower central California coast."

"Are they? That's odd…."

"How did you turn off your signal, Mr. Worthington?"

"I didn't do anything…."

"Do you have a jamming device?"

"I don't know what that is."

"Pleasure or pain, Mr. Worthington?"

"Excuse me?"

"Which do you choose?"

"Not pain."

"Pleasure then?"

"Well, yes."

"Then tell the truth."

"I told you, I don't know why the signal went out."

Nash tapped a code into Sam's controller, and Sam screamed like the top of his head was coming off.

"Fucking holy shit!" he yelled when the searing pain came to an abrupt stop.

"Pleasure or pain?" repeated Bruckner.

Nash stared into Sam's eyes, still gripping the controller.

"Pleasure," said Sam.

"And what's your pleasure?" Bruckner asked.

"I like.... I'm.... I like Cloud 10."

"Cloud 10. Popular choice. Yes, I've heard of it. Would you like some now?"

"Now? Yes. God, yes."

"Absolutely. Nash, give this man what he wants."

Nash activated Cloud 10 and Sam immediately fell back in his chair, covered in a blanket of cozy gratification. His face relaxed and his mouth broadened into a big smile. His hands fluttered, then caressed himself.

"Give him one minute," Bruckner instructed.

After one minute, Nash halted the feed.

Sam stirred back to full consciousness, as if awoken from a deep and wonderful dream. His good feelings were quickly replaced by renewed angst.

"Did you like that?" Bruckner asked.

Sam nodded.

"Want to go back?"

Sam nodded again, more vigorously.

"Then talk. There are things you're not telling us."

Sam was filled with dread and anxiety, reeling from the abrupt transition from heaven to hell.

He wanted to speak but he couldn't find the words. He didn't want to make a choice. He wished he was dead.

After a long silence, Bruckner spoke. "You know, I heard something interesting the other day. The makers of Cloud 10, they've been testing a new chipfeed to take to market. It's like Cloud 10, but even better, stronger. It's like Cloud 10 on steroids. It sounds pretty amazing. They call it...Cloud 11."

Sam straightened in his chair and listened, interested.

"Now, it won't be rolled out for a few more months, but, if you are able to help us out and answer some questions, I know I can get you access to Cloud 11. Maybe even a lifetime subscription, ahead of anyone else. A couple of phone calls and I can get you hooked up. Cloud 11. Imagine that."

Sam slumped his shoulders and hung his head. He hated himself.

"You can have Cloud 11," Bruckner said, "or we can restrict your chip menu so that you never again have access to Cloud 10...or Bliss or Rapture or anything else that makes you feel good. We can control your feed at a micro level – what you can access and what is locked off. Are you prepared to face life that way?"

"Will you really get me Cloud 11?"

"Yes, yes, of course. I'm a man of my word. Trust us."

And then Sam told them everything he knew about the Santa Barbara Sanctuary.

CHAPTER NINETEEN

The Santa Barbara Sanctuary Council Meeting began precisely at nine a.m. The first item on the agenda was a proposal for the next game night by Annabelle, the director of social events. In addition to the four tables dedicated to poker, a popular tradition, she suggested Twister. A complete Twister set – the large plastic mat and spinner – had been recently discovered in a battered box at a thrift shop. In addition, one of the sanctuary members had come up with an idea for 'book aisle bowling' – transforming a long, narrow alley between two rows of bookshelves into a bowling lane, using a soccer ball and ten empty wine bottles filled with sand.

"I'm also fleshing out an idea for a scavenger hunt with clues hidden in books, and each clue takes you to the next book. For instance, 'Richard was the long name for this big whale.'"

"Moby Dick!" excitedly answered Sylvester, head of budget.

"My husband is missing!" a woman's voice shrieked. Beatrice Worthington ran into the council meeting room, her hair up in a frazzled bun, wearing a pink nightgown.

The council members looked at her, startled.

"My husband Sam. I can't find him. I woke up, and he was gone. I figured he was wandering the library, but I've been looking, and I can't find him anywhere."

"He's a former chip addict," Aaron said, stating out loud the first thought that ran through his head.

"He's got to be here," said Colette, the manager of sanctuary property and operations. "We secured all the doors after the incident with Flynn Beaman. You can't leave without requesting a key, otherwise you set off the alarm."

Jacob, sanctuary council president, said to Beatrice, "You told us your husband hasn't had a relapse in years. Do you have any reason to believe he might—"

Then the council president halted midsentence. Another interruption arrived. One of the members serving on Sanctuary Watch came running into the room. "We have visitors," he said breathlessly. "There are jeeps outside. It's the patrol."

"Oh, shit," said Aaron.

"Double shit," Jacob said.

Everyone jumped from their seats and scattered from the room to activate the emergency plan they had rehearsed in drills.

Aaron ran over to a small opening in a window covering that allowed him to view the street without being seen. He watched several jeeps carrying patrol soldiers in combat fatigues. The soldiers dismounted the vehicles. They were armed.

"It's a raid!" Aaron shouted, pulling away from the window.

Panic rippled through the library in waves of loud commotion.

Jacob got on the intercom system. He turned the volume all the way up.

"Attention sanctuary residents. Code Red. This is a raid. Repeat. This is a raid. Regulatory patrols are at the front of the building. They are armed. Code Red. We are under attack. Follow the Code Red Emergency Response Plan."

Sanctuary residents ran in different directions to various destinations. The defense team reported to the sanctuary arsenal. Class A inners ran for the tunnel. Class B outers began evacuating through the rear of the building. In the midst of all the chaos, Aaron called out for Clarissa. He had not seen her since they woke up together that morning and had a light breakfast of microwave waffles in the staff room.

As he was looking one way, she grabbed his arm from behind. "Hey!" she shouted at him. "What are you doing standing there? We have to get our guns."

Aaron's heart pounded. He had received general weapons training but not actually fired a gun yet. The forces outside undoubtedly had better firearm skills. But there was no way he would surrender to them and be chipped – at best – or imprisoned for life for federal crimes.

Aaron and Clarissa ran to the American History section of the library and joined the growing line at the Civil War shelves.

The books had been dumped to the floor, revealing the hidden bounty of guns behind them.

Max distributed the weapons with a fierce speed, as if he had been waiting his whole life for this moment.

"Magnum .44…Colt .45…Remington 700 rifle…PARA USA Black Ops Combat Pistol…Ruger Precision Rifle…."

Aaron was stunned to see skinny, seventy-two-year-old Gertrude Ackerman accept a Smith & Wesson revolver with a firm grip and determined scowl.

Max handed Aaron a Beretta M9A3 black pistol, the gun Aaron was most familiar with from his weapons orientation class with Max.

"Give 'em hell," Max said enthusiastically.

Max handed Clarissa a much larger gun, a semi-automatic rifle with a sixteen-inch barrel. "Armalite M-15." He grinned. "Fully loaded," he said, giving her an extra thirty-round cartridge.

"What the hell?" said Aaron, staring at Clarissa's big, sleek rifle. "Really?"

"Really," Clarissa said. "Let's go. There's no time for gun envy."

"Jesus."

A loud pounding could be heard at the front of the library – they were breaking down the doors. Clarissa shouted, "Follow me!" She hurried forward, advancing past rows of bookshelves. She came to a stop behind a shelving unit of old New Releases near the entrance. She pulled out books to create an opening and shoved the barrel of her rifle through the hole.

With a violent, persistent banging, the invading forces smashed through the double doors. Glass shattered. Clarissa took aim.

Aaron created his own perch, dropping books to the floor to clear a space. He inserted his gun between a celebrity memoir and a vegan cookbook.

The regulation patrol burst into the library. Clarissa almost squeezed off a shot but stopped herself when a group of sanctuary members immediately rushed the soldiers to surrender. It was a young family with kids. "You can chip us, please don't hurt us!" cried the mother.

They were immediately apprehended. The young children broke out into tears.

A steady stream of armed patrol officers entered the building and their numbers made it obvious that fighting them would be a losing proposition.

One of the patrol officers in particular stood out because he was well over six feet tall and built like a massive football player with stringy red hair. An older sanctuary male ran up to him and hurled a dictionary at his chest. The red-haired giant immediately punched him in the head and knocked him out cold.

Clarissa turned to look at Aaron. "Let's get out of here. We've lost the library. We can't stop this."

"Agreed," said Aaron.

Carefully staying out of view, they moved through the maze of towering bookshelves, retreating deeper into the library. Clarissa shouted instructions: "We'll go out through the Children's Room. There's a side door, it leads to an alley. We'll get outside and run for it. If they shoot, we shoot back."

"Sounds like a plan."

"Are you being sarcastic?"

"I don't know."

"You got a better idea?"

"Yeah, let's not bicker right now."

Suddenly a peppering of gunfire erupted around them. Bullets tore into books and bounced off metal shelving units.

"Hit the floor!" Clarissa said, and she fell hard, with Aaron nearly toppling over her.

As bullets zinged overhead, Aaron scoped out his surroundings as best he could through the open spaces in a bottom bookshelf.

He heard Max shout, "Take this, you bastards!" It was followed by a mad cackle and more shooting.

Aaron glanced at Clarissa, who stared back.

The shooting was getting louder, closer.

"Let's go," Clarissa said. "Ready to run?"

"I can run."

"Meet you in the Children's Room."

"Got it."

Clarissa returned to her feet, rifle in her grip. She took a quick peek, then dashed out of the bookshelves and into an aisle. Aaron followed close behind, clutching his pistol.

The gunfire around them increased. They advanced fifty feet, dodging other scrambling, panicked sanctuary residents, and ducked into another aisle of bookshelves.

For a short moment, Aaron had a good view of Max, who had a gun in each hand and a thick belt of ammunition hugging his waist. He had tossed away his cane.

"Oh my God," Clarissa said. "He's like an eighty-year-old Rambo."

"He's providing great cover for the rest of us," Aaron said.

Max pulled a grenade from his belt. He plucked the pin and hurled the explosive at his enemies.

"Cover your ears!" said Aaron. The ensuing blast shook the library so hard that books tumbled off shelves. A 'Quiet Please' sign with an illustration of a shushing librarian fell off the wall.

With the momentary distraction of the explosion, Clarissa and Aaron slipped out from between the bookshelves and resumed running toward the Children's Room.

The library was in smoky chaos, a tangled mix of people fleeing and people joining Max's crazed assault on the intruders. Bullets crisscrossed in every direction, tearing into everything in their path. Aaron and Clarissa encountered the bullets' first victim. Beatrice Worthington lay crumpled on the carpet, having taken a shot to the head. The puddle of blood under her cheek was rapidly expanding.

The reality of the violent outbreak struck Aaron hard. Should they have even attempted to fight back with guns? Did they provoke the violence or merely prepare for it? He cursed and continued running.

Aaron and Clarissa passed the Reference Room, where a group of panicked inners pushed into the tunnel that led to the garage where Miles kept the special van. The chipped sanctuary members were the most vulnerable to being identified and located after fleeing the library.

The evacuation plan called for outers to flee in designated vehicles stored in a nearby parking garage. Aaron and Clarissa possessed the keys to an old, battered Nissan sedan that was an eyesore but remained drivable.

Staccato gunfire mingled with shouts and screams throughout the library. Aaron and Clarissa ran a crooked path around the obstacles in the Children's Room. They slammed hard into an exit door – locked.

"Damn it!" shouted Aaron. He whirled to face a large, nearby picture window. The window was decorated with colorful paper cutouts of animal characters holding books. "We'll break the window!"

Aaron grabbed a green toadstool chair from a set of children's furniture. He hurled the toadstool at the glass and it bounced off without making a crack.

"Move out of the way!" Clarissa said. She lifted the semi-automatic rifle and squeezed the trigger, unleashing a spray of bullets.

The picture window shattered to pieces. Shredded animal characters dropped to the ground with tinkling shards of broken glass.

Aaron and Clarissa climbed out of the window. They started running across the grass toward a multilevel parking garage one block away. But then a patrol jeep entered their path up ahead, blocking their escape route, and they had to cut sharply in another direction.

"*Stop, you must turn yourself in!*" boomed a voice through a loudspeaker.

Aaron and Clarissa slipped into a nearby alley, out of the jeep's view. They ran along the uneven pavement with the backs of retail stores on either side of them. Many were closed for good, but there was a large pharmacy up ahead with a big truck parked at a loading dock. The delivery entrance was open.

"In here!" Aaron said, leading the way. They circled the truck and dashed into the building. Seconds after they disappeared inside, the jeep trailing them turned into the alley. Aaron and Clarissa tucked themselves out of view, standing near the open door.

"They're going to figure out we're in here," Clarissa said.

"Let's go out the front. We'll cut through the store."

"Carrying these guns?"

Aaron shrugged, then nodded.

"Sure, why not," muttered Clarissa.

They resumed running. They dashed past confused workers in white smocks in a stock room. They burst into the brightly lit store and ran up the cosmetics aisle, scaring several customers. At the front of the store, a hefty female checkout clerk screamed. She offered all the money in the cash register. Aaron and Clarissa ran past her, pushing away a shopping cart and reaching the front door.

They stopped at the door for a moment and looked out at State Street, a main strip cutting east-west through Santa Barbara.

Blue skies. Empty sidewalks. The scene appeared peaceful and calm.

But only for a moment.

"Wait," Clarissa said.

They heard a crackle of gunfire. Then the roar of speeding vehicles.

Aaron froze, feeling his chest tighten.

Suddenly the white sanctuary van burst into view, swerving wildly. The tires had been blown out. The sides of the van had been pierced with a scattering of bullet holes.

The vehicle lost all control and jumped a curb across the street, crashing through the storefront of Francis, an upscale women's clothing store. The back doors of the van split open and people started spilling out and fleeing. Some moved slowly, injured. Two green jeeps quickly pulled up to the van and groups of patrol forces hopped out.

Clarissa lifted her rifle. She wanted to defend the sanctuary freedom fighters but those who hadn't escaped were quickly corralled. Aaron motioned for her to lower her weapon.

"It's too late," he said.

They watched through the window glass as the patrol officers rounded up prisoners. Some sanctuary members had fled inside the clothing shop. The van had obviously been packed very tight and people were still emerging from it, hands held high in surrender. Those who attempted to run were chased. One young man pointed a gun, and he was promptly shot in the chest.

"Oh my God." Clarissa brought a hand up to her mouth as the man died before her eyes.

"Miles was driving the van," Aaron said.

"I haven't seen him come out."

"Do you think he's…."

A rapid thumping of footsteps could be heard approaching from inside the pharmacy.

"Shit," Aaron said.

"They're over there!" shouted a panicked customer to a pair of patrol officers who hustled up a center aisle of dusty greeting cards.

"Go out and to the right," Clarissa told Aaron. She stepped on the black mat to trigger the electronic doors to pop open. They advanced to the sidewalk, took a hard right and ran up the street.

The patrol officers swarming the crashed van were preoccupied, but one of them glimpsed the fleeing duo. He shouted to alert the others.

"I don't like this," said Aaron, and then bullets began to bite into the pavement around them. He accelerated his pace and Clarissa kept up with him.

After half a block, she said, "Fuck this. I'm not getting shot in the back." She ducked inside the doorway to a closed pizzeria. Aaron joined her, panting.

Partly shielded by a corner of the building, she lifted the semi-automatic rifle and took aim at two patrol officers coming her way.

She fired a round. One of the men was hit in the leg and went down.

"Oh my God, did you see that?" she said.

Aaron, feeling obligated, took a shot of his own. It went nowhere near the rush of oncoming patrol officers but the sheer act of firing at them slowed their pursuit.

"We can't stick it out here, we're going to run out of ammo before they do," Aaron said.

"Let's cut through this pizza place," Clarissa said. "Your turn. Break the glass."

Aaron fired a bullet into the glass door of the pizzeria. It split into a massive web of cracks but stayed intact.

Clarissa kicked the glass with her boot and it shattered.

"Oh shit, here comes a whole jeep of them," said Aaron, seeing reinforcements approaching from down the road.

Clarissa and Aaron entered the dark pizzeria, kicking aside chairs. They moved into the kitchen, which smelled awful. Rats scurried across the floor. They hurried through a short maze of angular shadows, made it to a rear exit and spilled out into an alley.

The rumble of jeep engines circling the area created a steady noise in the background.

"We can't be spotted out here," Clarissa said. "We have to hide somewhere."

There was a tall, blank-faced building across the alley. They ran alongside it until they encountered a single windowless door.

"I don't know where this leads, but let's give it a shot," Clarissa said.

She tugged on the door and it opened to pitch darkness. The roar of a jeep engine quickly grew closer. "In we go," she said.

Aaron and Clarissa jumped into the blackness and shut the door moments before the jeep entered the alley.

For a minute, they stood still in the dark. They heard the jeep rumble past without slowing down.

Aaron felt along the wall for a light switch, found one, and flipped it. Nothing happened. The building had no electricity.

"You still have your old cell phone?" asked Clarissa.

"Yeah, but I'm offline. Nothing connects."

"For the flashlight."

"Oh, right."

He pulled out the phone, turned it on and tapped until the flashlight app set off a beam of light. He pointed it around their surroundings. They were in a narrow passageway that was cluttered with old cleaning supplies – mops, brooms and big plastic garbage buckets on wheels.

"Let's see where this leads," Aaron said.

He advanced along a windowless route and took a right turn into a new corridor. This one led to a door with a bar handle. He listened for a moment, heard nothing, and pushed open the door.

"I know where we are," he said. He aimed the flashlight at a huge white screen and then across deep rows of seating that disappeared into the darkness. "It's a movie theater. I didn't recognize it from the back." They had stepped inside the Santa Barbara Cinema.

"I could really go for some buttered popcorn," Clarissa said.

"I'm guessing it's a little stale by now."

They cautiously walked up one of the aisles, surrounded by long rows of thinly cushioned chairs. "We never knew this place when it was open," Clarissa said.

"Yeah, mental movies pretty much put it out of business."

"Turn off your light. Save the battery."

He tapped it off, plunging them back into darkness. "Want to sit for a moment?"

"Yes."

Aaron entered a row of seats, feeling his way around. He started to sit down but the seat of the chair broke and he landed on the floor.

"God damn it!"

Clarissa giggled.

Then a door banged loudly somewhere in the building.

Aaron froze. Clarissa whispered, "Somebody's here."

They remained very still.

Aaron clutched his pistol. He had fired it twice, hitting inanimate objects. He was fully prepared to shoot a living target next, especially if that living target intended to shoot him first.

A side door into the theater creaked open slowly. Aaron could see two shadowy figures behind a tiny flashlight with a narrow beam.

"Should we shoot?" Clarissa whispered. She aimed her rifle.

"I can't tell…" Aaron whispered back.

"We can hide in here," said one of the entrants, a familiar woman's voice.

The other shadow, skinny and male, said, "Okay."

"Who's there?" Clarissa asked.

"Clarissa?"

"Lorraine?"

Aaron aimed his light at them and their faces came into view as they stepped forward. It was the hippie mom and her teenage stoner son, Flynn.

"You escaped," Aaron said.

The four of them met up in a center aisle. Aaron could see that Lorraine had a bloody gash on her forehead.

"We were in the van," she said. "It crashed. We were right by the door, so we got out first and ran and ran, but most of the others—" She looked like she was going to start crying any minute. "They were stuck."

"What happened to Miles?" asked Aaron.

Now the tears flowed. "He died…in the crash."

"Oh my God."

"Why does it have to be so violent?" Lorraine said.

"Where's your gun?" asked Clarissa.

"We don't have one," Flynn said.

"We didn't take the weapons training," Lorraine said. "We don't believe in it."

"Well, believe in it now," said Clarissa in a hard voice. "Because if they get ahold of you, your chip is going to be programmed for maximum obedience."

"They're probably tracking us right now," Lorraine said, clamping a hand on the back of her neck. "Jesus, I'm a walking GPS!"

Aaron and Clarissa exchanged glances.

Lorraine recognized their concern right away. "You shouldn't be standing here with me. I'm a magnet. If they come for me, they'll find you. I can't have that on my conscience. We're leaving."

"Wait," Clarissa said. "You can't leave here without some protection. We'll give you one of our guns. Take the pistol." She nudged Aaron.

Aaron handed his pistol to Flynn. Flynn took it and stared at it in his hand. Aaron gave him a quick lesson on how to operate it – the hammer, the safety, the magazine. He gave him his extra box of bullets.

"I've shot things…in video games," Flynn said.

"I can't believe this," said Lorraine.

"The key for you is to keep moving, since they can track you," Clarissa said. "Go up into the hills, into the mountains, someplace where you might be able to lose the connection."

"We'll do that," Lorraine said. "We'll do that now." She began to step toward the front of the movie theater.

"Wait a minute," Clarissa said. "We'll go first and make sure the coast is clear. Don't go yet."

Lorraine looked at Flynn. She nodded. "Okay."

"Thanks," said Flynn. He held the pistol awkwardly, an unnatural appendage.

Aaron and Clarissa advanced up the long aisle. Clarissa carried the semi-automatic rifle. When they reached the door to the theater lobby, Aaron opened it a crack and peered inside.

The lobby was lit up from the outside glow of daylight piercing the big, dirt-clouded windows. The area was messy with trash and clutter, but void of any people as far as he could see.

"I think we're safe," he said softly.

"Let's make sure."

Clarissa and Aaron cautiously stepped into the lobby. The carpet was crusty and stained. The candy counter was a shell of empty glass, populated with faded advertisements for forgotten brands. An old soda dispenser with multicolored stains sat on a back counter, alongside a large popcorn machine with a layer of rotten brownish popcorn.

They glanced around the lobby and looked through the windows, seeing no outside activity.

Clarissa turned to face Aaron. "Maybe they should come with us. They can't protect themselves. We'll get them someplace safe."

"Yeah, but where is safe?"

"We need a car."

"Where will we—" Then Aaron's words cut off with a sharp gasp as he stared past Clarissa at a large cardboard display promoting the last movie in the *Star Wars* series. A very big, red-haired man stepped out from behind a life-size standee of the character Chewbacca. He placed a gun to Clarissa's head.

"Drop it," he growled.

Clarissa's mouth fell open and she stiffened. She slowly held out her arm with the rifle, and the giant man took it from her.

Aaron said, "Don't hurt her."

The giant said to Clarissa, "Turn around, real slow." She did. Aaron and Clarissa stared at him. Aaron recognized the stringy-haired giant from the raid on the library – he had been leading the charge.

"My name is Nash. I'm with the Regulation Enforcement Command. You two are under arrest. You will be chipped and placed into government housing for transgressors."

"You mean jail?" Clarissa said.

"No," said Nash, and for the first time he smiled, displaying broken, discolored teeth. "Don't get your hopes up."

At that moment, Aaron noticed movement behind Nash.

Flynn Beaman had quietly entered the lobby from another door. Aaron watched without changing his expression.

Aaron could sense Clarissa noticing, too. She remained silent and obedient to Nash's commands.

Flynn stepped slowly and quietly toward them.

"You think I don't know who you are?" Nash said. "You're Aaron Holt and Clarissa Harper. Two of the leaders of the underground resistance. Organizers of the anti-government movement, disruptors of the peace."

Flynn continued to approach, wide-eyed. He lifted the pistol. His face was white with fear.

"You two can say goodbye to the California sunshine," said Nash. "Because where you're going, there will be no windows, just four walls, to give you plenty of time to reflect—"

Flynn stepped on a candy wrapper. It made a crinkling sound.

Nash immediately turned around. Clarissa screamed.

Flynn fired a bullet into the giant's chest.

Nash staggered for a moment from the blow, stunned. But he did not topple. Blood leaked through his shirt. He began to raise his own gun.

Aaron jumped on his back.

Nash roared and spun around with the smaller man clinging to him, his arms around his neck. They crashed into the candy counter, shattering the glass.

As they untangled, Nash punched Aaron hard in the face. Flynn and Clarissa joined the battle, pulling Aaron free from the giant. Nash fought to retrieve his gun. Flynn fired the pistol again, missing Nash, piercing the popcorn butter dispenser and spraying a thick yellow goo.

Clarissa scrambled to grab her rifle, which had landed on the floor.

Nash lunged out of the pile of flattened shelving and broken glass, shards embedded in his body. He grabbed her leg, causing her to fall. With his other hand, he regained a grip on his gun. He was preparing to blast Clarissa in the face when Aaron came at him with a metal stanchion post, lifting it like an off-balance baseball bat with the round base high in the air. He slammed it into Nash's head, crushing a portion of his skull. Nash fell back into the smashed candy counter. His stringy red hair began turning redder. His chest was an expanding sea of blood. He fought to struggle to his feet.

Aaron hit him again in the head.

Then Clarissa pushed Aaron aside and let loose with a spray of bullets, peppering the giant up and down with piercing shockwaves.

When her gun went silent, no one said a word.

Clarissa, Aaron and Flynn stood over the dead giant, a heap of bloody flesh.

"Holy crap," said Flynn quietly.

His mother came running at him and hugged him. "Oh my God, Flynn. Are you hurt?"

Flynn shook his head, stunned.

"Good work, kid," Aaron said.

"I used to play Call of Duty a lot when I was younger," Flynn said.

"Until I made him stop," said Lorraine.

"So you got those video-game reflexes," Aaron said.

"This was…a lot more gross."

"We need to get out of here," Clarissa said. "There will be others. Let's take his gun."

"We're going to split off from you now," Lorraine said. "We're traceable, you're not. I won't have your blood on my hands."

"I like the idea of living in the mountains," Flynn said.

"I do, too, honey," said his mom. "I do, too."

The four of them stepped over to the theater's front entrance and looked outside. For the moment, the coast was clear.

"We'll go first," Aaron said. "Watch closely. If no one attacks us, you're probably safe."

Clarissa handed Lorraine a car key. "You need this more than we do. You have to get out of Santa Barbara fast. There's a silver Nissan Altima on the third level of the parking garage one block over, plates ZK 1124. Level three, silver Nissan, got it?"

She took the key. "Thank you. But what about you?"

"We can hide, if we need to," Aaron said. "You just need to run."

Aaron and Clarissa cautiously exited the movie theater and stepped out onto the sidewalk.

For the moment, the immediate surroundings appeared silent and empty.

Aaron turned toward the windows and signaled thumbs up.

Then he and Clarissa began walking east, away from downtown Santa Barbara.

Lorraine and Flynn slipped out of the cinema and headed west, toward the parking garage.

As Clarissa strolled down the sidewalk, she saw a smattering of pedestrians up ahead. "This rifle is pretty conspicuous."

"Just act casual."

"Right, like nothing's—"

Suddenly a huge explosion shook the pavement. Aaron and Clarissa whirled round to see a fireball reaching up into the sky, just a few blocks away, followed by a belch of black smoke.

"Holy shit. Is that the—?"

"It's the library!"

"Oh my God, they blew it up."

"We better start running."

Aaron and Clarissa began to race farther away from the scene. As they reached the next block, they could hear the roar of an oncoming vehicle.

"God damn it," Aaron said.

"Run, just run," said Clarissa.

Then there was the sound of squealing tires coming closer.

"Oh God, now what!" Clarissa shouted.

Aaron kept running as fast as he could, crossing another street, but he was losing steam. He quickly surveyed the scene around him. He faced a series of closed shops. "Let's keep going."

They crossed another block.

"Should we stop and shoot?" Clarissa asked.

"I can't run any further."

They slowed down and turned to face the vehicle bearing down on them, fully expecting to see a patrol jeep loaded with officers.

But it was a red pickup truck.

"Who the—?"

"It's Max!"

The pickup truck pulled up to the curb. Max stuck his face out of the driver's window. "Hop in!"

There was an old woman with silver hair in the front passenger seat. She held a Smith & Wesson revolver. It was Gertrude Ackerman from the sanctuary.

Aaron and Clarissa scrambled into the open back of the truck. Max accelerated the vehicle with a jolt.

"Yeeehah!" he whooped in elation.

Gertrude cackled with excitement alongside him.

Aaron and Clarissa glanced at one another, still breathing hard from the long run.

Max reached an intersection and took a hard right. Aaron slid into Clarissa.

"We'll lose them jeeps in the hills!" Max shouted. "We'll have lots of cover up there."

"I can't believe it, they blew up the library," Clarissa said.

"This really is war," said Aaron.

Clarissa noticed a shard of broken glass still stuck in his arm. She gently pulled it out and rubbed the bleeding wound.

"I don't think it's going to get any better," she said.

★ ★ ★

Sam sat alone in the bleak, secured interrogation room, staring at blank walls, too tired to think straight and too anxious to sleep. After he provided the compliance agency with the information they wanted, Sam's inquisitors had immediately cleared out, locking the door to keep him contained.

Many hours had passed, and in those hours his brain tormented him with heavy guilt. He had confessed everything they wanted to hear, a pathetic stoolie. Because of his weak, selfish addiction, the secrecy of the sanctuary was over, and he had endangered his wife.

When the door abruptly opened in a sudden bang, Sam nearly jumped out of his skin.

Bruckner entered the room. "Stay seated," he ordered. He shut the door behind him.

"What happened? What's going on? Can I go? I gave you what you wanted."

"Yes, you did. Your information was accurate. You have done a great service to your country."

"What about – what about my wife, Beatrice? Is she okay? Can I see her?"

"Your wife is fine," Bruckner said. "Everyone is fine. They were just... ticketed for unauthorized disconnection from the signal feed. We enrolled them back into society."

"So...where is she?"

"Your wife? First things first. We haven't discussed your reward."

Sam stared at Bruckner, and his heart accelerated. "My reward? What... now?"

"Cloud 11, the most fantastic mental and physical experience ever created. The powerhouse sequel to Cloud 10 that will send you higher than you've ever dreamed was possible. Oh, it's good stuff. Would you like to go there now?"

Sam thought about his wife, but then the urge for Cloud 11 overtook all other interests. He felt the itch. He needed to scratch.

"Yes...yes.... I would love to try some Cloud 11. It's really good?"

"It's *wonderful*."

Bruckner reached inside his suit jacket. He began circling the table where Sam sat. "Close your eyes," he instructed.

Sam shut his eyes and rested his hands on his knees. He awaited heavenly delights.

He heard Bruckner's soothing voice move around him. "You are going on a journey.... I'm sending you to that special place.... Are you ready, Sam? Are you ready to lift off and float on Cloud 11?"

"Yes, yes. I'm ready."

"All right then," said Bruckner, and his voice was directly behind Sam now. "Here you go...."

Very briefly, Sam felt something cold and metal press against the back of his head. There was a moment of surprise and then a split second of realization—

—before Bruckner pulled the trigger and blew Sam's brains out.

CHAPTER TWENTY

Max's new girlfriend, seventy-two-year-old Gertrude Ackerman, was well connected. She secured a sly hiding place: Sunset Gardens, a nursing home just outside of Santa Barbara in the town of Monticello. Under pseudonyms, Max and Gertrude moved into adjacent rooms in the eighty-person facility. Aaron and Clarissa, also using fake names, became a custodian and caretaker respectively. They settled into a vacant room with a small bed, formerly occupied by a ninety-six-year-old man who died from liver cancer.

Gertrude's niece ran the place with her husband, and she promised to keep them 'off the books' and protect their identities.

To fit in, Max discovered he had to slow down both physically and mentally. He was alarmed to see so many patients living out their final years with a premature departure from reality, humming along on soothing chipfeeds that made them happy zombies without aches or ambition.

"It's a despicable way to live out your golden years," Max said to Aaron and Clarissa as they sat down to a bland meal in the dining hall. "I refuse to be all doped up like that. Look at me, I still know how to live!"

"Yeah, by shooting people," Clarissa said.

Gertrude hobbled over to them, gesturing emphatically. "You need to come with me. The library raid is on TV. Sheridan is talking about us!"

The three immediately left the table and abandoned their dinners. They followed Gertrude into a private staff office, where video footage of the burning library filled the screen of a television mounted on the wall.

"Oh my God," Clarissa said.

Then the images became even more horrific: dead bodies crumpled on the pavement, including what appeared to be a teenage girl.

An emotional male voice spoke over the visuals: "This is a dark day in our country's history. Clearly the mandate of citizen tracking has gone too far, with freedom fighters subject to violence and destruction."

The Breaking News story cut to the man behind the voice: Senator Dale

Sheridan. He spoke from a wheelchair, still recovering from the shooting that had damaged his spinal cord.

His face was hardened with fury. He was calling upon Americans to rise up against the social injustices created by the chip technology.

"I beg of you, each and every one of you who still has some common sense, a shred of human decency, to look upon what we have become as a country, as a people, and reject this way of life before we are brought down as a nation. We were once the strongest, most admired country in the world. Now, because of our obedience to the chip, we are looked down upon as weak, subservient, without ambition or true leadership. We are so distracted by the fake pleasures of the chip that we cannot see our own decay. The burning of the Santa Barbara Library, a place of refuge for freedom fighters, is a symbol of a much larger attack on the United States of America from within. We must replace our complacency with outrage. Capitalism, our core strength as a nation, is dying all around us. We are losing the trade war, our gross domestic product is plummeting, the economy is in ruins. We are experiencing free-fall in manufacturing, in education. Auto plants are closing. Farms are abandoned. The military is disengaged. Schools and churches are neglected. The American work ethic is dying. Our desire to learn and innovate is gone. We have become a nation of lazy, stoned, do-nothings getting a free ride off the government's brain candy. Where is our pride, our patriotism, our backbone? The time has come to take back our country. Those images, going viral around the globe, of the burning of the Santa Barbara Library, the bodies in the street, brutality against children...we will never forget. Today is the day that the radicals in Washington have gone too far. They can control us with their laws, their regulations, their taxes... but they can't control our minds. Take back your brains, people! Rise up and fight! Never forget the Santa Barbara freedom fighters! Those flames today are a wake-up call for every citizen of this great country. The burning you see should create a burning in your heart...for something better...something stronger...something that brings us together, not sends us apart to hide in our self-absorbed little worlds. *Bring back America!*"

Sheridan shook with rage. He clearly wanted to rise out of his wheelchair but could not. His hands gestured wildly, his eyes blazed and occasional spittle flew from his lips.

He called upon the nation to fight back in massive protests in every city and community.

"You *cannot* wait for the next election. The vote will be manipulated through the radio waves to your brain. We must take back the government now, by sheer force, through your outrage and passion to be better than this!"

From the look of the news footage that followed, he was getting some traction. A wave of resistance was building. People were starting to gather in large numbers to protest and fight back.

In the hours that followed, chipping clinics were bombed in Houston, Cincinnati and Denver. Angry swarms of people gathered outside the White House and the New York headquarters of Dynamica.

Aaron, Clarissa, Max and Gertrude stayed glued to the news coverage all day, while the rest of the nursing home residents remained lost in peaceful oblivion.

"The tide is turning," said Clarissa.

"Thank God," Aaron said.

"Thank Gertrude," Max said.

Aaron turned to look at him. "What?"

Max smiled. "Who do you think created that explosion? Who do you think shot that video and sent it to the senator?"

Gertrude said, "Sometimes you need optics. Something bold, something big and colorful. You need to go viral to wake people up."

"Wait – you started the library fire?" Clarissa asked.

"I will not be bullied by the government, and I will raise awareness any way I can."

They continued to watch the news unfold.

"So where do we go from here?" Aaron said.

"Prepare for civil war," said Max. There was a tinge of enthusiasm in his voice.

Gertrude took Max's gnarled hand. Max turned and smiled at his new girlfriend. She smiled back through wrinkles and weary blue eyes.

"I can go to the grave knowing I did something right for my country," she said.

CHAPTER TWENTY-ONE

Dirty, silent and resigned, Lorraine and Flynn Beaman rode the long yellow bus to Chip Prison Ranch. They sat on padded seats with broken springs and stared out barred windows, packed alongside four dozen other enemies of the state.

The hippie mother and son had eluded the regulation patrol for nineteen days after fleeing the Santa Barbara Sanctuary, hiding out in the hills with other anti-chip activists, but unable to fully avoid sending signals that reported their location on the national grid.

Unfortunately, data pulled from the government satellite and Santa Barbara transmission towers placed them at the scene of the killing of Nash Wenzel, one of California's leading compliance enforcers. The tracking system recorded their presence with Nash inside an old movie theater at the precise moment he died from shooting and bludgeoning. There was no need for a judge or jury; the chip analytics did not lie.

Lorraine and Flynn Beaman were immediately found guilty of murder and sentenced to live the rest of their days in a forced stupor on a large, barren plot of land in the Mojave Desert.

At the Chip Prison Ranch, inmates sluggishly roamed the dry soil like groggy herds of cattle, offered minimal shade, food and water in the grueling heat. Simple wire fences surrounded the prison yard, easy to penetrate except for one deciding factor: the chipped inmates were programmed to receive a vicious shock if they crossed the perimeter. They learned, by instinct, to stay within the designated confines. Prisoners also received a heavy cocktail of Obedience and Dim Bulb chipfeed signals, essentially rendering them slow and stupid, oblivious to even the notion of escape.

Lorraine and Flynn knew what to expect. They had been informed, in cruel and graphic detail, upon their arrest.

They understood that upon their arrival at the ranch, they would receive a download of nasty ingredients to neuter their brains. They would be lucky to still remember their names or relationship to one another.

Lorraine remembered hearing a horror story from one of her friends who told the tale of driving past a Chip Prison Ranch in Nevada and witnessing a sight that gave her nightmares for months afterward. "It was just this one big field with all these people…and they were just standing there…moving very slow…and they had those horrible blank expressions, like they were dead…but they weren't, not physically anyway. It looked like a big pen of zombies. It was like they weren't even human anymore. Just dead-eyed, slow-moving zombies. They stayed away from the fence, because they knew it would shock them…and they just milled around like cows."

As the reality of her fate drew ever closer during the long bus ride, Lorraine remained stoic. She could no longer cry, she was all cried out. Her eyes felt like big, dark, sunken sockets. Her throat was raw. Her heart ached.

Flynn didn't speak. Words could not express his terror. He was too scared to move. He stared at the other prisoners around him. They were equally glum and silent, chained at the ankles to prevent running.

When the sun was high in the sky, bright and blazing, the bus arrived at the Chip Prison Ranch. It was the most haunting, desolate, oppressive environment that Flynn or Lorraine had ever witnessed.

"Maybe if we're lucky," Lorraine said, "really, really lucky…we can step on a rattlesnake."

Four rows ahead, there was a sudden eruption of screams. One of the prisoners, a Hispanic man, fell out of his seat and landed in the aisle. A steady stream of his blood moved down the center of the bus to pool in the back, passing Flynn and Lorraine.

Later, they heard the man had killed himself by tearing the chip out of his neck with his bare hands.

PART THREE
ONE YEAR LATER
CHAPTER TWENTY-TWO

Marc drove one hundred miles per hour because his was the only active car on the highway. Every other vehicle had pulled over to the side of the road with their drivers and passengers slumped and motionless. It was as if someone had placed the world on pause, and Marc alone had escaped. The incredible stillness continued for dozens of miles as Marc cut through the state of Ohio. He shot past stationary cars and trucks and buses. The anonymous people inside were shadowy blurs. The afternoon sun illuminated the surrounding forests and farms with rich Midwestern colors. Marc was immersed in a still-life painting. He would have been amused by the thought if he wasn't afraid for his life.

The fact that he was conscious and alert was an open violation of the law.

Fortunately, there was no one to arrest him, because anyone currently able to do so was also violating the law.

Foot firmly pressed on the accelerator of his old 2017 Ford Fusion, Marc was making excellent progress toward his destination. The time on his watch said half past two. He decided to briefly leave the highway and enter a small town for a food break. He was hungry.

Marc reduced his speed and took the next exit. He followed a long, straight road that split through a lush countryside under open blue skies. He felt as though it all belonged to him, not seeing another soul.

After several miles, Marc reached the simple town square of Crane, Ohio. It was marked by a hearty welcome sign planted in a roundabout that featured an elegant, bubbling fountain – the only hint of animation. Marc circled the fountain, observing a collection of minor shops and businesses with colorful awnings and empty sidewalks. An old man with a hat and baggy trousers sat motionless on a bench, like a mannequin, eyes half shut. Marc caught a glimpse inside a barbershop and recognized human shapes slouched in the chairs, not moving. A lone black dog, running loose and peeing on a lamppost, provided evidence that Marc was not entering a static photograph.

After nearly completing the circle, Marc turned onto a side street and found what he was looking for – a restaurant offering real food.

While Body Fuel bars with simulcast flavors dominated the food industry, 'nostalgia' meals still existed, and most communities retained a few traditional eating establishments for the sake of variety – or novelty.

Marc parked the car and entered Fran's Diner.

Inside, a plump woman in an apron, with gray hair and wrinkles – possibly Fran herself – sat behind the counter, not moving. Her eyes were half shut, hands in lap, staring forward at nothing.

Marc knew he could reach over and help himself to the contents of the cash register but chose to take a menu instead.

He said, "That's all right, don't get up. I can seat myself."

Marc walked into the eating area, two long rows of red booths. Several of the booths were occupied with immobile people, including a family of four with a young boy and young girl. The young boy still had a crayon in his grip, and there was a half-finished drawing on his children's placemat. His face was frozen in an open-mouth grimace, as if he had still been talking when his brain was turned off.

Marc sat in a booth by the window, where he could keep an eye on his car. He checked his watch: it was nearly quarter to three. He stared into his menu, lost himself in the lunch photos and found something that looked good: an 'old-fashioned' grilled cheese sandwich with 'blast from the past' french fries.

He was ready to order, once his waitress came back to life. She was currently preoccupied like the others, receiving chip updates.

This was the third 'reboot' of the past four months. Like any other operating system, the chip technology required occasional upgrades. This meant a countrywide shutdown lasting for a short period of time, heavily communicated in advance so citizens were prepared. Today's reboot required everyone to go into a passive mode for forty-five minutes, beginning at two fifteen p.m. Central time and concluding at precisely three p.m.

Even if someone didn't want the upgrade, they received it anyway. You could not 'opt out'.

Marc, still without the chip, remained unaffected but his 'untethered' status put him at considerable risk. He had been very careful not to reveal his true condition to anyone, keeping a low profile and growing his hair long to cover up the absence of a chip bump on the back of his neck.

The number of chipless citizens had dwindled steadily in the past year as the government continued to pursue one hundred percent compliance with an aggressive commitment.

President Sheridan, once a fierce opponent of the chip, had unexpectedly flip-flopped his stance upon taking – or, rather, seizing – office.

The 'Santa Barbara Massacre' had been a catalyst for turning the tide against the previous administration. The huge swell of government opposition had become unstoppable and led to a successful takeover of the White House by Senator Sheridan and his rabid supporters.

"This is not a coup!" Sheridan insisted in his first address from the bullet-riddled Oval Office. "This is a reclamation of America by the people."

While many expected Sheridan to disassemble the chip technology's firm grip on society, he surprised the nation by taking it in a new direction. Some blamed the assassination attempt that crippled him for also crippling his mind, while others declared it was his intent all along.

Sheridan stuck to his promise to put an end to a 'sloth society' where the population was perpetually high on government-subsidized 'brain candy'. He maintained that America would no longer be an embarrassment, subject to the ridicule of the rest of the world.

"After careful consideration, I have chosen not to abolish the chip but use it for more noble purposes," said Sheridan as commander-in-chief. "We will strengthen our military. Rebuild capitalism. Restore our faith in God. Bring back the basic values of discipline and work ethic. Eliminate wasteful, irrelevant pursuits and idle hands. I have learned this: the chip is not the enemy. *How* we use the chip is the difference between right and wrong. It is a power that must be applied toward a greater good that makes us better and stronger, not weaker. We are putting America back on track!"

The first reboot of the chip technology, described as 'the cleansing', wiped out most of the games, recreation, entertainment and intoxicants. The uproar was immediate, but short-lived. The second reboot introduced mandatory aspirations of worker productivity, civic duty and military service.

The third reboot, now underway, focused on security patches to resolve the various bugs and viruses from the first two system refreshes. One of the fixes closed a hole that had allowed hackers to display pop-up ads in the minds of unsuspecting citizens. One ad in particular led to a huge surge in purchases of time-share condominiums on a nonexistent island in the Bahamas.

Until very recently, Marc had remained in New York City living in secrecy among the 'chipped'. But lately the dangers of being discovered were too high. 'Chip resisters' were routinely rounded up and taken away in big buses, returning twenty-four hours later with a fresh, pink lump where the brain connected with the spinal cord. Marc scaled back his hours at the animal shelter to reduce his visibility. He limited his time outdoors partly out of fear of being captured and partly over his disgust at New York City's continued physical decline. It was sliding back to a grittier state from generations ago, filthy and neglected. Even worse: famous landmarks and attractions, like Central Park Zoo and Carnegie Hall, had closed down.

President Sheridan promised a major cleanup of America's top cities, including New York, Los Angeles and Chicago, but his tactics involved forced 'civic appreciation' service hours mandated through chipfeed signals. Marc didn't want to stick around long enough to witness the rollout of technology-enabled slavery.

He needed a new destination.

Then, one day, Kathryn Sedak, the kindly manager of the animal shelter, arrived at work in tears.

She wouldn't talk about it at first, but finally confided in him when Regan, Marc's nosy teenage coworker, wasn't around.

"My daughter is gone, she left home today," Kathryn said. "She…she's leaving the country."

"Where is she going?" Marc asked.

"Canada."

"Canada?"

"Promise you won't say a word."

"Of course not. You know you can trust me."

"I know I can, Bob," she said, and Marc tried not to wince at the irony of her statement. "I'm going to let you in on a secret. But you can't say anything to anyone. They would come after me. They would go after her."

"I don't talk to anyone. You know me, I'm a loner. I just like hanging out with the animals."

She moved closer and her voice became a hard whisper against the barking of dogs in the next room over. "My daughter – she – she doesn't have the chip."

"Oh."

"I don't blame her. If I could go back in time, I never would've gotten this damned chip stuck in my head either. I know you feel the same way. You've told me."

"I have the chip, yes, and I don't like it," Marc said carefully.

"She left today with a small group. They've been in hiding together. None of them have the chip. The dangers of getting caught keep getting bigger. So they heard about this secret escape route – up in northern Minnesota – across the Boundary Waters. No border patrol, no federal agents. A clean getaway, out of the country."

"Wow."

"We said our goodbyes this morning."

"I promise I won't tell a soul." He certainly meant it because he immediately felt compelled to take the same route himself out of the country.

Unchipped individuals could not legally leave the United States and when they were caught, they were chipped and jailed. Emigration officials enforced the law at airports, seaports, and Mexican and Canadian border crossings.

That evening, at home, Marc began his quest to uncover more about this secret escape path. He hopped online, entered secured chat rooms for chip resisters and left coded inquiries that only made sense if you knew the answer. He probed people in his personal network of sympathetic naturalists and traded encrypted messages.

Finally, someone behind the avatar 'Hobojoe19' gave him the information he needed.

There was indeed a managed escape route through the Boundary Waters and within minutes Marc had precise instructions.

He packed up that night and drove out of New York the next morning.

His timing could not have been better: shortly after he left the city, the government announced its intention to install chip readers at all tunnels and bridges leading in and out of Manhattan. It would go live in two weeks. Vehicles that did not emit a chip tracking signal would be immediately detained and searched for 'illegals'.

Eventually, the same system would be installed in toll lanes for every major highway, casting more nets for the chipless.

Marc knew that staying in the U.S. in his present condition was no longer an option. He needed to get to the Boundary Waters. Sitting in the eerie, motionless Ohio diner, he checked his watch anxiously. It was one minute to three p.m. He was starving.

"Come on, people, wake up," he muttered, taking another look around the diner at the frozen, blank-faced customers and employees.

It was a creepy feeling, like being the last man on earth.

Abruptly, at precisely three o'clock, the people inside the diner sputtered back to life. They made strange coughing, gasping and wheezing noises. They blinked rapidly, wiggled their limbs, shook off the stiffness and returned to their existences after a brief intermission.

Marc smiled and sat up, stretching a little to fit in, as if he had just emerged from a short coma as well.

After a minute, a thin, freckled waitress approached with a notepad.

"Hello, I didn't see you come in," she said to Marc.

"Oh, I arrived just before the upgrade."

"Such a nuisance, isn't it? And they probably just dumped a bunch of new spyware on us."

Marc chuckled. "Well, nothing they download can beat a fine home-cooked meal at Fran's Diner."

"You're too kind. What can I get you?"

Marc ordered a grilled cheese sandwich, fries and a lemonade.

After the waitress left, Marc pulled out an old-fashioned paper road map of the Midwestern United States. It was ripped and stained, a relic, but still a dependable depiction of the driving route to his destination: Ely, Minnesota. Once there, he would arrange a meeting with a private guide who would prepare his trek through Superior National Forest to a hidden area of canoes that regularly crossed the Boundary Waters to reach Quetico Provincial Park in Ontario, Canada.

The waitress delivered his lemonade. "Oh, a paper map. Do they still make those?"

"No, it's just for fun, a collector's item."

She left, and he continued studying the map to estimate the time it would take him to get to his destination. Suddenly a lanky, mustached man with a crooked nose dropped into the seat across from him with a thump.

Marc looked up and stared at the man. He wore a black leather jacket covered in patches with slogans like LET'S ROLL and images of eagles and the American flag.

"Can I help you?" Marc asked.

"Yes sir," said the man with a sharp nod. "You can answer a question for me."

"Okay."

"Are you serving your country?"

Marc hesitated, unsure of where this was going. "Yes," he said, guessing it was what this man wanted to hear.

"I don't think you are."

"I beg your pardon?"

"You don't have the chip."

Marc felt his skin prickle. He tried to stay cool. "Yes, I do. Of course I do."

"I've been sitting in the booth just over there." The man pointed two booths down, behind Marc, to another table against the window. "I have a new bike, a Harley. Right before they shut us off for the upgrade, I was staring at my bike. I love my bike, you understand? It's brand new. It's a thing of beauty."

Marc said nothing.

"So, at two fifteen, when everyone goes into passive mode, the last thing I see is my bike. At three o'clock, when we all boot up together, I'm in the same sitting position, staring out the window…and all I see is that stupid Ford."

Marc wouldn't turn to look. He continued to listen with a fixed expression.

"So that means that sometime between shutdown and reboot, that there Ford pulled up into the parking spot. It wasn't there before. And me, sitting close by, I'm pretty sure I didn't see you here in this booth, either."

"I arrived just before the shutdown."

"No. No, I don't think so."

"Why are you bothering me?"

"Because I believe you don't have the chip."

"How about you leave me alone?"

"Yeah, right." The biker leaned back in the booth, not going anywhere. "That's how it is with you people."

"'You people'?"

"What's the matter, don't you love America?"

"I want to."

"Face it, you're the deadweight that President Sheridan talks about. You expect to live here, on our land, but not serve your country. The chip is allegiance, you get that? It's going to put us back on top. We've been sick, we got lazy. You want everything to be made in China?"

"The chip isn't patriotism."

"What have you got against the chip?"

"I think it's ruining this country."

The biker chuckled. "Pretty strong words. Well, let me tell you something. I work for Dynamica, the greatest company in the world. The biggest and the strongest."

Marc was tempted to reveal he used to work there, too. Instead he simply said, "A lot of people work for Dynamica. It's the biggest employer in the country. What do you do?"

"I repair the local transmitter towers. You know, the towers that help relay the signals from the satellite to the chips, these chips right here." He tapped the back of his head. "I help keep it all in good working order. You seen the tower on the outside of town?"

"No, but I'm familiar with them." Marc wanted to blurt, *I know more about Dynamica than practically anybody. I know your boss's boss's boss's boss.*

Marc thought about Brandyn Handley, Dynamica Incorporated's head of operations. The man who risked everything to help Marc escape from the chip's control. They had fallen out of touch in the past two years, probably for the better.

"Let me tell you, it's the best company, the best job I ever had," said the biker. "I used to work in the sewer. Literally. *That* was a shit job. But I worked. I worked hard. I've always seen myself as part of a bigger picture. We're all connected to make this country great, you know? Except people like you. You want to be different. Independent. You want to play by your own rules 'cause you're special, you're better. And you sneer at the rest of us who are coming together to save this country, not betray it. You think you're too good for the chip, don't you?"

"That's not it at all…."

"Well, we're going to get this little matter taken care of." He reached inside his jacket and pulled out his cell phone. "You see, there's a reward for people like you. You're going against the law. I turn you in, I get a thousand dollars." He tapped his phone to life.

"No, you won't get a thousand dollars. Because I have the chip."

"I don't believe you."

"You want me to prove it?"

"Yes." The biker paused from dialing. "Prove it right here, right now."

"All right." Marc dug into his pocket and pulled out his device controller – the prototype version for law enforcement that Brandyn Handley had given him. It had come in handy, many times, to disarm threats.

"See, I have a controller for my chip."

"Having that in your pocket – it doesn't mean a thing. Maybe you stole it."

"I'll show you that it works on me," said Marc. "I'll send a signal to my chip. Something obvious, that you can see."

"How do I know you're not faking?"

"Hold on." Marc worked the controller quickly. He selected the nearest active chip. He called up a bestseller list and found something.

"Do you like rock 'n' roll?" Marc asked.

"Rock 'n' roll? Yeah, sure, of course. I subscribe to some music feeds. I get the classic rock station. They beam songs into my head. I have a bunch of playlists."

"Have you ever wanted to be a rock 'n' roll drummer?"

"What does that have to do with anything?"

"I hear it's a great workout, too." Marc jabbed a selection and sent a signal to the biker's head.

The biker's eyes glazed over, and then he became lost in his imagination. He transformed into the greatest rock 'n' roll drummer of all time. His hands moved through the air, clutching invisible sticks, pounding out an elaborate rhythm on a nonexistent drum kit.

The waitress arrived with Marc's sandwich. She gave an odd look to the air drummer.

"He's in the zone," Marc said.

The waitress nodded and put down the plate.

"Can I get this to go?" Marc asked. "I'm on a tight schedule, and I need to hit the road."

"Certainly. I'll bring the check." She took the plate back.

The biker continued to flail, drawing attention from others around the diner.

Marc received his sandwich in a Styrofoam container, paid his bill and departed from the restaurant. He had ordered a fifteen-minute drumming session and wanted to be long gone when the biker emerged from his virtual reality.

Marc climbed into his car and backed out of his parking spot. He hesitated for a moment, then swung the car forward to strike the back of the shiny, new motorcycle. It toppled over and hit the pavement, breaking a mirror and the headlamp. Marc drove away with a dented front hood, a small price to pay for the freedom he felt. He returned to the highway and now it was busy with vehicles. The pause button had been lifted. He joined the streams of traffic and added more miles to his progress as the late-afternoon sun dipped into the horizon.

CHAPTER TWENTY-THREE

After a long day of driving more than seven hundred miles, with two brief stops for food, including the grilled cheese sandwich in Ohio, Marc needed to pull over and find someplace to sleep for the night. If he had the chip, he could have ordered Buzz, a signal that ensured he would stay awake and alert, but without it he was simply and naturally very tired. He had plenty of cash cards to pay expenses anonymously, so getting a hotel room was no more difficult than filling up on gas. He was equipped with fake identification and as long as he kept a low profile, he was okay.

Headlights probing the dark, Marc exited the highway and entered Yorkville, a small town in northern Indiana. He didn't encounter a hotel right away and wound up driving deeper into the rural community than he expected. As his surroundings grew darker and more desolate, he contemplated turning around and returning to the highway. Ultimately, the paved road turned into bumpy gravel and then a mixture of mud and flattened grass. Marc swore, on the verge of getting lost, and decided to turn around and backtrack.

He made an awkward U-turn in a tight space, struggling with poor visibility as cloud cover concealed the moon and stars. The Ford hit an awkward dip in the road. Soon after, it became sluggish and off balance when he picked up speed.

Marc immediately sensed something was not right: the car was making a thumping sound.

"Oh God, please don't be a…."

Marc stopped the car and climbed out. He circled the vehicle and spotted his nightmare: a flat tire.

Now what?

Marc sighed and hung his head. He knew that his car lacked a spare tire – the prior owner had warned him about it, but Marc didn't care at the time because he was simply happy to be acquiring a working vehicle in cash from a private individual without the nuisance of a paper trail.

Marc wanted to yell at himself for being so stupid. Instead, he stood alone in the dark and listened to a gentle, lonely breeze. And crickets.

He slowly turned in a circle, looking in every direction. He needed a sign of life, anything, that might indicate people and help. He was willing to bribe his way out of any predicament – and use his rogue controller to counter any threat.

In the murky distance, through a long stretch of wilderness, Marc glimpsed a faint, flickering light. It gave him a tiny surge of hope. Reaching it would require leaving the road and his car and creating his own path in the dark through the wild brush. He could think of no other option. He cursed, locked up the Ford and began his long hike into the unknown.

He kept his hands in front of him as the brush got denser, pushing away the branches that scraped at his skin. The ground was muddy and uneven, causing him to stumble repeatedly. He didn't know what kind of creatures lurked in the dark and really didn't want to find out. Assorted insects flew into his face, and he kept his mouth shut to avoid breathing one in.

Most importantly, the light in the distance was slowly growing closer.

After pushing his way through tall grasses for nearly thirty minutes, Marc reached a clearing. The ground became level, and he could see what looked like a single building with a pitched roof, like an old church or one-room schoolhouse. A flickering light, like a candle, illuminated the square frame of a single window. He crept closer to get a better look. Was there someone inside?

He reached the side of the building and inched toward the window for a peek. For a brief instant, he could see children.

Then a crashing pain struck his skull, and his vision flashed white and immediately turned black.

★ ★ ★

Marc regained consciousness, stinging with a throbbing headache. He slowly sat up and found himself surrounded by shadowy, staring faces. The faces belonged to children, more than a dozen, from very young to upper teens. Their features were partially lit by a lone candle in a brass holder held by a frowning little girl who couldn't have been older than nine or ten.

A teenage boy with a crew cut leaned in and placed the blade of a sharp hunting knife one inch from Marc's throat.

"Don't move," he instructed.

"What did you…hit me with?"

"A brick."

"Where am I?" Marc could sense he was inside the mysterious building now; there was a roof with crossbeams high above his head and a big, open space around him that rapidly disappeared into shadows.

"Are you a spy?" asked the teenage boy.

"No."

Then the cluster of children parted to allow a lone adult to step forward. He was a middle-aged man with wavy blond hair and a medium build, wearing a simple blue sweater over a button-up collared shirt.

"That would be the obvious answer, given your predicament," the man said.

Marc peered down at the glistening knife blade. "Yes, but it's true."

The man motioned for the teenage boy to pull back the weapon. He immediately obeyed.

The man kneeled before Marc to stare into his eyes. "My name is Father Cusack. These are my children. We are a community. We don't take kindly to unannounced visitors, especially at this hour. Who do you represent?"

"Nobody," Marc said. "I'm alone. I have no authority. I'm just a person. My car broke down."

"Out here? That's not a good story. There's nothing out here. There's no reason to be driving anywhere near here."

"I was looking for a hotel."

"Should I kill him?" said the teenage boy, with a tone of practicality.

Father Cusack didn't answer. The fact that he didn't serve up a simple 'no' pushed Marc's anxiety level even higher.

He chose to make a run for it. He didn't have a clear sense of his surroundings, so the only hope of escape was to put everyone on equal footing – sightless.

Marc pretended he was adjusting his seated position on the floor. Then, with an immediate lunge, he shoved Father Cusack out of the way and leaped toward the girl with the candle. He knocked it out of her hands, snuffing the flame and sending the building into complete darkness.

Marc pushed through the sudden entanglement of confused children. He scrambled across the hardwood floor, hands stretched in front of him, banging into occasional objects, unable to see anything in his path. He couldn't sense the location of an exit, and the room filled with the sounds of children shouting, shrieking and scurrying to find him.

Reaching a wall, Marc realized his only hope was to use his controlling device on as many people as possible, sending them brain signals to disrupt their pursuit. He pulled out the controller, popped it on and immediately discovered....

It did not register any chips in the vicinity. None. Was it broken or—?

The dim light of the controller attracted a mob of children. They pounced on him, knocking him down, punching, kicking and pulling his hair. They screamed at him in shrill voices.

He curled up on the floor as they beat him. He yelled at them to stop, which they didn't.

Then Father Cusack ordered them to stop and they did.

Marc lay very still on the floor.

Several of the children lit candles and now the large indoor space was illuminated from multiple points.

Marc sat up against the wall, feeling blood trickle from his nose and lips. Now he had a better look at his environment. One side of the massive room had a series of bunk beds, a living quarters. The other side had old-fashioned school desks and a large blackboard. He also glimpsed a kitchen area with benches and a wood stove.

Father Cusack and the children surrounded Marc. Many of the kids held knives or clubs. Marc realized there were even more children than he originally surmised – they were several layers deep, at least twenty or thirty of them.

The largest child stepped forward. He was bulky, built like a football player, sixteen or seventeen years old. He wore a simple tank top that displayed big, rippling arm muscles. He sneered at Marc and leaned in toward him. He lifted his thick hands and wrapped them around Marc's throat.

Marc started to shout, to plead, fully expecting to be strangled on the spot.

But the big fingers didn't press on his throat. They gently caressed the back of his neck.

"I don't feel a chip," the boy said out loud to the group. He backed off.

Marc said, in short breaths, "Yes...I admit it.... I don't have the chip.... I'm not...."

Father Cusack reached down and snatched the controller from Marc's hands. "Then why do you have this?"

Marc's arms lifted to grab it back, but it was too late. "I need that.... It's not...it's not for me. It helps me protect myself. I can send signals to others who are chipped."

They stared at him, perplexed.

Marc said, "You didn't show up on the device. You don't – none of you – have the chip?"

The children all looked to Father Cusack, waiting for him to respond on their behalf.

"That's right," said Father Cusack. He tossed the device back into Marc's lap. "We don't have the chip. What's your story?"

"I had the chip removed years ago."

"That's not possible."

"It was...but I had to see a special expert, someone working for the chip company. I had one of the earliest chips, I'm sure today it's a lot harder—"

"Today it is fatal to tamper with the chip."

Marc nodded. "My story is true. I've been on the road. I left the highway, I took an exit to find a hotel, but I got lost, there was nothing out this way. Then I got a flat tire, and I walked through a field and this was the only building...."

Father Cusack nodded, staring into Marc's eyes. "I believe you," he said.

He turned to the gathering of children. "Prepare for bed, everyone. The excitement is over. You must get rest for tomorrow's lesson plan."

The children obeyed, peeling away from the group and reporting to their bunk beds. They opened the lids to large trunks on the floor and changed into sleeping clothes.

Father Cusack said to Marc, "You and me, let's have a drink."

⋆ ⋆ ⋆

As the children retired to bed, Marc and Father Cusack moved to the opposite end of the large, barn-like structure. They sat on hard benches at a long, wooden table, drinking red wine.

Marc told Cusack about his journey of the past several years, including betraying his employer, Dynamica, to reject a chipped society.

Cusack described his 'children for tomorrow' congregation.

"We have twenty-eight young people here between the ages of four and twenty-four. They've never been chipped and never will be. I'm the main adult in their lives. They've lost their real parents. In some cases, they were abandoned. Their parents died, became chip addicts or were jailed. In other cases, they escaped an abusive home life. This is a chance for them to be reborn, outside of a diseased society, before they're corrupted beyond repair. My goal is to continue growing this congregation – with young people – so we can change the future through a generation of people who reject the chip and *all* of technology to return to a simple, natural life, the way God intended. That is why we have very strict rules here. The children understand, and they will become better people because of it. No chip. No computers. No Internet. No TV. We're returning to our roots, back to the basics. The earth. The sky. Natural living. We grow our own food. There's a farm down the road. The children help manage it. We live by candlelight. We read books. We teach and learn through human interaction and dialogue. Imagine that. No one has their face stuffed in a cell phone or a laptop. No one is watching foolish videos or playing irreverent games. We live in the real world, and we appreciate it. Every blade of grass. Every star above us. Everything we touch and feel and taste. That's why God placed us here, to marvel over His world, not some artificial circus of distractions generated by machines. Let me be direct with you, Marc. I hate what technology has done to this world. I'm proud you chose to take a stand and leave that company. We need more people like you. And the most powerful thing we can do is start with the children."

* * *

Marc spent the night, sleeping on the floor with a blanket and pillow. The congregation woke up early the next morning, at the first strains of daylight, to embark on their daily duties. Many of the children left to tend to the farm. Father Cusack stayed behind and served Marc a hearty breakfast of eggs, bacon, hash brown potatoes, toast and organic black coffee.

Marc had told Cusack about the escape route into Canada, but Cusack politely declined the opportunity for the congregation to join him.

"You go ahead," Cusack said. "We belong here. We can't influence change by running away. I know I have a lot of work to do. Maybe it's hopeless, but I have a mission. It's what keeps me going. But I wish you well."

"Aren't you afraid of being discovered?" asked Marc. "They're rounding up people every day. They can inject people with the chip on the spot. They have a device that operates like a gun. Your entire congregation could be chipped in ten minutes."

"It will never happen," Cusack said, "because we're equipped with an escape if that threat becomes real."

"An escape?"

"A pill. The children each have a pill in a small case that they carry with them at all times. I have one, too."

"What, like a cyanide pill? Poison?"

"If the day comes when we're forced to live a life we do not want, then we will take the appropriate action. If the future belongs to technology, rather than the human spirit, it's not worth living."

When it came time for Marc to return to his car and find a way to replace his flat tire, Cusack offered an alternative. "There are some old cars on the property. They don't get much use. They pollute the air. You can take your pick. They're behind the barn."

Marc walked over to the farm with Father Cusack. The children were already hard at work, feeding livestock, milking cows, collecting eggs. The older kids were tending to the fields.

Marc chose a dusty Acura sedan. It appeared to be in good running order. He said his goodbyes and drove off, kicking up dirt on the gravel roadway. He returned to his Ford with the flat tire and transferred his belongings over to the new car. It was just as well – the front of the Ford was dented from where he had struck the motorcycle. It drew attention.

Marc returned to the highway and continued his journey to Ely, Minnesota, which he calculated was another eleven hours of driving.

He never expected the delay that awaited: being forced to work in a steel mill in Gary, Indiana.

CHAPTER TWENTY-FOUR

Without warning, the traffic on Interstate 90 switched from light to heavy. Marc found himself trapped in a thick congestion of cars.

"Where the hell did all these people come from?" he griped into the windshield. He was still in sleepy northern Indiana, not yet approaching Metropolitan Chicago. It didn't make sense. Was this some kind of massive evacuation? He studied the faces in the other vehicles, and everyone appeared calm.

Orange cones and large blockades with flashing arrows directed all traffic into the far right lane.

Marc watched his speedometer dip to ten miles per hour, reducing his progress to a crawl. Then he grew alarmed: all cars were being funneled to an exit ramp. He did not want to leave the highway, but everyone else was doing so, willingly. Then he observed the traffic flow on the other side of the highway, coming from the opposite direction, also being diverted to an exit ramp at this same location.

There was no way to escape this convergence of cars. It was like a tight, massive funeral procession.

As Marc left the highway, he could see the traffic up ahead, and it continued on a very controlled path. Flashing police cars blocked side streets, and police officers in orange vests waved everyone in the same direction.

The huge crush of drivers barely inched forward in a stop-and-go rhythm. While his car sat idle for an extended moment near an intersection, Marc lowered the window and called out to a fat, nearby policeman with a thick mustache and droopy expression.

"Excuse me. *Excuse me!* I don't belong in this line. I need to get back on the highway."

The policeman stepped over to the car, frowning. "What are you talking about? Of course you belong here."

"I know that I don't. What's going on?"

"You have the chip, don't you?"

Marc didn't hesitate to produce a lie. "Yes, yes. Of course."

"You are in an official Work Zone. Everything will be explained when you get inside."

"Inside?"

"The steel mill."

"Steel mill?"

The cop rolled his eyes, exasperated over having to explain something that he felt shouldn't be questioned. "Anyone in a ten-mile radius is officially engaged to revitalize the steel mill."

"What?"

"Listen, you don't see anyone else questioning it. Are you sure you have the chip?"

"I do. Yes. I understand. I was just confused."

"Confused isn't an option. *Go*."

Then the traffic began moving again, and Marc advanced toward his forced destination with uneasy resignation.

He had seen the steel mill's distant silhouette in a haze of dark clouds from the highway, but had not linked it to the traffic jam. As he got closer, he grimaced at the hideous magnitude of the manufacturing plant. It looked like a dreary industrial castle against an orange-red sky. Railroad tracks circled it like a moat, busy with freight cars for transporting raw materials in and casted products out. Towering chimneys spewed smoke from the blast furnaces. A flare stack expelled flames to burn off gases like a fire-breathing dragon.

Marc's windshield became fogged with a layer of blackish soot. In the murky pollution, the steel mill transformed into a strange, silvery beast, oozing a winding trail of piping, jutted balconies and jagged staircases. It beckoned its victims and swallowed them whole.

Marc followed the rest of the cars into an enormous employee parking lot, adjacent to a yard of monster trucks loaded with giant steel coils. Extended cranes hovered nearby. Parking lot attendees waved arrivals into tight, perfectly aligned spaces.

Marc parked and decided the safest course of action was to fit in with everyone else and not draw attention to himself. He followed a line of people walking toward the factory and hid his fear among the surrounding blank faces.

The crowd gathered inside a large, open room the size of a gymnasium.

Marc stood shoulder-to-shoulder with hundreds of others, facing a podium and back wall with two large logos hanging from the ceiling: Great American Steel Works and Dynamica.

The Dynamica logo, cheerful and colorful, made Marc sick to his stomach. He had helped to oversee its design a long time ago, when it represented a happier, more innocent technological breakthrough.

Once the room had filled to capacity, the doors were shut with a succession of loud booms that echoed to the rafters.

A smiling, older man in a blue suit approached the podium with an energetic bounce in his step. He greeted the crowd in a voice amplified through stacks of powerful speakers.

"Welcome to the rebirth of the American steel industry!" he shouted, and his audience broke out into loud collective applause. Marc quickly joined in.

"My name is Merle Gregory, president and CEO of this proud facility. We are gathered here for a major milestone. All of you are part of something special: the launch of Work Zones, a partnership between business and government to take this country's gross domestic product to a whole new level. We are one of twelve Work Zones starting today across the United States. Our goal is to revitalize critical industries that need a boost to regain our dominance in world trade. The first wave of Work Zones is focused on steel, auto manufacturing, oil, plastics and computer components. In the coming months, more Work Zones will be introduced, based on the learning we generate from the pioneers, the innovators, the superstars in this room and eleven other locations."

He broadened his smile and spread his arms. "Look at all this talent! You are phenomenal! When you were summoned here, with the magical efficiency of the chip, I'm sure you were wondering, 'What's this all about?' You knew you had a duty, a calling, but the exact nature of the request was unclear. What a wonderful surprise, to show up today and claim this prize. Every man and woman over the age of eighteen within a ten-mile radius of this facility is now gainfully employed with the dream job of a lifetime. You will love it here. It was a mistake we ever had to close this facility down. The grand reopening comes with a full-on commitment at the highest levels. You will have good pay and good benefits in exchange for eight-hour shifts of good, hard work. We will have three shifts each day, so that we may run at maximum efficiency, twenty-four hours a day, seven days a week. Each worker is committed to forty hours a week and not a minute more. But those forty hours will be maximized to bring out your best. You will go home each day feeling proud, feeling fulfilled, feeling purposeful. This is a return to the roots of our great-great-grandparents and a time when America was admired, not scorned. The patriotic pride is back, my friends. Can you feel it?"

"*Yes!*" shouted the crowd in unison.

One beat behind, Marc offered his own, thin 'yes'. It stuck out embarrassingly, and he nervously looked at the floor.

Merle Gregory made more statements to rally his audience. Then he introduced the next speaker: Gerald Lufken, Midwest director of operations for Dynamica.

Marc did not know Gerald, but he was immediately sickened by him. He was slick and glib. It anguished Marc to consider that this man probably reported to his old friend, Brandyn Handley, the head of operations at Dynamica.

"How are we feeling today?" Lufken shouted, pacing the stage like a would-be entertainer.

The crowd cheered wildly.

Joining in half-heartedly, Marc produced a fake smile and waved his hand lazily.

"Dynamica is proud to enable this partnership between government and industry to take a giant leap forward for the American economy. I must tell you, a moment ago I checked the stock market to see Wall Street's reaction to today's big news…and guess what, the Dow Jones is at an *all-time high.*"

More cheering.

Marc found the joyful response odd; how many of these people truly had robust investment portfolios that would benefit?

"I am thrilled to represent my company at today's ribbon-cutting for the reopening of the Great American Steel Works in Gary," Lufken said. "But I am even more thrilled for all of you. Because you are winners, each and every person in this room. That's because, as part of your employee benefits package, you will receive, *free of charge*, a bundle of Dynamica premium chipfeed subscriptions. This includes some of our biggest sellers: Ice Cream Sundae; Cozy Afternoon Nap; Tender Family Feelings; and Summer Beach Sunshine. Now, granted, they are strictly prohibited during work hours, ha ha. I think you all understand that. Work is work, play is play."

Marc heard the grizzled, pot-bellied man next to him respond with glassy-eyed awe. "Summer Beach Sunshine. I love Summer Beach Sunshine. It feels like getting a tan. You can practically feel the sand between your toes."

Finally Lufken left the podium to thunderous applause, and the last speaker stepped up to the microphone. He introduced himself as Jon Tchon, the head of employee training and orientation.

It was time to break up into small groups and receive job assignments and start safety classes.

"Your safety and well-being are of utmost importance to us," said Tchon. "You will receive your very own hardhat, gloves, boots and protective clothing. Some of you will work the blast furnace, making iron from ore, coke and limestone. Temperatures can get as high as four thousand degrees. Others will work the basic oxygen furnace or be assigned to the rolling mill. We will be producing six thousand tons of molten iron per day, minimum, to start out."

Tchon instructed the crowd to exit through one of the four main doors around the room. At each doorway, a company representative would be handing out manila envelopes containing randomly dispersed assignments.

"If you believe you cannot fulfill your assignment because of a medical condition, we have physicians on site that can help assess the accuracy of your reservations."

The people in the crowd obediently began to break up and head to the nearest door, murmuring agreeably.

Marc knew one thing for certain: he was not accepting a job assignment. He remained standing for a moment, stomach in knots over what he had just witnessed.

He watched Merle Gregory, Gerald Lufken and Jon Tchon exchange self-congratulatory handshakes by the podium.

As Dynamica's former head of marketing, Marc could not have felt more distanced from Lufken, the grotesque new breed of Dynamica lackey. He wondered how his old friend Brandyn Handley could have possibly remained loyal to this absurdity, the concept of mandated 'Work Zones' that essentially forced people into jobs they did not choose.

It filled him with anger.

Marc saw Lufken abruptly reach into his suit jacket's inner pocket, pull out a cell phone and look at it. Lufken gestured to the other two men that he had to step aside to take a call. They nodded and moved on.

Lufken stepped through a private door at the back of the stage to get away from the noise of the crowd.

Marc followed him. As he walked, he took out his chip controller device.

Inside a small corridor, Lufken stood alone, leaning against the wall, cheerfully talking into his phone.

"Tell President Sheridan that it's going great," he said to the caller. "We've got full engagement and compliance."

Then Lufken sensed someone had joined him in the small space. He turned his head to glance at Marc for a split second before an immediate curtain of drowsiness overtook him.

Eyelids heavy, then shut, Lufken gently lowered his body to the floor. He curled up and went to sleep in the fetal position.

Marc had sent him one of the chip signals that had just been touted as an employee benefit: Cozy Afternoon Nap.

As Lufken slept, Marc took away his phone and hung up the call. He quickly advanced down the corridor to where it split into three directions and picked one. After hurrying through a maze of passageways, isolating himself from the bustling commotion elsewhere in the building, he spotted a Men's Room and slipped inside.

It was empty.

Marc entered a stall, latched himself inside, and sat on the closed toilet lid.

Using Lufken's phone, he called Lufken's boss, a name listed prominently in the Recent Calls log.

"Brandyn Handley speaking," answered a familiar voice.

"You piece of shit."

"Gerald?"

"No, this is not Gerald. This is a name from your past. A former friend. Someone you once helped."

"M-Marc?"

"What the hell is going on? 'Work Zones'? Are you kidding me? This is slavery. How far back in time are you taking this country in the name of technology?"

"All right. All right. I understand. I – I don't like it either. I'm just – it's my job. I can't just run away like you. I have a family. I have children. They already threatened me once before. About the controller that got stolen. I'm lucky I'm not in jail because of you."

"Listen, at some point you have to say, 'This has gone too far.'"

"Of course it's gone too far."

"Then do something about it! You're the God damned head of operations!"

"That doesn't mean I have any power. We're the government's tool now. You think I really run the show? Not even the CEO runs the show. They run us. And, yes, some people here, leaders in high places, have fought back. And do you know where they are? Gone. Locked up. They dialed down their brains and took all the fight out of them. They're vegetables. I can't take that risk. Wait— Where did you say you are?"

"Gary, Indiana. The steel mill."

"Jesus."

"Exactly. I got scooped up in one of your Work Zones. It appears I'm the only person bothered by it. Your chip operation is very effective at mind control."

"I can't – I can't be talking with you."

"Fuck you."

Marc hung up the phone. He stood on the floor, opened the toilet lid and dropped the phone into the bowl. He flushed.

Then he contemplated his next move. Lufken would be waking up from his nap soon, without his phone.

But leaving now would be obvious – a lone figure sprinting to his car, ditching work. He needed to wait for the current shift to end, so he could lose himself in the mobs of people departing at the same time.

The toilet stall wasn't a great hiding place. Marc looked around and then glanced up – at the ceiling tiles.

Why not?

He stepped on top of the toilet tank, reached up and shifted one of the squares to create an opening. He climbed the stall wall and entered the ceiling. Inside the ceiling, in the dark, he moved carefully on the cross beams, minimizing his weight on the tiles themselves. He closed the opening he had made.

Then he waited.

Over the next several hours, he had to endure occasional visitors to the bathroom and the odors they produced.

Finally, at five o'clock sharp, he heard a loud factory whistle.

"The slaves have been freed," he muttered to himself.

He dropped out of the ceiling, stepping back onto the toilet tank. He hurried over to a clouded glass window. He opened it as far as it would go and squeezed outside, falling to the dirt.

Marc joined a large throng of tired but complacent workers returning to their cars in the massive parking lot.

A fresh traffic jam ensued. A new shift arrived to the steel mill as the nine-to-five crews departed. Marc patiently endured the horrible traffic, inching closer to the highway. The sun set in front of him, creating a hazy orange glow in the murky, polluted air.

Finally, he reached the highway entrance ramp. Marc aimed his car for Minnesota. With each mile he advanced, the highway opened up a little more. Before long, he was speeding comfortably at seventy miles per hour.

He was glad he escaped but could not stop thinking about the rest of the workers, who would report back to work the next morning, already locked into a routine.

★ ★ ★

Gerald Lufken sat in a small room of monitors with Merle Gregory, CEO of the Gary steel mill; Jon Tchon, head of employee training; Craig Hess, the steel mill's head of security; and James Summaria, director of citizen tracking and compliance for the state of Indiana. Summaria was in close contact with his superiors in Washington, trading messages.

For the seventh time, they watched the security camera footage that showed a lone individual breaking from the rest of the employee orientation group, following Lufken out of the room through a doorway at the back of the stage.

"Somehow that son of a bitch knocked me out. I'm not sure how he did it – I don't have a bump, a bruise, nothing." Lufken stared hard into the black and white footage on the monitor. "The bastard took my phone."

"We'll take care of it," said Gregory. "It happened at our facility, and I take full responsibility."

"I don't think this is a random robbery for your phone," Summaria said. "There's something else going on here. We think someone may have hacked into your chip signal."

"But why? Who?"

"I sent this footage to agency headquarters. It looks like it could be the same guy who was hacking into chipfeeds in New York City, about a dozen cases over the past two years."

"Some random hacker?" Lufken asked.

"No," said Summaria. "We believe it could be someone who was formerly employed at your company."

"Dynamica?"

"Do you know the name Marc Tefteller?"

Lufken thought for a moment. "The marketing guy?"

"He's been on the government watch list ever since he abruptly left the company two years ago, after removing his chip. We believe he might have certain tools at his disposal."

"I barely got a chance to look at him...but if you can show me a picture."

Summaria quickly called up a headshot of Marc Tefteller on his tablet and showed it to Lufken.

"The guy I saw, his hair was a lot longer. But yeah, could've been him. What the hell is he doing here? Spying?"

"We've been after him for quite some time," Summaria said. "Now we're going to elevate the search. Clearly he's up to something. We'll find him. And when we do, we'll put him down."

CHAPTER TWENTY-FIVE

Marc stared into the mundane window display of Simon Hardware in Duluth, Minnesota, finding it hard to believe he was standing at the gateway to freedom. Perhaps the sheer ordinariness of the setting accounted for its suitability. He faced stacks of paint cans; bags of fertilizer and birdseed; an array of ladders, shovels and rakes; durable tools; and special sales on lightbulbs, grills and propane tanks. A handcrafted sign also promised the presence of a locksmith. However, there was no banner promoting human smuggling across the border.

Marc took one last look around, continuously paranoid of being watched, especially after his adventure in Gary. He saw a perfectly normal downtown strip of commerce, with its mixture of shuttered and surviving storefronts and a few unassuming northerners strolling in no particular hurry on the sidewalk.

His heart pounded from the knowledge of a big secret. He took a deep breath and opened the door. It jingled.

Marc pretended to browse the tool section for a bit. Then he approached the tall man at the cash register, maybe thirty years old with a full head of dark hair, a minor mustache and dark, attentive eyes.

"Hello," Marc said.

"Hello," said the clerk.

"I'm looking for a drill bit."

The clerk nodded, leaning forward to hear more.

"Um…it's a specific drill bit. I have the code. Um…6XB427."

The clerk stared at Marc. "Would you mind repeating that?"

Marc did.

"Okay. That's a special part. I need to take you to our staff expert."

"Sure."

The clerk glanced up into a large circular mirror that reflected the activity in the aisles. He saw no other customers and said, "Follow me."

The clerk led Marc past a selection of lawnmowers and snow blowers to a private door in the back, marked *Employees Only*.

The clerk knocked four times in a specific rhythm.

After a moment, the door opened halfway.

"In you go," said the clerk.

Marc advanced into a back room crowded with supply shelves and a long counter for small repairs. A man and a woman faced him. The man had a gray and black beard and black-rimmed glasses; the woman had curly, flowing blonde hair and wire-rimmed glasses. She spoke first: "Stand right where you are."

Marc stood very still, and she closed the door behind him. The bearded man approached with a hand-held scanning device similar in size to a metal detector security wand, but definitely with a different intent.

The bearded man brought it to the back of Marc's neck. The device remained silent.

"If you had the chip, it would have started beeping," the man explained, dropping his arm. "Welcome to our office. My name is Thomas. This is Heidi."

"Welcome," Heidi said.

"Thanks," said Marc.

They showed him to a wooden stool, and Marc sat down. Thomas and Heidi settled in folding chairs on either side of him.

"We start the process with an interview," Thomas said. "What brought you here. How you've managed to avoid the chip this long. Your intentions. Your character."

"Whatever you want to know," Marc said. "And let me tell you one thing upfront, because I know it will cause some concern. I don't want you to get the wrong idea. I am one hundred percent independent and removed from my professional past."

Thomas and Heidi listened carefully as Marc told them about his prior life as head of marketing for Dynamica.

He could see them tense up at first and then gradually relax as he talked through his story: leaving the company, escaping from government agents, staying off the radar under a false identity.

He chose not to tell them that he possessed a special device that could hack into the chips of other people. That was a power he possessed that no one else needed to know about, aside from Brandyn Handley, the man who gave it to him.

Once Marc had completed his life narrative and secured the confidence of his hosts, they filled him in on their mission and the process.

Thomas stated, "We believe strongly in freedom from the chip, the right to remain independent without surrendering access to our thoughts and feelings. We don't care if it's big government or big business, we stand firm against the use of technology to influence our minds, interfere with our physical sensations and re-interpret our experiences. Enforcement of the chip is the ultimate violation of human rights. We believe in the individual, not a manufactured collective mindset."

Heidi said, "This coalition is dedicated to helping as many people as possible escape from this corrupt environment to lead lives of their own choosing. We've been doing this for six months now. Seventy people a day. That's more than twelve thousand prisoners freed. They've escaped prosecution and can now live a natural, organic life without fear. We're part of a much bigger team that helps move refugees through various checkpoints. There are seven interview locations like this in northern Minnesota. After the interview, subjects stay in one of five holding stations, where they're eventually tapped in small groups to go to Ely and enter the Boundary Waters by canoe. We have a special route to Canada – not an easy one. There's a lot of portaging between bodies of water. It takes you through forests and islands where you won't be detected. We travel only at night. You'll need to paddle and carry your belongings."

"There's a heavy restriction on the volume of what you can bring," Thomas said. "Everyone brings too much. You just need a few days worth of clothing, some food and water, then a couple of valuables or mementos – like jewelry or a photo album."

"That's no problem," said Marc. He was already traveling light. His only valuable was the controlling device. And his stash of cash.

"Good," Thomas said. "Now we will give you directions to your holding station. It's about thirty minutes from here. It's a mattress store."

Marc's eyebrows lifted. "A mattress store?"

"It's closed down. It's a good space. You'll see."

Marc had to ask, "What's – what's the cost for all this? How much do you want?"

"We don't take money," Heidi said.

"We do this – everyone in this network runs this escape route – because we believe in it, deeply," said Thomas. "If you make it safe to the other side, that's our reward. It's our purpose and our passion."

"Wow," said Marc quietly. "I didn't know people like you still existed."
"It's easy," Thomas said. "We don't have the chip to tell us otherwise."

★ ★ ★

Later that day, Marc arrived with a bag of personal belongings to the boarded-up entrance of SLUMBE MATTRESSES. The first 'R' had fallen off the sign. The windows were covered with 'Lost Our Lease' posters. Marc could not see in. He simply stood in the designated spot at the designated time and waited.

Finally a heavyset, rugged man with a curly beard and wool hat approached on the sidewalk. He stopped and stared at Marc. Then he stared at a photo on his cell phone – a profile picture taken by Thomas and Heidi at the hardware store.

"You're Marc?" asked the big man.

"Yes, that's me."

"I'm Willard. Come with me. We're going to enter from the back."

Marc followed Willard to the gravel alley behind the store. They entered a service entrance and walked into a rear storage room.

Willard closed the door behind them and turned to Marc. "Give me your key."

"Excuse me?"

"Car key. You're done with the car. We'll dispose of it so no one can trace you here."

Marc nodded, nervous to surrender his transportation but trusting in the process. He handed over his car key.

Marc and Willard advanced to the main showroom: a dimly lit sprawl of dozens of bare-mattress beds. Most were filled with people sitting or sleeping.

"Welcome to your hotel room," Willard said with a stab of sarcasm. He brought Marc to an empty bed with a sticker on the frame to identify it: number 22. "Settle in, get a good day's sleep. I can't give you an exact time of when you'll be tapped, but we take people in shifts after nightfall, every hour. Be ready to go at a moment's notice."

Marc nodded and placed his small carrying bag of cash and clothes on the bed. The room did not smell good – it was obvious there was no shower on the premises. The other refugees looked up at him for a moment or two, revealing tired and fearful faces, and then went back to their reading or dozing.

"No going online," Willard said. "No phone calls. No doing anything stupid. If you get bored, in the corner over there, we have a television. We keep it on a news channel."

"All right."

"We have classes, several times a day, to go through the canoe trip logistics. Basics, orientation. We'll have maps and instructions on who you will meet at the other end. Oh – and if there's a raid, it's every man for himself." He glanced around the room at the diversity of occupants and corrected himself. "I'm sorry – every man, woman and child."

Willard left, and Marc sat on the edge of his designated bed. He was too wired to sleep but well aware he needed rest, especially if he was going to be paddling a canoe for miles and miles in the middle of the night.

He noticed a young couple entangled on the bed next to him. They shared a Queen mattress, lying down together but very much awake. They studied him with alert eyes.

"Hi," Marc said with a short wave.

"Hey," said the male.

"How's your mattress?" the female asked.

"Firm," Marc said.

"We've got memory foam," said the female with flat enthusiasm.

Marc smiled. Then he introduced himself to the couple, "I'm Marc."

"Hi, Marc, I'm Aaron."

The female introduced herself without rising. "I'm Clarissa."

"Hi, Aaron. Hi, Clarissa. So how far did you travel?"

"We're from L.A.," said Aaron. "It's been a long, strange journey."

"I'm from New York," Marc said. "Same."

"I'm Max!" said a grizzled voice from a nearby mattress.

Marc turned to look at him. A dirty, weathered old man with heavy wrinkles sat up. "I'm with them," he said, jabbing a thumb toward Aaron and Clarissa.

"Yeah, he's our stray dog," Clarissa murmured, face still half-pressed into the mattress.

"Where'd you say you were from? New York?" Max asked.

"That's right," said Marc.

"I was in New York once, back in the seventies."

Marc wanted to say, "Not much has changed," but refrained.

"Did you hear about the bombing of the Santa Barbara Library?" Max asked.

Marc said, "Sure, the thing that sparked all those protests? It went viral all over the place."

"We were there!" Max said proudly.

Now Aaron sat up on his bed, rubbing his face. "Yes. Yes, we were. It was one of fifty times we were nearly killed."

Marc nodded in sympathy. "Yeah, well, did you hear about these new Work Zones where they're using the chip to send people into factories as slave labor? I almost got stuck working in a steel mill that's been brought back from the dead. They swept me in for new employee orientation without asking."

"No shit," said Clarissa.

Over the next two hours, Marc and his three new acquaintances shared their stories.

Aaron and Clarissa spoke of their journey from California to Minnesota, stopping at various sanctuaries along the way, finding some of them open and others emptied out and destroyed after being raided. They described several close calls with regulation police, including an episode where they lost a member of their group. Max talked about his girlfriend, Gertrude, who was captured in Idaho and injected with the chip.

"It was a big shootout," said Max. "I got several of them. And then – then I had to shoot her. They stuck her with the chip. They would have gotten her to turn on us. She had all the information about the escape route. I had to do it." Max's eyes welled with tears as he told the story. "She always told me, 'If they catch me, put me down. I don't want the chip. I don't want to live like that.' So I did what she wanted…but it still hurts. Damn, it hurts something awful."

Marc tried to console him. Aaron and Clarissa said nothing; they were clearly familiar with his grief and simply frowned in silence.

"You need a gun?" Max asked Marc, brightening. "We got guns."

"No, but thanks. I have something better."

Max looked at him quizzically, but Marc declined to elaborate. The controller device remained in his pocket, ready for quick action if needed.

* * *

Marc, Aaron, Clarissa and Max joined several others in a far corner of the mattress store, seated along the edges of a King bed, watching the news on a loosely mounted flat-screen television.

President Sheridan was speaking to his chip-captive audience, seated in his wheelchair in the Oval Office.

"The Work Zone initiative is a big success," he declared. "We will open twelve more Work Zones in the next few weeks, revitalizing the U.S. economy and ending the long slump in manufacturing. America's factories will struggle no more!"

Marc thought about the Gary steel mill pulling in thousands of obedient workers each day, like a giant magnet. The country had gone from government-sponsored laziness to forced productivity, a societal whiplash.

"I can't believe I trusted this turkey, that he would abolish the chip," Marc said.

"Me too," said Aaron. "I supported him. I thought he would turn things around for the better. But he's using the chip to push his own agenda, and it's getting crazier every day."

"He's just picking up where others have left off. It's the same old story, using technology to spread influence. But now it's way more dangerous. People barely know they're being manipulated."

Clarissa said, "Why did we think he would be any better? Once they seize power, it messes with their minds."

After touting the success of his Work Zones initiative, President Sheridan delved into his next priority: ramping up America's military.

"Through the power of the chip, I have delivered on every one of my promises, and this one will be no different," he said. "I am tripling the size of our military forces. I can stand here now before you to guarantee that every one of our new and veteran soldiers will be one hundred percent committed and fearless. With the ability to unite behind a single, collective mindset, we will be unbeatable. We will fight to the death in every battle. We will confront our enemies aggressively. As a united front, we will not stand by silently as our enemies take advantage of a history of softness and tolerance.

"The first threat we will abolish is the new satellite created in partnership between Russia, China and North Korea. We have all heard the denials, that there is no partnership, that the satellite is used for one country's domestic security, not international spying. That is a lie. I am absolutely positive the purpose of this satellite is to hack into our systems and hijack our chip technology to steal control of American minds. Make no mistake, this is the biggest threat our country has ever faced. This evil alliance has three days to dismantle the satellite, or we will destroy it. We will blast it out of the sky. We are locked and loaded, with our military leaders on full alert. We have the missiles prepared, and we have complete alignment in the Pentagon, in Congress, and with the American people. We are a true *United* States of America. So this is my final warning. All it takes is the press of a button. If the satellite does not come down, we will take it down. We will go to war. That is my promise. And I have yet to break a promise."

As Marc watched President Sheridan deliver his remarks, he felt nauseous.

The news subsequently reported on the response from the countries identified in the president's accusations. All three denied any alliance or intention to hack into the U.S. chip signals to influence the American people. All three also promised dire consequences if the satellite was destroyed, issuing a joint statement: "You will experience a war to end all wars."

"Fabulous," muttered Clarissa. "World War III is just around the corner."

"Probably a good time to leave the country, before we all get nuked," Aaron said.

"How did things get out of control so fast?" Marc asked. The whole scenario made him dizzy. Sadly, he knew the answer. He had witnessed firsthand the fast rise of Dynamica. He had contributed to its dominant presence. He had successfully promoted its product across the country until it became the most popular brand in American history. He had deployed maximum-strength advertising, marketing and public relations to spread the technology like a blanket across society until it became deeply embedded in the daily lifestyle.

Marc felt a lump in his throat. *I did this.*

No one goes to work thinking that what they do might one day create a worldwide crisis and kill innocent lives. We just do our jobs.

At that moment, Willard stepped over to the group and tapped a young African-American couple for the next ride to the Boundary Waters.

"Time to go," he said simply.

The young couple, looking very fatigued and anxious, broke out into excited tears. They quickly began to gather their belongings.

Aaron watched them go, and Clarissa took his hand in a rare display of affection. "Don't worry. Our turn is coming."

CHAPTER TWENTY-SIX

In the middle of the night, Marc was awoken by a big hand shaking his shoulder.

"It's time."

He immediately sat up, surging to full alert. His heart pounded. He was going to escape. It was real now.

Willard also gathered Aaron, Clarissa, Max, and four others: a pair of middle-aged women and a soft-spoken father with his young teenage son.

They collected their things and slipped out of the rear entrance of the mattress store, moving quickly and silently.

It was cool and very dark outside; there was no light in the back alley. A large SUV waited. It took time to squeeze everybody in: two in the front seat with the driver, three in the second row, and three in the third row. Modest-sized bags of personal belongings were placed in laps.

"It's a ninety-minute drive to Ely," announced the driver. "Sit tight, take a nap, don't turn on your phones."

He advanced to the main road.

The passengers were too excited to sleep. They engaged in quiet conversations. There was continued fear over the war that would break out if President Sheridan fulfilled his promise to destroy the international satellite. Marc talked for a while with the female couple, Emma and Nico, and they explained they were fleeing the country because they were gay, and President Sheridan had made allusions to using the chipfeed signals to 'reshape' minds that displayed 'unnatural tendencies', singling out homosexuality more than once.

"Eighty years ago, people in the gay community were subject to electroshock therapy to 'fix' their brains," Emma said, holding her partner's hand. "It was barbaric, and all these years later, we haven't made any progress. People who don't understand still want to 'fix' our brains."

Aaron and Clarissa sat up front with the driver, studying the road and the very sparse traffic. In the row behind Marc, the gentle father spoke in reassuring tones to his son, trying to calm his nervous fidgeting. Only Max slept – nothing fazed him anymore. He snored.

Eventually they reached a very dark, abandoned Boy Scouts camp. Dozens of small cabins populated the grounds. The main lodge sat on the bank of a broad river. The river identified itself through silvery streaks created by the moon's reflection. The walking paths had long ago succumbed to wild grasses and natural debris. The entire Boy Scouts organization had collapsed once Dynamica offered a Boy Scout Experience chipfeed. It was just another 'development' to create a sinking feeling in Marc's gut.

Four rugged-looking men, the appointed guides, greeted the arrivals as they approached the river. A husky northerner named Eric explained that each guide would take two passengers in a canoe. "Everyone paddles," said a guide named Vance in a deep voice. "The trip will take two to three hours, including portaging. We will leave you on the other side and bring back the canoes for the next group."

As they stepped along the riverbank together, Aaron noticed shapes on the water's surface coming toward them from the distance.

"Don't worry," Eric said. "That's some of our men returning."

Four large canoes soon came into view, each occupied by a lone paddler, having dropped off a group of refugees.

"We each do one shift a day," Vance said. "Technically, at night. We sleep during the day."

The arriving canoes were secured to posts on a long dock. The tired incoming crew passed along their well wishes to the outgoing crew and their passengers, and then headed off for some rest in the scout cabins.

The four guides for the new shift quickly assessed the carry-on luggage. They made two people – Emma and the father of the teenage boy – reduce their loads. Both did so without argument.

Max had a small, heavy backpack. "What do you have in there?" Vance asked him.

"Guns," said Max.

"All right."

Eric began to assign the group to canoes: Aaron and Clarissa together, the father and his son together, Emma and Nico together, and Marc and Max together.

Max beamed at Marc. "Howdy, partner. I got your back if you got mine."

"Of course," Marc said.

Everyone slipped into green-and-gray lifejackets. On the hill above the Boy Scout lodge building, Marc could see the SUV departing to return to the mattress store, headlights probing a gentle fog.

The four guides – Vance, Eric, Leon and Gio – each commanded an eighteen-foot, three-man canoe. They assisted their passengers on board, handing out long, wooden paddles.

"I hope everyone remembers their canoeing lessons," Eric said. "Depending on which way the wind blows, it could get rough."

Before long, the canoes were untied from the dock and pushed off to begin the long trek to freedom. The wind picked up, chilling the bones of the eight refugees, who fought to stay warm through vigorous paddling.

The moon and the stars provided the only light.

No one spoke, except to pass along directions when the route veered from a straight line. The primary sound was paddles dipping into the water in steady rhythms.

The canoeing was tough, but the portaging was even tougher, hauling the canoes across dark, bumpy terrain and trying not to sprain an ankle. Marc cursed himself for being out of shape. Aaron and Clarissa were doing fine, more athletic than the others. The guides gave extra assistance to Max, who hobbled on a bad leg.

Marc felt immersed in a surreal dream and recognized the irony because this was probably the most 'real' environment he had ever encountered. If he could forget his physical discomfort and mental fears, he could fully appreciate the mesmerizing beauty of his natural surroundings and absorb the organic sounds and sensations. The path unwound through dense woods, dirty and timeless, stubbornly stuck in an alternate universe that knew nothing about computer chips, satellite signals and virtual reality.

Marc felt a chilled perspiration coat his body and a healthy aching reach across his bones and muscles. He actively listened to the soundtrack of buzzing insects, fluttering birds and scampering creatures rustling in the brush. On several occasions, the group spotted deer, along with beavers and otters. Confronting a black bear was not out of the question.

Marc experienced a Zen-like spiritual feeling. An environment like this could never truly be recreated for stay-at-home imagination prompts. To be fully appreciated, it needed to be honestly experienced. It was a true nirvana effect.

No one in the group complained about the cuts, bruises, bug bites or exhaustion. They endured, and they felt better for it.

At the other side of the small forest, they returned to a body of water.

Soon they were back in their canoes, paddling together in close proximity across another wide, shimmering lake.

Conversation was sparse. Eric announced they were reaching the halfway point. Then the young teenage boy mentioned he heard thunder.

"Shouldn't be any rain," said Eric. "Skies are clear."

But then the others heard it.

As the rumbling grew louder, Eric said, "Shit." Then, "Stop paddling." In the ensuing stillness, they listened to the audible disturbance with rising dread. The thunder no longer sounded like thunder.

"What is it?"

"Is it—?"

"Sounds like—"

"Helicopters."

The reality of the source struck everyone simultaneously. A fierce pounding filled the sky. The noise came from helicopter blades, hammering a steady rhythm, rapidly growing closer.

Stuck in the middle of the lake, everyone in the four canoes froze in collective terror, with hands on paddles, eyes looking skyward.

THWAP-THWAP-THWAP-THWAP!

"No fucking way," Clarissa said.

"Son of a bitch," said Max.

With a monstrous roar, three attack helicopters charged into view. They arrived in a line formation, then split apart to create a hovering triangle directly above their targets. Bright, piercing spotlights beamed down on the canoes and their occupants, revealing them in a bathing illumination of white. It was so blinding that Marc had to shut his eyes.

A booming voice shouted down from a loudspeaker. "STAY WHERE YOU ARE. YOU ARE UNDER ARREST."

"Like hell!" said Max, and he abruptly sprung up in the center of the canoe, causing it to rock violently.

"Hey!" Marc shouted, grabbing the rim of the canoe, fearing they would capsize.

Max began firing bullets into the sky.

The loud *cracks* echoed across the lake. They were answered immediately by a rapid return of staccato shots, sounding like the bang of fireworks.

The gunfire cut up Max with a line of bullets across his torso, puncturing his life vest. He fell overboard.

"Holy shit!" Marc said. He dropped his paddle and scrambled for his controller device.

From one of the other canoes, Clarissa lifted a gun and began firing at the nearest helicopter. It fired back, creating bursts of water between the canoes. The canoe with the father and son was hit, sprouting a fast leak. The son cried out for help.

Marc fumbled with the controlling device. He called up the nearest active chips and immediately sent them into sleep mode.

The helicopter hovering directly above the canoes stopped firing. It wobbled awkwardly. Then it slid through the sky in a steady sideways descent across the lake and toward the forest.

Marc braced himself, knowing what was about to happen.

The helicopter crashed into the trees. It exploded into a massive red fireball that illuminated the lake in a wide-reaching flash of light.

The explosion's powerful force created instant, turbulent waves that rocked the remaining three canoes. The fourth canoe had sunk from the surface, leaving its occupants floating helplessly in the middle of the lake.

With one helicopter destroyed, the other two swarmed in with extra aggressiveness, firing a rapid spray of bullets downward.

One of the bullets struck Emma in the neck, and Nico screamed in anguish.

"Everybody – out of the canoes!" Eric shouted, balanced in a standing position at the back of Marc's canoe. "Go for shore – get under cover – go as far and deep as you can—"

Then his shouting cut off with a grunt as bullets tore into him from his head to his legs. His body jerked involuntarily before dropping with a thump inside the canoe.

Marc scrambled to call up more chips on his controller device, but the canoe was rocking wildly, disrupting his ability to tap out commands. More bullets struck his canoe and then it began sinking.

"Oh God, no, no, *no!*" he said, fumbling with the controller, desperately trying to bring down another helicopter.

Then the controller device slipped out of his hands and fell overboard. It sank into the inky, black waters.

"*Fuck!*" he screamed. His voice echoed across the lake and into the shadows of the surrounding forests.

In the distance, small pairs of lights appeared on the water's surface. They rapidly grew closer, accompanied by a layered roar. After a moment, Marc recognized the sound: motorboat engines.

Aaron and Clarissa jumped overboard. They began swimming toward the shore, escaping the direct beam of the helicopter spotlights.

Marc decided to take their lead. He jumped out of his sinking canoe, splashing into the cold, rough waters. The life vest kept him afloat, and he immediately began swimming for land.

As he swam, he looked back for a moment and witnessed something he did not want to see: Nico remaining in her canoe, cradling her dead lover. She sobbed, and Marc wanted to yell out for her to swim to shore, but then it was too late.

The canoe was hit with a missile and exploded to pieces in a booming flash of red and orange, kicking up a huge spray of water.

Marc frantically thrashed through the waters, away from the violence. He passed a lifeless body in a life vest, bobbing in the waves, but couldn't identify who it was. The patrol boats zoomed toward the sinking and broken canoes. Marc couldn't tell how many people were dead and how many had survived.

As Marc got closer to the shore, he entered a thickening haze of black smoke coming from the burning helicopter. It had landed about a half mile inland, igniting the trees to start a full-fledged forest fire.

Out of the frying pan into the fire, he thought, but he wasn't laughing.

The smoke grew worse, and by the time he crawled onto the shore, he was coughing and clutching at the ground as his chest heaved. He staggered to his feet and ripped off the wet, heavy life jacket. He began to move down the shoreline, away from the fire.

As he stepped quickly in the dark, stumbling over terrain he could barely see, he looked back for a moment and saw several others reaching the shore in their life jackets – more survivors. They were vague shadows, but he thought he saw Aaron, Clarissa and possibly the young teenage boy.

He was relieved for them, then alarmed. A helicopter spotlight rediscovered the trio, beaming a wide net of piercing white light to reveal their presence once again.

A voice on a loudspeaker announced their location: "ON THE SHORELINE. THREE FUGITIVES. ON LAND. THREE FUGITIVES."

The patrol boats in the distance were getting closer, advancing at breakneck speed. Marc could see the outlines of soldiers with guns standing in the backs of the boats. He shuddered and fought his way forward.

The wind shifted and a thickening haze of smoke rolled his way. He began coughing again. His lungs hurt, every muscle in his body hurt.

He didn't know where he was running to. He didn't know who from his group would survive, if any of them. He was no longer armed with the one thing that protected him. And his bag of money was gone.

The pounding of helicopter blades continued relentlessly, like a jackhammer. As Marc ran with wet shoes over the bumpy ground, his foot struck a thick root, and he fell. He hit the ground hard, striking his head on the side of a big rock. He saw a flash of stars. He rolled over on his back in pain and felt a wet trickle of blood move from his hair to his cheek.

Marc briefly slipped out of consciousness.

He awoke to a firm command.

"Don't move."

He opened his eyes. He could see someone standing over him in the dark, outlined in the lingering smoke and swaths of helicopter searchlights. He could not see the person's features. He could only see a long gun – pointed at his face.

"You move, I shoot."

"I won't move."

"You're under arrest."

"I figured."

"I am a regulation officer with the authority to kill you on the spot."

"Great, then just do it," mumbled Marc. "Why talk about it?"

"Because killing you lets you off the hook too easily."

Marc didn't like the sound of that. "Great."

"Turn around."

"What?"

"On your stomach."

"Stomach?"

"Do it."

Marc twisted his torso until he was on his stomach, facing the dirt. His head throbbed from where it had struck the rock.

"Okay, now what?" Marc murmured into the ground.

"This," said the regulation officer. He pressed something to the back of Marc's neck.

Marc knew exactly what would happen next. It was the inevitability he had resisted for so long.

With a hard, sudden jolt, Marc received the chip.

CHAPTER TWENTY-SEVEN

"If our demands are not met, we go to war in two days," President Dale Sheridan said.

Brandyn Handley, eyes glued to the television, let out a small gasp. He stroked his beard.

In another room, his two boys were playing – tussling loudly – with their usual back-and-forth bickering over who got to use the children's pod. In the kitchen, his wife, Letty, was preparing dinner for Real Meal Monday. The kids would complain – they loved their candy-flavored Body Fuel bars.

The president's declaration was a double down on the previous day's promise to blow up an international satellite he was convinced posed a threat to American security.

"Make no doubt about it, the purpose of this satellite is to interfere with signals transmitted to American citizens," he said. "If we allow it to continue, we jeopardize our freedom of thought. We open the door to a Trojan horse of devilry to enter our consciousness."

World leaders from Russia, China and North Korea vehemently denied Sheridan's allegations. They dismissed it as a paranoid man's conspiracy theory. Russia's president explained that the satellite was solely intended to serve his own country's communications and security infrastructure. He vowed the satellite would remain operational. That caused President Sheridan to reiterate his commitment to blow it up.

The response to Sheridan was equally strong. "If the satellite is attacked in any way, we will take it as a declaration of war," said the Russian president, with the backing of international allies.

"Dinner in five minutes," Letty announced from the kitchen.

Brandyn Handley did not feel hungry. His stomach had become a tight rubber ball.

And his worries were only beginning.

His cell phone rang.

He slid it out of his shirt's breast pocket and looked at the caller ID.

It was Dynamica CEO Jeff Reese.

Brandyn assumed Reese was calling to discuss the rapid escalation of tensions on the world stage related to Dynamica's chip technology.

But it was something else.

"He's been captured," Reese said.

"Who's been captured?"

"Tefteller! Our rogue CMO. They finally nailed him!"

Brandyn felt a wave of shock. He immediately thought back to his brief phone conversation with Marc just a few days ago. He had told no one about it. If there was any evidence that connected the two of them recently, Brandyn knew he would be doomed.

"He's been on the run for what, nearly two years now," Reese said. "They caught the son of a bitch trying to cross the border into Canada. He still had our jamming device. He crashed a helicopter with it, he killed people. They retrieved it in some lake."

"Oh my God," was all Brandyn could say.

"I've got our PR team on it. If this gets out, it's bad for the brand."

"Where…where is he?"

"He's chipped, he's in custody. That's where I'm headed now. I'm in my car. He's being held in a federal building in lower Manhattan for questioning. What he did is disastrous. It's treason."

"You're going to see him?"

"There's a group of us going, to help with the investigation." Reese rattled off names from the Office of Citizenship and Compliance, as well as representatives from Dynamica's security team.

"You're welcome to join us, it's going to be a real party," Reese said with sarcasm.

"Yes. I want to join you. I do."

"Seriously?"

"I owe it to the company. It happened under my watch, too."

"It's probably the last time any of us will see him. I'm pretty sure he's headed to termination."

Brandyn shut his eyes tight at the impact of the word.

'Termination' was the term used for modern-day executions. Criminals on death row were swiftly put down through a quick and painless signal sent to their chip that essentially flicked off their existence like a light switch.

Brandyn almost choked on his words as he tried to sound unmoved. "Yes – yes – he's probably headed to termination for sure."

His wife called out: "Dinner, Brandyn. Dinner, boys."

Brandyn touched the back of his neck and resisted the urge to send himself artificial happy thoughts to wipe away his crushing dread.

* * *

Brandyn met with Reese, U.S. Compliance Regulation officials and the head of Dynamica's security division in the lobby of the Vanover Federal Building. They were joined by Wilbur Kepling, the head of the U.S. Department of Citizen Affairs.

There was a general familiarity across the group, but Reese made quick introductions to reinforce the roles across his team. When he came to Brandyn, he said, "Brandyn is our head of operations. He worked closely with Tefteller back when Marc was our Chief Marketing Officer. How long did you two work together?"

"Ten years…" Brandyn said quietly. They had risen through the ranks together.

"Let's move to a conference room, we'll give everybody the full debrief," said Kepling.

In a windowless room upstairs, seated around a long table, Kepling delivered the details. Brandyn listened in silence.

"We raided a major smuggling ring in the Boundary Waters between northern Minnesota and Canada. They were funneling illegals out of the country. It was a highly organized operation and has been going on for at least six months. We put a spy into their pipeline and got a full look at their methods. We busted it up big time, arrested everyone in the network. We captured a group of refugees who were halfway to Canada by canoe. It turned violent. There was a battle and lives were lost on both sides. We have five people in custody, including your man, Marc Tefteller. Four of them are being held here. The fifth, a teenage boy, is in a Minnesota hospital."

Kepling distributed a document to everyone at the table. "These are the names of the individuals in this facility. They're secured in a temporary holding cell, strictly classified. With everything else that's going on in the world, we don't need the publicity right now. Two of the captives come from that Santa Barbara cult and you know what a political hornet's nest that is. We also have one of the guides who were helping to transport the illegals. And, of course, Tefteller. Their names are on this sheet, along with their chip codes. They have all been freshly chipped. The chips cannot be removed. We are looking at likely termination for the four of them. The teenage boy will receive a prison sentence."

Brandyn stared down at the sheet of paper. His eyes scanned the list of service codes assigned to the prisoners. The blocks of numbers dehumanized them. Brandyn read the identities attached to the codes. Seeing their full names made them and their fate all the more real and heart-wrenching.

Marc Douglas Tefteller.

Aaron Jay Holt.

Clarissa Margaret Harper.

Vance Shane Wyatt.

"Our top priority right now, the reason we are gathered, is to interview your man, Mr. Tefteller," said Kepling, looking directly at Jeff Reese. "He had a device in his possession that threatened national security. It was used to kill American officials, beginning with the murder of one of our compliance men at his apartment. He used the device to send the man over the rail of his balcony to his death. I personally delivered the news to his widow, and it's a murder that still affects me and my team to this day. It was an act of terrorism. Who knows how many other people he's harmed between that killing and the two men he killed when he brought down that helicopter. We know he gets around. Earlier this week, he was discovered spying at one of our new Work Zones, a steel plant in Gary, Indiana. We believe he was planning an act of sabotage. He's a dangerous man, and obviously he had some help. How did he obtain the jamming device? Who gave it to him?"

Brandyn felt woozy. He had an urge to flee the room. But he kept his exterior façade as cool as possible.

"I believe we'll get some of our answers today," Reese said. "Are we ready to meet with him?"

Heads nodded around the table, including Brandyn, who was merely mimicking the mood of the others, playing along, being the good corporate stooge, a role he performed so well.

Kepling summoned an armed guard. The guard led the group across a hall, down some stairs and into a well-secured area of holding stations for special government prisoners.

They gathered in a room divided in half by a sheet of bulletproof glass. Kepling, Reese, Brandyn and the others took their seats, facing the glass partition. A moment later, a door opened on the opposite side of the room. Marc Tefteller entered in an orange prisoner jumpsuit, hands cuffed in front of him. A bulky guard led him to a stool, facing the group. He was positioned in front of a small, round opening in the glass that allowed for the exchange of audible conversation.

Brandyn studied Marc as he sat down. Marc's eyes looked weary, his expression was a blank, his face was full of dirt and stubble, and his hair was long and disheveled.

Marc lifted his head to scan the people presented before him. He had little reaction until he saw Brandyn.

Then his eyes widened and his body stiffened, as if to say *What the hell are you doing here?*

Brandyn attempted to remain nonchalant.

"Hello, traitor," said Wilbur Kepling.

Marc's eyes moved to Kepling. The two men had met briefly when the government partnership was first communicated to Dynamica's senior leadership team.

Marc said nothing.

"We will discuss your crimes against your country momentarily," Kepling said. "But right now, we've brought representatives from your former company who would like to ask you about an act of theft you committed against them. To be specific, they want to know how you got hold of a top-secret jamming device, an extra one that was not logged in any company records. It's been a source of great concern for Homeland Security. The tool is very powerful, as you're well aware. It can be used to confuse, harm and kill people. Your acquisition of this device must have required some inside assistance. An ally inside Dynamica. Someone, perhaps, who is still at the company and continues to pose a threat. So, without any further ado, Mr. Tefteller, we are here to ask a simple question, and we expect a direct answer. Who helped you steal the jamming device?"

Brandyn couldn't help but stare into Marc's eyes. He was terrified Marc would implicate him. In Marc's position, it was the only thing to do. Why wouldn't he?

"I don't remember," Marc said.

The group watching Marc began muttering among themselves.

For a brief moment, Marc looked at Brandyn. Brandyn felt horrified and ashamed. He did his best to remain unflustered.

"We will ask you now for a second time," Kepling said. "You will not like it if we require a third. So, tell us – be forthright, do the right thing. Who helped you get the jamming device?"

"No one," said Marc. "I just took it on my own."

"How did you even know about it?"

"Word spreads."

"The marketing department was not privy to the testing of this tool."

"I don't remember."

Kepling sighed. "All right, gentlemen. He has the chip. Let's make the most of it."

One of the regulation officials at Kepling's side pulled out his own shiny jamming device, the latest model. He poked it a few times, calling up the service code for the brand-new chip installed at the base of Marc's head.

"This will hurt," he said.

He sent a signal of piercing pain.

Marc screamed out loud in uncontrollable anguish. He nearly fell off the stool.

Brandyn felt sick to his stomach.

When the pain ceased, Marc swooned, as if recovering from a searing electrical shock.

"Now," Kepling said. "Are we going to be cooperative?"

"Don't be an idiot, Tefteller!" Reese shouted at him. "Tell us your source and get it over with. Who was your mole inside Dynamica?"

"Yeah," chimed in Brandyn, echoing his boss and faking anger. "Say the name. Spit it out!"

Marc looked straight at Brandyn, gave him a hard look and said, "No."

"Just do it," Brandyn said. He wasn't even sure if he was playing along or really did want Marc to confess. He knew the next zap was coming, and it wasn't going to be pleasant.

Marc received a bigger shock of pain and screamed so loud it seemed to vibrate the sheet of glass separating the room.

"Give us a name!" shouted Kepling, growing more impatient.

"You must tell us!" Brandyn said, trying to sound angry while fighting back tears. Now he really wanted Marc to surrender. He wanted Marc to shout out the truth: "It was Brandyn! It was the head of operations! He did it! He gave it to me in a jazz club on Fourth Avenue! He covered it up, he made sure there was no paper trail. He gave it to me to *protect* me!"

But Marc simply accepted more shocks until he was barely conscious and his body rendered unusable.

"Forget it," Kepling said. "We retrieved the device. We captured the bastard. He'll be terminated in a couple of days. Let's just leave him. Interview over!"

The interrogation group left their seats at the glass partition and slowly began moving out of the room.

Brandyn stepped back toward Marc and looked him in the eye. "You really disgust me!" he said, voice shaking.

"Let it go," said Jeff Reese, leaving.

"He needs to hear this!" Brandyn said, louder, pumping out fake rage.

Once the others had left the room, Brandyn seized the short period of privacy before the guard on Marc's side of the room came to escort him out.

"Listen, I gotta talk fast," said Brandyn in a low voice. "I promise they won't hurt you anymore. I – I'll turn off your chipfeed."

"How?" Marc said numbly, still stunned into a stupor.

"I'm the head of operations, I can do anything. Just don't let on. Pretend like they're in control at all times. Then when you see your chance, *go for it.*"

Marc nodded slowly.

Jeff Reese poked his head back into the room, and Brandyn quickly resumed his phony tirade against Marc. "So long, asshole! You'll get what you deserve. Dynamica was so good to you, and this is how you treat us. Go screw yourself, Tefteller!"

"Come on, give it a rest," Reese said. "The guy's toast."

"Yeah, you're right," said Brandyn. As he left the room with Reese, an armed guard grabbed Marc off the stool and began escorting him back to his cell, half holding him up to prevent him from collapsing on rubbery legs.

"Stupid bastard," Brandyn muttered. But he meant it for a different reason.

CHAPTER TWENTY-EIGHT

The next morning, Brandyn Handley woke up early and headed for The Brain.

The Brain was the private nickname given to the Dynamica Core Applications and Systems Center, an inconspicuous but heavily guarded flat, brick building located in Princeton, New Jersey, just a few miles from Princeton University. The signage out front didn't even identify Dynamica – it simply said 'CAS Center'. The reason for downplaying the company's presence was that it was actually a critical element of the Dynamica technology infrastructure.

This is where the chip-coding databases lived, hosted on massive servers that were meticulously backed up on other servers around the country. The best and brightest worked here in total secrecy to ensure every citizen was properly active in the system and receiving the appropriate communication signals from transmission towers that linked to the Dynamica satellite.

Brandyn parked his car in a guarded lot that required an ID badge for the highest level of corporate security. He proceeded through five more layers of clearance to get inside the building and to the core systems room, including codes, thumbprints, face scans and an old-fashioned sign-in with a team of heavily armed, no-nonsense lobby guards.

He had no problems because, despite this being an unscheduled visit, he was the head of operations. He ran the day-to-day technology needs. This was his domain.

Brandyn received warm greetings and immediate respect. He had not been inside the CAS Center for a few months, but he was accepted without a trace of curiosity or suspicion.

It helped settle his rattled nerves because he was here to do something highly illegal.

He entered a massive sea of monitors filled with rolling data on every citizen in the country. As he walked the long aisles of the sprawling systems room, the employees who recognized him stiffened a little with intimidation and made sure to demonstrate total focus and hard work, tapping diligently at their keyboards. One older fellow in the mix of hunched programmers said, "Hello, boss!"

Brandyn chuckled. "At ease, everybody."

A manager rushed up to welcome him. He had a tidy, small mustache and enlarged eyes behind big glasses. "So good to see you, sir. We weren't expecting you."

"Just a short visit, a spot check." Brandyn continued to walk a long aisle of faces buried in computer screens. Then he found what he needed: an empty desk with a blank monitor.

"Are we down head count?" he said, pointing to the rare gap in productivity.

"No sir," said the manager. "That's Andy. He left this morning. His wife is having a baby."

"How wonderful!" Brandyn said. "Do you mind if I sit at his desk? I need to run a quick systems check on something. It's routine. Won't take long."

"No, no, of course not," said the manager, rubbing his hands together nervously, eager to please a corporate leader. "Whatever you need. No problem at all. Can I get you some coffee? We have real coffee. If it's not fresh, I'll make a new pot."

"No need," Brandyn said with a gentle laugh, dropping into Andy's chair. "Please, don't let me interfere with your day. Pretend I'm not even here."

The manager lingered for a moment, until it was obvious Brandyn had no more words for him, and then he obediently scooted away.

Brandyn looked to his left. He looked to his right. He craned his neck to look behind him.

Everyone was deep in their work, putting on a good show for the Executive Vice President of Operations. They knew better than to stare.

Brandyn used his personal access code and password and entered the system.

He reached into his sports jacket pocket and pulled out a sheet of paper.

It was the list of names and service codes of the prisoners scheduled to be terminated – the sheet given to him by Wilbur Kepling at the federal building.

Brandyn let out a small, barely perceptible sigh, then got to work.

He called up Marc Tefteller. Marc showed up as a line of code linked to the satellite.

Brandyn deleted him from the system.

A pop-up window immediately appeared requesting confirmation of his action. He poked YES.

Brandyn disengaged everyone on the list from the signal feed. He deactivated their chips. It was a highly unusual action to take, unless there was a technical or health problem with a chip and it needed repair. Brandyn knew these deletions would go in a report for scrutiny and recordkeeping.

But he also knew how to keep these names off the report.

After disconnecting the four individuals sentenced to death, he called up a few additional service codes to erase from the system.

His wife, Letty.

His two sons.

And then himself.

"I can get you a more comfortable workspace, something private," said a voice behind Brandyn, and he nearly jumped out of the chair.

He did his best to downplay his startled reaction, facing the eager-to-please manager with an abrupt shake of the head. "No, no. Really I'm fine. I'm almost done."

He positioned himself toward the manager in a way to block his view of the monitor. He made a mild expression of annoyance to signal the manager should just leave him alone.

"Yes, of course," the manager said. "No worries. If you need anything – I sit right over there. Anything at all."

"I'm good. I'm really good."

"It's so nice of you to visit from corporate. We really appreciate it."

"It's my pleasure."

Fifteen minutes later, Brandyn was several blocks away from the CAS Center in his car, pulled over to the side of the road, making a frantic phone call to his family.

Letty answered. Brandyn could hear the boys crying in the background.

She immediately said, "It's a crazy house here. The chipfeed just stopped working. The kids are having a meltdown. I thought we had premium service. What the hell, Brandyn, this is *your* company."

"I did it."

"What?"

"*I* turned it off."

"What do you mean you turned it off?"

"Listen, I can't explain right now. Just do as I say. Take the boys and get out of the apartment. You need to leave. This is serious."

"What on God's earth is going on?"

"We're going off the grid."

"Excuse me?"

"Meet me – meet me—" He hesitated, not sure if the conversation was being bugged. Nothing was private these days. "Go to where we had our first date."

"You mean the—"

"Don't say it out loud. Just go there, now. As quick as you can. I'll meet you there. Then I'll explain everything."

"Brandyn, you're scaring me."

"That's because I *am* scared."

She took in the panic of his tone. "Okay. Okay. We'll leave now. And we'll go there. See you soon."

"I love you," said Brandyn, and he hung up the phone.

★ ★ ★

Marc suddenly felt normal.

It was a startling sensation. He felt like a huge weight had been lifted off his shoulders, because that's what had just happened.

For the past eight hours, the four prisoners in the holding cell at the Vanover Federal Building had been 'sandbagged' – a chip signal sent to their brains and nervous system that effectively created the sensation of being weighed down to an almost total lack of mobility.

Marc, Aaron, Clarissa and Vance – the sole surviving guide from the attempted canoe escape – lay slumped against the wall in the small holding cell, awaiting their fate. The room was locked and guarded from the outside, but this was an extra measure on the inside to solidify their captivity by giving them a physical affliction that felt like being stuck in cement.

The two guards who occasionally visited them got a big kick out of it. They stood over their prisoners and poked and taunted them, knowing they were helpless to fight back.

It was like being strapped down by invisible chains. It wasn't total paralysis – they could move, just barely, but every tiny motion was an enormous, exhausting strain.

"Tough tittie, honey," one of the guards had said to Clarissa's face, spewing bad breath into her nostrils before he groped her breast with a twisted smile. "Guess you can't do nothing about it." Clarissa had gritted her teeth, bugged her eyes, turned red and fought as hard as she could against the virtual barrier, vibrating like she was having some kind of convulsion as she struggled to unleash her pent-up fury. But she could barely raise her hand an inch. Her fingers could not curl into a fist. Her butt remained on the floor. The guard had laughed in her face.

But now the guards were somewhere else and the 'sandbag' signal had been abruptly cut off.

Marc regained normal motion. He moved his limbs. He looked at the others.

They, too, had returned to a full range of mobility. Clarissa started to stand up.

"Wait," Marc said. "Stop."

In a low voice, he instructed them to continue acting as though the 'sandbag' signal was still in effect. He told them about his conversation with Brandyn, the connection to Dynamica and the ability to secretly disable their chips.

Brandyn Handley had succeeded.

"Follow my lead," Marc said very quietly. "Act like nothing's changed. Don't let them know. We'll find our moment."

He gradually slumped back to a limp, helpless position.

Clarissa slid back down to the floor. She sat passively, propped up against the wall, arms dropped at her sides. She exchanged a glance with Aaron, who nodded.

Vance said, "They still have guns and we don't."

"I'll take that chance," said Aaron.

"No more talking," Clarissa said. "Everyone sit still and shut up."

An hour passed, and then the door opened.

The two guards reappeared. They stepped into the room with big smiles.

"Good news," said the slimy guard who had previously groped Clarissa. "We just received our orders. The president has approved your terminations."

"Yep," said the other, older guard with a trace of a southern accent. He patted the gun in his holster. "I would prefer the old-fashioned way, sticking you all in a firing line. But this'll be a lot cleaner. The wonders of technology!"

"Time to go bye-bye," the groper said. He held a jamming device, similar to the one Marc had previously owned. "A press of a button, and you are done. Easiest executions ever."

He stepped over to Marc and said, "You first."

In that moment, Marc had a flash of terror. What if his chip became operational again? What if only the 'sandbag' signal had been cut? How did he know for sure the termination command would fail?

The groper said to Marc, "Okay, asshole. Any final words?"

"I'm sorry...."

"Those are good final words," said the groper.

"I'm sorry you're a fucking idiot," Marc said.

"Whoa."

"I'm also sorry I had anything to do with this technology. I regret it, and I'm prepared to pay the price."

"You're just a douche bag. I'm turning you off now." With a dramatic flourish, the groper tapped a command on his handheld device.

On cue, Marc slumped over on the floor and didn't move.

He acted dead.

However, his mind was very much alive, filled with gratitude for Brandyn's actions to save his life.

Marc made his breathing as shallow as possible, trying not to create any small movements in his chest.

From his 'dead' position on the floor, he was able to keep his eyes slightly open in thin slits. He watched the groper approach Aaron.

Aaron glared with simmering anger, remaining pseudo-paralyzed.

"Any last words?" the groper asked.

"Yeah," said Aaron. "I want you to know—"

"Ah, shut up," the groper said, and he poked the jamming device with his index finger.

Aaron, seeing the motion, promptly went limp and shut his eyes.

"Two down, two to go." The groper stepped over to Vance. The second guard watched nearby with a big grin, fully entertained.

"Any last words?" asked the groper.

"No," Vance responded.

"That counts as a last word." Then the groper's hands became engaged with activating the termination.

Vance tipped over and did not move.

The groper froze for a moment, startled. "I didn't send the signal yet."

Oh shit, thought Marc, witnessing the scene unfold.

The groper took a step toward Vance, curious, studying him. Vance remained very still.

Then the groper broke out in a big laugh. "Ha, the son of a bitch must've fainted before I terminated him!" He positioned his finger above the jammer's interface and said, "Well, as long as you're asleep, let's just keep you there." He poked the command on his device and said proudly, "Terminated!"

This left Clarissa.

The groper stepped over to her. She stared at him with a cold, dark stare. She pretended to struggle with lifting her arms.

"Last but not least," the groper said.

"Yup," chuckled the older guard, grinning, looking forward to watching one more body drop.

But the groper sent him away. "Terry, I'll take care of this. I need you to go get the medical examiner. We need to declare some deaths. We don't want any lingering comas here. We want fully, one hundred percent *dead*. Go get him, please."

"Will do." The older guard left the room, closing the door behind him.

The groper stared down at Clarissa. "I sent him away, because I think we need a moment of privacy." He smiled, displaying dark teeth. He unbuckled his pants. "I like a good-looking young woman who submits passively to her man. I'm gonna give you a send-off, honey. Before you die, there's going to be a happy ending."

He started pulling down his white cotton underwear.

Aaron punched him in the back of the head from behind.

The groper stumbled and fell to the ground.

In a split second, all four prisoners attacked the groper and hammered him into unconsciousness, slamming his skull against the hard floor.

"Holy shit, is he disgusting," Clarissa said.

"I'm getting his gun," said Aaron, removing it from the guard's holster.

"And I'm taking his jammer," Marc said.

"You know how to work that thing?" Vance asked.

"Let's just say I have some experience."

The cell door opened, and the older guard appeared with a skinny man in a white smock, wearing rubber gloves and a stethoscope.

"You're all supposed to be dead!" said the guard, entirely perplexed.

"No, sorry," Aaron said, and he shot the guard squarely in the hip. The guard dropped to the floor like a sack of potatoes. The medical examiner turned and ran.

Clarissa quickly snatched the fallen guard's gun as he squirmed.

"We gotta move fast, there's gonna be a whole lot of people on our ass," Aaron said.

Marc, Aaron, Vance and Clarissa escaped from the holding cell. They entered a long corridor and began running. They could hear loud voices up ahead. They rounded a corner and immediately found themselves facing three more security guards with guns drawn. One of them fired, striking Vance in the forehead and spraying blood out the back of his skull. He went down hard. The remaining three prisoners immediately turned and retreated the way they came.

"Dammit, *dammit*," exclaimed Aaron as he ran, shaken by the shooting he had just witnessed. "We need more guns."

"No," Marc said. "Follow me." He led the others down a short side passage and ducked inside a recessed doorway that hid them from view for a moment. "We've got all we need right here."

Marc activated the jamming device he had stolen from the groper. He called up the active chips in the immediate vicinity and began sending them signals from a special menu of law enforcement commands.

Clarissa screamed. A pair of security officers was suddenly on them, guns drawn.

In an instant, they lost all coordination as horrible, painful shocks jolted their brains. The two officers shrieked, dropped their guns and clutched their heads in unspeakable agony. They fell to the floor in thuds and writhed in anguish like worms speared on a hook.

"Nice," said Clarissa, looking down at them as they squirmed at her feet.

Marc continued to work the jammer, sending powerful signals to every chip code within a three-hundred-foot radius. Marc heard pained reactions from multiple locations in the building, near and far. The range of yelps, shrieks, grunts, howls and hollers sounded like some kind of demented avant-garde chorus.

"Unbelievable," Aaron said. He watched in awe as Marc rapidly activated each shockwave, disabling a dozen or more threats to their escape.

"Are you killing them?" Clarissa asked.

"No, just giving them a very big migraine."

After a couple of minutes, Marc paused, still staring at the jammer. "I think that's all of them for now. Let's get out of here before they send the entire Army."

* * *

As Brandyn Handley drove to his next destination, he listened to his car radio with a sinking feeling in his stomach. The country was headed toward World War III.

"Negotiations are in full collapse," President Sheridan said. "Therefore, we will launch our missiles in exactly twenty-four hours. I will keep my promise to the American people."

Brandyn pulled into the parking lot of a shuttered strip mall in Kearny, New Jersey. His family was waiting for him. They climbed out of the silver SUV. His wife was confused, the kids were whiny.

As Letty approached her husband, he was lost in a moment of nostalgia. He gestured to a recently shut down Walmart following the company's bankruptcy. "This is it," he said. "It was right there. It must've been fifteen years ago or more."

"How could I forget?" Letty said.

"The Stardust Bowling Alley and Pinball Arcade," Brandyn said. "Our first date. I had such a crush, all those amazing feelings for you – and not one of them came from a chip. They came from here." He pointed to his heart. "Real love, what a concept."

"So what's going on?" Letty asked. "Everything is crazy enough with this war looming, and now you're acting like a nut case. Please tell me why we're here."

"We're going into hiding. We're going to move into a motel a few miles from here. We'll stay there for a while under an assumed name."

"But why?"

Brandyn struggled to find the right words. "It might not be popular, but I think I need to save the world."

"Oh great. You *have* gone crazy."

"No. I've finally come to my senses."

Letty turned to face the two boys, who were arguing and tussling over something meaningless at the other side of the car.

"Kids, I was right. Your dad is insane. Do you want a new dad?"

"Okay," said one of the boys.

Brandyn smiled at his wife. "You don't really mean that?"

"I don't know," she said with a sad sigh. "I really don't know anything anymore. You turned off my chip. Now I have to think for myself."

CHAPTER TWENTY-NINE

Brandyn received a cryptic text message from a 'Joan Stone', requesting his immediate presence at an unfamiliar address in Midtown Manhattan. The meeting request was on behalf of 'Big Be Bop Buddy'.

He instantly recognized this to be a reference to Marc, who had taken him to the old-fashioned Big Be Bop jazz club more than two years ago for their final, secret meeting after Marc quit Dynamica.

At the same time Brandyn received this text, his phone was exploding with messages from Jeff Reese and the Dynamica security team with the news that Marc had escaped custody.

"The fun never ends…" said Brandyn, and he quickly drove into Manhattan after securing his family in a motel room under false identities.

He found a parking spot and walked the sidewalk until he reached the address he was given.

"What the hell. Really?"

His ears were assaulted by the loud chaos of dozens of barking dogs, everything from deep woofs to high-pitched yips. The sign in the storefront window said: *Furry Friends Pet Rescue.*

He stood at the door for a moment, staring at a big picture of a doe-eyed Shih Tzu. He was stuck in uncertainty. Then the door opened a crack and a familiar voice said, "Get the hell in here!"

He entered.

Marc was inside the pet shelter with three other people and about sixty dogs and cats, many of them roaming freely in a happy, tail-wagging commotion.

Brandyn stepped through the animals and reached Marc with a rough embrace. "It worked."

"You saved our lives."

"For now, anyway."

Marc introduced Brandyn to Aaron, Clarissa and Kathryn Sedak.

"Don't worry," said Marc about Kathryn. "She's anti-chip."

"Nice place you got here," Brandyn told her, trying not to trip over a poodle.

"She got us a change of clothes," said Marc. He and the other former prisoners were no longer wearing the orange jumpsuits.

"You should keep away from the windows – go in the back. There's a small office, just past the kennels," Kathryn said. "No one will see you."

"I don't like cats," Clarissa said, staring down at the furry sea of animals swarming around her.

"They sure like you," Aaron said.

The four of them gathered in a small, messy office beyond the maze of animal cages. It had a couch, two chairs and a desk. Everything was coated in animal hair.

"Who's Joan Stone?" Brandyn asked as they settled into the room.

"It's just a phone I stole," Marc said. "I used the jammer on a woman on the sidewalk. I didn't hurt her, just distracted her and took her phone so I could text you."

"I have to ask you something. Why didn't you tell them?"

"Tell who?"

"At the interrogation. Why didn't you just tell them it was me who gave you the jammer device?"

"Because I made a promise not to."

"But they were torturing the shit out of you."

"I made a promise the day you gave it to me."

"You're weird."

"Oh no," Clarissa said. She faced a TV monitor mounted on the wall, displaying the news. "It's Bozo."

Dale Sheridan was continuing his countdown to war.

"In eighteen hours, we will launch our missiles. If there is any retaliation or interference, we will broaden our attack to hit our enemies fast and hard at strategic targets in ways they will deeply regret."

"Do you think it's really a spy satellite?" Aaron asked.

"Who knows?" said Brandyn. "Maybe yes, maybe no. In any case, it's going to start a big war, and we don't have a lot of global allies right now."

On the television, Sheridan continued: "Through the power of technology, our military is second to none. Unified by the chip, loyal to every mission, fearless in the face of danger, our fighting men and women will be unstoppable. If war is inevitable, I say *bring it on*."

"We're blowing up the wrong satellite," Aaron mumbled.

The statement caused Marc to cock his head. "You're right." He looked over at Brandyn. "He's right."

"I know," said Brandyn. "It's sad, but true."

"So can we do something about it?"

"Blow up our own satellite? What, the four of us?"

"Maybe."

"How?"

"Can we redirect the missiles?"

"How are we going to do that?"

Clarissa faced Marc and Brandyn. "You guys are so good at getting into people's heads…get into somebody's head and change their minds."

"It's not that easy," Marc said.

"Well, wait," Brandyn said. "Maybe it is. Let me think."

On the television news, a countdown clock began running at the bottom of the screen, displaying the number of hours, minutes and seconds before the promised missile launch.

Brandyn began pacing the small room. "There's…there's a test in the works. It's part of the way we code. We can program for moods, feelings and perceptions, but not at the level of specific actions. We're working to create a way to trick the brain into believing a piece of information and taking action through a line of code. It's meant to treat people with phobias and mental blocks, but…."

"So how do we do this?" Aaron asked.

"We don't do anything. It's being developed by our scientists. I – I'm not a programmer," said Brandyn. "I just know the players. It's an initiative led by Dr. Higgins."

"Higgins?" Marc said. "The 'Father of the Chip'?"

Brandyn nodded.

"So let's get this Higgins guy to help us," Aaron said.

Marc said, "It's not that easy. He's not on our side. I tricked him into removing my chip, and it was not good. He was part of the raid at my apartment that tried to stick it back in. I had to subdue him…with a laughing fit."

"What?" said Aaron.

"He's not going to be on board with this," Marc said. "Not at all."

"How about," Clarissa said, "if we persuade him?" She held up the gun she had taken from the security guard at the federal building.

Brandyn gave her a long look. Then he shrugged. "Could work."

* * *

Dr. Rance Higgins awoke to a gun in his face.

"Don't move."

"Can I – can I put on my glasses?" he asked, trying to discern the fuzzy images in front of him. He lay flat in his bed, head sunk in a big pillow.

"Slowly."

Higgins reached over to his nightstand for his glasses and put them on.

The faces before him came into view, forming a semi-circle around the bed.

"You," he said.

Marc made a half smile and shrugged. "Yeah. Me."

"We need your help with something," Brandyn said.

"Looks like I don't have a choice."

Clarissa kept the gun pointed at his head. Aaron stood at her side.

"No," said Marc. "But we'd like to think you'll want to cooperate for other reasons – like saving your country and maybe the world."

"That's quite a pitch, marketing man."

"How would you like to prevent World War III?"

"It's two o'clock in the morning. Can it wait?"

"I'm afraid not."

"Is this about the missile launch?"

"Yes."

"The president is just protecting the people. He's protecting our chips. We don't want our brains to be hacked into by other countries and force-fed their agendas, do we? This is a serious threat."

"We know another way to stop the threat," Brandyn said.

"And what's that?"

"We blow up our own satellite. Bring down the whole system."

Higgins took a long moment to absorb this statement. Then he let out a big exhale. "That's…a brazen concept."

"We blow it up. We disable every chip so there are no signals to hack. We render the entire chip system inoperable."

"I don't like this," said Higgins.

Marc held up a jamming device. "We can make you like it."

"You son of a bitch, that laughing fit you gave me nearly ruptured my spleen."

"Listen," Brandyn said. "We don't have a lot of time. This is the best solution we have."

"But how are you going to redirect the missiles?"

"You're going to write a line of code."

"For who?"

"For the president, the secretary of defense, the Pentagon."

"How naïve are you? That's not possible. You would need the personal access numbers of every one of those individuals, and they're highly classified. It can't be done. Sure, I could write a line of code to influence a specific desire to redirect those missiles. But I don't have access to President Sheridan's personal account. I can't hand-select who gets a signal. The only way to do it would be to send the code to *everybody* – everyone who receives the satellite feed in one massive go."

Marc brightened. "Sounds good to me."

"What?"

"We send it to everybody. That way we know he gets it and anyone else who needs to support this."

"Gentlemen," said Higgins, and then he nodded toward Clarissa, who still pointed the gun at him, "and lady. Please listen to me. All of this brainstorming is cute, but the reality is we're still in a test phase with this. I can't guarantee any of it is going to work."

"Do you agree that it's worth a try?" Aaron asked.

Higgins made an uncomfortable, noncommittal face, and finally said, "Not really."

Clarissa brought the gun closer to his head. "Do you agree that you'd like to continue living?"

Higgins looked down at his burgundy plaid flannel sleepwear. "Can I change out of my pajamas?"

"If you can do it fast," Marc said.

* * *

The five of them crammed into Brandyn's car and sped to Princeton, New Jersey to enter The Brain, AKA Dynamica's Core Applications and Systems Center.

Brandyn responded to messages on his phone from his employer, agreeing that it was horrible to hear about Marc Tefteller's escape and explaining away his own absence from the office as a bad bout of the flu.

He knew it was only a matter of time before they realized he had disconnected the signal feeds and linked him to Marc's escape. Until that happened, he was making one more visit to the high-security facility that managed the nation's chipfeed accounts and coding.

They arrived as the night shift was turning over and the day shift was arriving. Brandyn and Higgins used their maximum security clearances to also gain entry for Aaron, Clarissa and Marc. The latter was disguised in hat and dark sunglasses to conceal his identity so no one in the building would recognize him as the company's former Chief Marketing Officer and current Public Enemy Number One.

As they made their way through the endless aisles of programmers and monitors, looking for an empty chair to fill, Clarissa noticed television screens on the wall displaying the news with the countdown clock prominently featured.

"*We have less than thirty minutes*," she said in a harsh whisper.

Aaron took her hand. "It's okay. We're going to make it."

"You're certainly optimistic," growled Higgins. "And it's not your experiment."

Brandyn found an open chair. "I'll log in here," he said. "I'll get us in – then Rance, you do your magic."

"There are no guarantees…" he started.

"Except for the guarantee we will blow your brains out if this doesn't work," Clarissa said.

"No pressure," muttered Higgins.

Brandyn used his access badge and codes to enter the core systems application. Then he surrendered the chair to Higgins.

Higgins sat down as the others crowded around him.

An ongoing flow of programmers walked by, reporting to work, giving curious glances to the huddled group and moving on.

Then one of the arriving programmers stopped at the desk and stared. He was a young man in his twenties with a ponytail.

"You're in my spot."

Brandyn quickly turned and addressed him. "No worries. I'm Brandyn Handley, head of operations."

"Is everything okay?"

"Absolutely. But we need your station for a moment. Why don't you get a donut or some coffee, we won't be long."

"I don't eat donuts or drink coffee."

"As the highest-ranking leader in your division, I order you to go get yourself a donut and coffee, *now*." Brandyn flashed a don't-mess-with-me expression.

The young programmer nodded, shrugged and left in search of donuts and coffee.

"How long is this going to take?" Aaron asked.

"I don't know," snapped Higgins.

"The countdown clock says fifteen minutes."

"You're not helping!"

Brandyn stepped back and motioned Marc over for a private conversation.

"I just realized what we're doing," he said.

"What do you mean?"

"We're doing the very thing that scares us about this technology. Mass distribution of a single thought to manufacture a point of view – it's brainwashing."

Marc nodded. "I don't disagree."

"We're going to brainwash the entire country with one forced perspective. That's a pretty dangerous concept."

"But not for long," Marc said. "Because after we blow up the satellite, it's never going to happen again. This is the last time."

They continued to hover over Higgins. The countdown clock steadily advanced toward the deadline. Higgins worked with intense focus, fingers moving swiftly across the keyboard. Perspiration dotted his forehead.

"Eight minutes!" Clarissa said.

"Stop doing that in my ear!" Higgins said.

"How close are you?" asked Aaron.

"I don't know. Maybe five minutes, maybe ten."

"Ten won't do."

"You think I don't know that?"

Then Brandyn said, "Oh, shit." His eyes locked on something at the far end of the room.

Marc followed his gaze and discovered activity at the front entrance to the data center. There was a swell of people filling the doorway, prepared to burst in.

They were soldiers, dressed in green-and-gray combat fatigues. They were heavily armed.

"I think we've been discovered," Marc said.

"Do you still have the jammer?" Brandyn asked.

"Yes, but there are so many of them, I don't think I can—"

Clarissa whirled to face the other end of the data room, reaching for her gun.

Company programmers witnessed the sudden commotion with armed soldiers and quickly pulled away from their stations in a confused panic.

"Shit, they have a lot of guns," said Clarissa. "Really big guns."

"I think I've got it!" Higgins said.

"Send the code!" shouted Marc.

The soldiers stormed the room. The entire area erupted into pandemonium.

Aaron grabbed Clarissa's hand. "Pretend you're a programmer!"

"What?" she said.

"Hide the gun, follow me."

In the chaos of stampeding soldiers and scattering programmers, Aaron led Clarissa to a couple of nearby workstations, recently abandoned.

"Play on the keyboard, pretend like you work here," Aaron said.

Clarissa did as she was told. The soldiers ignored them. They rushed at the Dynamica trio of Marc, Brandyn and Higgins, who were still huddled at the workstation. The three of them were tracking a rapidly scrolling line of code, representing the release of a forced perspective on the full body of chipped citizens in the United States.

"Hey, I think it worked," said Higgins, pleased with his own successful execution. Then he was grabbed by two soldiers and thrown to the ground.

Marc and Brandyn were also apprehended and shoved to the floor. They landed alongside Higgins. Angry voices shouted at them not to move. Rifles were pointed into their faces.

Marc shut his eyes, expecting a bullet to the brain.

But then everyone was distracted.

The soldiers and the programmers all froze in the moment to watch the large television monitors mounted on the walls.

The president's countdown clock had reached zero.

Live cameras captured the launch of the missiles.

The cavernous data-systems room fell into an immediate, eerie silence as everyone watched.

Aaron and Clarissa stared from their neighboring workstations, bridged by holding hands.

Marc, Brandyn and Higgins watched from the floor, trying to get a good look past the guns obscuring their vision.

On the television monitors, accompanying live footage of missiles soaring into the sky, a Breaking News statement flashed at the bottom of the screen.

PRESIDENT DECLARES NEW MISSILE TARGET: DYNAMICA SATELLITE.

At the appearance of the president's proclamation, the entire room broke out into loud cheering.

From the floor, Higgins said proudly, "It worked. It worked. I'm a genius."

Still pressed into the ground, Marc and Brandyn exchanged smiles of relief. "We did it," said Marc. "We got inside their heads."

Aaron and Clarissa watched the news coverage, eyes glued on the screen.

The camera feed showed fiery slivers of light against the blue sky, representing the missiles as they climbed ever higher into the atmosphere.

Clarissa squeezed Aaron's hand tighter. And then:

The missiles struck their target.

A big, dramatic, colorful explosion filled the screens across the data center.

The crowd cheered again, this time louder and more raucously, dancing and waving their arms.

The screen read: DYNAMICA SATELLITE DESTROYED.

With everyone extremely distracted, including the soldiers who had apprehended them, Marc, Brandyn and Higgins quietly removed themselves from the floor. They slipped out of the nest of soldiers, who continued to obsessively watch the live coverage of the satellite explosion as it replayed in slow motion like a celebratory fireworks display.

Aaron and Clarissa recognized their opportunity to escape as well and quickly left the workstations to join the others on their way out of the building.

Once outside, they ran for the car and they squeezed inside.

Brandyn started up the engine. He turned on the radio as he peeled out of the parking lot and headed for the main road.

A newscaster delivered the latest developments with uncontrollable enthusiasm. "All of America is rejoicing following the president's decision to bring down the satellite that once captured our imaginations…."

"I think we just united the country," said Marc.

"By giving everyone one last common thought," Aaron said.

"At least we know there won't be any others."

"Just our own thinking and feeling for a change," Clarissa said. "It's about time."

"I guess I'm out of a job now," Brandyn said.

"And you've pretty much killed my career," said Higgins.

"So we'll start a new venture," Marc suggested. "Some kind of start-up."

"I'm on board," Brandyn said. "As long as it's something small."

"Aaron, Clarissa, want to join our startup?" Marc asked. "I don't know what it is, but if we're lucky, it won't become as successful as Dynamica."

"No way," Clarissa said. "If it has anything to do with technology, you can leave me out."

"Same here," said Aaron. He looked over at Clarissa and smiled. She smiled too, which he hadn't seen in a long time. He couldn't help it then – he leaned over and gave her a long kiss.

"My chip is receiving some incredible signals right now," she said.

"Oh really? How'd you like to subscribe?"

"Sign me up."

CHAPTER THIRTY

The day the satellite died marked a new era for society.

The adjustment jolted people out of their stagnant comfort zones and forced them to deal with something they had effectively avoided for years: reality.

In the Elysian Valley neighborhood of Los Angeles, three roommates simultaneously stirred from deep, immersive trips inside their imaginations to confront their physical surroundings.

Scotty now weighed four hundred and twelve pounds and everywhere he walked created a crunch as he stepped through layers of trash around the house. He tried to articulate that his chip wasn't working but had a difficult time putting the words in the right order – he barely spoke out loud to anyone anymore. His voice sounded strange and foreign in his ears.

"Chip…stopped."

"Me, too," said Larry, walking precariously on shaky, rarely used legs. His beard now stretched down to the middle of his chest. His clothing, unchanged for weeks, stuck like a second skin. He recalled a fading thought. "Satellite…bad."

Desmond joined them, also foggy and stuttering. He had been comfortably living in another world and someone had switched it on him, sending him into this familiar setting from a distant memory. "Satellite go boom," he said. Desmond wore no pants and his genitals dangled.

Vaguely recalling an urge for the satellite's destruction, Larry, Scotty and Desmond moved in baby steps toward the front door of their house. The stench inside was quickly making them nauseous, and they remembered that out on the front lawn there was something known as 'fresh air'.

They stepped outside and immediately shielded their eyes from the bright sun.

"Whoa," Larry said. "Eyes hurt."

They walked out on the grass. Scotty moved with difficulty, still adjusting to his enormous weight gain. Larry scratched at his beard and insects emerged. Desmond felt the breeze on his exposed privates.

They witnessed a remarkable sight: up and down the street, dozens of other people were emerging from their homes, too, staggering as if awoken from a multi-year slumber. They were equally disheveled and confused, gawking at the big, open sky.

"Did we order this?" Larry said.

"I don't know," Desmond said.

"Who are all these people?" asked Scotty.

Larry studied the strange, alien creatures learning to walk and talk again. "Looks like us."

* * *

In the massive tent community beneath a stretch of Los Angeles freeway, residents began emerging from their shelters, realizing the ineffectiveness of their controllers.

"We blew it up!" shouted Michael Harper, kicking past a mound of Body Fuel wrappers as he circled his tent, clutching the handheld device that no longer sent signals to his brain. Instinctively, he held it up to the sky to see if it would reconnect, without any response.

Others also spilled into the open air, slowly rediscovering their true surroundings. Soon the entire tent community was inside out, a mob of reborn lives.

"Let's go!" Michael cried out. He began to move across the dense sea of poorly propped canvases that created an illusion of green, gray and blue waves.

The population appeared to merge into a single, moving mass. They left their makeshift neighborhood under the freeway in search of a new destination.

"Where are my thoughts?" yelled out a bug-eyed woman with wildly unkempt hair and a torn T-shirt. She struggled with the broken chipfeed. "What should I think? How do I feel?"

Michael followed the hundreds of homeless moving in the direction of downtown Los Angeles, drawn by the mesmerizing sight of bold skyscrapers reaching into the sky.

"What is that place?" a scraggly, dirty man asked Michael as they trudged forward through the trash in their path.

"I know it," said Michael, and he struggled to remember it. "Angels. Angeles. Lost. Lost Angeles."

"Oh," said the scraggly man. "Is it real or another head trip?"

Michael studied the city skyline carefully as he weighed a decision. "Not sure. I don't know. It's not very realistic – looks phony to me."

⋆ ⋆ ⋆

Wendy Holt woke up in a clear, plastic casket. She was connected to various tubes that had kept her alive while she spent her days in an eternal loop of heaven. However, suddenly and without warning, heaven ended. She had risen.

And it freaked her out.

"Bring it back!" Wendy screamed, and no one answered. She was angry, disrupted, confused.

Her Living Casket rested on a shelf in a small room with two chairs for guests. She looked around, taking in her surroundings. She had no idea how long she had been here – days, weeks, months, years. She remembered intentionally ordering up the chipfeed that put her into a happy coma. More recently, she recalled a dreamlike urge for an exploding satellite. She had a faraway, vague recollection of a husband, who was mad at her. What was his name? Started with an A.

Abe. Andy. Aaron. Alex. One of those.

As it became obvious that the eternal loop of heaven was not resuming, she decided to break out of her box and raise a complaint with someone.

This was a most rude awakening.

She pounded up on the clear casket and shook the lid loose. She kicked it off with a loud clatter. She pulled the tubes and wires out of her skin.

She climbed out of the casket.

Her arms and legs were weak and not used to any of this, and she fell gracelessly to the floor.

"Ow!' she yelped. She felt a sensation she hadn't experienced in a very long time – pain. It made her angry.

She crawled to the door of her tiny, closet-like tomb. She grabbed the handle and pulled herself back up. She held on to the walls and the doorframe for support.

She exited her personal space and entered a long, white corridor. The corridor was lined on either side with doors for other Rip Van Winkles.

People were slowly emerging from their afterlife, groggy and uncertain. They looked like hell – pale, withered, atrophied.

Wendy staggered toward the elevator. She started to yell out in a dry, hoarse voice. "Somebody! Anybody! What the hell is going on! Where's my heaven? I want a refund!"

When the elevator was taking too long, she chose to enter the nearby stairwell.

"This is a travesty," she said. "Heads will roll. You can't just yank someone off the feed like that. Terrible!"

She slowly began descending the stairs on shaky legs, having a hard time maintaining a firm grip on the banister.

"Give me back my heaven!" she yelled. "Living is shit. I hate it. Who's in control around here? I hate this world! *Get me the hell back to heaven, God damn it!*"

Then she stumbled and fell down the stairs. She tumbled hard, smacked her head, broke her neck and died.

* * *

Lorraine and Flynn Beaman quickly found each other on the well-trodden plot of desert land known as Chip Prison Ranch. They pushed past other joyful, re-animated prisoners regaining their clarity.

"Something happened to the signal," Lorraine said excitedly to her son. "I feel like a fog has been lifted from my head. I can think clearly. I can move normally."

"Me too," said Flynn.

They could see groups of prisoners already climbing through the flimsy wire fence that penned them in. No one was showing signs of being shocked when they broke through the perimeter. In a matter of minutes, the inmates had transitioned from captive zombies to regular human beings again.

"The chips aren't getting a signal anymore," Flynn said. "Something happened to the feed, it just stopped." He recalled feeling an intense desire for the chip satellite's destruction. Was it a premonition?

"Let's get out of here," Lorraine said. She looked around at her surroundings. No one was coming to stop them from escaping.

"I'm with you all the way."

The two of them hurried for the fence. They easily slipped between two wires stretched across wooden posts. They ran off into the open desert with clear heads under clear skies.

Flynn began laughing at the ease of freedom. He let out a yelp of joy and didn't look back.

★ ★ ★

The children came running from multiple directions, across fields, over hills, down the gravel road.

Father Cusack gathered his clan on his Indiana commune for a special daylight announcement. Big and small, they hurried in from their chores around the farm to gather in the one-room schoolhouse.

They listened in silence as Father Cusack delivered the news.

"Every day we pray. We pray to God for acceptance. We pray to escape the relentless grip of technology on our flesh and blood. We pray that we may once again worship the natural beauty of God's earth over the cold hardware of the computer. We know the Antichrist bears a birthmark and it is the chip. I am blessed to tell you today that your prayers have been answered. God delivered a miracle. I have received word that the chip no longer controls the soul. The devil in the sky has been brought down. God is victorious once again. He has heard your prayers. We may now reenter society without being demonized. The world is blessed again with the Lord's grace."

★ ★ ★

In the months that followed, Marc Tefteller, Brandyn Handley and Dr. Rance Higgins launched their new business venture, Null and Void Incorporated.

The company specialized in 'chip scrubbing' – wiping implanted chips clean to fully deactivate and neutralize them so they could never again be used to receive controlling signals from a third party.

The demand was huge.

Common paranoia persisted that a new U.S. chipfeed satellite could be built – or that perhaps another country's satellite really would be used to hack into the minds of the American people and subliminally influence their thoughts and actions. No one wanted the chip anymore.

Old and new generations rediscovered the richness of reality and, freed from the chip, they became inspired to build a better world. They faced their fears and challenges head on, rather than hiding in escapism. They engaged in group problem-solving instead of seeking isolation and personal pleasures at the expense of the broader community.

The people took back the government, removing Dale Sheridan from office and working swiftly to undo the damage created by him and his predecessor.

The forced labor initiative ended, freeing thousands of workers to find their own roles in the world rather than be told.

It was a nationwide awakening.

Null and Void Incorporated created hundreds of thousands of jobs. A portion of the company's profits was committed to rebuilding resources and institutions that had fallen into neglect: libraries, playgrounds, museums, schools.

Best of all, Marc slept soundly at night and it didn't require calling up electronic signals.

He reconnected with family and friends and found time to start dating again, something he had not done in a very long time.

On a blind date with a thoughtful and kind brown-eyed woman named Kelly, he found himself struggling to describe himself, deliberately avoiding any mention of the chip technology.

"So what is it you do?" she asked innocently with a real smile as real drinks were served with real dinner entrees, and real music played in the background.

"I live life," he said simply.

* * *

In a rustic log cabin in the mountains of Montana, Aaron and Clarissa started a new chapter entirely of their own design. They immersed themselves in a natural environment with simple comforts and a strict rule of no computers of any kind. They returned to the basics, and it allowed their senses to bloom like never before.

They created art, they read books, they hiked, they cooked, and occasionally they watched old movies on VHS tapes. They enjoyed the classic films of Aaron's old friend Madison Reddick, even though the special effects were unconvincing, created before CGI could fake anything the mind could imagine.

Clarissa became pregnant, and they felt the time and place was right to bring a new life into the world. They looked forward to becoming parents.

Occasionally they went into town for simple supplies and to engage with others at community events: fairs, festivals, lectures, plays and sports. They enjoyed horseback riding. It was not a big town, but they got to know almost everybody.

One day there was a knock at their door, and they opened it to face an unfamiliar jolly man in a colorful flannel shirt, clean overalls and a khaki cap.

"Howdy, I'm your new neighbor," said the man. He introduced himself as Orville Hastings. "I live just up the road from you. Moved in last week."

Aaron and Clarissa welcomed him to the neighborhood and invited him in for a drink. He graciously accepted.

They sat together in the living room, getting to know one another, as a warm fire crackled in the fireplace. Orville was an oil company executive from Chicago and had bought the house down the road as a vacation home to 'get away from it all'. He marveled over the scenic beauty of the area and the abundance of wildlife. "Just beautiful, everywhere you look," he said.

Aaron and Clarissa were starting to like him, but then something bad happened.

In the middle of the conversation, Orville pulled out his cell phone. He stared at it, smiled and nodded.

Then he said, "You gotta check this out."

"Check what out?" Clarissa asked.

He stood up and walked over to show it to her. "This great new app. Just downloaded it the other day. It keeps track of all your personal data up in the cloud and sends you push alerts—"

Very quickly, Orville Hastings was thrown out of the house. Aaron grabbed him by the collar and shoved him across the room.

"*Out! Out!*" Clarissa shouted as she pulled open the door. Aaron pushed his new neighbor outside, where he tumbled into the dirt with his cell phone bouncing on the ground alongside him.

"And don't ever come back!" said Aaron. He slammed the door.

FLAME TREE PRESS
FICTION WITHOUT FRONTIERS
Award-Winning Authors & Original Voices

Flame Tree Press is the trade fiction imprint of Flame Tree Publishing, focusing on excellent writing in horror and the supernatural, crime and mystery, science fiction and fantasy. Our aim is to explore beyond the boundaries of the everyday, with tales from both award-winning authors and original voices.

•

Other titles available by Brian Pinkerton:
The Gemini Experiment

You may also enjoy:
The Sentient by Nadia Afifi
American Dreams by Kenneth Bromberg
Second Lives by P.D. Cacek
The City Among the Stars by Francis Carsac
Vulcan's Forge by Robert Mitchell Evans
The Widening Gyre by Michael R. Johnston
The Blood-Dimmed Tide by Michael R. Johnston
The Sky Woman by J.D. Moyer
The Guardian by J.D. Moyer
The Goblets Immortal by Beth Overmyer
The Apocalypse Strain by Jason Parent
A Killing Fire by Faye Snowden
Fearless by Allen Stroud
The Bad Neighbour by David Tallerman
A Savage Generation by David Tallerman
Ten Thousand Thunders by Brian Trent
Two Lives: Tales of Life, Love & Crime by A Yi

Horror titles available include:
The Haunting of Henderson Close by Catherine Cavendish
The Garden of Bewitchment by Catherine Cavendish
Black Wings by Megan Hart
Those Who Came Before by J.H. Moncrieff
Stoker's Wilde by Steven Hopstaken & Melissa Prusi
Stoker's Wilde West by Steven Hopstaken & Melissa Prusi
Until Summer Comes Around by Glenn Rolfe

•

Join our mailing list for free short stories, new release details, news about our authors and special promotions:

flametreepress.com